How to Impress a Marquess

SUSANNA IVES

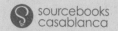
sourcebooks
casablanca

Published by Sourcebooks Casablanca, an imprint of Sourcebooks,
Inc.
P.O. Box 4410, Naperville, Illinois 60567-4410
(630) 961-3900
Fax: (630) 961-2168
www.sourcebooks.com

Printed and bound in Canada.
MBP 10 9 8 7 6 5 4 3 2 1

One

London
Spring, 1879

A DAY WITHOUT LILITH DAHLGREN WAS A FINE DAY indeed, George, Marquess of Marylewick, mused as he eased back in his brougham seat.

He was finally heading home after surviving another insipid musical evening of delicate young darlings in dainty gowns gently butchering Bach or Mozart. He removed his top hat, tugged his tie loose, and gazed out at the night. Gold halos glowed around the gaslights, turning the London night a silken deep gray. The moody atmosphere reminded him of Joseph Mallord William Turner's paintings. Turner was a real painter, unlike Lilith's ramshackle bohemian friends whose art resembled the plum jelly drawings a four-year-old George had created on his nursery walls. These new artists should be punished for their pathetic attempts at art the same way he had been: their hands dipped in iced water and then slapped with a leather strap. Indolent wastrels, all of them.

George released a long stream of tired breath and reviewed his day to make sure he had squeezed every drop of productive juice from it. He had attended the boxing parlor as he did every morning. He had danced about the ring, thinking about the metaphorical punches he needed to deliver in the heated debate of the contentious Stamp Duty Extension Bill. After a brief breakfast with his sister, he had reviewed estate, bank, and stock accounts with his man of business. Then he had legged over to White's to pass the remainder of the morning making political battle plans with the lord chancellor. Two more hours had been allocated in the afternoon for the business of his numerous wards and dependents, including the sugar-coated orders from his mama as she readied Tyburn Hall for the upcoming house party. Three Maryle relatives had appointments and were each given fifteen minutes. George believed that was sufficient time for them to express the matter at hand without lapsing into tears or drama. He abhorred sentimentality and rapturous overtures of any kind—all the things that characterized Lilith.

After his relatives had left, he had lingered in his study a few minutes longer, in case Lilith graced him with an appearance. Acting as her trustee was a taxing and thankless responsibility. She never bothered with appointments, but breezed in as the mood struck her, staying well beyond her allotted fifteen minutes. She always had a new ploy to wheedle money from her grandfather's trust to help some degenerate artist pollute society with his rubbish. When George was convinced that she wasn't calling, he had breathed a sigh of relief, donned his wig, and headed for Parliament with an extra spring in his step.

Now, having survived a grueling session of Parliament and the equally grueling musical party, he could look forward to donning his nightshirt, sliding under crisply ironed sheets, and reading *Colette and the Sultan*.

The latest chapter in author Ellis Belfort's serial had been wagging on everyone's tongues that evening. How would Colette escape her evil pursuer, Sultan Murada? The story had set London society ablaze, but George had been enthralled with Colette from the very first installment. In a sense, he felt her story was *his* for having discovered it before everyone else.

As his carriage rolled along Piccadilly, George imagined the gentle Colette. He envisioned her possessing ebony locks that flowed over her breasts, almost reaching her waist. The black waves shone like onyx in sunlight. Her enormous eyes were the green of country fields after rain. He chuckled to himself. Colette didn't exist, yet in his mind she seemed so real. As if she rubbed elbows against him in Trafalgar Square, or had just left the circulating library as he entered. As if she—

"Damnation, Lilith!" he thundered.

Down Half Moon Street, bright light and raucous laughter and music—loud enough to penetrate the inner sanctum of his carriage—blared from the home Lilith shared with her late father's cousins, Edgar and Frances Dahlgren.

"Hell's fire!" He should have known he couldn't have a day free of Lilith.

He had a good mind to ignore her and drive home to his crisp sheets and fictional Colette, but then a horrible image of being summoned to police court for Lilith filled his mind.

He rapped the carriage window with his cane. Without his having to issue a command, the groom, reading his master's mind, turned the brougham. George prepared for battle, rebuttoning his collar and retying his white tie. The carriage lurched to a stop before a brick townhouse. On the door was a brass plaque that read "Dahlgren Ateliers." George stabbed the walk with his cane as he stepped unassisted from his carriage. "Around the block," he ordered his groom.

At the door, George was impeded by two young men reeking of a distillery.

"Art is death, my good fellow," declared one of the gents. He wore a crumpled coat, a loose scarlet cravat, and a tragic expression on his pallid face. "The loss, the separation, the mystery."

"Death, death, death," retorted the other man, shaking his Byronesque locks. "You are obsessed by death. But there is no meaning in death as there is in life. Art is the lost, sensitive soul grappling for meaning amid our meaningless, empty existence."

"*You* are meaningless!" cried the scarlet cravat. "I ask this chap here." He stumbled into George, giving him a shot of his liquored breath. "Is art about death or finding meaning?"

George paused, having never had the absurd question put to him. "It's something pleasing to look upon while dining or passing time at a tedious musical evening," he mused. "Anything beyond that is the conjecture of selfish, grown boys unwilling to contribute to society except to aggravate it with their indulgent, nansy-pansy rantings. Good evening." He brushed them off as if they were lint on his immaculate sleeve. He knocked at the door.

Was art about death or finding meaning?

He pondered the question while waiting. When he found himself pondering for more than thirty seconds, he started to knock again but the door swung open. A blond woman in a revealing purple gown peered at him.

"Aren't you handsome?" she purred. She removed his top hat, letting her finger draw a tiny circle on his cheek. "A Donatello in the flesh. Simply exquisite. Absinthe?"

"No, thank you." George reached for his hat.

She laughed and hid it behind her back. "I meant, do you have any absinthe, my dazzling Donatello?"

"No, ma'am. As a general rule, I do not willingly ingest poison. Please restore my hat."

"Hmmph." She tossed his hat against the wall with a flick of her hand and sauntered away, her bustle wagging behind her.

He stepped inside, retrieved his hat, and dusted it off. People crammed the parlor and adjacent back room. They conversed in small circles, drinks dangling from their hands, eyes lit with animation. Their conversations merged to form a loud roar over the music. Their energy soaked into his veins. A thought bubbled up—"Damned sight better than that blasted musical butchery"—before he could pop it. He had to remind himself that these were artists and Lilith's friends, never a good recommendation. They were probably rapturous over the subtle depth in a certain shade of blue or the hidden symbolism in some obscure poem or other such nonsense.

He edged along the wall. *Just find Lilith*, he told himself, trying to keep his mind from straying into the guests' ridiculous conversations. Then he heard a female voice say, "Colette? Why, it's all about coitus."

He halted.

"Coitus. Fornication. All of it," the woman prattled on, affected cynicism oozing from her words. "See how the author cleverly disguises his meaning: 'Kiss me, dearest, know the sweet nectar of my lips.' I daresay the uneducated masses assume he is referring to the lips on her mouth."

His innocent Colette's lips. *Those* lips. How dare someone suggest that of his pure Colette? Had these so-called "artists" no respect for what was decent and honest? No, they were obsessed with carnality and the darker aspects of human desires and viewed all humanity through their warped lens. He was about to say as much when someone shouted in his ear, "Do you like the painting?"

George swiveled and found himself staring at a painting of what appeared to be the blurred image of a woman with flowing hair. Or was that a flowing gown? In any case, something was flowing around her. Blobs of blue and green paint were splattered along her feet and around her head—if that indeed was her head and not another random blob.

"Good heavens, what blind sot vomited that?" George wondered.

The man's jaw dropped. Tears actually misted his eyes. "I—I did."

Damn. George should have known as much. "I'm sorry, my good man, I didn't mean… It's most color-ful," he grappled. "I admire the subtle depth in the shades of blue and so much symbolism in those…well, whatever those splotches are at the bottom."

"Water lilies, Lord Marylewick," a familiar dusky voice said. Behind the man, Lilith materialized in all her brilliance. "It's *A Muse Amongst the Water Lilies,*" she stated as if it were readily apparent Dutch realism.

Whenever Lilith appeared, George had the sensation of walking from a pitch-black room into the piercing sunshine. He needed time for his eyes to adjust. When they did, he didn't approve of what he saw. Her lustrous auburn locks, adorned with flowers, were loose and flowing over her azure robe and gauzy shawl. From the way the thin silk of her robe rested on her ripe contours, he could only guess that she wore no semblance of undergarments. That tiny vein running over his temple began to throb, as did another part of his body.

"There, there." She hugged the distraught artist. "Don't let the horrid Lord Marylewick distress you. He has the sensibilities of a dishcloth."

She impaled George with a glare. "You see, Lord Marylewick, it's about capturing the ethereal and fleeting. Those moments when the beautiful morning light illuminates the garden in all its blues, greens, and golds. It is not a representation of reality, but a sensation captured in time. A sensual impression of a moment. And philosophically, we could argue that all we have are mere impressions of a greater reality."

George's mind had left off after the "impression of

a moment" part. With Lilith now standing beside the painting, he could see the resemblance in the flowing gown and hair and splotches.

"Lilith!" he barked. "That had better not be your impression in those ethereal blobs."

By God, she was a grown toddler. He couldn't turn his back on her for a moment or she would be playing near fire or gleefully shedding her clothes for some filthy-minded artist. He didn't wait for her answer but seized her wrist and dragged her through the nearest door, which led to a paneled study with a leather sofa stacked with pillows. Cluttering the walls were paintings of pale-skinned, nude ladies gazing off to some sorrowful horizon. Luckily, these paintings appeared to be from King George III's reign, when Lilith hadn't been born yet to pose for them.

He shut the door behind them. She sauntered to the mirror and began to curl her locks around her finger and then let them unfurl in spirals about her cheeks. There was a dangerous, ready-for-battle tilt to the edge of her mouth, lifting the little mole above her lip.

"Lilith, did you pose for that…that…*Tart Amid Blue Pigeon Cack* painting? And in a rag even a Covent prostitute would think twice about wearing for fear of attracting the wrong clientele?"

Anger flashed in her eyes for a half second, and then a delicious smile curled her lips. A warm shiver coursed over his skin.

"And what if I did?" Her eyes, the color of coffee, gazed at him from under her thick lashes. He couldn't deny their sultry allure. "What would you do? Tuck me away to another boarding school? But I'm all grown up." She shook her head and made a clucking sound. "What to do with a grown woman who dares to have a mind of her own?" She snapped her fingers. "Ah, why not control her by taking away her money?"

With gentlemen and ladies of his set, he might say that he "spoke on the level" or "gave the news straight." There was nothing straightforward or level about Lilith. She was all curves and turns. Conversing with her was akin to Spanish flamenco dancing with words.

"I never took your money away," he said, feeling like a weary father cursed with an errant, irresponsible child. "And if I truly controlled you, I would never have consented to your living with your father's cousins. Your grandfather warned me about the Dahlgrens. Nor would I have consented to use his hard-earned money for this ridiculous party. Or allowed you to pose for illicit impressions of fleeting moments."

"Good heavens, I never posed for anyone! The painting was in the man's imagination—that mental faculty you are woefully missing, darling. I merely dressed as the muse in the painting as a lark for the exhibit opening." She tossed back her wrists. "You know, a muse who inspires artists to great heights of fancy."

"Lilith, the only people you are inspiring are unsavory men to low depths of debauchery."

"Unsavory men?" She raised her arms and draped her gauzy shawl across his head and over his eyes. "I didn't know you found me inspiring, Georgie." The peaks of her unbound breasts lightly brushed against his chest. Ungentlemanly desire pooled in his sex.

"Lord Marylewick," he corrected in a choked voice

and pulled her garment from his person. "And try to behave with some semblance of propriety."

"Propriety, propriety, propriety." She tapped her finger on the side of her mouth, as if she were searching her memory for the meaning. "I remember now. It's when you address a lady, such as myself, as *Miss* Dahlgren."

"I'm sorry," he said. "I didn't realize I had addressed you inappropriately. But if one insists on acting like a child… You are, what? Three and twenty, and continuing to romanticize this ramshackle lifestyle that any lady of good sense would—"

"It's the Lord Marylewick patronizing play!" She clasped her hands. "I adore it! In fact, I know every line. Wait. Wait. No, don't continue." She withdrew the cane and hat from his hand, letting her fingers flow over his skin. "Allow me." She placed the hat over her head, the flowers sticking out around the brim. She scrunched her eyebrows. "It's high time you grew up, my little lamb, and threw yourself to the wolves of high society." She croaked like a stodgy man of seventy-five, not George's thirty-one years.

He regretted coming here. He should have driven home to gentle, fictional Colette. And when they hauled Lilith into police court, he would say to the judge, "You see what I must suffer?"

"You need a husband to temper your reckless ways, young lady," she continued her performance. "One who meets my approval. Someone like me— controlling, overbearing, starchy, and unbending." Her old man voice began to fall away as her pitch rose in a crescendo. "A husband who will dress you in lace, place you on a cold marble pedestal, silence your voice, bleed your wild heart dry, and destroy your gentle, yearning soul." After delivering this melodrama, she pressed the back of her hand to her forehead and fainted onto the sofa.

He crossed his arms and gazed at her supine and curvaceous body. "I don't recall using the terms 'destroy your gentle, yearning soul.' It has always been my objective to 'shatter' or 'squash' your wayward soul. And I have never fainted in my life."

She opened one eye and regarded him. "Ah!" She jumped to her feet and pointed at his face. "I saw it. Don't deny it. Your lip trembled. You wanted to smile." She clenched her hands into tight balls. "Fight the urge with that iron will of yours. Fight it! First smiling, then a tiny chortle, and then before you know it, full-blown, vulgar, belly-deep laughter! And then where would you be? Almost human."

He really did have to squelch a smile. "Miss Dahlgren, I am not devoid of proper emotions. But unlike you I temper them with sense, you know, that mental faculty you are woefully missing, darling," he said, splashing her own words in her face.

"What would I do with something as horrid as sense? I want wild, overpowering feeling, passion, zest. 'More happy love! more happy, happy love! / For ever warm and still to be enjoy'd, / For ever panting, and for ever young; / All breathing human passion far above…' That's Keats, dearest," she said. "I know you wouldn't recognize it."

"But I recognize what you are doing."

"Oh, but I do many things." She fluttered her

eyelashes, sending a heated tremor through him. "What particular *thing* is this?"

"Last week, you came to me with a sob tale of not having enough funds to buy clothes or pay the grocer. I advanced you ten pounds. And here you are in indecent rags, pretending to be a ridiculous muse, and throwing a party—"

"Exhibit opening, not a party."

"Don't try to distract me from the matter at hand. Ever since you were a child, you have teased and danced around the matter of your atrocious behavior."

"And you know so much about my childhood from those few days I was allowed to leave school and visit Tyburn at Christmas." Fire flashed in her eyes, but her voice remained creamy. "Such special times. They were like a beautiful illustration in *Town and Country*."

"I would hardly call it that."

"I would." She waved her hand as if she could conjure the scene in the air. "The children are gathered around the adorned tree, speculating about the gifts Mama and Papa have given them this year. Maybe it's a bicycle or that lovely china doll from the shop window. An enormous Yule log roars in the fireplace while the adults, their cheeks and noses reddened from spiced wassail, laugh over old stories of Great-Aunt Millicent and the recalcitrant poodle, Lord Bertie and the silly hat, or such." Her chuckle, at first light and musical, turned bitter. "Only I wasn't in that lovely picture like you, the golden boy, and my adored, precious half-siblings. I was ten pages over in the tiny article 'Ways to Hide the Child Who Doesn't Fit into Your Shiny New Debrett's-Worthy Family.'" She spun on her heel, putting her back to him.

She had the smallest toehold on his family, having issued from the unfortunate elopement of his aunt by marriage and her first husband, the roguish John Dahlgren. When Lilith was five, her father had died in a duel after cheating at cards. By then, he had already lost his wife's substantial dowry on poor business investments. When her mother married George's uncle, Lilith, the human embodiment of a bad memory, had been sent away and fair-headed, beautiful babies created in her place.

Her shoulders now drooped as she pressed her hand to her mouth. Several beats of silence passed. He had never seen her serious. She was always scheming, teasing, or flying into a rage. He hadn't witnessed one of her famous tantrums, though, since her youth. The last he could recall was when he was a young man and she was being physically forced by his uncle and his manservant onto the train back to school, after she called her young half-siblings vicious names and marked up her chamber walls with shoe polish. "Too wild to handle," his uncle would say of his stepdaughter as the men watched the train chug off and her, finally inside, screaming "I hate you" and banging her hands against the train-carriage windows.

After her mother and stepfather had passed away, her grandfather, fearing for the welfare of his estranged and unruly eighteen-year-old granddaughter, set up a trust for her. He named George as the trustee, thereby keeping her under the Maryle mantle.

"What do you want?" he asked quietly. "What will make you happy?"

"What will make me happy?" She turned and gazed at him with large liquid eyes that reflected the hurt in her voice. He had the absurd urge to draw her into his arms.

"A world without war," she said. "Where every child is tucked into bed with a full tummy and a kiss from his mama and papa, where artists have respect and can earn a living. To visit the moon in a hot air balloon. To time travel and have tea with Leonardo da Vinci and Sappho. To live in the Sistine Chapel. But on a more realistic scale, I'll just take five hundred pounds of my own money and then you can leave me alone. Forever." Her lush lips gave a tiny good-bye kiss to the air.

The low lamplight deepened the contours of her high, full cheekbones and the tiny cleft in her chin.

He cleared his tight throat, stepping back. "You would run through the money in a year giving it to this and that poor artist whose parents couldn't afford to tuck him into a comfortable asylum. Impressions of water lilies, indeed! Your grandfather entrusted me with his monies, earned from decades of brewing."

She released a put-upon sigh and flicked her eyes toward the heavens. No doubt old-fashioned hard work and responsibility was a bit dull for her taste.

"I will not be accountable for losing it." He waggled a finger before her nose. "If you want that money, my lady, then follow the terms your grandfather laid out in his trust: find a responsible, well-situated husband of whom I will approve. A man who will not destroy your so-called gentle yearning but temper your wild spirits and provide you a respectable home. At which time I will thankfully leave you alone forever. Until then, you will dance to my tune."

Anger flashed in those dark eyes. She raised the edge of her mouth, the side adorned with that teasing mole.

"Dance to your tune?" She began to sway her hips and wave her hands like an exotic belly dancer. "Like this?" She lifted the sides of her hair high over her head and then let the glossy curls fall around her breasts. All the while, she kept her head low, watching him from under her lashes. "Is this your tune?"

George swallowed. The courtesans dancing in the gentlemen's clubs weren't half so wanton…or entrancing. "Stop that," he choked.

She only sashayed closer, picking up an orange pillow from the sofa. She held it just below her glittery eyes. She continued to sway in steady rhythm, like a hypnotist's swinging watch. His tongue moistened as blood pooled in his male apparatus. She let the pillow drop lower, revealing moist, gleaming, open lips. The cushion continued its progress over her creamy throat and then down, down, down to her exquisite, ample, succulent br— "Ouch!" In a quick, unforeseen move, she had whacked his chin with that cursed pillow. "Lilith!"

"I don't dance to your tune or anyone else's." She whapped him again, this time on his chest, displacing the white rose in his lapel.

"You little devil." He lunged at her.

She shrieked and ran around the sofa, her wild laughter streaming behind her.

He snatched up his own pillow.

"Oh no!" she cried, those eyes now alight with mischief.

"Oh yes!" He smacked her nimbly but gently on the shoulder, giving her a little taste of her own medicine. They commenced a childish swordplay game of lunge and parry with pillows.

Her laughter was infectious. He knew he should stop, but then the white feathers would no longer billow in the air and fall around her lovely face and that weight that had lifted from his chest would settle back to its usual position. And before he could stifle it, a chuckle escaped his mouth.

"I heard that!" she cried and raised her pillow high. "You can't deny it. It was mirth. You laughed."

"I deny everything." In a swift move, he gained the strategic upper hand by knocking the pillow from her grip. Unarmed, she attempted to flee. He leaped over the sofa's back, halting her retreat.

"Surrender, Lilith. You know you can never defeat me." He threatened both his cushiony weapons over her.

"Never! I'll fight you to the death!"

"So be it." He lunged forward for the deathblow, trapping her in the pillows. She laughed and fell back onto the sofa, almost taking him with her. He balanced his knee on the cushion and studied her. She lay with her dark hair splayed wildly around her head, flower petals and little white feathers trapped in the locks. Her shoulders shook with silent laughter, causing her breasts to jiggle beneath the thin fabric of her costume. She was doing something he had never seen her do before: smile. A true, unguarded, non-manipulative or -malicious, luscious smile. It heightened the color in her cheeks and softened her eyes. They now gazed at him with an expression he wouldn't have associated with Lilith: tenderness.

It seemed the most natural thing in the world to lean down and kiss her, as if he had done it a hundred times before. Her skin was warm silk and her lips were like tasting honey, leaving him wanting more of their sweetness. The peaks of her full breasts rubbed against his chest as she shifted beneath him when his tongue slipped inside her. She met the pressure of his mouth and released a hum as her fingers tangled in his hair, pulling him even closer. Her scent of citrus and vanilla overpowered his senses and erased any rational thoughts from his mind. His cock hardened, straining against his pantaloons. He hadn't felt this hunger for a woman in months. All those days of endless parliamentary sessions, lines and lines of estate accounts, and dull musical evenings. He suddenly felt sick of it all. He released her mouth long enough to murmur, "Sweet Lilith."

"Lord Marylewick!" She shoved him away and bolted to her feet. Her eyes were dilated with horror.

Reality hit like freezing hailstones pelting from the sky.

"I'm sorry!" he gasped. What had he done? Where was his brain? "I'm truly, honestly sorry. Forgive me."

"Oh God!" She rubbed her lips with the back of her hand. "It was just a game. What have I d—You're the…" She fled the room.

He raked his fingers through his hair and paced, his heart thundering. He had never lost control like that before. What had come over him?

Black shame wormed in his gut. He hadn't been a gentleman. In a matter of seconds, he had managed to breach his code of honor, his integrity, all the things around which he ordered his life.

He snatched up his hat and cane, and opened the door. Lilith wasn't in sight, thank heavens. He couldn't face her. He needed…he needed air. He couldn't breathe. He ripped opened his tie and yanked at his collar buttons as he pushed through the raucous crowd.

The cool air outside offered no relief. The two gentlemen, Byronesque locks and scarlet cravat, were still engaged in their drunken philosophical debate.

"Art is about finding meaning in the gaping chasm of meaninglessness."

"Death, my friend. It's all death and dying and—"

"For God's sake, lads," George bellowed. "It's about coitus. Every bit of it. Coitus, copulation, fornication, shagging." He jogged down to meet his approaching carriage. "Take me home," he ordered his groom.

Two

LILITH TORE THROUGH THE GUESTS, MURMURING HER apologies to the people beckoning her to join them. Her body quaked. What had happened? How could that man, after disparaging her manners and her person, dare to kiss her?

More to the disturbing point, how could she have kissed him back? Why did his body feel so safe and snug atop hers? Something was very wrong with her. For God's sake, he was the Sultan Murada in flesh and blood.

She had to get to the sanctuary of her bedchamber. Words, sentences, and phrases of vitriol burned in her mind. She had to commit them to paper before they incinerated her.

She closed the door to her garret bedchamber, shutting out the party raging below. She patted about until she found her matches and then lit her lamp. Light illuminated her walls adorned with copies of paintings by the Pre-Raphaelite Brotherhood and French Impressionists.

Her writing desk remained in the disheveled state in

which she had left it. A drained pot of oolong tea and an empty box of toffee sat atop her beloved volumes of Keats, the Brontë sisters, and Christina Rossetti. Telltale signs of a fruitless morning and afternoon spent staring at the page as a deadline loomed, and her mind was incapable of none but the most uninspired and tepid of words. When her unreliable muse failed to make an appearance, Lilith had decided to dress like the one in the painting. It was supposed to have been a fun joke.

The joke didn't seem so funny when only a thin layer of silk had separated her body from Marylewick's muscled, aroused one.

Her fingers were shaking as she fished her portfolio and key from her desk drawer. She unlocked the portfolio's tiny latch and slipped out her latest pages. Only her cousins, Frances and Edgar, knew she was the author of *Colette and the Sultan*. Heaven forbid that George would find out she wrote the sensational stories. Since she was too old to be hidden conveniently in another boarding or finishing school, he would tuck her away in an asylum. He was painfully old-fashioned in his views on women. And by old-fashioned, she meant Roman. In his mind, women should never venture from their homes, much less have their names venture into journals.

She grabbed her pen, jammed it into the inkwell, and under where she had written: *Colette's tale was abruptly ended when in her confused state (and much to the dismay of her publisher, a character heretofore unmentioned but always looming in the background) she accidentally stepped in front of a herd of angry camels and was trampled to death,* she now penned:

Lord Marylewick's powerful body trapped Colette beneath him. His caftan was of the finest silk and gold embroidery. Its delicate beauty was wasted on his hard, brutish face and body. Colette refused to give in to fear. She would not give him the pleasure of her terror.

As always, she would change Marylewick's name to Sultan Murada before she gave the clean copy to her publisher. She would remove any incriminating vestiges of Marylewick's annoying mannerisms and alter his handsome features to a better reflection of his true ugly personality. Marylewick's pale gray eyes were changed to vacuous, cold black. The graceful arch in his brows flattened to severe slashes. His lips, which she now knew to be as lusciously soft as they looked, were reduced to a cruel line. However, the sultan sported Marylewick's unyielding jaw.

For now, she didn't need to think of the trifling details of appearance. She was a mere scribe to her fast-flowing muse.

He lifted her veil. The vivid sunlight burned her eyes.

"Your father is dead," he growled. "But my spies know you carry his secret. The formula for Greek Fire. Give it to me, woman."

"I would rather follow my father in death," she answered in Persian.

He drew the sword from his sash and held it above her thundering heart. The blade penetrated the thin fabric of Colette's peasant caftan, in which she had disguised herself in her attempt to flee the sultan and his army. She could feel the sharp point poised on her skin.

"Death is too merciful and does not achieve my aim," Marylewick spat. "I will make you my slave. Your life is my possession."

"Do what you will." Her voice remained steady despite the rapture in her breast.

"Wait! What? Muse, did you say 'rapture in her breast'?" Lilith asked. "No, no. For God's sake, he's making her his slave. She can't feel anything but abhorrence for him."

But her muse continued on this dangerous path.

"You've already taken my home, my books, my art, all I have known," Colette cried. "But the contents of my mind cannot be possessed. You will never know the gardens of my heart."

"I won't?" His voice was creamy and low. "My fair Colette, it's not your lush, flowering heart I desire but the sweet nectar from your wet lips."

He dropped his sword.

A hot, heady wave coursed through Colette's body as his mouth descended upon hers—

"What! No, no, Muse, you are wrong. Pick up the sword this instant and aim at her heart again."

Lilith's mule-headed muse refused to listen.

His rough fingers gently caressed her—

"Dammit, Muse! You stop that!" Lilith leaped

back from the desk and stared at her words as if they had come alive—ugly Frankensteins shocked to life. "Muse, you had better have a devious plan in mind, because Colette is far too intelligent and possesses too much taste to find Marylewick the least bit alluring."

"But, darling, Lord Marylewick *is* alluring," a female voice said.

Lilith wheeled around. Her cousin-in-law, Frances, had opened the door and ambled in. A tipsy smile played on her unnaturally cherry-red lips. "Terribly alluring," Frances said. "Why, when he walks into the room, the heavens open and angels sing." She waved her hand, jangling her paste diamond bracelets. "But then he insists on speaking and—"

"Hell opens, choirs of demons sing, and Satan falls. Paradise lost." Lilith began to quote from Milton's masterpiece. "'Me miserable! which way shall I fly / Infinite wrath, and infinite despair? / Which way I fly is Hell; myself am Hell; / And, in—'"

"Darling, darling, you know I get a headache when you become dramatic."

Frances's blond curls were twisted around ostrich plumes. Pink fabric roses clustered at the bodice and down the bustle of her purple gown. She was vivid and vibrant, and Lilith worshipped her.

After years of the Maryle family sending her from one boarding school to the next, Lilith had finally managed to escape to her paternal cousins, Edgar and Frances Dahlgren. They took her in and kept her safe from George's controlling clutches. Lilith savored their exciting world of artists, musicians, and writers. Just being amid the stunning art was as close to heaven as she could get on Earth. She had always wanted to dwell in a story or painting. As if she could step out of her anxious life and into the paper and canvas and exist in a better world.

She'd learned at a tender age that books and art offered a kind of escape from the loneliness and fear she suffered amid the strict, uniform living of boarding school life. At seven, she taught herself to read while hiding behind the curtains in the alcove of the school's study. She remembered laughing aloud when reading Dickens's *Pickwick Papers. So this is laughter,* she had thought, reflecting on the rise and release in her chest and the peace that flooded her body. What the outside world couldn't provide her—a true home, loving parents, kindness, companionship, and laughter—she had found in books.

Later, after she grew older and bolder, having learned to make friends, conceal sweets in her mattress, smoke a cigar, and sneak out of the seventh floor dorm windows at night, she still craved to escape into art, this time into the darker reflections of Mary Shelley, Emily Brontë, and her beloved Keats. She found kindred spirits in the works of the Pre-Raphaelite Brotherhood. She spent hours studying their paintings of beauty seemingly locked away behind an invisible wall—perfection so close, but never attainable.

"I saw you fly away." Frances clutched the bedpost. "Has odious Marylewick vexed you again? Did he say anything about your money?"

Lilith rested her pen on the tray. "Of course he did! The man can't mutter three sentences without reminding me. 'Hello. What fine weather we've been having. Did I mention that I control all your money and expect you to grovel for it?'"

"He isn't stopping your allowance, is he?"

"Until next month, you can be sure."

"Dear God! But we need—" Frances visibly checked herself and began again in a calmer voice. "What happened?"

Lilith's face heated. She glanced at her pages, where Colette remained trapped beneath the sultan. "He, er…he was angry because of the exhibit opening, what I was wearing, and that I had lied to him—which I hadn't." Lilith couldn't sit still and began tidying her empty toffee papers. "You see, when I begged for extra funds on Monday, I told him that we had outrun the grocer, which was true, and that I had outrun my gowns, which was also true, because I can hardly get into them anymore due to my little toffee problem. I couldn't tell him that I needed money for the gallery. I didn't have the fortitude to sit through the denigration of me, my lifestyle, and my bohemian friends, only to be told no. He detests you and Edgar and thinks you're a terrible influence upon me."

"We try our best, darling."

"I meant to go to the shops directly after I spoke with him. Truly. Except that Monday was particularly gray and soggy, and you know how low I become after meeting with George. He makes me feel horrible about myself. I thought a tiny spot of tea and toffee in my favorite teashop would brighten my spirits. And what do you know, I smashed into Figgy."

"You didn't tell me about Figgy."

Lilith sank into her chair.

"The poor man. He hasn't written a poem since his wife died. He was a dreadful sight, disheveled and unshaven. My heart bled for him. How could I not help? So I gave him a few pounds."

Frances groaned. "You are too generous, and it's dreadful. Charity, luv, begins at home. *This* home." She waved about her.

"But I gave the rest of the monies to you for the exhibit opening. Don't tell me we need even more."

Frances bowed her head. "Edgar hasn't sold a painting, whether his or other artists', in a month."

Oh no! Their little household rolled along on tenuous finances. Lilith gave money for rent, coal, and groceries from her monthly allowance, but running a gallery and supporting a community of underappreciated artists stretched their meager funds.

"Frances, I simply can't crawl back and beg George after he kissed—" She faltered, realizing what she had admitted aloud. She moved hastily to cover her mistake. "I can't—"

"Wait, did you just say *kissed*?" Frances lit up.

"No." Lilith gazed at Frances with wide, guileless eyes, a trick she had perfected in school.

Frances, keener than Lilith's old schoolmistresses, would have none of it. "Yes, you did. You said 'after he kissed.'"

Frances crossed to Lilith, her eyes aglitter, and knelt before her. "Did he kiss you? Truly? On the lips?"

Lilith removed her beloved volume of Keats from under the teapot and hugged it to her chest. The worn leather binding gave her comfort. "I don't want to talk about it."

"No, no, my darling, you don't say 'he kissed' and then leave me in suspense. Now tell me all that happened, starting from the beginning and then lingering about the kiss part. Leave nothing out."

Lilith released a long breath. Frances was quite tenacious and wouldn't let up until Lilith threw her a scrap. "It was the usual banter. You know I behave dreadfully around that man. I taunt, I tease. I say the most outrageous things to keep him at bay. I can't let him near the real me, because he would only mock and hurt me in the deepest way. So it's always veiled barbs and games, except this time the game took a turn out of my control. He kissed me, and his male part, it…it…never mind."

Frances clapped her hands and gleefully laughed. "No, no, this is delicious. What did you do to that man's instrument?"

"Nothing. It engorged of its own accord. I did nothing." Well, maybe a few things she wouldn't admit despite Frances's demand for detail—the mocking play, teasing dance, pillow fight, and how for a moment, he appeared like an adorable boy when he laughed. Nor would she reveal that briefly, she had actually desired to know the feel of him deep inside her.

"Was his manly shaft very big?" Frances relentlessly interrogated.

"What! How can you think about such a thing as that?"

"I always think about such things. I make a practice of it. "

Normally Lilith would have laughed, admiring Frances's unabashedly naughty mind. But Lilith wasn't accustomed to thinking of George in such intimate terms. It was disconcerting and made her painfully self-conscious. "I suppose so. I'm not personally acquainted with any *real* male parts."

"George could remedy that."

"What? Absolutely not!" Nonetheless, Lilith's mind filled with images of her and George's bodies entwined like in those vivid illustrations in *Love's Wondrous Positions* that she had found when she was fifteen, hidden inside the schoolmistress's copy of Hannah Moore's lectures. Lilith had "borrowed" the guide and showed it to her friends over jellies and giggles late that night in their room. These were the mysteries that proper girls would only know once wedded. However, in Edgar and Frances's liberal circles, marriage hardly signified. One needn't be married to enjoy Love's Wondrous Positions. And Lilith had received a handful of casual propositions since living with her cousins that she had readily turned down.

She wanted something more. She desired to give herself to a love that was worthy of Keats—unfettered and all-consuming love. She had been waiting years for such an attachment and was beginning to think it was too pure to exist. Perhaps her dream was merely the leftover yearnings of a lonely child who wanted to be loved completely.

"So after his ardent showing, what happened?" Frances refused to let the subject drop.

"I leaped away. I felt…" Wild? Throbbing? Exhilarated? Terrified? Ashamed? "*Repulsed*, of course. Then he apologized."

"He apologized!"

"Yes, profusely." She didn't describe the horror

twisting his features. No doubt he was disgusted to have lowered himself to touch her. A stinky gutter rat would carry less taint than lowly Lilith.

"This is very, very good, darling. You have the upper hand now." Frances began to pace in the small space between Lilith's bed and her desk, her brows lowered in concentration. "You must play upon his guilt."

Lilith was taken aback at her cousin's scheming. "Pardon?"

"Don't you see, George prides himself on always being proper and right. But, alas, he has tumbled from his self-righteous throne. Trust me, dearest, this is the perfect time to ask for more money."

"The perfect time is never! But since we live in an imperfect world, I'll just wait until my allotted fifteen-minute appointment next month. I won't go back before then. "

Frances's features tightened to angry lines. She opened her mouth to say something, but stopped. She tilted her head. "Are you sure you didn't enjoy that kiss and arousal?"

"What?"

She sashayed toward Lilith. "Maybe you're ashamed of your own feelings for George?"

"No! Never!"

Frances ran a strand of Lilith's hair between her thumb and index finger. "Were his lips soft, my dear? Does his body feel as exquisite as it looks?"

"I'm not playing your game."

"But I wager you played for him, didn't you? Look at you, all flushed."

"What?" Lilith yanked away from Frances. She

didn't know why, but tears welled in her eyes. "Pray, do you realize how much pain George and his family have caused me? I came to my new papa with my young, tender heart open. I didn't understand such things as title, wealth, and ancestry. I thought this new papa might be kind and love me. And we would be a true family. And…and my stepfather ordered my mother to send me away. But I was never good enough for the Maryles. And now George controls me like a puppet because of that bloody trust. He becomes irate when he tugs a string and I refuse to leap." She covered her face. "And I kissed him. I kissed my very tormentor. I'm not humiliating myself before George by asking for any more money until my next allotment. I refuse."

"The gallery, darling," Frances whispered. "We are struggling. I don't know how much longer we can continue."

"I'll write more!" Lilith cried. "I'm finally inspired tonight. See? Words." She held up her page. "Good words…well, some of them. My elusive muse is rather obstinate."

"Damn your muse!" Frances balled her fists. "We can't live on three pounds a chapter, let alone support a gallery!" She pressed her hand to her mouth, catching herself. "I'm sorry, darling. I didn't mean to raise my voice." Her lips trembled.

Lilith rushed to her cousin and embraced her. Frances and Edgar had taken her into their hearts and the company of fascinating artists. If she lost her home and Frances and Edgar, she had nowhere and no one to go to…but George. "Let me talk to the publisher," she implored. "The story is very popular now. Maybe I can get more money, or write another story. Several stories."

"What? Six pounds a chapter? It's not near enough." Frances studied Lilith with her shiny, wet eyes. "Sometimes we must let go of our childish, unattainable ideals. Sometimes we must kiss the fusty patron frog for our art's sake, and pretend that he is a prince."

Lilith pulled back. "George isn't even a frog. He is much lower. He's the sultan. He and his family have broken my heart again and again. L-let me ask the publisher tomorrow. If he won't give me enough money, well, then I'll go to George. Will that do?"

Frances kissed Lilith's cheek. "Thank you, my love," she whispered and left.

Lilith trudged to her desk, her shoulders slumping under the weight of worry. "You heard that, Muse, I need money. No more rapturous breasts or sweet nectar on lips."

She dipped her pen and began to write.

When the sultan's lips touched hers, she was surprised at their softness.

"Muse! I warned you. If you don't behave…I'll…I'll…"

Hmm, how does one punish a muse?

"I'll force us to eat eel pie and ale in a dirty tavern full of drunken dockworkers who think they belong on the Royal Opera House stage."

Colette submitted to his kiss as her fingers patted

about the ground until she found what she desired:
the ivory handle of his sword.

"Oh, that's brilliant, Muse!"

Her chamber, the party below, Marylewick's stiff manhood, and her scary emotions all scattered from her mind. She became lost in the rushing current of her story, her hand flying as she scribed her muse's words.

∜

George was relieved to learn his sister had already retired for the evening when he returned to Grosvenor Square. He didn't want to speak to anyone. He removed his tie and collar on the way to his study. A golden fire was burning in the grate and his decanter of brandy had been refilled. His secretary had piled a fresh crop of correspondence with a new letter from his mother concerning the Maryle annual house party on the top. He didn't have the wherewithal to read her latest demands, so he poured a glass of brandy and sank into his leather wingchair by the fire. He studied the flames on the liquid surface. The lulling reddish-brown tones of the alcohol and black shadows of the dancing flames. He squinted his eyes until all the colors seemed to sparkle on the glass.

He couldn't explain what happened on that sofa between him and Lilith. He had been weak. No matter how wild, alluring, and infuriating, she was his trustee and responsibility.

Maybe the months of the Stamp Duty Extension Bill going back and forth between the houses in conference and the pressure from Disraeli to make the bill pass had worn him down. George was a Tory from the egg, as his Maryle ancestors had been before him, and like any dutiful political warrior, he fought his party's wars without question.

Maybe the upcoming house party frayed his nerves. A major yet subtle battle would be waged at it in the midst of waltzes and croquet. The party was a treacherous affair of political and romantic maneuvering as ambitious leaders tried to foist their ideas—or their daughters—upon George. He rolled his burning brandy on his tongue and thought of his young female guests.

Maybe it was finally time to get married. Perhaps the lack of consistent female attention lay at the root of his problem with Lilith. After all, he hadn't had the best of luck with his last mistresses. They were all lovely ladies and the first weeks with each had been spectacular, but his restlessness soon returned after the initial lust had burned out. He kept craving more, wanting something they couldn't provide and he couldn't articulate. Maybe he should concede that this restlessness would always be a part of him, stop expecting a woman to sate it, and marry.

Maybe.

However, he knew one thing with certainty. He had to apologize to Lilith. He was a gentleman, and would not cower from his obligations, no matter how odious. Of course, she would lord it over him for months and use it as leverage to wheedle more money. But it couldn't be helped. He had been in the wrong.

In the morning, he would send out his secretary for flowers that said "I'm sorry. I assure you that it won't happen ever again. However, I still don't approve of your wild ways." Was that hyacinth and Venus flytraps? He would personally deliver them to Half Moon Street after his meeting with his man of business and be done with the bad business before Parliament.

But for now, he didn't want to think anymore. He reached for an old issue of *McAllister's Magazine* to let the story of Colette wash over his troubled mind. He opened to the very first chapter in the series. Colette learns of the encroachment of the sultan and his army on her Greek village. The sultan desires her ailing father's discovery, the components of the fabled Greek Fire—a fire born of water and difficult to extinguish. The sultan has suppressed the surrounding regions through a regime of cruelty and terror. Colette knows that the secret of Greek Fire would make him unconquerable. She attempts to escape to the safety of Northern Greece with her dying father.

If only Colette existed in bodily form: loving, true, compassionate, and intelligent. She would be his wife.

Three

Lilith burst into the dining room that morning, her mind whirling from drinking cup after cup of unadulterated oolong tea through the night. She wore her lucky lavender gown for the upcoming meeting with her publisher. To fit in it required lying face-down on the floor as their only maid shoved her foot into the small of Lilith's back and tugged mercilessly at her corset laces. In the crook of her arm, Lilith carried her new, clean chapter, devoid of references to Marylewick.

Frances slumped over a plate of untouched toast and a cupful of steaming tea. Her pallid forehead rested in her hand. Across the table, her husband, Edgar, assumed a matching pose of overindulged, paying-the-piper agony.

Lilith was too hopped up on tea to be brought down. She gazed around to make sure the servant girl wasn't lurking about and then raised her pages. "My darling cousins, I present you with a masterpiece of sensational fiction. You see, when you threaten your muse, lovely things can happen." Lilith spoke in that fast, charging clip brought on by caffeine-induced euphoria. "My publisher will adore this chapter and certainly shell out more money. Just listen—'Colette hold the veil to her scared, tremble head and crouching down in tiny cave made by a collapsed tree. Over her head, she could hear the sultan barking orders rudely at his reticule and'—oh God!" Her face heated. "I wrote this rubbish! The verbs are wrong and the words...this is terrible. Did I really say he barked orders at a lady's valise? I can't show this drivel to anyone!"

"No!" Frances bolted up and then swayed for moment, muttering something about never drinking punch again before saying, "I felt your words deep inside me. They stirred my soul."

Lilith looked at her askew. "Poor grammar stirs your soul?"

"Darling, how can you be provocative and inventive when you use language like everyone else?" Frances linked her arm through Lilith's and began leading her toward the hall. "Passion knows no bounds or rules. Don't be a slave to grammar. Live and write freely." She opened the front door and gently nudged Lilith onto the pavement. In the stark sunlight, Lilith could see the network of tiny wrinkles under her cousin's tired eyes.

"Is something wrong?" Lilith asked. "Aside from the punch, that is."

Frances gazed down. "I didn't want to say this in front of Edgar. But he and I had a dreadful row after the party. He's terribly worried about money."

"I'm so sorry." Lilith embraced her dear

cousin-in-law. "I'm going to find what quids I can. I promise. What more can I do? Tell me."

"He and I just need to be alone for a little reconciliation today. Do you mind staying away until after two o'clock? Please."

"Of course, whatever you require." Lilith put aside her vision of returning victorious from the publisher and celebrating by curling up in her bed until the evening parties began.

"Now you go sell your chapter, make a wagonload of money, follow your dreams." Frances kissed her cheek. "Good luck, my darling. I adore you." She turned away, stepped inside, and quietly shut the door.

Lilith hurried down the walk, muttering under her breath, "Get quids," then added, "get wagonloads of quids. Mountains of quids. All that matters are quids." She practiced the words she would say to her editor all the way to Fleet Street. But when she reached the imposing brick building with *McAllister* written across the top, she felt like a scared child again, arriving at a new school, unsure of what her life would be like. Would she make friends, would the teachers be kind, or if not, could they be easily bamboozled, would the library have many books? She clutched her pages and remembered Frances's worried expression when she left that morning. Lilith couldn't allow her fears to paralyze her. She must face the publisher and demand more money for the sake of her cousin's marriage and the gallery. But still she remained planted on the spot. A tiny voice in her head reminded her: *It's either McAllister or Marylewick. Choose.*

She forced herself to take a step forward, and then

another, feeling her confidence rise. A determined smile spread her lips by the time she was ushered into Mr. McAllister's office.

❦

A half hour later, Lilith emerged from Mr. McAllister's office nine pounds richer and holding a document outlining the terms for another story. She wondered why she had been so afraid to ask for money from the publisher before. He was all too happy to agree to her terms and enthusiastic about her new story ideas.

Sunlight gleamed off the roofs and tops of carriages. Lilith released a long breath. She had money, true money, to give the gallery, not a measly shilling here and there. Money that she didn't have to beg, tease, plead, or lie about to squeeze from George. A small, fragile root of hope burgeoned in her heart: perhaps one day very soon she might be able to support herself as a writer, as well as help Frances, Edgar, and their gallery. She might not need George after all.

She halted in the current of human traffic, raised her head, and laughed. The idea of independence felt like cool rain on a parched desert. "*I sing the body electric.*" She cried out Walt Whitman's line and smiled at the confused stares she garnered.

Of course, her writer's imagination ran wild. As she wove through the crowds, she daydreamed of reaching Charles Dickens's and Victor Hugo's literary status. Having her bestselling novels cram the bookshop windows and demands for her to read passages to packed auditoriums. Without monetary concerns, she could marry a chimney sweep if she pleased and have her name appear in fat bold print on a leather-bound book and no blustering Marquess of Marylewick could stop her. In fact, she would send George copies of her bestselling books, signed "Keep the money (and your stiff man part), Lilith Dahlgren." What would she do with all her delicious money?

But the more pertinent question at hand was *where would she pass the time until Frances and Edgar had thoroughly reconciled*?

A silly question, really, she thought as she stepped into a bookshop.

The smell of leather, ink, and pages crowded out her thoughts. She was in paradise. All around her were shelves and shelves of glorious books which whispered *read me, escape into my delightful world*.

She found a vacant chair, as if waiting for her, by a second floor window. For the next three hours—or was it four?—she was lost in the intrigue of Tolstoy's Russian aristocracy or giggling at the droll irrationality of Alice's Wonderland.

That she managed to restrain herself from buying a book, or journal, or toffee was a singular miracle. She was very proud of herself. As she headed home, she kept her head and hat low to avoid recognition by any needy artist acquaintance who wanted money to finance a brilliant project. But she couldn't resist the desperate plea from a barefoot street waif under the draper's shop window and gave him several shillings.

When she turned onto Half Moon Street a little after two o'clock, all she wanted was to be released from her corset so that she might crawl under the covers. Yet something had her neighbors aflutter.

They milled outside their doors, their gazes fixed on an enormous wagon pulled up beside her home.

"What in all that's good in the world?" Lilith muttered and hastened her step.

As she drew nearer, two boulderlike men clad in workmen's clothes strode from her house. One held a stack of books while the other, sporting a brown cap, read from a book open in his hands. Her volume of Keats's poems!

"Aye, Keats was known for his visual imagery," the man in the cap said. "Whereas his contemporaries Byron and Shelley—"

"That's mine!" Lilith raced down the street and tried to rip Keats from the stranger. The book fell to the ground, spine cracked and face open—all the lovely words that had sustained her through the dark times, in the mud. When she bent to save the volume, her eyes caught the contents of the wagon. Her other books, prints, and her writing desk where she hid her locked portfolio! "My art! My things!" She released a strangled cry. "Help me!" she begged the crowd.

No one moved to help. A few neighbors snickered behind their hands.

Gripping her wounded Keats volume to her bosom, Lilith attempted to climb into the wagon.

"Another Bedlamer," a deep male voice said. The powerful, rough hands of the two workmen drew her back. "No, miss, you mustn't do that."

Again her beloved Keats poetry fell onto the manure-drenched road.

"Frances! Edgar!" She kicked her captors.

"Now, now," brown cap said. "Violence is never the proper course."

"I'll be as violent as I blooming well please," she shouted. "Someone fetch the police."

The neighbors only laughed as if this was a merry game. "Frances! Edgar!" she called again. "Where are you? Help me!"

"Lads, ain't this a pretty picture?" said a third man exiting the house. He held Lilith's treasured etching copy of Millais's drowned *Ophelia*. Unlike his companions, this workman was thin and wiry. His mouth was the slack type that hung perpetually open. "Why would she drown herself?"

"My *Ophelia*!" Lilith cried.

"Who?" said the thin man.

"That's Ophelia from *Hamlet*, Ronald," the capped man explained in a calm voice, despite Lilith's kicks.

"Aye, little Ophelia," Ronald said. "Hamlet was a right blackguard to her."

Lilith flung up her feet and then slammed down her boot heels onto the men's hard shin bones. The grip on her upper arms loosened, she yanked free and raced forward, shrieking, "Let go of my *Ophelia*!"

The slender man yelped, dropped the print, and slumped onto the steps, crossing his arms over his face. "Don't let her hurt me!"

She snatched up the print and raised it over her head as if it were a club or sword. "Ophelia might enjoy a little bloody revenge, if you and your friends don't return my things."

"What is happening here?" a familiar baritone demanded. Oh no!

She spun around, her picture still poised for striking. George stood in a precision-tailored gray suit, gleaming shoes, top hat, and holding a vase of purple hyacinths and hazel flowers. The edges of his nostrils were quivering and his lips thinned in a scowl.

"I'm being robbed, George! Help me!"

She watched his gaze move from her to the man crumpled on the ground, shielding his face and pleading for mercy, to the men rubbing their shins, to the crowd, and then back to her. The muscles at the back of his jaw pulsed. "Get inside this instant," he hissed.

"Aye, I'm sorry, guv'nor, but I'm afraid she can't do that," said the man in the cap. "Me and me mates work for Mr. Villiers, who owns this row. Seeing how the occupants at this residence are seven months behind on rent, we've been ordered to remove the contents of the home, lock the doors, and take everything to Mr. Villiers."

"Seven months!" Lilith exclaimed. "But I gave Frances and Edgar money every month for rent. They would have told me. Mr. Villiers has made a terrible mistake. Let me speak to my cousins and you will see. Then you must put back everything exactly or I'll call my solicitor." Lilith didn't actually have a solicitor, but the men didn't need to know that.

"Aye, miss," said the man. "There ain't no one in that house. No servants. Nobody."

She grabbed the iron railing, feeling her legs weaken. "Impossible."

"Lilith, did I not warn you about them?" George barked.

She was about to scream *Shut your stupid mouth, Edgar and Frances could never leave me*, when the man hunched in terror on the steps lowered his arms and ventured, "Are you Miss Lilith?"

"Yes."

"I found this letter with your name on it on a table." He shifted to reach deep into his pocket and fished out a crumpled letter. "Lilith's a pretty name," he told her, holding out the missive. "I love lilies."

But it was George who snatched up the letter. "I shall have this," he announced in his authoritative tone. "I'm responsible for Miss Dahlgren."

"You are not responsible for me. Hand me the letter this instant. It is mine." She tried to seize it but was hampered by her cumbersome print of *Ophelia*. In a flicking motion, he snapped open the letter. She could only peer around his arm to read:

> *Dearest Lilith,*
>
> *I'm sorry, my love. Edgar and I must retrench, and we can't take you with us this time. My darling, remember what I told you last night. Keep tempting stiff-rumped George, play upon his guilt. Kiss the fusty frog, and he'll give you a golden ball.*
>
> *Sincerely,*
> *Frances Dahlgren*

"Right, then," George said. "I'm a gullible frog. I see it clearly now."

Lilith sank onto the step, clutching drowned *Ophelia* tight to her chest.

They had left her.

She had brought them into her life, trusted them, shared her secrets—for God's sake, they were the only people who knew about *Colette and the Sultan*. These were the facts of the situation, but she couldn't feel them. They didn't feel real. Maybe she had fallen asleep at the library. Maybe this was a nightmare brought on by the Edgar Allen Poe short story she had read.

Wake up, Lilith. This isn't happening. Wake up!

She stretched her eyes wide, but the nightmare remained. Then the emotions came down like a nasty mudslide. The last fifteen years fell away, all the lessons learned, all the barricades erected around her fears. She was eight again, scared, hurt, and angry. Just this afternoon, she had thought the universe had finally tilted her way. She was going to be the famous, rich writer, liberated from Lord Marylewick and his family. She could live on her own terms.

She bowed her head. Colette had lost. She couldn't escape the sultan. He had her from the beginning. It would all end tragically.

"There, there," soothed the worker whose life she had previously threatened.

She was vaguely aware of George striding about, carrying on in his usual commanding manner. "I am the Marquess of Marylewick. My secretary shall see directly to this inconvenience. Please restore the contents of the home to their rightful place. Miss Dahlgren, go inside immediately. Miss Dahlgren. Lilith?"

She pointed to his shoe. "George, y-you're stepping on John Keats." She heard a ripple of laughter through the crowd. What was funny?

"What?" She watched him glance down to where a page of Keats's poems had fallen from its binding and was crushed under his heel. "For heaven's sake," he hissed. He bent down and, with the hand not holding the flowers, snatched the page from under his shoe and then the book that rested nearby. He handed her the volume and page. "Go inside. You've entertained your neighbors long enough."

She slowly grasped the poems and then pressed them and the *Ophelia* print to her heart. She refused George's offered hand and managed to rise to her feet in jerky, flailing motions. As she turned to enter her home, she stopped. "I'm sorry if I hurt you. Please forgive me," she told the workmen, and went inside.

❧

"Lilith, sit down," George ordered her, trying to keep his anger reined in. He pointed to the only piece of furniture left in the parlor: the sofa where last night they had enjoyed that notorious kiss. Just looking at the pillows heightened his fury. He wasn't a stiff-rumped, fusty frog! Is that how she—everyone—viewed him?

Well, Lilith had gone too far this time. He wanted nothing more than to wash his hands of her. She must marry. He refused to be her trustee frog to kiss and misuse any longer.

She shrank into the sofa's corner, still gripping her print and book, her inky eyes large and glassy with unshed tears.

For a quiet moment, he forgot his rage, struck by the picture she formed by the curves of her profile against the hard jut of the wooden frame and the horizontal

line formed by the sofa. Her mouth was drawn, her
skin almost white; tired brown shadows had formed
under her eyes. Even so, she was beautiful, like a gem
showing different facets depending on the light. He
wanted to rage at her, but at the same time he wanted
to study her quietly until he could capture her essence.

Damn her!

He had to get her away from him.

"Lilith, this is it." He set his arrangement of purple
hyacinths and hazel—or, according to the language of
flowers, *I'm sorry* and *let's make up*—on the mantel.

"This is the last time I'm pulling you from the
suds." His voice boomed around him. He sounded
like his own father when he'd lectured young
George. "You *will* get married. I've given you
enough time to find a suitable, responsible gentleman
and all you've managed to do is cavort with half-wit
artists and your dubious Dahlgren relatives, all the
while spurning my wise advice. And you see where
it has gotten you. Nowhere."

He saw no change on her face, nothing to register
that his words had made any least impression on her
ramshackle brain. "I dislike being medieval about the
matter, but you have persisted in your wild and foolish
ways, leaving me little choice but to arrange a marriage
for you."

He expected a fight or a tease. The usual dance. She
only gazed out the window. The light illuminated her
pale skin and strands of red in her loose hair beneath
her lavender hat.

"Once established in a sound marriage, the money
is yours, and you'll become the responsibility of

another man, a new frog to kiss and manipulate," he continued, trying to goad her into a response. "Until that time, you will remain under my care and tutelage. You *will* obey me."

She closed her eyes.

"I expect you to be angry," he said, unsettled by her silence. "I expect you to say that I'm trying to control your life, shattering your soul. What have you to say?"

"'O Rose thou art sick!'" Lilith murmured. "'The invisible worm, / That flies in the night / In the howling storm: / Has found out thy bed / Of crimson joy: / And his dark secret love / Does thy life destroy.'"

"Please, Lilith," he implored. "No more Keats. No more melodrama."

"It's Blake, you idiot," she cried, shaking her spread palms. "William Blake! *The Sick Rose*."

"Can you just say what you mean and stop playing games?"

"I'm not...playing... I'm not..." She closed her eyes again and shook her head, as if she had given up on words. On him. "You don't understand that poem, do you? Your dry, inflexible mind can't even conceive its meaning?"

"Of course I do!" he replied. "You believe the vulnerable place in your heart, the wellspring of your tender passion, has been destroyed by what you sought to protect yourself from. And I am the invisible howling worm."

He halted, unsure where the ridiculous words he spoke originated. It worried him that he was capable of such inanity.

But she stared at him now, straight at him and only him. Her eyes, in their glorious gold and brown tones, were luminous.

He slipped onto the sofa beside her. "Why don't you want a true gentleman to take care of you?" All the hardness had drained from his voice. "To keep you safe? To honor you?"

"I do."

"Then why do you feel you must manipulate and lie to me? Why do you think I don't have your best interests in mind? Can you try to trust me?"

"How can I?" She shook her head. "You're a Maryle. All you and your family ever wanted to do was send me away, pretend that I never existed. How can you have my best interest at heart if you don't know or care who I am?"

"Then tell me who you are." He tugged at her print of dead *Ophelia*, trying to remove it from her white-knuckled grip. "I dearly want to know the real Lilith."

She tightened her hold on the frame before she slowly released it. He carefully set it at their feet and then reached for her broken book. "Just try to refrain from the poetry for a while." He chuckled softly, a little white flag that he meant no harm.

"They left me." Her words were a brittle whisper. "They left me, George." In the briefest moment, he felt her pain all over him, the years and years of rejection and estrangement. Then she turned her head, closing herself off again.

"But I'm here." He grasped for her hand. "I haven't left you."

Tears welled in her eyes again, pooled in her lashes, and ran down her cheeks.

He panicked. "No, Lilith."

She brushed off his hands and turned, hiding her face as she wept.

His mind contained one thought: *Make Lilith stop crying*. Make her angry, annoyed, anything but this. He reached to touch her shoulder, but stopped, unsure. He waited in this awkward, impotent place for several painful seconds, his fingers hovering just above her. She swiveled around.

"Be quiet!" she cried.

"I didn't say anyth—"

She crushed her head into his chest. Her hat poked his chin and the feather tickled his face. For all his dislike of emotional outbursts and wild displays of emotion, he wrapped his arms around her shaking body.

"I'll make sure everything is well for you," he whispered in a soothing voice he didn't know he possessed. Meanwhile, his rational mind was shouting *What in the hell are you doing*? Was he being a gullible frog again? Was this a trick? And did he care?

"It won't be." Her lips brushed the skin above his collar as she spoke, sending a current of wild energy over him. What magic did she possess? It made no sense that the most annoying female in his life felt like the old ragged blanket he had slept with every night as a child until the nursemaid was ordered to toss it in the fire.

She pulled away.

"I want to be alone." She gazed at her hands, where she rubbed the palm of one hand with the thumb of the other. "I need to wri—I want to be alone."

"That's not wise."

She jerked her head up, her brows down, eyes hot. "What do you mean?"

"It's not wise to be alone to stew in dark thoughts when you're upset."

She stared at him for a beat more. Then a fragile but devilish smile wavered on her lips. "How would you know? Do you have dark thoughts, George? Is there a black stain on your soul that you have never revealed?"

"Of course," he quipped, easing back against the cushion. "When I'm not fighting with you, I'm excessively moody, brooding, and brimming with dark desire. Keats and those other chaps are mere shades of gray compared to my opaque blackness as I scribble parliamentary bills and orders for estate plumbing repairs."

"Stop making me chuckle. I'm very upset. I've lost my family…again."

He rested his hand on hers. "I'm your family."

"No, you're not."

He shrugged. "It says so on the trust paperwork. Bloodlines be dammed if the Bank of England says you're related."

"Well, I don't like you."

"So you see, we are family. True family members detest each other through thick and thin."

"You jest. You Maryles are a perfect family. You are idle summers of fresh berries and glacé, fluffy cakes, Sunday strolls in the park with a bouncing baby in the perambulator."

None of George's memories included such nostalgic memories. In fact, when he thought of his childhood, he remembered standing terrified before his father's enormous oak desk. He had waited there, chin down, resigned to the harsh punishment that his father would exact for painting a bright yellow and pink parrot on his wall. A good paddling to ensure his son didn't grow up to be an embarrassing molly of a man.

The memory made him restless. He desired to get away from this room and into the daylight.

"Let us go to the park." He reached for her elbow. "A little sunshine will bleach out all the dark spots in your heart."

"Thank you, but there is something I must...I need to do." She pulled away. "I just want to stay home and sleep."

"But Lilith," he said gently, "you can't stay here alone. This isn't your home anymore."

"What?" she cried, visibly surprised by his words. "You told those men to put everything back. This is my home!"

"I had the furniture and art returned because I have no other place to store it at present. I can't in good conscience allow an unmarried lady of three and twenty to be on her own."

"You are not my owner!"

He studied her fierce, defiant face and bit back his sharp retort about how she needed one.

"Do you have any notion of proper society, Miss Dahlgren?" The enormous amount of polishing that she would require before he could pop her off to a respectable gentleman sank in. "You don't, do you? No. You shall come to my home where you shall be under the wise chaperonage of my sister. While there, you shall practice wholesome habits and enjoy proper company. My sister and I will endeavor to teach you the finer points of manners, polite conversation, and the delicacies of better society—graces a gentleman of proper station will require of a wife."

Her mouth dropped open as if he had slapped her rather than saved her hide again. He only wished someone would take such good care of him—that he could set down his mantle of worry and responsibility for a day.

"I know all about the so-called finer points of manners, conversation, and delicacy." She was on her feet now. "I was sent to finishing school not once but twice."

He refrained from commenting about the waste of good money because he didn't care to sport a blackened eye to Parliament.

"Has it ever occurred to you, George, that I am the way I am because I desire to be? I am not an ignorant yahoo or a freakish aberration. I know this is shocking to hear, but not everyone finds membership in your elite circle of society the pinnacle of human existence."

She couldn't be worked on in this state. Now she waited with her eyes glittering and hands clenched, ready for the battle that he refused to fight.

"Right." He snatched up a pillow from the sofa and aimed it.

"Don't you dare!"

He shot her a smile and tossed the cushion in the air. She had to catch it, else it would land on her head. In the meantime, he seized her book of poetry. "Why don't you tell me what constitutes the pinnacle of your existence during a little stroll in the park," he said. "You can take Keats along, of course." But he didn't relinquish the volume. Instead he walked away with it, using it as a lure.

Four

"Isn't it a stunning day," George declared. The sunshine glistened on the lush grass and sparkled on the water. He protected Lilith's Keats volume in the crook of his arm and beat a steady rhythm with his walking stick. "It inspires one to write poems about the beauty of nature and such."

"Hand me my book, you vile toad," Lilith spat. She trailed a foot behind him.

"That's Lord Vile Toad to you. Or perhaps Lord Vile Fusty Frog is more appropriate. I will also answer to Your Exultant Fusty Frog and Your Fusty Frog Eminence." And he couldn't help but add with an arched brow over his shoulder, "And it's rumored that if you give me kisses, I'll dispense golden balls."

"Is that what you call your little surprise last night?" A challenging light burned in her eyes.

That devil inside him, who always came out to play in Lilith's company, volleyed back. "*Little* surprise?" His words were inappropriate and ungentlemanly, but he enjoyed seeing her mouth drop. *Don't play with fire or my manhood and not expect to get burned. Frog, indeed.*

Alas, his humor was short-lived. Ahead, a cluster of fashionable people strolled, surrounded by several ladies and gentlemen on horseback. George could make out Mrs. Pomfret, the wife of a powerful Tory MP from Yorkshire, and her daughter Cecelia. Guests at his upcoming house party. If he continued down this path, introductions would have to be made, evoking curious inquiries. Lilith, in her angry state, might make a scene. Correct that thought; she *would* make a scene even if she didn't open her mouth. She was like a rare white tiger. Stunning, but deadly. He couldn't release her into genteel society until he had properly trained her.

He seized her arm and veered onto a smaller path protected from view by spreading trees.

She wasn't fooled.

"Oh, Georgie, were those some of your dear society friends?" Her voice was all saccharine and innocence. She tugged at his arm. "Shall I ask them if they know about your little golden balls? Or will you give me my book back?"

"Truce." He offered up the book.

"Victory." She closed it to her bosom.

For several minutes, they walked in silence. He struggled to keep from glancing at her, taking in the way sunlight, filtered through the leaves, fell like lace upon her skin and how the breeze blew her hair willy-nilly about her cheeks. He wanted to somehow preserve this moment. He remembered her words from the other evening: "It's about capturing the ethereal and fleeting…" In his mind he saw this moment painted, all the colors and textures of the brushstrokes.

"George, why are you staring at me?"

He didn't realize he had fallen down a rabbit hole of thought. A mental leather strap slapped his wrist, and he hastened to cover his slip. "I'm thinking about what kind of husband would suit you."

"You mean what kind of husband would suit you for me? Does England have a bachelor diplomat in Siberia or Bangkok?"

"You may laugh, but now is your chance. What kind of man do you desire? What respectable man's society would represent the pinnacle of your existence so that I may find a genteel version of him for you? Or you can leave me to my own devices. Tell me, how do you feel about musty cigars or reading religious tracts?"

He casually chuckled to hide his curiosity. If she had ever fancied a man, she had never told him about it. He wondered what she found desirable.

"You're a bachelor and a marquess. It's more important for you to marry than me, so you can get busy creating a little marquess, and spare marquesses and daughters to barter for powerful clanlike alliances. Tell me what kind of wife you desire."

"No more games, Lilith. It's your future we are deciding."

"It's not a game. You tell me about you, and I'll tell you about me. A fair trade."

"Very well." He stopped walking. Behind him, ducks skimmed along the water's surface.

"I prefer…" He paused. On the tip of his tongue was Colette. But he wouldn't admit he desired a fictional character. That bit of lunacy he kept to himself. "I prefer…a gentle lady possessing pleasing manners and a clear mind," he said. "She must be charming but never vulgar. She must never embarrass me but assert herself in quiet ways."

This was harder than he thought. He couldn't explain that what he wanted was a woman to hold him safe to her body, soothe the restlessness inside him, say the words he couldn't express, tell him that she loved him only and fully. Instead, he said, "She should be tasteful and understated in her appearance."

The edge of Lilith's mouth hiked up in a way that said *Are you jesting?* "I'm shocked that you are not already married. There are many eligible ladies, as well as sofas, chairs, and ornamental rugs that fit that description."

"I answered your question," he said hotly. "And you mocked me."

She flinched as if he had stung her. When would he ever learn to stop playing her games? He was so busy mentally berating himself that he almost didn't hear her speak. She was using that unsettling quiet voice again. "I prefer a man who is kind."

"Merely kind? Not wildly romantic? Handsome in a severe Gothic manner? Brooding? Poetic—a modern Keats? A misunderstood artist?"

"You don't know me at all." The wind blew a strand of hair across her mouth. Again he felt the sensation that he was staring at one of those insane Impressionists' paintings. All the beauty and light assaulted his senses.

"Kindness," she continued, "loyalty, and a home."

"Only kindness, loyalty, and a home?"

She thought for a few seconds more. He could see the machinations of her mysterious mind working behind her eyes. "Yes."

"What about love?"

"I didn't realize it was in the offering."

"It could be. I could introduce you to a brooding poet of excellent breeding, competent accounting skills, and deep funds, and you could fall madly in love with him. And then you would have me to thank."

She walked on. "I think your definition of love and mine are very different."

"What is your definition?"

"You wouldn't understand, and you would mock me if I tried to explain."

He clasped her elbow, halting her progress. "I promise to be deadly serious."

She clutched her book tighter. On the river, a male duck raised high in the water and beat his wings to challenge another duck. George studied her as she watched the ensuing water fight and heated pursuit across the river.

"I'll just take kindness and loyalty in a husband," she said, still looking out at the river. "He must provide me a home, a true home, and he can't leave me."

"You should have told me this earlier. There are many more-than-suitable gentlemen who meet the bare requisites."

"Are there?" she whispered, no hint of the usual derision in her voice. When she turned her head, her large eyes earnest, the tears were starting to collect in the corners. He felt her pain in his own heart again. He longed to hold her, comfort her. Good God, this woman lit up his emotions. One minute he was furious at her and the next filled with sadness.

"Lilith, you could have...bloody hell!"

"What?"

"It's the Duke of Cliven and his son, Lord Charles." He nodded to two men strolling down the path. Both men sported canes and carefully tailored clothes.

The elder was tall with powerful shoulders, well-trimmed gray lambchop whiskers, and somber eyes in a lined face. He said very little, but when he did, bills were passed, prime ministers made, and treaties signed.

His third son, Lord Charles, was trim and athletic. Lord Charles was the most dashing, most witty, most sought-after man in London, according to George's sister. George knew him as his tormentor at Eton, rallying the other boys to ape George in the corridors and hide his Latin work. Now he and his father were the most powerful Whigs in Parliament, their influence spanning both houses. They sat on the fence regarding the Stamp Duty Extension Bill, enjoying letting George toad-eat them.

George had to make a decision of national importance in a matter of a few seconds. Stay, introduce Lilith, and put the tax bill in jeopardy, or hurry along and pretend not to see them.

He seized her elbow and spun her around. "Time to go back."

"Afraid to be seen with me?"

"Not at all," he lied, affecting a pleasant voice while trying to drag her along.

"Hello there, Lord Marylewick," Lord Charles called. "Wait up, my good man."

"Fuckery," George growled under his breath.

Lilith giggled. "I didn't know you were capable of such vibrant language. I rather like it."

"This is no laughing matter," George hissed under his breath. "I need their votes for an important bill. I'm begging you, Lilith. For once in your life, behave."

He affixed an amiable expression on his face and waved at Lord Charles. "Fine day, is it not?"

"You think I can't behave?" Lilith asked.

"I really don't have the time for this discussion," George growled through his pleasant countenance. "Don't ruin this bill for me, Lilith. Or you will regret it."

"Are you threatening me?"

"Yes."

What happened next took on that odd sensation George always experienced when tumbling from a horse. Time slowed so that he could notice every detail: the mischievous smile that snaked over Lilith's lips. The father's and son's expressions as the dazzling lady turned her mesmerizing gaze on them. The guile darkening Lord Charles's eyes. The burning fist twisting in George's gut when he bowed and the fatal words fell from his lips. "Your Grace, Lord Charles, may I present my...er...cousin, Miss Lilith Dahlgren."

Time returned to its normal speed as the conversations collided.

"Miss Lilith Dahlgren!" Lord Charles stopped in his tracks. His predatory expression was momentarily knocked away before returning stronger than before. "We meet *at last*." He bowed, a head-flinging, hand-sweeping act worthy of the stage.

"At last?" She blinked and performed a graceful curtsy.

"You attended school with my sister, Evangelina. For years, all we heard was Miss Lilith Dahlgren said this, Miss Lilith Dahlgren wore that. You made quite an impression on her."

"I had no idea." Lilith smiled, a gracious, polite one that George hadn't seen before. "Miss Evangelina certainly didn't require my fashion sense. She is quite the beauty. And so thoughtful and kind." This last compliment she addressed to the father, melting his usual grave countenance.

"Ah, she is but a slave to society's whims, a mere follower, not a leader such as yourself," Charles said. "All these last months, I've walked into art galleries to find to my dismay you had just been there. In fact, we missed each other by mere minutes at Paris last summer. I met your cousins instead—Mr. and Mrs. Edgar Dahlgren, no? I hope I don't put your nerves on edge when I admit I've been quite desirous to meet you. But you know, the more you desire something, the more elusive it becomes. I was beginning to believe that you were a dream."

"But now you have met me," she said, a bright twinkle in her eye. "Do you not think our dreams are far better than harsh reality?"

"Even in my dreams I could not imagine such magnificence as you."

Lilith laughed, a musical sound.

George was offended. He would never dream of being so fast with one of his sister's classmates whom he had just met. But the duke only chortled at his son's outrageous behavior, clearly as bamboozled by Charles as the rest of London society.

"Ah, I've made you blush prettily, which was really my objective," Charles said. "How has it escaped my notice all these years that you were Lord Marylewick's dear cousin? Marylewick, I demand that you meet me at dawn. You, my lord, must eat grass for this unpardonable offense of omission."

The man needed a proper set-down, but damned if George could deliver it.

"You are deliciously absurd," Lilith told Lord Charles. How easily she slipped into his breezy urbanity.

"Absolutely absurd," Charles assured her. "I once tried sense and rationality, but I stuck out like a sore thumb in society."

"I, for one, don't understand a word of sense and rationality. Lord Marylewick keeps trying to teach me, but alas, it is going as poorly as the time I tried to teach myself Siamese. However, I'm quite fluent in absurdity, and proficient in ridiculous, should I find myself traveling there."

"Ridiculous is my favorite holiday spot," Charles declared. "The views are stunning and the locals utterly charming."

George wished they would stop this silly conversation at once. He hated when people talked in this nonsensical manner. Say something of value or say nothing at all.

"My dear, I see that you have a book," Charles observed. "I must know what it is so that I might purchase it immediately." He slid it from her hands and examined the cover. "Ah, Keats. And well-loved, if I may judge from the worn condition." He began to quote: "'O Goddess! hear these tuneless numbers, wrung / By sweet enforcement and remembrance dear, / And pardon that thy secrets should be sung

/ Even into thine own soft-conched ear: / Surely I dreamt to-day, or did I see / The winged Psyche with awaken'd eyes?'"

"Very nice," Lilith said of his recitation.

"What is your favorite Keats poem?" asked Charles. "I must learn it by heart."

George expected her to break out in quotes as she usually did. But she remained elusive, drawing her book back and cradling it to her chest. "I do not give away such things so easily."

"You leave me a mystery that I cannot resist," Charles said. "I must endeavor to solve it at Lord Marylewick's annual house party."

"House party?" She blinked and then raised a brow at George. "*Annual* house party?"

"The zenith of the season, of course," Charles answered for George. "Politicians and young debutantes alike swoon to receive an invitation. It's all political and romantic intrigue, and lawn tennis."

Lilith continued to gaze at George. The words "why have I never been invited to this party?" hung in the air. George tugged at his tie. He had always assumed she knew about the party but would rather lose an eye and limb than attend. And his mother had made it clear that she would sooner be laid in her cold grave before that "atrocious, recalcitrant girl" Lilith Dahlgren would cross the Tyburn threshold again. Thus he never mentioned it.

But he could tell from her expression she now included "omitted from family annual house party" to her list of perceived injustices he committed against her.

Charles's glance flickered between Lilith and

George, a realization lighting their shallow depths. "Father and I have been looking forward to it with great anticipation," he said slowly. "We are having our gowns done up, so to speak. But this year, let the other guests chase balls with racquets or sticks. I shall monopolize Miss Dahlgren's company until I discover her secrets, for I am an intrepid detective."

Blooming Hades! Lord Charles's little political maneuver was insidious. He knew full well that Lilith wasn't invited, and he subtly moved his bishop and knights, boxing in George's king.

Lilith couldn't go to the house party. He hadn't properly educated her yet. In her current feral state, she was capable of single-handedly destroying the entire Tory party's agenda, not to mention killing his mother.

George had to be subtle, protect his king with the few pawns he had left. "I'm afraid that Miss Dahlgren has a prior en—"

"Why, of course I shall be there!" Lilith cried. "After all, it's the annual Marylewick house party and family is family. I take my familial obligations very seriously," she assured Lord Charles. "I should never want a Maryle member to feel shunned by me. How it would break my heart." George received a hurt flash of her eyes.

"It shall be a fine party," the duke said. "Come, let us walk and enjoy the day. You look anxious, Lord Marylewick. You are far too serious, my boy. It will do you a world of wonder to relax in God's creation, listening to the birds chirping and bees buzzing."

If the birds chirped and bees buzzed, George didn't hear them. The duke immediately dove into a deep political conversation about the war in Afghanistan, which George, and Samuel Johnson, would hardly define as relaxing. Behind him, Lilith and Charles were engaged in violent flirtation.

If Charles had been George's son, he would be mortified by his offspring's outrageous conduct. The duke only laughed indulgently and waxed about the short, bright days of youth. Whenever George tried politely to check her behavior, Lilith would say something such as, "Lord Marylewick, you are a darlingly old-fashioned chaperone," or "Yes, Papa, dearest." The duke would chuckle.

The small, private path turned out to be a tiny tributary trickling to hell. It merged into a larger lane that was clogged by the cream of society out sunning themselves. The duke was knee-deep in a discussion of the proposed rectification of a boundary between Greece and Turkey, leaving George no room to wedge in a polite *How interesting, but we really must be going*. Stuck in the conversational mud, he was powerless to stop Lord Charles from dragging Lilith into the crowd. She glanced back at George, and her smile widened to its full gravitational force. He knew she was putting on a little production to vex him. A tiny revenge. She turned around and allowed Lord Charles to present her.

She was all "How enchanted to meet you," "What a stunning gown," "I attended school with your daughter. Such a kind girl. How is she doing? A new baby? You must be very proud," and "Why yes, I shall be at the Marylewick house party. How lovely that we should meet again." All the while, Charles kept a possessive hand on her shoulder, as if having finally met her, he was determined to keep her captive.

When His Grace finally paused a moment to rub his whiskers and contemplate the tariffs on New South Wales, George dove into the conversational hole. "Thank you for suggesting the stroll. I say, listening to the chirping birds truly relaxes the soul. Unfortunately, I have some papers to read over before attending Parliament. I'm afraid I must whisk my cousin away."

"A high-spirited filly, that one." The duke gazed to where his son had wrapped Lilith's hand around his elbow. "But she'll make a fine lady when she's tamed."

Lilith would most certainly be tamed and *not* by Lord Charles. George would be the one to "bleed her wild heart dry" and "destroy her gentle, yearning soul."

The duke turned to George. "I look forward to your house party and meeting the charming Miss Dahlgren again."

George bowed and muttered a nicety to excuse himself, instead of the curse he wanted to utter.

His plans to polish up Lilith over the course of a few months and quietly pop her off had exploded. He plunged into the crowd to fish her out before she could make any more of a mockery of him. It was no easy task. He had to answer as to where he had been hiding her all these years. And yes, she was a dear lady. And so very charming.

"Enough of this little show," he hissed in her ear when he finally reached her.

He managed to untangle her from Charles and forcibly escort her away until he had put a safe distance between her and her impassioned suitor.

"You did that on purpose," he accused.

"Did what?" she asked, so innocently. "Martyr myself for your political career? Really, you should be grateful. A tiny 'thank you' wouldn't be out of order."

"You did no such thing. You're angry because..." He faltered. Admitting the truth was too damning.

She stopped and faced him. "What reason would I have to be angry? That you've ejected me from my home? Or the little *annual* Marylewick house party to which *annually* I wasn't invited? In fact, I hadn't even heard of it. You said you were my family, but we are not related after all. Stop pretending."

"Did you not once say—no, shout is the better word—that Tyburn was the tenth circle of hell—that Dante had forgotten one? I hope you are quite satisfied with yourself. And don't think of displaying yourself as boldly as you did with Lord Charles ever again."

"Why? Am I too lowly for him? Could you not believe that I, Lilith Dahlgren, supposedly devoid of all proper manners, could win the admiration of a duke's son?"

"I have no doubt in the powers of your charm when properly directed. But the simple truth is that Lord Charles is neither kind nor loyal, although he may give you an impressive home."

"Really? What terrible thing has he done?"

She searched his face. He heated under her scrutiny. "He...he made sport of me."

"In Parliament? Isn't that what you're supposed to do?"

"No, at Eton." He couldn't explain the humiliation of having books hidden so Charles and the band of school boys who orbited him could delight in knowing George received the paddle, hearing snide little ditties made up about him echoing in the corridors, or wiping dog defecation from his bedcovers. Those episodes really shouldn't matter almost twenty years later. He shouldn't still think of them.

"Eton! George, people change from when they were twelve," she said, as if he were an idiot.

"Truly? Because you're still as unmanageable and hard-headed!" he fired back out of frustration.

She flinched. "I—I don't want to talk to you for a while," she said slowly. "You've hurt my feelings."

She spun on her heel and walked away—her shoulders drooping. Her gown was so tight that it formed tight creases along her back. She appeared frail and sad. He wanted to run to her and assure her that he would make everything well. But he checked himself.

Then she peered over her shoulder at him. The sunlight formed a halo of light around her, like a medieval painting of the Madonna. The beauty flooded his senses and he hastened toward her.

"I'm sorry," he said. "I don't know why, but when I'm with you, I'm—"

"A consummate arse!"

"I would say unbending and prone to anger in certain situations."

A burst of laughter shook her body. "Certain situations?"

"You're not innocent either. And historically, you have never liked Tyburn—"

"Historically, it's been made abundantly clear to me that I was never wanted at Tyburn."

George couldn't refute the hard truth. So he said nothing. Words didn't seem to be helping their situation.

"I'm so tired," she said, finally. She closed her eyes and somehow all her wild, magnetic energy drained away. It was like watching a play end, the audience leave, the usher snuff the lamps, leaving an empty theatre and a bare set. "I want to go home." She pressed her hand to her forehead. "But I don't have one anymore."

Five

LILITH DIDN'T SPEAK TO GEORGE FOR THE REMAINDER of the walk to Half Moon Street. She turned over all that had occurred, as if by mental force she might make it unhappen. Frances and Edgar, whom she loved and trusted, had deserted her. Her heart hurt as it had when her mother explained that Lilith couldn't stay with her any longer because Mama had a new family. Lilith had told George that people changed from when they were twelve, because she wanted to mock him. But inside she still felt like a scared child, only now she was better at concealing her fears and hurt.

At home—or what once was her home—the wagon was gone from the door and the neighbors had returned to their houses. All the large pieces of furniture had been restored, but the candlesticks, silver, gewgaws, and Edgar's own paintings were missing. No laughter or energy infused the house. The rooms were like cold corpses.

"I had told my groom to return in two hours," George said. "We have but a few minutes left. I shall have your personal items fetched in the morning.

Can I assist you in packing anything you need for this evening?"

"No!"

He raised a brow at the violence of her reply.

She couldn't allow him in her room with all her beloved books and personal possessions, including the portfolio containing the vile words she had scribed about him. She couldn't let him see *her*. The real her. "I, um, need to pack for my feminine ailment."

"Ailment? Are you ill? Shall I take you to a physician?"

Was the man that obtuse?

"My *monthly* feminine ailment."

"Oh." That properly scared him. His face and neck turned scarlet. "Oh," he said again. He backed toward the door. "I had no idea—I mean, not that I should have known." His skin tone continued to creep across the red color spectrum. "I'll…I'll wait outside." He hurried away.

She slowly mounted the stairs. In her chamber, her belongings were back in their proper places, neater than she had left them this morning. Soon they would be packed up again. Another hope dashed and another unknown future looming. She had loved living here. She'd had so much hope that she had finally broken from her past.

She sank into her desk chair, hung her head in her hands, and broke into tears. For tonight, she would go to George's home. She could sort out her life in the morning and make her escape. She just didn't have the strength at the moment.

She wept until she heard the carriage draw up and George's rich voice booming her name and carrying on about needing to attend Parliament. She drew her portmanteau from her trunk—the one that had been with her through four different boarding schools, two finishing schools, and across the channel last summer with Frances and Edgar. She nestled her locked portfolio and Keats's poems inside. With tear-blurred vision, she pulled two gowns, three chemises, fresh pantalets, and stockings from her clothes press. She folded them together and placed them on top of the book. Then she added her toothbrush, paste, hairbrush, and a tin of hairpins. Despite what George thought, she required very little. She could hear him pacing about below, no doubt growing impatient. She had far exceeded her allocated fifteen-minute appointment.

At her door, she turned back and gazed once more at the chamber where she had spent so many beautiful hours lost in the imaginary world of Colette and Sultan Murada. She whispered the final lines of Tennyson's poem *Break, Break, Break.* "'But the tender grace of a day that is dead / Will never come back to me.'"

Lilith adored walking about the city, rubbing elbows with its inhabitants. The rush of the metropolis exhilarated her. She delighted in mounting the top of the omnibus and gazing up at the buildings as the cumbersome vehicle lumbered through the streets. However, George wheeled about London in a lonely bubble of glass and luxury. Being inside it made her feel even sadder, as if she had been plucked from her colorful life and put in a sealed, hermetic bottle.

As she gazed out the window, her eyes burning and head aching from lack of sleep, her thoughts tangled up. Her own life fused with Colette's.

The sultan, having finally captured Colette, bound her with silken sashes. She was his slave to do with as he pleased.

"You shall eat proper meals," he growled in menacing tones. His brows drew down in a hawkish manner. "You'll receive plenty of sleep each night and do calisthenics each morning."

A shiver ran down Colette's back at his unsavory demands. He may be the master of her body now, but her spirit would soar free from its bodily cage.

"Are you even paying attention?" the sultan demanded.

Colette answered in a broken whisper, "Ahhbuhh," and bowed her head.

"What? You're not making sense," the sultan spat. "This illustrates my point. You've beaten your wings to exhaustion because you've had no proper guidance. Well, that has changed."

He seized her elbow as the carriage rolled to a stop. She tried to protest his brutal treatment, but his retinue descended upon her, ripping her from the carriage. His enormous tent was ablaze with torches.

"Show her to the parlor." His powerful voice thundered in her ears.

Colette was taken inside the tent, ordered to wait upon plush cushions for her master's cruel bidding, and asked if she required "a spot of tea or a biscuit."

She tried to speak but her lips wouldn't move. Her eyelids were closing fast. The sultan must have poisoned her. She fought to remain conscious.

She heard a female voice behind the tent door. "Lilith is staying with us! No, no. What will Mother say?"

Ah, yes, Lady Marylewick, that beautiful, perfect valide sultan—queen of the harem.

"Hush, my dear Penelope, she will hear you," the sultan barked.

Penelope, Lady Fenmore? Why was the sultan's sister with him and not with the harem of her husband? Those were Colette's last thoughts before being carried away in the swift, black undertow of sleep.

◈

George entered the parlor to inform Lilith of her waiting bedchamber. He found her collapsed on a sofa, sound asleep. Her hat had toppled from her head, freeing her auburn hair. Her lashes cast shadows on her face. A beautiful sleeping tigress. He knelt beside her and studied the lines and planes of her face. Her symmetry.

She hummed and shifted onto her side.

"Miss Dahlgren," he whispered. He rested a hand on her shoulder and squeezed. "Lilith."

She clasped his hand, slid it under her cheek and cuddled around his arm. Warmth flowed from her body into his.

The clock on the mantel chimed five. Parliament had begun. Outside, the long shadows of the afternoon were beacons of the coming gloaming. After Parliament, he had several balls to attend. Today's adventure had set him behind in his estate work. He had a multitude of reasons to hurry on, but he couldn't stop gazing at the picture she made and enjoying the tingle of his skin where it touched hers. "What am I going to do with you?"

She drew up her legs and snuggled even closer. "So tired," she mumbled and rubbed her cheek against his arm, as if settling into a pillow.

He knew it was improper and unwise, but he wanted to feel more of her. He brushed a stray lock, the color of brandy and firelight, from her face. How could he make her mind as delicate as her nose, her manners as pleasing as her lips, and her ways as soft as her silky hair? If only he could find a way to temper her wild, disorderly nature and keep her as gentle as this moment.

He lingered five minutes longer, savoring the soothing rhythm of her breath on his face, until he couldn't put off his responsibilities any longer.

"Come." He tenderly gathered her up. "Let's tuck you in bed."

❧

George's carriage rambled through the streets as he contemplated the Lilith problem. Away from her, cold reason set in again. The truth was she was too great a risk at the house party. Politics was a careful, subtle dance in a house of cards. One jarring move, one misspoken word, and all his good work would fall apart.

He couldn't let her attend, no matter how this might deflate Lord Charles. In fact, George took secret pleasure in thwarting the man.

He straightened his parliamentary wig and made his decision. On the eve of the house party, Lilith would contract a chill and be temporarily removed to a nest of spinster relations housed in Chester, where she would adhere to a strict regimen of improvement as laid out by George. Then, for the rest of the spring, she would remain under Penelope's feminine tutelage, with George acting as the firm authoritarian whenever Lilith strained Penelope's delicate countenance. By late summer, he hoped to have Lilith's wild tendencies ironed out. Then he would quietly establish her.

Yes, that would be the best plan of action, he thought as he stepped out of the carriage at the Palace of Westminster.

Six hours later, he had different thoughts as he stood by the dance floor at Lord Winterston's ball. He seethed inside but kept his features composed in a pleasant, nonmurderous expression. *The best-laid plans of mice and men often go awry. And if Lilith Dahlgren is involved in said plans, they go spiraling down into the pit of hell.*

He just waited for yet another powerful member of Parliament, whose vote the Tory party had been courting since the winter, to approach him and say, *Lord Charles tells me that you have a delightful cousin attending your house party. I will enjoy making her acquaintance,* or *Lord Charles tells me that Miss Lilith Dahlgren will attend your house party. How wonderful that I shall finally meet her. My sister sang her praises at school,* or the oddest one of all, coming from Lord Harrowsby, the oldest member of the House of Lords, *I hear from Lord Charles that you've kept a charming little dove hidden from us; we are all actually looking forward to your house party this year.*

What did that mean? Did no one enjoy his house party?

George thought he was the better man, but he couldn't help feeling a twinge of jealousy.

He had spent months trying to bring the Stamp Duty

Extension Bill to people's attention. Meanwhile, Lilith showed up at the park one afternoon and suddenly England's politicians were on fire. But he knew the truth of Lilith. She dazzled people in bright, short bursts, but if they lingered any longer, her charming facade soon began to melt and there would be George, behind the glitter and glow, mopping up her mess again.

On the dance floor, the waltz had ended and partners were beginning to form for a quadrille. George's temples ached. He wanted to go home and crawl in bed with Colette, but he needed to dance with the Whig host's daughter, play a rubber with an MP from Sheffield, and then drive five blocks to another ball and dance with more daughters and play more cards. It was no use standing here, silently cursing Lilith and letting her steal any more of his precious time. He turned and headed for the host. He preferred the old-fashioned, courteous method of asking a lady to dance: inquiring of the father.

He had not gone two steps when he heard, "Lord Marylewick, dear boy."

Lord Charles sauntered over, his blond-red hair shiny under the huge chandelier. In an easy motion, he grabbed two champagne glasses from a passing servant, handed one to Marylewick, and then took a sip from the other. "How is it that Miss Dahlgren was in your possession all this time? You could have been a regular fellow and mentioned it earlier. I'm quite cut up at your shabby treatment of me."

"Don't be ridiculous. I've made no secret of Miss Dahlgren."

Charles's azure eyes glittered as they had when he

had cheered on his schoolmates to toss George's shoes and coat up in the trees. "Don't tell me you have your own plans for her—down on one knee in an orangery, babbling of undying sentiments and devotion."

"Don't be daft! I'm her guardian," he said, simplifying the complex relationship. "I oversee all aspects of her life."

"Ah, I see. Then I must romance you, if I'm to romance her."

"You seem quite taken by a lady you met just this afternoon." George didn't hide his incredulity. He knew Charles cut a wide swath with London's more willing ladies. Now the man seemed to be waging a campaign for a woman he hardly knew.

Charles pressed his fist to his chest. "But in my heart, I've known her an eternity. I'm rather romantic."

"I'm sure that in a week's time you will have forgotten about Miss Dahlgren and found another quarry."

"There is no other woman but Miss Dahlgren. All is Miss Lilith Dahlgren, I assure you. Come now, consider my suit: I'm the third son of a duke and that makes me a lord with all the usual paraphernalia— estate, funds, and so forth, but without the stringent matrimonial requirements of my elder brothers. I stand in Parliament, so I'm not a completely useless fribble. I vote on issues of national importance, such as stamp duties. You know about those. I believe you and your Tory kind in the House of Commons are trying to shove one down this nation's throat."

His true meaning flowed beneath his drollness. *You have something I want romantically, and I have something you want politically.*

George drew a long sip of bubbling spirits. "My cousin is not a political pawn."

"I'm not sure what prompted you to say that. How could I sully pure, innocent affection with filthy politics? I merely tell you that my intentions are honorable, and I ask that I be allowed to pursue them at your house party."

Charles's gaze met George's—a challenge more than an entreaty. George felt that gut-churning sensation of having been bested by Charles again. Except this time the victory was more subtle than young George sniveling in his dormitory bed, his backside aching from a paddling, and all the candies Penelope had sent him stolen.

"I warn you, you have much worthy competition." George couldn't deny Charles, but he would be damned if he'd let the man roll over him.

"As I understand. All the eligible politicians are sharpening their jousting sticks, ready to win the fair maiden's hand. Which gallant knight shall succeed, Lord Marylewick?" He gestured to the room. George found the eyes of young men watching their conversation with great interest.

Damn Lilith Dahlgren, he thought. *Damn her to her own special frigid hell of white empty walls, books without words, poems without meter, and Schumann on a harpsichord.* He was backed into a political corner. Lilith must attend the house party.

"We shall see," George replied coolly and bowed. "Good evening, Lord Charles."

George wanted to stomp to the cloakroom, retrieve his hat and other accoutrements, and go home to Colette. But as Admiral Nelson said, "England expects that every man will do his duty." And George unflinchingly performed his. So he approached the host, complimented his daughter, Lady Cornelia, and asked her for the next dance.

&

Four hours later, George stalked into his library. He had learned several enlightening things that evening. First, no one really enjoyed the Marylewick annual house party, and second, if Lilith didn't attend this year's painfully boring party, the earth might stop going around the sun.

He poured a glass of brandy, sank into a wing chair, and rubbed his temple. He had only a few days to turn Lilith into some semblance of a proper lady. It was impossible. He sipped and stared at the glowing coals. How to create a meek lady out of that termagant?

His father's voice echoed in his head. *I'm going to turn you into a man, Goddammit!* What was George supposed to do? Obviously his father's solutions wouldn't work. He couldn't force her into the boxing ring to be pummeled while he shouted *Fight back, damn you,* or give her a rifle and order her to shoot the orphaned fawn, or pour brandy down her throat until she vomited. He wasn't making a man, but the ideal female.

What was the ideal female, anyway?

His eyes lit on *McAllister's Magazine* resting on the table beside his chair where he had left it the previous evening.

Colette.

She was the perfect woman. Most likely because she was created by a man.

He carried the journal to his desk, picked up a pen and tapped the page. How could he create a modern Colette in a matter of days? And out of Lilith?

He rubbed his tired, burning eyes, dipped the pen and scrawled on a piece of his stationery: *The Education of Lilith Dahlgren.*

Six

THE MORNING LIGHT WARMED LILITH'S FACE. SHE wasn't ready to wake up yet. She wanted to loll in this peaceful, drowsy feeling longer. She snuggled into the soft sheets and drifted back into her dream where she was clad in Colette's robes and veil and dancing in a flower garden. She was completely free, her spirit unencumbered. She lifted her smiling face to the brilliant sky.

Tap tap.

Colette stopped. How did a door suddenly appear in her garden?

Tap tap.

"Miss Dahlgren, Lord Marylewick requests your presence at breakfast," a timid female voice said.

Lilith's lids shot open. Brilliant light flooded in from two huge windows on the opposite wall, hurting her eyes. She wasn't dancing in a garden. Where was she? And how did she get in this nightgown?

"Shall I help you dress?" the voice said.

Lilith pressed her hand to her thundering heart. What was happening? Her sleep-dulled mind slowly sharpened. The previous day's memory returned. She had been betrayed again. Frances and Edgar had deserted her. Her lovely life in the world of art and words had been ripped away.

She drew her knees to her chest. She didn't have the strength to get up.

"Miss?" The determined young servant slipped into the room. "Are you well?" she cried when she spied Lilith huddled on the bed.

An anxious thought exploded in Lilith's mind. *The story! Where was the story? If George found out…*

Lilith bolted up. "Where are my…my things?" *Oh God!* She studied her chamber—a bright, airy room in George's Grosvenor Square prison. She had slept in a large mahogany canopy bed. On the left wall stood a mirrored wardrobe, and on the other wall, a washing stand and carved bureau writing desk sandwiched the chimney-piece.

"I put your clothes and toiletries in the wardrobe," the maid said.

Lilith rushed to the wardrobe and tore open the doors. Her gowns and chemises were neatly pressed and hung. Her reticule dangled from a hook. The drawers housed her folded stockings and pantalets. But her portmanteau and portfolio remained missing. She released a panicked squeal.

"I'm Lucy," the servant said, not commenting on Lilith's frantic fossicking. "I thought your nightgown was too worn. Lord Marylewick's sister kindly lent one. Shall I help you dress?"

"My portfolio!" Lilith cried. "Dear God! Where is my portfolio? Did George take it?"

Lucy blushed. "I-I don't recall Lord Marylewick visiting your chamber last night. I placed it in the bureau. I thought that's where you would want it, miss."

Lilith pulled down the bureau desktop to find the portfolio still locked and resting in a cubby below her volume of Keats. She yanked them out and hugged them.

"Thank you, Lucy," she whispered, sinking into the chair. Tears formed in her eyes. "Thank you."

Lilith picked up the pen from the inkwell. Her fingers were shaking around the point. She had to write. It was the only way she knew to make sense of what had happened, else she would fall apart. "P-pray, tell Lord Marylewick that I'm indisposed and desire a nice pot of tea—and toffee if available—brought to my room."

The servant's mouth dropped open as if she had been asked to climb onto the roof and then jump. "You…you really want me to tell my lord that? Are you quite certain, miss?"

"Yes, please."

Lucy swayed on her feet as if waiting for Lilith to change her mind. When Lilith didn't, she curtsied and edged fearfully out of the room.

Lilith felt sorry for Lucy. No doubt Lord Marylewick marched about his house like Lewis Carroll's Queen of Hearts, cutting off the heads of anyone who dared to defy him.

She couldn't face him yet. She had to gather her emotions and plant them in neat rows of prose. She crossed to the wardrobe and pulled out her key from her reticule. Back at the bureau, she unlocked the portfolio and then grabbed a piece of stationery with a big gold M embossed on it.

She marked through the M until she couldn't see it anymore. "Please be present for me, Muse. I need you."

Colette blinked, drowsy from the poison the sultan had forced her to drink. She could make out vivid drapes in deep reds and purples and the gleam of gold ornaments.

A shadow moved from the dim corners of the tent. "You're awake, my fair one." The sultan came into the sparse light.

She struggled to rise, clutching at the blanket to cover her bare skin. She had never felt more vulnerable in her life—her clothes, her identity, everything that was hers, stripped away. "What are you going to do with me?"

He shrugged. "Take you to my palace."

"You're not going to...to..."

He raised a black brow. "To what, my lovely dove?"

She raised her head boldly, refusing to show fear. "Ravish me?"

He chuckled darkly, a strangely musical sound. "You think me a monster." He twined her hair about his finger. Her body trembled with terror... and pleasure. "I will ravish you in good time," he growled. "Rest now, soon we will travel." He strode to the tent's entrance. "And don't think of escaping." He opened the flap with his sword and strolled out. She heard him order the guards outside, "Give her anything she desires, but don't let her leave."

Colette buried her head in her hands and wept…
and wept…
and wept…
and wept some more.

"Muse, I realize she's distraught, but how does she
get out? She needs a plan. She needs hope."

"Why have I lived only to know pain?" Colette
cried out. "I can go on no longer. My soul is tired
and desires to rest in the heavens."

What? Lilith stared at the pages. Colette couldn't
die. "No, no, Muse. She must live. This can't be a
tragedy. Tell me she escapes."

Her pen waited, poised on the page. But no words
came.

"No." Her eyes grew moist again.

Tap tap.

"Pardon, Miss Dahlgren," Lucy called.

She jammed the pages into her portfolio, locked
it again, and wiped her eyes on the nightgown
sleeve. "Yes."

The door cracked enough for Lucy to slip through.
"His lordship still requests your presence downstairs."
She kept her gaze averted.

"Tell him that I'm sorry, but I prefer my presence
in this chamber."

"He said…" Lucy swallowed. "He said that we
don't practice the loose and lazy hours you are accustomed to. If you don't come to the dining room, he
shall personally drag you there."

"Ooh," said Lilith after a beat. "Very well, then." She rose and marched from her room.

"Miss Dahlgren, wait!" Lucy scurried behind her. "You're still in your nightclothes. I think your blue gown would be lovely. Shall I put it on you? And your hair? Please, miss, please!"

Lilith continued down the grand stairs. "I'm sorry, Lucy. But I would be loath to keep Lord Marylewick waiting over something as trivial as clothing."

❦

Lilith flung open the dining room doors. She interrupted what appeared to be a serious conversation between George and his sister across the vast table. Stacks of books crowded about a plate set between sister and brother.

"Good morning, Georgie!" Lilith cried. "Isn't it a glorious day?" She twirled on her toes, the motion lifting her hem.

The ever proper Penelope shrieked and then pressed her hand to her mouth, no doubt shocked to have emitted a sound above a feminine whisper.

George shot up from this chair, splashing his tea onto the pristine tablecloth. "Lilith, go put on decent clothes immediately."

"But I had to hurry down in terror of being *dragged* to breakfast. Really, George, you are positively barbaric."

"Y-you shouldn't say such things about Lord Marylewick, especially after all he's done for you," Penelope ventured and then looked to her brother to see if her words met his approval.

"Is this my seat?" Lilith asked. "By these books? How lovely, I shall be hidden."

"Lady Fenmore has graciously lent those to you," George said through his tight jaw.

Lilith picked up a volume. *What Every Young Lady of Quality Should Know Upon Entering into Society and Marriage: A Guide to Gentle Breeding.* Then she saw the document resting beside her plate—*The Education of Lilith Dahlgren.*

1. Daily calisthenics. 2. Practice manners of better society...

Lilith's mouth dropped.

"Shall I pour some tea, Miss Dahlgren?" the footman asked.

"No, I'll have hemlock with two lumps of sugar." Lilith turned to George, her face aflame with anger. "What is this?"

"It is a schedule for your improvement," he responded, taking his seat again and placing his linen back in his lap.

"My improvement!" She rattled the paper in the air—written proof that she wasn't good enough for the Maryles. Yet she was no longer a hurt, turned-away child but a woman with her own mind and sense of worth. "George, this is insulting!"

Penelope's jaw dropped. No one was supposed to speak harshly to George. "Now, Lilith..."

"Insulting, assuming, and ridiculous," Lilith expounded.

George calmly sliced into a mushroom. "If you desire to attend the house party, then you shall adhere to those items."

Ah yes, that stupid house party that she'd used against George yesterday. "I may have been rather hasty on that point. And coming to stay here, for that matter."

His face jerked up. "What do you mean? Where else would you go? Who would take you in?"

That was the heart of the problem. "I know of s-several colonies where artists—"

"If you care to see a penny of your monies, you will not set foot in an artist colony." He was on his feet again. Cordlike tendons bulged on his neck. "I'm tired of your antics, Lilith," he thundered. "You shall attend the house party, and you shall behave like a proper lady for its duration."

Penelope flinched. Lilith narrowed her eyes. This was the unyielding, arrogant George—a typical Maryle silverback ape—to which she was accustomed. Now that he had entrapped her in his home, he assumed he could do what he may with her. Just like the sultan.

She knew better than to get in a shouting match. She would plan her escape later when she could think. For now, she needed to buy a little time.

"I'm sorry, Lord Marylewick," she said sweetly, gazing up at him, pouting her lips. "I didn't mean to upset you. I especially love item four, *Ensure that Miss Dahlgren only consumes appropriate literature and art*. I'm certain I'm the way I am because of all the bad art I've consumed."

He studied her, his eyes suspicious slits. "You will not distract me from the issue at hand. I am not a tyrant, but you will not listen to reason. You don't know what is good for you. You have proven that over and over."

"I'm such a mindless little thing." Lilith directed a giggle at Penelope, who appeared to be relaxing now that no one was shouting and all the women had returned to their proper submissive places.

George continued to stare suspiciously. Lilith continued to smile sweetly.

"I'm going to the club early to converse with the Prime Minister," he said slowly. "You will don proper clothes and meet Penelope in the garden for calisthenics. Afterwards, when the shops open, she will assist you in having gowns made—I have given Penelope a description of the types of gowns I find acceptable."

"You don't dictate how I dress."

He raked her up and down. "I must, if this is your idea of appropriate attire. No, aside from unbecomingly popping at the seams, your current gowns are the wrong color and fit. Then in the afternoon, you shall review the books before you. I shall check your progress upon returning from Parliament. If you give Penelope any difficulty, a footman will be dispatched to me, and I shall deal with you personally."

"Personally?" Lilith arched a brow. "What are you going to do if I misbehave? Spank me? Maybe a little whack with the pillow?"

He opened his mouth, but thought better of whatever words he was about to utter. A beat passed before he spoke again in a measured manner. "I'm not going to play your games, Lilith. I'm not your frog. There is no golden ball. I did not advance your money to pay for your late rent. I paid for it out of my own funds. You are indebted to me for sixty-five pounds."

Hang Edgar and Frances for leaving her! Hang her mother for marrying into the Maryle family, and hang Lilith for allowing herself to come under George's control again. She blinked back the tears daring to form in her eyes. That hideous tyrant would not see her cry again. He would not enjoy that luxury.

"A proper, respectable gentleman courts a well-behaved lady," he prattled on. "That is the way of the world. And the only way you will receive your trust money is if you marry according to my approval. Many eligible gentlemen will attend the house party. I suggest you follow my counsel or..." He opened his palms.

"Or?" she spat.

"Beg on the street. Now eat your breakfast. You need regular, nourishing meals." He signaled to a footman, who rushed forward to help Lilith into her chair.

The sultan must die, Muse! Not Colette.

Lilith jammed her fork into a poached egg. *Colette will plunge her knife into the sultan's heart, piercing it like an egg yolk, his lifeblood spewing forth.*

❦

George stalked from the dining room and ordered his hat, gloves, and coat. He could see the terror in the footman's eyes and he realized how harsh he sounded—like his father.

"Thank you," he said quietly.

He peered back at the dining room. He hadn't intended to be so severe, but she had dared to appear in that flimsy nightgown that silhouetted her luscious contours to mock him. He had been up most of the night worrying and writing out her plan of improvement. He had panicked when she said she didn't care to attend the house party. Typical Lilith behavior. Yesterday, she was aflame to go. But now that London society waited with bated breath for this house party because *she* was attending, she casually tossed the party aside.

Yet was he making her pay for his own frustration? He remembered the pain in her eyes when she realized her cousins had left her. No doubt learning she had been excluded from the house party for years had hurt. She was orphaned again, drifting, scared, and trying to survive, a bit like Colette but with sharp claws and a vicious tongue.

He considered returning to the dining room and explaining his intentions more calmly. But Lilith would only mock him if he showed weakness. She needed to learn the harsh lesson of responsibility that he had fortunately gained at a tender age. "Spare the rod and spoil the child," his father oft said. George would never physically hurt Lilith. Or any lady or child, for that matter, but he wouldn't spare Lilith the painful rod of his censure if it helped her.

He turned and headed out the door.

❧

Lilith stood in the tiny courtyard, hefting a metal hoop over her head, and pondering which artist colony might take her in, how many pages she needed to write to earn sixty-five pounds, and ways to have Colette kill the sultan.

Across from her, Lady Fenmore lifted a matching metal hoop. Her stiff smile appeared tabbed on like a cut-out doll's. The two ladies had enjoyed a strained relationship since Lilith, in one of her childhood tantrums, cut off several of Penelope's beautiful spiral curls after Penelope refused to let Lilith play with her pristine doll collection. "You will ruin them like you ruin everything," Penelope had sniped, prompting Lilith to reach for the clippers.

Penelope leaned her hoop to the left. "To the left, back to the center, now to the right," she ordered like a soft-spoken drill sergeant, seemingly unaware of all the stable hands peering around the corner to enjoy the spectacle. "Do try to straighten your posture, Lilith. Turn your head to gaze up and keep your limbs slightly apart."

Lilith couldn't bend, much less breathe, in her corset. "I feel like a yogi from India."

"A yogi?"

"A person who ponders the meaning of life while assuming different positions with his body."

Penelope wrinkled her nose. "I don't know if George thinks you should say such things."

Lilith raised her hoop. Given her emotional instability at the moment, she opted to change the subject before she blew up in fury over the subject of George's censorship. "Why are you not residing at your husband's London home?"

Penelope's brow creased, but her smile remained intact. "Lord Fenmore is at his hunting lodge. My husband loves horses and hunting. Always hunting."

"I didn't think it was hunting season."

A cloud passed across her eyes. "I just adore my brother," she said, steering the conversation away from her husband. "He requires a lady to keep his home. He unselfishly puts everyone else's needs first. Now bend to the left."

"A regular Atlas."

"Atlas?"

"The Greek god carrying the weight of the world on his shoulders." Lilith lowered her hoop to demonstrate.

"I don't know if George thinks you should say such things."

"I don't care what people think I should do or say," Lilith replied, no longer able to hold her tongue.

Penelope flinched as though free will were a terrifying concept. Hers was a flat world and ships that ventured too far fell off the edge. "Ladies should always seek to please their brothers or parents or… or…husbands in all matters."

"What if your husband, brothers, or parents are cruel monsters?"

Penelope's eyes turned hot. "I hope you aren't suggesting my brother is a cruel monster. He only wants what's best for you. He's so caring. You know nothing about him."

Lilith, who was bending to the right, burst out in incredulous laughter, causing her to lose balance. Her staystrings popped as she fell to the ground and the giant ring crashed upon her. Penelope gazed down with a smug expression that said *See what happens when you say terrible things about Lord Marylewick.*

Seven

WITH THIS AUSPICIOUS BEGINNING TO LILITH'S education, she could only assume the trip to the clothing shop would be disastrous. George sent his carriage to drive the ladies about. Heaven forbid they should rub shoulders with the great unwashed.

Madame Courtemanche's shop exuded wealth. Delicate fabrics and handmade lace were draped in the front window amid gold-framed paintings of gowns adorned with intricate ruffles, bustles, trains, and pleats.

Lady Fenmore allowed the footman to help her down without looking back at Lilith. If she did, she would surely see the panic seizing Lilith's features.

Once on the pavement, Lilith reached for Penelope's elbow. "I'm sorry, Lady Fenmore, but I— I can't, that is, I don't have enough funds for this modiste."

Why did admitting poverty feel like a crime?

"My brother will pay," Penelope replied and entered the establishment as the footman held the door.

"But—"

Penelope couldn't hear Lilith anymore. She was

being greeted by a fashionable woman with a lovely French accent.

"But I don't want to be further beholden to George," Lilith whispered to no one.

Nor did she desire to become further entrenched in that ridiculous house party. She nervously entered the shop's lush parlor of mahogany furniture and white, lace-trimmed cushions.

Penelope made a curt introduction of the ladies.

"Your cousin is a beauty." Madame Courtemanche curtsied. "I shall make a gown worthy of her." She clapped her hands and a young seamstress appeared from the back rooms. "Bring the English fashion book," she ordered in French, which, if Lilith translated correctly from the subtle inflection, meant *Bring the uninspired fashion book.* Madame reverted to English and gestured to the sofa. "Please, please, sit down, my ladies."

Penelope took a seat on the edge of the cushion, her expansive bustle commanding a great deal of space. Lilith edged in beside her. The modiste chose the wing chair on the other side of a low marble table.

"Now, what lovely creations shall I make for you? Morning dress? Walking dress?" She leaned in to Lilith. "A ravishing ball gown to make a certain gentleman fall madly in love?" She shifted her gaze to Penelope. "You remember the gown I made for your debut ball? Did not Lord Fenmore fall in love that night?"

Penelope didn't respond, but opened her reticule and retrieved several folded pages. George's list for Lilith's education rested on the top. Lilith fought the urge to tear it into tiny strips useful only for bum fodder.

Penelope shifted the pages, handing several to Madame. "My brother sketched pictures of what he thinks are appropriate gowns for Miss Dahlgren."

What?

"Such magnificent pictures," Madame Courtemanche commented. "If I may—"

"P-pardon me," Lilith cried. "Did you say that Lord Marylewick sketched these?"

Penelope looked at Lilith as though she had lost her senses. "Of course," she said, and then returned her attention to the modiste. "His instructions were that the gowns should be made in shades of soft gold, reds, or browns. Also, if you could—"

"Pardon me again," Lilith cut in. "May I see them? The sketches. Please."

Lilith's fingers shook as she took the offered pages. She gasped. The images were fast renderings, but the style and the composition were exquisite. The top sketch displayed Lilith seated in a chair and wearing a simple yet elegant ball gown. Her hand dangled casually off the armrest and her head was slightly raised, a smile blossoming on her lips. The illustration below featured Lilith standing with her hands resting on a table behind her, thereby pushing up her breasts. Her hair was piled high, accentuating the long line of her neck. The sheer silk gown he had created flowed like smooth water over her curves. Her eyes had been drawn slightly downcast, a modest touch to a rather provocative image.

"And you said Lord Marylewick—your brother

George—sketched these," Lilith broke into the conversation between Penelope and Madame Courtemanche. "Using his own hands and a pencil?"

"Yes," Penelope affirmed, clearly annoyed at having been interrupted again.

"These could be the work of Edgar Degas," Lilith marveled aloud.

"Who?" Penelope asked.

"Edgar Degas?" cried the modiste. "*J'adore* Edgar Degas!"

"Me too," Lilith said. "I saw his work at the Impressionist Exhibitions in Paris last summer."

"I was there, as well! How sad that we missed each other."

Lilith and Madame laughed, each recognizing a kindred spirit. Penelope eyed the two ladies nervously and then tried to nibble on a fingernail through her glove.

The young seamstress returned, bearing the fashion book.

Madame Courtemanche waved her off. "No, no, this will never do. Please bring the French magazine." Her eyes glittered. "Those designs will better suit my fashionable guest."

The modiste was overjoyed to have a client who appreciated the more modern fashions. She carried on in fast-flowing French. Lilith did her best to keep up as she was being measured and various silks held to her face. Penelope added nothing to the conversation except to say what George would or would not approve of and to please remain true to the sketches.

Lilith wished she could steal the pictures and

examine them in solitary silence. She still couldn't believe George—overbearing, dry George—drew them. That he was capable of such imagination or beauty. He must answer for this artistic side he hid. What else had he drawn? Did he paint? Where did he keep his art? Her heart raced so fast that perspiration broke out around her temples. Good heavens, she hadn't time to worry about such trivial things as gowns when a great mystery demanded to be solved.

She was bereft when the sketches were taken to the back rooms to be used as references by the seamstresses. Despite George's claim that she had posed for paintings, she truly hadn't. In fact, these were the only sketches ever made of her.

As the ladies rose to leave, Penelope casually asked that the gowns be ready in two days. Lilith thought that wasn't enough time. The poor seamstresses.

"Of course," Madame Courtemanche said without a beat. "The gowns will be delivered. My girls and I will make the final fittings at your home, if your ladyship agrees."

Penelope nodded and then the modiste kissed Lilith warmly on both cheeks. "*Au revoir*. I shall make inspired creations for you. Edgar Degas with fabric. You will adore."

Penelope stared on, her expression unreadable.

When they stepped onto the pavement, Lilith was dying to ask Penelope about the sketches. She thought she would ease into casual conversation before she peppered Penelope with questions.

"Madame Courtemanche is a fascinating lady," Lilith said. "Did she really make your debut gowns?"

Penelope had made quite a societal splash with her debut, and Lilith assumed it would be a pleasing subject.

"Yes," Penelope replied and glanced away. So much for a cozy tête-à-tête. But Lilith couldn't give up. She spied a confectionery shop down the street. Toffee! That's what she needed to butter up the conversation.

"Please excuse me for a small moment." Lilith left Penelope with the footman and dashed along the walk to the confectioner's. Three minutes later she emerged with a box filled with tiny paradises. She gave two toffees, as well as several pence, to a hungry child under the shop window and hurried to catch up with Penelope. "These are little pieces of heaven. You put them in your mouth and they melt into something sugary and magical. Here, have one. Penelope? Penelope?"

Penelope stared across the street, her eyes large, mouth gaping, and hands clenched as if witnessing some bloody horror. Was there an accident? Were people hurt? A dozen or so dreadful images flooded Lilith's overactive imagination as she followed the line of Penelope's gaze. A beautiful woman in a vivid yellow gown smiled intimately at the man whose elbow she clutched as he opened the door to their pied-à-terre. Just another garish actress and her benefactor. An everyday sight in London. Lilith released a relieved breath. No one was bleeding in the street. Then the man turned and gestured for his little yellow lovebird to enter. Beneath his top hat Lilith recognized the features of Lord Fenmore, Penelope's husband!

Without thinking, Lilith shouted, "You blossoming arse!"

The only weapon she possessed was a box of toffee.

She threw it, raining toffee onto the street. "You bloody, blossoming bumhole."

The man's head whipped around as a small but strong hand clamped onto Lilith's shoulder, yanking her back into Madame Courtemanche's entrance.

"Don't make a scene," Penelope whispered.

"What!" Lilith cried. "He's a deceitful, turgid arse. He needs to know as much. You are the perfect lady and he dallies with…with that bright canary. "

Penelope pressed her fingers to her temple. "Don't make a scene." Her voice was breaking. "Don't!"

"Oh, Penelope," Lilith whispered and tried to embrace her. "I'm sorry." Penelope remained immobile, watching Lord Fenmore escort his mistress into a flat. When the door closed, Penelope yanked away from Lilith and rushed down the walk. Lilith and the footman hurried to catch up.

"We must do the next thing on the list," Penelope cried. "That's what's most important. Lord Marylewick gave me a responsibility." She opened her reticule with shaking hands and frantically rooted through it. "George's list! It's not here. I've lost the list. How could I have done that? I'm so stupid. Stupid! Stupid!"

Lilith retrieved the list from the ground where it had fallen. "Here it is," she said quietly. "You didn't lose it. You're not stupid. Don't ever think that. And look, item three is *teach Lilith to drink tea properly*. Let's find a nice tea shop." She took Penelope's hand.

Penelope didn't protest as Lilith led her. Shame poured into Lilith for all her mocking thoughts about Penelope. Her expression resembled that dazed, lost look that Lilith had worn the previous day, when the

outside world was a big blur and the only thing she
knew was how much her heart ached.

Two streets over Lilith found an establishment with
the words *Simon Brothers Tavern* painted in gold letters
above a large, paned window. Inside, well-dressed
men and women crowded around a bar and the tables,
drinking spirits and smoking. The ladies' enormous
hats shook with their happy laughter.

"Come," Lilith said to Penelope.

"This—this doesn't look like a tea house."

"Of course it is," Lilith lied and let the footman open
the door. The sunlight reflected on the brass fixtures,
stamped tin ceiling, and glasses on the tables, spreading
beautiful white light over the chattering crowd.

"I don't think George would approve of this place."
Penelope clutched her reticule to her chest.

"We must remember to ask Lord Marylewick if we
should not have come here when he returns this evening to check on my progress." Lilith dispatched the
footman to the bar for a pot of tea, teacups, a bottle of
wine, and three glasses. She clutched Penelope's elbow
and led her toward an empty booth in the back corner
of the narrow room.

Penelope sat and ran her finger over a stain in
the blue table linen. "Don't tell George," she finally
whispered. "About seeing my husband. Promise me."

"If you wish."

Penelope continued staring at the stain. As Lilith
studied Penelope's bowed head, loneliness washed over
her. She had a sense that Penelope wanted to talk and
that she had wanted to talk to someone for a very long
time—someone who understood and didn't judge.

The footman brought the wine and tea. Lilith poured the glasses of wine, gave the footman one, and asked him to leave the ladies for several minutes.

Penelope shifted her thousand-yard stare from the table to the deep red tones of the wine.

"My cousins on my father's side left me yesterday," Lilith shared. "I trusted them. I thought I had finally obtained the life that I had dreamed of. But they... they broke my heart."

"Fenmore broke my heart a few months after we were married." Penelope poured a cup of tea, took a small sip, and then reached for the wine.

"I'm sorry. How painful to witness."

"Yes." She drank more of her wine. "It's not the first time. I just wish I didn't have to see it."

Lilith ran her finger down the stem of her glass. "Have you thought about a divorce?"

Penelope's head snapped up, her eyes hot, as though Lilith had asked her to commit murder. "I couldn't do that to George. To Mama. It is wrong. What would people think?"

Lilith only shrugged. "I think it's wrong to sacrifice your happiness for something as trivial as another's opinion. Your mother should desire your happiness. And Lord Marylewick is fully grown. You shouldn't feel the need to please or protect him."

"You don't understand George," Penelope fired back. "You never have. You're cruel to him like Pa..." She gazed down, not finishing her angry thought.

"Tell me about him. I'm mad with curiosity to know about this George who creates beautiful sketches."

Penelope resumed studying the stain on the cloth.

Don't shut down, Lilith thought. *Talk. I'm dying inside.*

"Tell me what you want to say, Penelope," Lilith said gently. "It's all right."

Penelope shook her head. "It's horrid to speak ill of your parents."

So George's problems began with his parents.

"Oh dear," Lilith said. "Pray, my father was a handsome wastrel and foolishly died in a duel after cheating at cards. My dear mother abandoned me to boarding schools so she could start a new and better family. And my stepfather—your uncle—had a higher opinion of plague-ridden sewer rats than of me." Lilith lifted her glass and gestured to Penelope before taking a sip. "There, I daresay you can't possibly be as horrid as I am. You are absolved."

Penelope flashed a tentative smile, like a fragile, tiny sea crab venturing from under its shell. "George is like you."

Lilith couldn't help but spew the wine from her mouth in the most unfeminine manner. She grabbed a napkin and dabbed her lips. "Sorry. I just find that, well, a little more than shocking. And pray, never tell George you think we are alike, the man would have an apoplexy."

"I mean he enjoys art, or at least he did. When we were young, he was always drawing pictures and painting. This was before your mother married Uncle Reginald, so you wouldn't know. George would make strange sculptures from twigs and objects he found about the estate. He painted on boards, on walls, on his clothes…anything he could find. When I was sad, he made books for me, all illustrations of my favorite stories because I couldn't read then."

"George? Big, tall, booming, all-things-proper, don't-you-dare-be-different George? Are you quite sure you don't have another brother named George you've kept hidden from me?"

Penelope laughed. A true, easy laugh.

"He wasn't always big and tall. He was once small for his age and ever so thin. He didn't want to ride horses, shoot, or play cricket—all the things my father loved. Papa was positively terrified that George would turn into what he called a…a…" She looked about to see if anyone was listening.

Lilith leaned forward. "A what?"

"Molly," Penelope whispered. "You know, a man who—"

"Yes."

"Father was quite different when other people weren't around. To everyone else he appeared congenial but…" She paused.

Lilith could tell Penelope struggled to articulate emotions she couldn't fully comprehend.

"We had responsibilities because of our birth," Penelope continued. "We had to be examples. We couldn't be…" She gazed up, hunting for words.

"Human," Lilith supplied. "You were actors in a play. You couldn't stray from the lines of the grand stage production *We're Britain's Most Admired and Distinguished Family*."

"Yes." Penelope lips curled into a relieved smile. "I shouldn't say that, but yes."

It was Lilith's turn to be silent. The only time she had visited Tyburn Hall was for holidays. Young and so full of anger, and desiring to feed that churning, simmering rage, she had only seen the Maryles as she wanted to: perfect. Was it all truly a play? Had she been buying a ticket all these years?

"That's sad," Lilith said. "I'm sorry. I didn't know."

"George received the brunt of it. He was supposed to be manly like Papa. If he didn't ride his horse correctly or refused to shoot his rifle, he was spanked and not fed dinner. Then Father became so frustrated with George he told Nurse to toss all his art in the grate."

"No!"

"But she couldn't, at least not all of it." A devious grin that Lilith had never seen before lit Penelope's face. She slid forward in her seat. "Because I hid it."

"You did!"

She nodded her head, her eyes gleaming at her act of rebellion. "I could be rather naughty then."

"You? Naughty? Have you met this horrid little girl named Lilith Dahlgren? I understand she is a hellion of mythic proportions."

"Pray, I was quite naughty and wild. Only, George would take the blame for things I did, so no one knew. He figured he was going to get punished for something else anyway."

Lilith's throat burned. "W-where did you hide the artwork?"

"In a trunk in the back attic room of the original fortress wing. No one goes there."

Penelope sipped her glass of wine and fixed her gaze on a spot on the wall behind Lilith. "After that, George stopped painting. He turned quiet and did everything Father told him. Papa was finally proud."

Lilith's heart hurt for young George. Did a tiny bit

of him still remain in adult George? Could she find it? Could he be saved or was too much damage done? She made a vow to herself that she would be nicer to George, no matter what he said to her.

"Penelope, I'm sorry I cut your lovely hair all those years ago," Lilith said.

"I'm sorry I didn't let you play with my dolls. I had outgrown them by then."

Lilith flicked her wrist back. "I would have ruined them anyway."

Both ladies chuckled and then an awkward hush fell over them, both unsure how to maneuver now that honesty had spilled onto their relationship.

"I dread this house party," Penelope mused. "Fenmore will be there, and Mama, she doesn't understand."

"Well, I shall be there," Lilith said, truly committing herself to the party. "And we can always sneak away to a tea shop and have wine. We naughty ladies."

"Yes, let us," Penelope said, her eyes bright. She finished her wine and fished the crumpled list from her reticule. "So what is the next item on the list?"

Lilith resisted saying, *I think it's "toss this list in the fire and go to a gallery."*

"Ah, millinery!" Penelope grinned, all her delicate features at ease.

Lilith returned her smile. "Wonderful!" she lied.

Eight

GEORGE EASED BACK IN HIS CARRIAGE'S SQUABS AND watched the wet blur of buildings and pedestrians passing outside his window. The beautiful afternoon had ended in abysmal gray rain. He had remained out as long as possible, keeping himself away from her because he knew any conversation between them would flame up like a match to dry straw. He had forced himself to concentrate on the business at hand, because in any idle moment, Lilith came to his thoughts. Yet all day, he turned at the sound of hurried footsteps, thinking his footman had come rushing with news of some Lilith-related disaster which required his immediate attention.

But he had received no word. He hoped a minor miracle had occurred and that the warnings he had issued to Lilith that morning managed to keep her in check for the entire day. But he wasn't an optimistic man. He had a niggling fear that Lilith was waiting, biding her time for some enormous revenge that probably involved destroying the Stamp Duty Extension Bill, not to mention his family's honor.

He circled his hat in his hands, feeling both dread and anticipation as the carriage rambled into Grosvenor Square. Parliament had run until seven. He had just enough time to check Lilith's progress and then he could safely remove himself to another insipid musical evening.

Firm, he thought as the carriage halted. *I will be firm, calm, and fair.* He would not let Lilith's outrageous behavior provoke him and suck him into her little games.

As he stepped over the threshold into his home, his gut tightened, his jaw clenched, steeling for an epic battle of wills. But something was different about his home. Everything appeared in shipshape, gleaming precision, but the atmosphere felt light and relaxed.

As the footman removed his coat, hat, and gloves, female laughter rang out from the parlor. Penelope's laughter. A sound he hadn't heard in years. He edged quietly toward the parlor like some stealthy thief, afraid his presence would shatter the moment.

The door was open and Lilith, dressed in her blue floral robe—the one he remembered from that notorious night of the pillow fight—reclined on the sofa, holding a small square of paper before her. On the carpet, a bottle of wine and a glass rested atop the books he had asked her to study. Penelope sat on the opposite sofa, holding her wine, her other hand pressed to her giggling lips. The light from the lamps and fire bathed the ladies in hues of gold.

Lilith glanced up, catching him staring. Her expression faltered. He stiffened, waiting for the gentle glow in her eyes to turn to a dangerous glitter. Yet a small, welcoming smile curved her lips. "Good evening, Lord Marylewick. Did you enjoy a fruitful day in Parliament? How is that bill coming along?"

He stepped forward, feeling the pull of her magnetism, then stopped. Why was she being nice? What was her game?

"Have you completed your tasks?" he asked in a firm tone, determined not to give her an inch.

"I have completed your entire list for today." She drew the page from the side table and held it up. "I've checked off each item: modiste, millinery, shoes—ah, but we added bookshop, print shop, and confectionery—I appended those at the bottom. Now Lady Fenmore is tutoring me in etiquette. We've even made a game of it. Care to play?" She patted the empty place beside her on the sofa.

Who was this woman who outwardly resembled Lilith? "I don't think—"

"Do play, Brother," Penelope implored. "It's great fun."

With his sister, who had been so listless for months, who hadn't responded to any of his attempts to cheer her or let him inside her thoughts, now smiling, he couldn't refuse.

"Maybe for a few minutes." He took the seat Lilith offered. "I must leave shortly."

"You must select a question." Lilith picked up a stack of tiny squares of paper. She leaned in, close enough for him to smell her musk perfume. His pulse quickened.

"But don't look at the back, for it has the answer," Penelope cautioned.

"That's right." Lilith wagged her finger. "No cheating."

He cautiously picked a piece of paper so as to avoid any accusations of duplicity. A strange sensation, like painless, hot electricity radiated out from where their fingers met.

"You read it," he said, handing it to Lilith. He sat back in the cushion and tapped his fingers on the armrest.

"This is a very serious etiquette question indeed." Lilith's face grew grave.

A tiny giggle burst from Penelope, but she quickly composed herself again.

"You are at a dinner party," Lilith began in a somber voice. "And you can't help but notice that the gentleman or, in your case, the lady across from you is exceedingly handsome. How do you signal to her that you desire to rendezvous on the dance floor later?" Both women dissolved into giggles.

"What?" he cried. "This wasn't in the books I gave you!"

"We found those books rather antiquated," Lilith explained. "So we purchased *The Lonely Suitor's Guide to the Romantic Arts, or How To Get Married Within a Year—A Comprehensive Guide to All Areas of Flirtation Including Handkerchiefs, Parasols, Rings, Flowers, Gloves, Linens, and Utensils.* George, I didn't realize people flirted with their utensils. How could I have missed it all these years? I wonder if a man has been secretly signaling that he loves me and all the while I thought he was bathing his parsnip in cream. Have you ever flirted with your spoon or linen?"

He was about to say something censorious about mocking his instructions when his sister helpfully supplied, "Oh, George doesn't flirt with his spoon or anything."

He was torn. Which did he want more? For Lilith to obey his dictates or not to think he was a flat. All the while, Lilith waited.

"I see you don't know the answer," she said, as if she expected as much. "Now you must—"

"When I want to rendezvous with a ravishing lady on the dance floor," he said, "I draw my linen slowly through my hand as if I were caressing her as we dance."

Lilith's mouth dropped. She stared at him as if she couldn't believe he was capable of anything romantic. He winked at her to further discombobulate her.

"Lord Marylewick, you're right!" She gave his arm a gentle swat. "Have you read *The Lonely Suitor's Guide*?"

"I have not." He edged even closer. The phrase *moth to a flame* echoed faintly in his head. "These things come naturally to me. For instance, when I want to rendezvous in a quiet garden or *elsewhere*, I place my spoon atop my knife. Maybe give them a little rub together." He couldn't deny that how he used his fingers to illustrate might be deemed impertinent, but he enjoyed seeing how her blush and fluster erased the usual wry gleam in her eyes.

"George!" Penelope cried. "You're horrid. Lilith isn't married. You shouldn't say such things."

"I'm sorry, Miss Dahlgren," he said, but felt no contriteness. After all, she had asked him to play. Maybe it wasn't so amusing when she couldn't control the game. "What is my prize for my table-flirting prowess?"

Lilith was still blushing as she reached over to open the box on the table. "You get a toffee." She held the little confection in her palm. "Penelope and I must drink from our wine, because you answered the question correctly."

"Wait a minute!" Realization dawned on him. "You've entangled my sister in some drinking game worthy of a gin palace?"

This was too much. He should have known Lilith would have no compunction about manipulating Penelope, turning her into a pawn in their greater battle. He should never have left them alone. Good God, was he going to have to cancel every engagement he had for the next few days and watch Lilith like a nursemaid?

"You were to study proper etiquette," he barked. "Not enlist my unsuspecting sister in making a mockery of my orders. I'm trying to help you."

Penelope's happy expression fell. "But it was…was my idea. I didn't know…I thought…I'm sorry." She bit her lip. "It seemed like a fun idea at the time."

George felt like the lowest cur. Penelope was finally laughing for the first time in years, and he had to ruin it by harsh remarks intended for Lilith.

"I'm very sorry," his sister pleaded. "Please forgiv—"

"Well, I'm not sorry." Lilith rose from the sofa. "It's a brilliant game. In fact, I challenge Lord Marylewick to play."

A word he never thought to associate with Lilith came to his mind: gratitude. She always fought even if the battles were foolish and unwinnable. He remembered her childhood tantrums when his father and uncle called her an unmanageable termagant. But this time she fought to vindicate his sister.

"I'm raising the stakes," Lilith continued. "We will not use *The Lonely Suitor's Guide* because Lord Marylewick disapproves of it and finds it a dead bore, being such an accomplished flirt. No, the questions shall come from the books he so kindly *ordered* me to study. Lord Marylewick will choose the questions and I will answer. Did you not say you would check my progress?"

George glanced at Penelope. Her face was pale, her eyes moist and glassy. "I did," he agreed.

"For every question I get right, Lord Marylewick must drink. However, we will not use the watered-down elderberry wine Penelope wisely suggested for our previous game. For as she aptly pointed out, it's rather unbecoming for ladies to become tipsy or, heaven forbid, bosky. No, no. For this game, we will have a more manly drink suitable for our manly marquess." She walked to the side table and picked up the crystal decanter. "Brandy. Hard, teeth-clenching, burn-your-mouth brandy." She arched a brow, daring him.

"You just stated that it's unbecoming to be foxed," he said. "You don't even follow your own wise counsel."

"But you see, Lord Marylewick," Lilith said, setting the bottle and tumbler on the table beside him, "I don't intend to drink. I shall sit here all proper and virtuous. See if I don't. Ask me a question."

He didn't approve, but held his tongue. Very well, then. No doubt a few sips of brandy in and she would be pleading for mercy. He poured a generous amount of brandy into the tumbler, enough to make Lilith regret her decision, and then opened the top book on the stack, *What Every Young Lady of Quality Should Know Upon Entering into Society and Marriage: A Guide to Gentle Breeding,* and began to scan the lines. The first chapters were prudish ranting on duty and modesty. Around page fifteen he almost picked up the tumbler of brandy for relief when the author finally decided to write something of concrete value. "Ha! What is the standard hour for luncheon?"

"The standard hour for luncheon. Ah, I must think." She closed her eyes and pressed her fingers to her temples. "Ooh, what is it? What is it? It's on the tip of my tongue."

"Of course it is. You don't know, do you?"

"Wait, I remember now." She snapped her fingers and a cool smirk lifted her lip. "Two o'clock in the summer, half past one in the winter, and always one o'clock in the country. Am I correct?" She held up the glass. Her dancing dark eyes were hypnotic over the rim.

"Yes," he admitted. In fact, Lilith was more thorough than the book, but he wouldn't tell her so. He couldn't cede any territory to his brandy-pouring enemy.

"So drink," she said. "No, no, not a tiny sip. The entire glass. Toss it back the way they do in the gin palaces where the etiquette drinking game is all the rage."

He had poured the glass, he had asked the question, there was nothing to do but take his medicine. The rush of liquid burned going down his throat, but for some reason, he enjoyed the pain. It was primal and heady. His blood rushed as he gnashed his teeth. Lilith retrieved his empty glass from his fingers. He tried to ignore the electric tingle where their skin touched.

"Another question, please." She refilled the glass.

He loosened his tie. "What time of year do country balls begin?" She wouldn't know this one. She'd lived in boarding schools or London for her entire life.

"When hunting begins in November, and they continue until Lent. Members of the aristocracy—that's you, Lord Marylewick, and your blue-blooded partner—safely stay at the top of the ballroom, whereas I, a member of the great unwashed, loiter about the bottom. And no invitations are necessary, but in certain circumstances you may require a voucher." Lilith tapped the glass with her finger. "I do believe you must drink again, Lord Marylewick."

What had he done? He steeled himself and gulped fast. No more burning in his throat, but his head was feeling lighter when he asked the next question. "What does a young lady—for instance, say you, if you behaved properly—do after every dance?"

She refilled the glass and handed it to him. "If, for some mad reason, I choose to behave properly, I would return to my chaperone." She stifled a feigned yawn. "Really, George, this is hardly challenging. For God's sake, don't bore me."

Penelope chuckled, color returning to her face.

Why did he think this would teach her a lesson? And he didn't need to learn the lesson of too much brandy yet again. He had to switch to more advanced etiquette studies before he was foxed out of his wits. He set *What Every Young Lady of Quality Should Know* aside and picked up *Letters to a Debutante and New Wife on the Subject of Correct Social Usage and Good Form.* But it was useless. Lilith made mockery of that and dissected *The Deportment of Proper Young Ladies in Society and Abroad*. Could he have conducted his exams at Oxford with such precision and thoroughness?

Seven questions later, Lilith held the decanter, threatening to pour more of that devil's brew. The words in the books were swimming about the page and Lilith's smile and hypnotic eyes were doing things they shouldn't be doing to his male parts.

"Shall I pour or do you surrender?" She let a tiny drop of brandy venom fall and pool on the bottom of the glass. His gut turned.

"No more, no more," he begged.

"Then say, 'Miss Dahlgren, you are the all-knowing goddess of etiquette. I humbly beseech your forgiveness that I should have doubted your social brilliance.'"

He would never utter such nonsense nor could he come up with a clever retort. A wave of brandy-induced lightness crested over his brain. "Ugh. I think I need some coffee and a sandwich."

"Good heavens, are you foxed?" Lilith scooted down to the end of the sofa and flicked her fingers in a shooing motion. "Stay away from me, you black rake. I am a well-behaved lady. Lord Marylewick would be furious if he knew I associated with low drunks. Penelope, call the butler and have this louse tossed into the street."

"I have met the devil and he is a woman," he moaned. "Penelope, my dearest, beloved sister, take compassion upon me and please ring the bell for a pot of coffee and a sandwich. I have a musical murder to attend this evening."

"Musical murder?" Lilith asked. "Are you going to bludgeon someone to death with a French horn?"

"A musical party," Penelope explained as she crossed the room to the bellpull. "George despises musical parties and calls them musical murders of Bach, Haydn, and such."

"I don't despise musical parties," he protested. "In fact, there is nothing I enjoy more than a good musical party." He pressed his hand to his temples, trying to stop the sensation of a rolling sea in his head. "And therein lies the problem."

"Then why not stay home with us?" Lilith said, surprising him. She nestled into the cushion, her blue floral robe flowing about her. With the fire behind her, her hair gleamed like reddish copper and dots of light shone in her cocoa eyes. "We shall have our own musical evening. Penelope, you play and sing so beautifully. What do you say?"

Penelope answered something, but George didn't hear because he continued to study Lilith. Something was missing from the lovely picture she made. The composition wasn't correct. There needed to be an object on the side table, maybe a lamp with copper fixtures, casting an orange glow to balance the left side of the would-be painting.

"George? George?" Lilith was saying, her voice seeming to be miles away. "Stop staring at me in that faraway manner and answer."

He bolted up in his seat, embarrassed to be caught gawking.

"We are asking you a question," Lilith continued. "Will you stay home and join us for our own domestic musical murder? Penelope says you've been looking tired lately and should rest. And I say you won't do Parliament any good if you show up bosky. No one likes to be romanced by a drunk, politically or otherwise. It's against all proper etiquette. And as you know, I am the all-knowing goddess of the subject."

"Then why don't you apply it?" he barked out of his own frustration and then instantly regretted it when Lilith's mouth fell open.

"George!" Penelope cried. The drowsy, lulling magic of the moment was seeping away again.

Damn Lilith serving him brandy and being so lovely, laughing, and taunting. And damn him for getting lost in her beauty again.

He rushed to salvage the old feeling. "Please forgive me, Miss Dahlgren. I *am* too bosky if I'm being rude to my sister and cousin. It wouldn't do to appear in public." What was he saying? He had made promises to converse with a certain MP tonight. He had confirmed his presence with hostesses. He had a responsibility to appear. He wouldn't say anything at the moment, but in half an hour or so, he would quietly steal away after sobering up.

Lilith linked her arm through his and smiled. Beneath the thin silk of her robe, he could feel the soft mound of her breast. Was she not wearing a corset again? He decided not to make a point of it but instead enjoy the pleasing sensation of her body brushing against his as they walked arm-in-arm to the music room.

Nine

THE COFFEE AND SANDWICHES WERE REDIRECTED TO the music room. George sat with his legs stretched out, enjoying warm bread, beef, and tangy mustard. Penelope played and sang in a gentle soprano, her voice blending with the low roar of the fire and the rain beating on the window. Lilith turned the music pages, yet often George would lower his coffee after taking a sip to find her watching him and not the music. She would quickly avert her gaze, but not before sparking him with the magic in those mysterious eyes. The mountains of work that had piled up over the last days and the parties he was missing seemed miles away as he relaxed in the hazy lull of brandy, the music, and Lilith's beauty.

Then Penelope told Lilith that it was her turn to sing.

"But my voice has been compared to a tone-deaf barn owl," Lilith protested. "And I don't think that is being fair to tone-deaf barn owls."

"Come, it's not as bad as that," Penelope assured her.

"It could potentially be worse."

"You are being modest," Penelope said. "Sing."

Unfortunately, Lilith wasn't being modest. Tone-deaf barn owls, unoiled hinges, and amorous bullfrogs were more melodious. George struggled to contain his laughter. He could see that his sister labored under the same problem but gamely continued playing until Lilith smashed into a high C, and then warbled down to a B flat. Penelope's eyes drifted to George and they broke down.

"This isn't fair," Lilith cried, hurt, but with a twinkle in her eyes. "You asked me to sing. I can only assume you wanted to hear." She continued singing with great zest, exaggerating her horrific, wobbly voice.

"Lilith, Lilith, you are beautiful," George said. "You speak the poetry of angels and you are the all-knowing goddess of etiquette, but dear God, you can't sing."

She stuck out her tongue. "Let us hear you, Lord Severe Critic. How nice to sit in a comfy chair, sipping coffee, eating sandwiches, and smugly judging others."

"George has a fine voice," Penelope said unhelpfully, "but he never lets anyone hear it."

"Does he, now?" Lilith cast him a glance from under her long lashes. "George is a man of many hidden talents, and we must bring them all to light. Sing for us. It's your turn."

"I'm afraid I can't be removed from this chair. Some viciously polite ladies plied me with too much brandy and trapped me in their musical lair."

"No?" Lilith said. "Well then, Penelope, what is a song with many sharps and flats that will best suit my voice? I shall endeavor to torture it for many measures. After all, we promised Lord Marylewick an evening of domestic musical murder and you didn't harm a thing with your beautiful voice."

"You are always going to have your way, aren't you, Lilith?" George rose from his chair.

"I especially adore having my way with you," she retorted. Penelope dissolved into giggles.

"Scoot over, my wicked-minded ladies." He slid onto the edge of the piano bench. "Pray, let me get my turn over with because I fear I won't get any peace until I do."

Penelope flipped through her hand-scribed book of songs. "Ah, '*Caro Mio Ben*' would suit you. Have you heard it?"

"Once or twice or a thousand times these few years," he dryly quipped.

He gamely sang along as Penelope played. Out of the corner of his eye, he could see Lilith watching with unguarded admiration on her face. Her approval split his emotions. Part of him wanted to spread his vocal feathers like a peacock, and another part figured if Lilith approved of something, it must be dangerously wrong.

To hell with it all. He closed Penelope's music book.

"George!" his sister cried.

"Enough of this boring music. Don't we have something more lively? Something even Lilith can sing." She made a face. He winked at her. "What about 'Nut-Brown Ale' or 'A Health to All Good Fellowes'?"

"Good heavens, drinking games and now tavern songs," Lilith marveled. "What low place have you brought me to, Lord Marylewick?"

"It's all part of the education of Miss Lilith Dahlgren," he replied, bland-faced. "You missed the last item on my list: tavern songs. I believe in a well-rounded education." He nudged his sister. "Come now, Penelope, spice it up."

Penelope's eyeballs rolled upward as she thought for a moment, then she broke into a raucous version of "Song of a Fallen Angel Over a Bowl of Rum-Punch."

Lilith clapped. "I didn't realize you had this in you."

"Just sing," Penelope ordered.

And they did. Lilith's voice was so wretched it was comical, but what she lacked in musical talent she made up for in fearless gusto. Competition and perfection characterized George and his world. Aside from Penelope, all the other ladies of his acquaintance vied for the prize of being the most accomplished, the most beautiful, the most charming. For now, he enjoyed basking in the shockingly terrible. (However, he would ask Lilith not to sing to a potential suitor until after the marriage, when it was too late.) Penelope continued playing, never putting a break between songs, and Lilith kept glancing at him. Being around her lightened his mind and pushed back the heavy mantle of his daily concerns and worries.

But then Lilith took her magic away. She rose, interrupting Penelope as she played the beginning notes to a new song.

"I'm sorry," Lilith said. "I'm rather tired. I should go to bed."

George didn't want to admit to himself the cold disappointment in his chest. What could he do to grow immune to this woman? Everything she did lit him up. He bit back the words *but you stay up until the wee hours every night at those wild bohemian parties you attend.* Instead he said, "That is wise, Miss Dahlgren. Sleep calms the excitable nature."

"But I rather enjoy being exciting." She rallied and then

said to Penelope, "Thank you for cheering me up today. I'm so happy…" She paused, as if searching for correct words. "I'm so happy I've gotten to know you better."

"And I'm so glad you are coming to the house party," Penelope replied. "*Dear* cousin." Some of the mysterious, unspoken female communication, the kind that always confused and terrified men, passed between the ladies. Then Lilith smiled and left.

He and Penelope were back to their own company. She tried to start playing again, but the spirit was gone.

"I wish she wasn't tired." Penelope's features had returned to the usual distressed lines. "The evening was perfectly lovely."

"You must be careful around Lilith," he cautioned his sister, but the warning was for him, as well. "Behind that dazzling facade are sharp fangs."

Penelope played a quiet G. The note reverberated and slowly died away. "I think there is only hurt behind the facade." She stared where her finger remained on the key.

"Talk to me, Penelope. You know you can tell me anything."

He tried to put his arm around her in a hug, but Penelope slid off the bench. "Good night, brother. I think the education of Lilith proceeded very well."

He now sat in the empty room. He pondered Penelope's words: *I think there is only hurt behind the facade.* He suspected as much, but whenever he tried to help Lilith, she lashed out. When he attempted to talk to Penelope about her life or marriage, she turned quiet. He wished he knew how to talk to them. Hell, he wished he knew how to talk to Parliament.

He glanced at the mantel clock: quarter past ten. It would be too late to attend the musical evening. To atone for his social sins he would make a stab at the mounds of work waiting on his desk. He headed to his study. His secretary had divided the documents that required the marquess's attention into three towering piles: Parliament, business, and estate. He felt tired and disinterested gazing at the stacks.

Nonetheless, he sat, withdrew his penknife, and opened the first letter on the Parliament pile. Prime Minister Disraeli had written that he was regrettably unable to attend the house party, but penned a lengthy outline of political points to be subtly discussed at the party and a list of the men whose votes George needed to romance. Somewhere in the middle of the letter, George's mind's eye wandered off the page and to the memory of Lilith on the parlor sofa, nestled amid the blues, reds, and golds. The light of the glass lamp had showed the contours of her neck and the mounds of her breasts beneath the robe. He remembered their softness and the rise of the nipples underneath his body that night at her party. He released a low, long breath as he imagined what waited beneath the blue silk. More creamy skin and peaks the shade of a faded rose. How would they feel as he swept his fingers over their tips? How would they taste if he teased them with his tongue? If he slipped her robe down, lower and lower, would her thighs be as ivory and silken? Would her curls be a rich auburn? How would his cock feel sliding into her snug body? His mind continued to wander down this dangerous path, fantasizing about Lilith's body in various love-making positions, until he glanced down to find he had idly doodled his fantasy of Lilith's nude body on Disraeli's letter.

What was he doing and thinking? He ran his hand down his face.

Of course he desired Lilith. How could any man of a healthy, lustful appetite not? She was a lush beauty, an ever-blooming garden. If he never touched Lilith in an intimate way again, delivering her tidy and well-trained to her future husband, at least he could reward himself by imagining her glorious breasts bathed in sunlight as she rode atop him, sliding up and down his shaft. His hand slid across his thigh to where his erection strained against his trousers and slowly began to pleasure himself as he imagined her. He could see the glow in her luminous eyes. Her hair would be loose and brushing his face like soft feathers as she moved above him, sinking him deeper into her—

The door creaked open and the object of his lustful fantasy slipped inside.

Bloody hell! He grabbed Disraeli's letter and shoved it in a drawer.

"Good evening." Her voice was breathy. He couldn't politely stand with his cock jutting in a stone-hard erection. And that damned blue robe clinging to her curves and the way her hair tumbled loose as he had imagined it didn't help matters.

She edged toward him. "I didn't mean to interrupt your work."

"Not at all," he choked.

"I must admit that I lied." She held up her hand. "I know, I know, you are about to say that you're not surprised or you expected it from me. I just…just had to be alone with you."

His penis almost popped his trouser buttons. "Lilith, I'm your guardian for all intents and purposes and it wouldn't be right if we…we…"

"If we?" she said, prompting him to continue.

"You need to be virtuous for your future husband."

Every visible inch of her skin turned crimson. "I didn't mean that! I meant…" The shock gave way to laughter. "That's rather funny."

He didn't know which was worse: mistakenly assuming Lilith desired him, or being laughed at for said mistake. In any case, the mortification destroyed his erection. "It's the usual reason a lady in a state of dishabille wants to be alone with me," he said for the sake of his wounded pride.

Lilith flashed a flustered smile. "I simply wanted to ask you something in private."

"Of course." He rose, now that he safely could, walked around the desk, and motioned to the sofa and chairs.

She settled onto the sofa. "It's like my fifteen-minute appointment."

"I'll give you a few more minutes this evening," he teased, taking the chair opposite her. "How can I be of assistance?"

She didn't answer but studied his face, her eyes narrowed as if she were searching for something. His body heated under the scrutiny. Then she surprised him by sliding from the sofa and kneeling before him. She seized his fingers and gazed up at him.

"I saw your sketches of me today. They were wonderful. Truly. I couldn't believe you sketched them. So I made Penelope reveal everything to me."

His stomach tightened. "What do you mean? I merely wanted to give the modiste a guideline, as, pardon my saying, sedate and understated have never characterized your fashion sense."

"No, not that." She edged closer, her belly pressing against his knees. "How you were all supposed to be the perfect family. How your father disapproved of your art. How you were paddled if you drew or painted." She squeezed his fingers to her chest. "I'm sorry. I wish I had seen. I was too wrapped up in my own anger. I could have helped."

"I don't recall needing help." He tried to retract his hands. "Penelope has a tender heart, but I'm afraid her version is most incorrect."

"Don't you see? You're an artist. You must draw again. You must make art. This is why you have been so...so...miserable all these years."

"Miserable? I'm not miserable." Yet with her so close, her eyes dilated with tender emotion, and wet lips glistening from the firelight, the last years felt painfully empty.

She placed her palm on his heart. "You're an artist. It's your calling."

Her touch burned. Sweat beaded around his hairline. He came to his feet, yanking at his tie until the knot came loose.

"My calling?" he scoffed. The words came out more derisive than he intended, but he could barely catch his breath.

"Yes," she said softly. "Don't look away from me. Don't dismiss me. Being an artist is noble. You should be proud of your talent." She opened her arms with a bursting motion. "You must draw and paint and sculpt and get out all the beauty that's inside of you. 'Then let winged Fancy wander / Through the thought still spread beyond her: / Open wide the mind's cage-door, / She'll dart forth, and cloudward soar.'"

"More Keats?" he asked.

"Yes."

He swallowed his desire to call her childish. He paced to his desk and pulled a letter from the estate pile—a bill from a stonemason regarding tenants' homes. "I'm afraid that all my fancy darted forth and left years ago. I think a better simile would be to say that my fancy has been put away, along with my toy soldiers and hobby horse. I had to grow up and face my responsibilities. My father made a marquess from an irresponsible, lackadaisical boy who would rather, I don't know, draw pictures of bird eggs than understand the intricacies of running an estate." He rubbed his temples, suddenly tired. "I know you enjoy your little art and poetry, but it's time you learned some responsibility, too. Let us discuss my expectations for you at the coming house party."

She crossed to the other side of the desk and began neatening the political stack.

He placed his hand atop hers to stop her efforts. "My secretary has put these in a specific order."

She glanced down to where their skin touched. "All those bird eggs you drew," she said quietly. "Fragile promises of hope. Maybe some will hatch, some will not. The mechanics of nature are beautiful and heartless. But that tiny boy caring for those eggs, no doubt checking their nest every day, lovingly drawing them... What an irresponsible, lackadaisical little boy."

He hated when she did that. As if she possessed some supernatural ability to look inside his memories. She held his gaze until he couldn't bear being stripped naked by her deep eyes and looked away.

He cleared his throat. "As for the house party, there will be some influential—"

"What happened to the eggs?"

He paced to his window. "I haven't the time for this inane conversation!" The bird had built the nest in the bushes leading to the labyrinth garden. The head gardener had it ripped out and the eggs smashed as George watched. He remembered the mother and father bird squawking and flying around the gardener's head, trying to protect their babies. He had drawn the scene at night in his bedchamber. He didn't know how to get the pain out of his young heart. The resulting painting was as ridiculous as the blotched painting at Lilith's party on the night of their notorious kiss. Just slashes of red and black paint.

"You want to know my calling?" he asked. "I have to help run a country, as well as take care of ten estates, and nearly a hundred relatives and tenants who depend upon me for food and shelter. I'm the guardian of numerous children. Then there's you. And you take up more of my time than most of those combined."

She drew a little circle with her finger on the stonemason bill. "It's always responsibility and duty, as if you are using them to keep you safe from something."

"Safe from something?" he thundered. "Do you know what happens when I don't see to my responsibilities? Families don't have enough food. Workers don't get paid. Governments don't function. You

gazed at the picture he had sketched. He ran his fingers along the lines. It wasn't enough. He hadn't captured her. He wasn't a Keats, nor was he an artist. He slammed the drawer shut and hung his head in his hands.

❧

What sadly misguided notion did you harbor? Lilith admonished herself in her chamber.

Why did she keep making stupid mistakes? She had thought her cousins were loyal. Quite wrong on that count. George drew a few sketches and suddenly she believed that under his starched exterior existed a soul-crushed little boy trying to break free. She humiliated herself in the process of learning how wrong that assumption was.

Her fingers were trembling. She needed to write. She had to direct this anger and frustration churning inside her somewhere or she feared that *poof*—she would spontaneously combust. All the coroner would find was the smoldering ashes of Lilith.

She dug out her portfolio and withdrew her last pages. She scanned over her previous work, all melodrama scrawled in a heated passion: Colette trapped in the sultan's tent, her heart broken, railing against God, threatening suicide, etc.

"Muse, we need a vast improvement. Some ideas of murder or, at the very least, accidental death for the sultan." She dipped her pen and began to scribe.

> *Colette could cry no more and buried her face in the pillows.*
> *She let her mind wander back to her home and her*

*father when he was well. Her heart ached for the love
she had then, so abundant, like the groves of ripe olives.*

*At first, she thought it was a trick of her mind, re-
membering the songs her father sang to her as a young
child, but the timbre wasn't correct. He had a weak,
reedy voice and what she heard was rich and resonant.*

*In the tent's dim corner, she made out the hard
lines of the sultan's powerful body. He continued
to sing, moving closer. His magnificent voice wove
a musical spell around them. Caught in its magic,
there was no anger and hurt from the past or fears of
the future. Only this moment.*

"Dear Muse." Lilith rolled her eyes. "Must we
be melodramatic?"

> *Colette smoothed a wayward strand from his
> savage brow and gazed into his black eyes, finding
> in their depths a frightened little boy.*

"Frightened little boy? Muse, no! Did you not
witness what happened? I thought we had cleared up
the matter of the little boy. He doesn't exist, just a
hardened villain. He can garner no sympathy."

> *"Who are you?" Colette whispered.*
> *"I don't know." Sorrow imbued his voice. "I
> don't know." He clasped her hand and pressed it to
> his mouth. "You must help me, Colette."*
> *"What can I give you? What do you need?"*

Lilith's pen hovered over the page. "Well, Muse,

why don't you tell me," she quipped. "How can Colette, who has almost died by this man's hands on several occasions, help him?"

Colette lowered the blankets, revealing her nude body.

"What? The publisher will never allow that."

"Touch me," she whispered, taking his hand and resting it upon her breast. "Fill yourself with love. Take it from me until you hurt no more. Only healing love will vanquish the evil in your heart."
The sultan flicked his thumb over her nipple. Colette gasped in pleasure.
"Rest upon me," she cried. "Find solace inside my—"

"Enough, Muse! Enough! I'm rather upset tonight and you have not been the least helpful. I don't know what journal you think will publish this lurid claptrap. He is the villain. Villains meet horrible yet deserved ends. That's how the stories go. I'll give you another chance."

He opened his caftan. His dark chest was striped with hard muscle all the way to his—

"Good night, useless, filthy-minded Muse." Lilith shoved her pages into her portfolio and locked it. "Maybe tomorrow you'll remember what proper literature resembles."

Ten

"PARDON ME, MY GOOD MAN," GEORGE CALLED TO THE newspaper and magazine vendor in Euston Station. "Has a new issue of *McAllister's Magazine* come out?"

The man shook his head. "No, guv'nor. Maybe tomorrow. Been asked about it all week. Everyone is mad for Colette and the sultan of 'ers."

Dammit. George needed the calming words of Colette to keep him distracted from the worries weighing on his mind.

He liked to believe that omens were the stuff of addled minds. Yet as they were about to embark for the house party, the drenching rain making a muddy slurry of the street and swelling the gutters left an uneasy feeling in his gut. Then added to that uneasy mix, he hadn't wired his mother that Lilith was attending.

Lilith hadn't spoken to him for the last several days. Even a brief flicker of eye contact seemed too painful for her to manage. Despite their embarrassing fight in his study, he thought it best not to give in to his urge to reconcile with her. He was her trustee, not her friend. Meanwhile, Lilith and his sister's relationship continued to blossom. He felt oddly jealous of their private jokes and shared secrets. If Lilith hurt Penelope, she would be beneath contempt in his mind. However, it soon became apparent to him that it wasn't his threats about money which had persuaded Lilith to attend the house party, but some loyalty to Penelope he couldn't understand. The two ladies had never been friends before.

Now the newfound laughter between the women was silenced. They appeared glum as they stood on the platform, clearly wishing they were anywhere else.

Lilith waited in her wet coat, holding her portmanteau and closed umbrella, staring at some nondescript spot on the station wall in that dazed, vacant manner indicative of lack of sleep or severe trauma. His sister Penelope clutched and unclutched the strings to her reticule, looking as if she might burst into tears at any moment.

"Come, ladies, it's a house party," he jested, trying to lighten the mood. "Not a sentence to Newgate."

Lilith finally decided to acknowledge his existence and flashed him a hot glower. "I would much rather spend the week in the congenial company of such established societal matrons as Nimble Fingers Nelly, Axe Handle Anna, and Mary Tart of All Seasons. And I wouldn't even need a new wardrobe."

It scared him to admit how much his body surged at the littlest scrap of her attention. "By Jove, I never thought to have you arrested," he retorted. "That would solve my Lilith problem quite nicely."

"Just stop bickering!" his sister uncharacteristically barked. "For goodness' sake, we're not five!" People further down the platform turned to observe them.

He and Lilith swapped startled glances.

"Penelope, are you well?" Lilith put an arm around his sister's shoulders. "I was only funning with George. I can't help it. He's always so stiff."

His sister's face colored. "I'm sorry. I didn't sleep well. And Mama… I should rest on the train."

As soon as they boarded their first class seats, Penelope turned her head and closed her eyes, shutting out her fellow passengers. Lilith mumbled something about catching up with correspondence, opened her portmanteau, drew out her Keats book, paper, and a pencil. She hunched over her work, shielding it with her body, lest George should spy a word.

He had brought parliamentary work along with him, as well as some letters from his solicitor which required careful reading. Between "wherein the party of liability" and "under the terms as found in exhibit A" he found his gaze drifting to Lilith and her peculiar behavior. For several pregnant moments, she would stare at her page with fierce eyes and then burst forth in writing as if the words were erupting from her mind. After the volcanic spew slowed, she would nibble on her fingertip as she looked over what she had written. Then with the same ferocity as the lines were written, she would mark through them. He wondered who might be the recipient of this passionate outpouring.

He returned to his boring letter, only to lift his head a minute later to find her studying him with two tiny pleats between her eyebrows and her pencil hovering over her page.

"Does something about my person offend you?" he asked.

She jerked her head as if waking from a dream. Her face flushed. "Of course, George. Everything about your person offends me." She wadded up her pages and jammed them into her portmanteau. He thought he heard her mutter, "You can go to fiery Hades, Muse." She opened her Keats book and dived in. And that composed the entirety of their conversation for the rail trip.

At the train station, George had a four-wheeler waiting to deliver them to Tyburn and a covered cart to carry their luggage. The rain had finally stopped, but trees still dripped. The pearly orange and blue tones of dusk lit the sky.

The four-wheeler sloshed along the rutted road through the village and then turned onto the long drive. After rounding a line of oaks, the great estate of Tyburn filled the horizon, a mountain range of masonry, vaulting windows, chimney stacks, and towers. His spirits waned. Although each Marquess of Marylewick had made his own mark on the structure, every inch of the estate reminded George of his father—intimidating, impassive, and larger than life.

Across the carriage, Lilith's chin trembled. She resembled the young girl she used to be, her eyes large and tense, her motions jittery like a nervous squirrel.

He wanted to squeeze her hand and tell her everything was going to be well. But he knew that might not be true. Instead he said, "Are you feeling well?"

"Every demon of my childhood is coming back to haunt me at the moment," she replied. "Otherwise, I'm just splendid."

Penelope released a puff of bitter laughter that she quickly hushed up.

It was clear that no one inside the carriage wanted to be here.

Lilith touched the carriage window with her finger and began to tick off the architectural history of Tyburn. "The original unadorned fortress wing built by the savage George I and the foreboding Tudor addition by the ambitious George III, the staid Jacobean wing by dour, uncompromising George IV, the dry, neo-Classical addition by painfully symmetrical George VI." She looked at him. "What will be your addition, George? What will you leave behind for future generations of Georges to remember you by?"

He didn't know why, but her question dejected him even further. "I'm thinking of making an Egyptian addition and adding a sphinx. When you come up the drive, you'll see just the massive stone head."

Lilith opened her mouth in shock that turned to laughter and Penelope joined in. He wanted to tell the driver to keep riding on this moment of good humor, getting far away from old family disputes, the Stamp Duty Extension Bill, political maneuvering, blushing young ladies with their ambitious mamas vying for his title, memories of his father, the despondency of his sister, his controlling mother, and the loaded gun that was Lilith.

❧

Lilith gazed up at the massive doorway. She hadn't been back to Tyburn Hall since the Christmas before her mother died. The extended Maryle family always gathered for Christmas and Easter, and Lilith only came home from school at those times, so her few family memories occurred within the walls and corridors of Tyburn. When she had been very young, she would enter the grand home, imagining that this visit would be different. By some Christmas miracle, her mother and stepfather would suddenly see a special spark in her that they had missed all these years and they would come to love her as they did her half-siblings. Her mother would be unable to part with her when school resumed. This sad delusion led to many tears and screaming tantrums. Later, as a sulky, withdrawn adolescent, she passed the torturous holidays by escaping into her mind, fantasizing about being grown and married to a radical, handsome artist in France. She would spend her days sipping wine and discussing art, writing, and the deep matters of life with other free-spirited artists in Paris cafés. That dream had yet to materialize.

All she truly wanted was to break from this family, to sever the tie forever. But the more she tugged at the string holding her, the faster she was snapped back. Now she found herself at twenty-three back at Tyburn Hall, as homeless and confused as ever.

Passing into the grand hall of marble staircases and massive portraits of Maryles, more and more old memories assailed her. Would their potency ever fade? Or did the bitterness remain with her forever?

"My darling boy," a majestic female voice cried.

Dowager Lady Marylewick entered the hall in a grand sweep followed by a thin, ungainly young woman who appeared to be a secretary, judging from the notebook and pencil she carried. Lilith hadn't seen the magnificent Lady Marylewick in years. In her presence, Lilith was reduced to the insecure girl who was intimidated by her ladyship's elegant countenance. Lady Marylewick's ivory skin had remained firm and unmarred by age spots, her pale eyes unclouded, and her lips still delicately curved in a pleasant smile. Her black mourning gown molded to her slender form and accented her platinum hair.

"George!" she cried. "George, my little—" She halted, her gaze landing upon Lilith. The pleasant expression on her face remained intact, but a perceivable coolness washed over her features.

"Lilith Dahlgren," she said slowly. Her smile lifted a fraction. "What a surprise. It's been so very, very long." Her eyes shifted to George. "You should have told me she was coming, my darling."

George hadn't wired his mother that she was attending? Lilith's face heated with embarrassment.

"The fault is all mine," he admitted. His hand clutched Lilith's elbow. "I begged Lilith to attend at the last minute. She kindly took pity on me and consented."

"Oh dear," Lady Marylewick said to Lilith. Her eyes grew large with concern. "I hope you haven't landed in another one of your infamous scrapes. I remember how my late husband always said that no one could cause a delightful uproar like Lilith Dahlgren." She gave a little tinkling laugh.

The typical words of greeting—how lovely to see you again, I look forward to the house party, and so forth—didn't make it to Lilith's lips. Did Lady Marylewick employ the malicious female trick of the sugar-coated insult?

Lilith gave her ladyship the benefit of the doubt. "Lord Marylewick most ardently wished my presence." She lifted a quizzing brow to him. "He just wouldn't let me refuse."

Lady Marylewick's sharp, glittery gaze shifted from George to Lilith to where he clutched her arm. "I see, a private joke. How simply darling. You must explain it to me sometime, so that I can find it amusing as well."

She held Lilith's gaze a few seconds longer, her eyes narrowing a fraction. Then she turned to Penelope. "Lady Fenmore, my precious daughter. You look quite worn. Does Lord Fenmore not accompany you? You are always abandoning that poor gentleman."

Penelope opened her mouth to reply, but George saved her the effort. "Lady Fenmore kindly arrived early to help you with the house party planning."

"She should have come before today," Lady Marylewick replied in saccharine tones. "But it is no matter. I've put together this whole affair by myself." She turned to her secretary and kissed her cheek. "Of course little Beatrice, the dear girl, has been such a lovely help. Like a grateful and attentive daughter she is to me."

"Beatrice!" Lilith cried. *Her half-sister Beatrice!* The last time Lilith had seen her, she was the angelic girl whom her mother had doted upon. Lilith always assumed Beatrice would develop into a beautiful, simpering version of their delicate mama, not this awkward lady with slightly bent shoulders, enormous eyes, and head full of wild blond curls. "You've grown so much. I didn't recognize you."

Lilith advanced to embrace her sister, but Beatrice made a quick sidestep, leaving Lilith to grasp the air.

"Good evening, Lord Marylewick." Beatrice curtsied stiffly.

"What is this?" George asked. "I can't pick you up and twirl you about anymore?"

Guilt colored Lilith's conscience as the situation's full implications sank in. She had tossed her innocent half-siblings, the adorable infants of whom she was so jealous, into the same mental box with her parents, who didn't love her. She had tied it shut and shoved it into a dark corner in her heart. She hadn't realized George had become more than a mere guardian to her orphaned half-siblings. He was their surrogate papa.

"Now, George, I'm teaching Beatrice the tenets of being a great lady," Lady Marylewick said.

"Beatrice will be a grand hostess, of this I have no doubt." George assumed the warm tones of a proud father. Beatrice blushed underneath the spray of freckles on her cheeks.

"I don't know," Beatrice responded. "Lady Marylewick thinks I spend too much time wandering about the countryside and thinking about, well, unnatural things. But I'm getting better, Cousin George. Truly, I am."

"Unnatural?" Lilith echoed. What a peculiar thing to say. Unnatural in Lilith's Bohemian set meant something quite risqué, indeed. "What do you mean?"

"Science," Beatrice whispered as though it were a foul word.

Lilith chuckled. "What is unnatural about science? It's completely natural. It's the very study of nature."

"It's not lady talk," Lady Marylewick explained. "Gentlemen speak of science, not ladies."

Lilith blinked. "Pray, I speak of science. I find the subject fascinating."

"Of course you do." Honey dripped from Lady Marylewick's voice.

What a subtle jab!

Was this really the same Lady Marylewick Lilith had remembered? The elegant lady who had seemed to exist in a serene sphere apart from everyone else? Had she always possessed this fissure of meanness? Lilith felt like Alice, falling down a rabbit hole to a world that appeared similar to the one she knew, except very different.

"Now, Beatrice, my dearest," Lady Marylewick began, "this perfectly illustrates what I explained yesterday. A good hostess must be prepared when a wonderful guest arrives unexpectedly."

"Mama!" George warned.

"That shan't be a problem at all," Beatrice responded. "We can put Miss Dahlgren in the Foxglove chamber."

Miss Dahlgren, Lilith noted. Not *my sister*.

"Foxglove chamber?" Lady Marylewick asked.

"Yes, in the southeastern wing or the old Tudor wing," Beatrice clarified. "Some of the wings and chambers share the same name. It confuses the incoming guests and servants. Therefore, I've created a consistent naming convention for the duration of the party." She opened her notebook to reveal a detailed blueprint of Tyburn that she must have sketched.

She possessed the drawing talent of her cousin George!

Beatrice pointed to a chamber with the letter F written on it. "Foxglove is really F. It's between the Elder and Geranium chambers. I thought flowers would be easier to use than Roman or Greek designations."

Before Lilith could examine the impressive sketch, Lady Marylewick closed Beatrice's notebook. "Thank you," Lady Marylewick said to Beatrice's eager face. "That is quite enough."

"W-what did I do wrong?" Beatrice's delicate features screwed in confusion. "I th-thought it would help."

"You've done nothing wrong, Beatrice," Lilith said kindly. "You've created such an impressive rendering. How talented you are. And I'm sure the precise naming scheme will prove to be most helpful. I'll be most content in the Foxglove chamber."

Beatrice appeared more confused than ever. Obviously, a compliment from Lilith could only mean a terrible thing.

"As you can see, dear Beatrice and I have seen to every trifling detail, every possible need, so there is nothing for you to do but to relax." Lady Marylewick cupped her hand on Penelope's cheek. "Do get some sleep, my poor dear, you are rather haggard. You will want to appear radiant when your husband arrives."

The obvious pain in Penelope's eyes sliced into Lilith.

"And Lilith, my dear child." Lady Marylewick sauntered toward Lilith, linking their arms. "It's been too long since I've seen you. Too long. Let us have a darling little chat to catch up. Just between us ladies."

Why did Lilith think there would be nothing darling about this "chat"?

Lady Marylewick didn't wait for Lilith's response but led her to the adjacent parlor. Lilith glanced over her shoulder to see George reaching to embrace his sister and Penelope escaping his sympathetic embrace. Then Lady Marylewick closed the door.

"Come, my dear." Lady Marylewick sat on the sofa and patted the cushion beside her. Lilith obeyed.

Tight wrinkles streamed from the edges of Lady Marylewick's smile. Her gaze drifted down Lilith's body. "You were a tiny, adorable thing when I last saw you. A little garden rabbit. Not a curve on you. But how you've filled out."

Was that a compliment? "Thank you."

"Now, my dear," Lady Marylewick continued, "I know you're a rather excitable lady. Wild ideas just pop into your lovely head. Pop. Pop. Pop." She laughed and then leaned in. Lilith could smell her floral perfume and the rose oil in her hair bandoline. "However, attending this prominent house party are gentlemen who influence Britain and the world. And my son, dear Lord Marylewick, so like his father, is one of the most powerful men in Britain. Wouldn't you agree?"

"Lord Marylewick shoulders a great deal of responsibility, indeed."

"He does, the poor man. Therefore it's essential that you and I do nothing to jeopardize his political aims or cause him one morsel of embarrassment. Nothing." Her ladyship drew herself up. "We shall ape the manners of our betters."

Lilith had no doubt that Lady Marylewick's use of the plural "we" meant the singular Lilith.

"Tell me that we are of one mind on this matter," implored Lady Marylewick. "For I assure you, I will be most displeased if George's honor is tarnished by another's unseemly behavior." She capped her menace with a harmless giggle.

Lilith was beginning to unravel this different version of Lady Marylewick. A younger Lilith, blinded by her hurt and anger, couldn't see the machinations holding up the smokescreen of perfection. She carefully considered her reply. "I seek only Lord Marylewick's true happiness."

Lady Marylewick studied Lilith, sensing something off-putting about her cool response. Then she gave another silvery laugh again. "By the by, I'm glad we had this tête-à-tête," she concluded, having injected her sweet venom. "I'm sure you're worn out from travel and desire to rest. Good night, my dear."

Lilith matched Lady Marylewick smile for smile. This battle wasn't over yet. "I wanted to inquire about your son's art."

"George's art?"

"I've learned the most remarkable thing: as a boy he created lovely pictures. Of course, like all loving mothers, I know you've kept his precious work to remind you of those tender years. How little boys love their mamas! I'm so desirous to see his art."

"Good heavens, that was so long ago." Lady Marylewick waved her hand with feigned casualness. "They have been put away."

"No doubt in a special place where they couldn't be harmed. How thoughtful you are. Can you direct me to this place? I promise that I shall take as good care of the treasures as you have."

Calculations worked behind Lady Marylewick's brilliant eyes as she chose her next tactic.

"Lilith, do you not see? You are enthralled in another of your wild ideas." She captured Lilith's hands and squeezed them. "My dear, had I not the great responsibility of a house party to oversee, I would indulge your fancy. Now, I desire you to consider in what docile way you will pass your time during the party. I suggest sewing. As I recall, you could have improved your technique. I shall be happy to show you the proper way to form a French knot, for truly yours were tangles of thread."

Lilith wasn't deceived by having the conversation turned against her. "You didn't save them, did you?"

Lady Marylewick's lips tightened and quivered. She quickly spread them back into a smile. "Perhaps after the party I shall have them taken out and viewed. Good night, Miss Dahlgren. May you wake up tomorrow in better humor. Traveling is quite tiring on a lady's delicate constitution."

Lilith had seen all she required. She strolled from the room, closed the door behind her, and leaned her back against it. She rubbed her temples.

"Pardon me," a female voice said. "I must speak with Lady Marylewick."

Lilith raised her head to find Beatrice before her, hugging her notebook to her chest, her eyes cast down. How long had she been there?

Lilith tried to push away her anger at Lady Marylewick and reached out to her sister. "Beatrice, I'm so happy to see you. We have much to talk about. You must tell me about your love for science. I want to hear all your wonderful thoughts."

Beatrice didn't look up. "I need to tell Lady

Marylewick the supper menu for the ball must be changed." She reached for the knob, but Lilith didn't move.

"Thank you for helping with this house party," Lilith said. "Lord Marylewick is correct, you will be a grand hostess." She paused and then slowly added, "If that is what you want, of course."

Beatrice's eyes turned hot, as if Lilith had insulted her. "Naturally, I should want to be a grand hostess someday. It is the proper thing. It is what I am to do. Lady Marylewick has been so kind to me." The words "and you have not" remained unsaid but loudly heard.

"Oh," Lilith said.

Beatrice glanced away.

"H-how are your brothers?" Lilith asked.

"They are *your* brothers, as well. Shouldn't you know? Perhaps you should write to them or…or me."

The words pierced Lilith's heart. "Yes, I should. I'm very sorry."

"Our brothers are away, studying at Eton." An odd plaintiveness ran beneath her words.

"Would you like to study, too?" Lilith guessed. "To learn more about, I don't know, astronomy or engineering?"

"Ladies shouldn't enjoy rigorous study. It's unnatural. It draws energy away from their nurturing regions."

"You don't truly believe that claptrap, do you?"

Beatrice paused for a beat. "Pardon me, I really must speak to Lady Marylewick."

Lilith stepped aside, letting Beatrice pass.

As Lilith trudged through the maze of corridors, her heart ached with that same numb, shocked hurt of finding Edgar and Frances gone. All the beliefs she had clung to these many years were being yanked from her grasp. She could clearly see the damage Lady Marylewick and her husband had done to Penelope and George, and now her half-sibling was trapped under the harsh Maryle influence. The family had problems, but did she really need to help solve them? Hadn't the Maryles caused her enough pain? To be mucking around in their secrets would sink her deeper into their lives. Some mysteries weren't meant to be solved.

Eleven

Inside the lush women's quarters of the sultan's palace, Colette's travelling robes were removed. Stained glass windows muted the light filtering into the great room. A fountain built into the mosaic floor trickled a low, lulling sound that blended with the quiet murmur of conversation among the other women—the sultan's concubines. They watched Colette curiously, whispering among themselves. Colette huddled in a corner upon a cushion and tried to remember her old home by the sparkling sea.

She had been weak several times on the journey and almost had given her body to the evil sultan when under the spell of his lovely voice, but Lilith Dahlgren, the author of this story, cruelly intervened.

The great doors flung open and a tall woman with blazing black eyes and a flowing embroidered robe and veil strode in. She was flanked by two powerful eunuchs. The concubines quickly rose to their feet. This woman paid no attention to them but headed to Colette.

"So you are the slave he speaks of." The woman's

voice was blunt as a dull knife. "The one who knows how to make Greek Fire."

Colette lifted her eyes.

"I am the valide sultan," the woman thundered. "I am the most powerful woman in the land. I manage every aspect of this palace. Humble yourself before me."

Colette bowed her head. The woman leaned over and hissed in Colette's ear. "You will never be more than a lowly slave. Not even a concubine. Don't think you can tempt him by withholding your secret."

Colette could only laugh at the woman's threats. "I want nothing of your palace or family. I want to go home."

"Hah! You will never see your home again, slave. But if you tell the sultan the formula, he may spare your life."

The valide sultan spun, her flapping robes creating a draft of air as she strode out. "Don't let her eat or drink or give her her clothes until she reveals the formula," she ordered the eunuchs. "I am not as merciful as my son."

Colette buried her face in her hands. Her life was over. It would end here, hundreds of miles from home among strangers.

She felt a kindly hand on her shoulder and raised her head to see a young green-eyed woman. "I'm from Greece too. I was so lonely when I was first captured and sold. But then the sultan took me in and gave me a kind home. Don't cry."

"This will never be my home," Colette said.

"But you can't leave unless the sultan marries you off to someone else," the woman replied.

A stunning woman with Nubian features stepped forward. "Or you find the secret box. Its contents will set you free."

"Shh," one of the concubines said. "We are never to speak of the secret box. We will anger the sultan, our exalted and kind master."

But Colette was unconcerned about the sultan's wrath. He would never be her master. What was in that secret box?

"Muse, no!" Lilith cried. "I know what you are proposing. It's quite transparent. You want me to go up into the attics to find George's childhood art that Penelope hid, for the sake of research. Well, I refuse. Now let's mark through this entire scene and return to the tent where Colette will make a daring escape—with her clothes on—and the sultan will be killed by a tiger or… or…some other deadly animal indigenous to Turkey."

Lilith kept her pen poised, waiting for her muse to behave. Several minutes passed. Black ink dripped onto the page.

"I told you, Muse, I'm not climbing into the scary and who-knows-what infested attics in the middle of the night, in my nightdress, so you will be inspired to write. I'm going to bed. When I wake up, I hope I find a new and more cooperative muse. You're horrible."

She replaced her pages, locked up her portfolio, and then hid it deep in the wardrobe. She placed her Keats volume on the nightstand, extinguished the lamp, and slipped beneath the covers.

Still the muse whispered, *Go to the attics. A real writer seeks the truth.*

Lilith smashed the pillow over her head, a symbolic gesture that she wasn't going to listen.

Then the muse turned vicious. *Keats would have gone in the attics.*

≈

At two in the morning, Lilith, holding a lamp, tiptoed through the corridors in a nightdress, shawl, and boots.

All those painted ancestors lining the halls took on sinister expressions in the dim, early hours. She ascended round tower stairs to the top floor. No one inhabited these rooms, but the scurry and scratch above her head and the tiny black droppings under her feet indicated that she wasn't alone. She lifted her lamp, casting an oval of light all the way down the attic corridor crammed with pots, bottles, and trunks. She edged along the tiny path blazed in the rubbish to the back garret room, where Penelope said she had put the art. Once there, she only found more trunks stacked almost to the rafters. Lilith's ambition flagged.

For the next two hours she dug through yellowing household accounts, absolutely hideous clothes from the 1830s full of enormous puffs and pleats, moldy shoes, cracked spectacles, ugly samplers, two sets of dentures, decades' worth of *Gentlemen's Quarterly*, old parliamentary wigs that now made cozy insect homes, and wall ornaments made of human hair, but no paintings or illustrations. At four in the morning, the lamp oil was almost gone and she was coated in dust and other things she preferred not to think about. Her arms and back ached, and she cursed her muse in terms that would have impressed the crustiest of dockworkers.

"One more trunk," she told the muse. "That's it. Because this little misadventure is making me question my sanity."

Penelope hid that art so long ago that a thousand different things could have happened to it.

Lilith slid one inspected trunk atop another to reveal an upturned blue floral chamber pot.

Eww!

She used her foot to slide the pot, but it wouldn't budge. Hmmm. Something was beneath it. She tipped it with her toes. Inside was a small trunk, the kind made for china dolls and their wardrobes. The words "Kep Out" were carved into the wood.

Lilith drew her lamp closer, her breath quickening.

She undid the latch. *Pop.* The lid sprang up to reveal another clumsily sewn child's sampler.

Bloody, bloody, bloody hell.

She pulled out the sampler, assuming she would find more embroidery or doll clothes. Instead, nestled in cotton was a roll of pages bound with a blue string.

Her fingers trembled as she undid the tie and unrolled the stiff paper. A picture in watery blues and lush greens jumped from the page. An enormous oak with sweeping boughs grew over a brook. A little girl in a blue dress sat against the trunk, smiling in the same joyous light that was shining on the water and leaves.

The night turned silent in Lilith's mind. She carefully turned the page. Written in black ink was one word, "George."

"Dear God."

She shifted through the pages as though they were four-hundred-year-old hand-painted holy manuscripts.

Below waited a scene of workmen in smocks ripping turnips from the soil. The field was symmetric lines against the men's rounded, hunched forms. An expanse of blue sky with gossamer whirls of clouds arched over them. Composition that masters had studied for years came instinctually to this young artist.

She had to wipe away tears to view the next painting: a servant girl perched on an upturned bucket before a blackened kitchen fireplace. The image was dim but for the warm gold light of the flames that reflected on the girl's silver sewing needle and the coppery tones of her hair.

"George," she whispered. "What did they do to you?"

Beneath the servant girl, Lilith found a tiny book Penelope had described. She smiled as she flipped the pages. George had painted beautiful dolls and playful kittens for his young sister. But the last image undid her. Hiccuplike sobs shook her body. Protected in jagged shrubbery rested a nest filled with vivid blue robin eggs.

She bolted up and cradled the pages to her heart. *That sensitive little boy. How could someone be so cruel as to silence this brilliant talent?*

She wanted to pull that hurt boy to her heart and assure him he was perfect just as he was. Rip out the seeds of shame that had been planted in him.

Did she possess the strength to help him? George would hurl vicious insults to keep her away. Whatever words or threats had been used to stifle his talent still waited inside him like an uneasy tiger, ready to lash out if threatened. She had felt his sharp claws that night in his study when she first asked about his art. She wasn't strong enough to break through his defenses, not after

Frances and Edgar had left her. She needed to lick her own wounds, not tend to someone else's.

And George, no matter the sensitive material of his soul, was a Maryle. No amount of pretty pictures could make up for the pain inflicted by him and his ilk. He could have no redemption.

Like the sultan.

She released a long breath while her fingers caressed the old pages. But at least she had to show him the pictures. He needed to see the beautiful parts of himself that he had rejected in order to become the unyielding man he prided himself on being.

However, she couldn't take the pages back to her room. They wouldn't fit in her portfolio and she didn't know how to keep them safe from nosy servants, no doubting working as spies for their controlling valide sultan. The trunk had been safely concealed for over twenty years and that shouldn't change overnight. She carefully replaced pages and doll trunk in their protective chamber pot shell and then shifted another trunk over them.

How could she lead George up here with an open heart? She couldn't approach him and say, *Hello, Georgie, I've found parts of yourself that are painful and that you refuse to admit exist. Care to see?*

She needed to be a little more devious.

And she needed an answer soon, for she was about to run out of lamp oil.

She paced in a tight circle. The lamp guttered. As if by instinct, she reached into the trunk of clothes from the 1830s and grabbed a handful of balloonlike sleeves and billowing skirts.

Oh yes! Simply perfect.

❧

That morning in the breakfast room, George regretted his words the instant they left his mouth.

His mother pressed her clasped hands to her heart. "Oh, George, grandchildren!"

Even Penelope perked up from where she stared glumly at her unbuttered toast.

"That's a bit premature, Mama," he said. "I merely said I'm aware that I need to prepare for my family's future and will consider, merely *consider*, courting one of our young female guests."

"I'm quite champing at the bit to hear the joyous laughter of children and the patter of their little feet at Tyburn again," his mother prattled on. "You know how I adore children. Penelope, my dear daughter, has kept me waiting all these years. Yes, you have, my darling, you know it."

George prided himself on keeping a neutral face in Parliament when some cabbage-headed Whig carried on with his fairy tale–like solutions to England's complex problems. However, his mother's utterance was more than even a man of his forbearance could stand. He made busy dissecting a sausage to keep his face concealed. Since when did his mother care for children? The minute they broke out in joyous laughter or left tiny mud prints behind the patter, she would be calling for the nurse to whisk them away, complaining of her nerves. And secondly, why did she assume she would continue to live at Tyburn once he brought home a wife?

And then there was the scary concept of being a father. What the hell would he say to his children?

All he had was what his own father had told him. He didn't want to be like that. No child of his should know the pain he had growing up.

"Where is Miss Dahlgren?" Penelope cried in a small, desperate voice. Yes, he wondered the same thing himself. At that moment, he needed her there, but he didn't know why.

"I'm sure she's found a lovely new scrape to detain her," Lady Marylewick said in complete amicability and sipped her tea. "Such an excitable young lady. No doubt she will find our respectable party a dead bore and wish she had never come."

George heard the subtle threat under the tinkling laugh.

He realized just how frayed his nerves were when he desired to bolt from the table and shout *Enough of this stupid house party*. Penelope was miserable, Lilith was beautiful, tempting, and insane, among other things, and his mother…well, Samuel Johnson hadn't precise words for a person possessing such sugar-laden malice. Only Beatrice, who appeared to be studying the water displacement and solvency by adding more and more sugar cubes to her tea, was all right and that was because she was too young to know better.

Then, as if strolling onto center stage of the hilarious farce *Lord Marylewick Throws a House Party,* or maybe the angst-ridden drama *Lord Marylewick is Hanged for Murder*, George wasn't sure yet, Lilith entered.

She wore a vivid pink satin gown that would have fit a woman several inches smaller. Her breasts appeared ready to pop out from the bodice and her ankles were in plain view. Massive puffed sleeves decorated each arm and her hair was piled high, resembling a bird's nest on the top of her head.

"What on earth!" his mother shrieked.

"Lilith, what…what are you doing?" Penelope cried.

"I'm going to make the 1830s all the rage again!" Lilith swished her abundant skirts. "I shall be big and bombastic. Everyone will talk about it." She studied her massive sleeves. "Hmmm, I wonder if I pumped these sleeves with hot air, whether I could float about. What do you think, Beatrice?"

The last of George's self-restraint cracked. He bolted to his feet, toppling his teacup. "Stop making a mockery of this family, Lilith! By God, I should never have let you come. You cannot be worked on."

Lilith's features fell. She gazed up at him with large, wounded eyes. "You don't like it?" she asked like a hurt child.

"Lilith Dahlgren, don't you dare disgrace us by appearing in those hideous clothes!" his mother hissed, her beautiful features pinched to sharp lines. "George, she intends to ruin everything. It's her raison d'être."

"Mama, please," George said. "I'll take care of Lilith."

He grabbed Lilith by the elbow, escorted her into the corridor, and shut the door.

"Lilith," he began, trying to keep his anger in check, "I thought we had an understanding—"

"Oh, George." All the mischief drained from her face. She pressed her palm to his chest. The sensation of her touch sank below his skin to the marrow of his bones. "I've seen your art. I've seen it. You're brilliant."

"What?" Just capital. She picked the morning of his house party to truly lose her wits.

"The art from when you were a boy. Penelope preserved it in the attics under a chamber pot. George, you should never have been stopped. It was cruel. The composition, the colors, the light. It's stunning. You must see."

Why the hell was she digging into his past?

"A chamber pot is its proper home," he barked. "I have serious—"

She clasped his hand, trapping it between hers, and held it over her heart. He released an uneven breath as blood rushed to his cock. "Don't get angry. You must recognize your talent. See all the beauty inside of you."

He bit back the harsh words waiting on his tongue and said, with all the control he could muster, "I know you sincerely believe your artist mumbo jumbo. But I've serious obligations, Lilith. Important men will be arriving at any time. I must persuade them to vote in their best interest. I don't have time for your silliness."

"You won't come, will you?"

"No."

"That part of you, that curious, sensitive artist, is shut away forever. You are all grown up. No room for so-called silliness."

"Yes. And I would like you to do the same."

"Would you?" Still holding his hand to her bosom, she started to sway, letting her full skirt swing about her hips. "Isn't this gown magnificent? I'm sure the guests will adore it. It will be written up in all the magazines. I think I shall perform my exotic Arabian dance in it." She lifted his hand and twirled underneath it.

Wasn't she clever? In a fast motion, he braced his arm across the small of her back and dipped her.

She released a surprised squeak.

"You've done this on purpose, haven't you?" He leaned over, keeping her body trapped beneath his. The vanilla and citrus scent of her skin, tinged with lavender soap, exploded in his mind.

"Unless you vow to see your art, this is how I will meet your guests." Her eyes held a bold challenge. "Do you think I'll make a good impression? Will I help your political ambitions?"

He took those words as an invitation to examine in the minutest detail how she planned to greet his guests. Starting from the loose locks falling from that ridiculous bun, then to her soft open lips, down the curve of her neck to where her breasts rose over the top of her bodice. He felt her shiver under his gaze, but she kept her dark eyes locked on his face. His cock grew harder. He released an uneven breath through his teeth.

His lips were so close to that silky skin. He was certain that releasing her breasts from this hideous gown, taking the tip of one into his mouth, licking and suckling it, could calm his anxious thoughts.

"I can't now," he growled between clenched teeth.

She lowered her head until it dangled beneath his arm. Her breasts slid from her bodice until the very tops of her rosy areolas peeked over the edge of the bodice just below his lips. "Promise me," she said, all low and creamy. "Meet me in the attics in the fortress wing at two in the morning, when everyone has gone to bed."

He released a tight groan. "Good God, I promise," he cried. "Stop this game."

She was too much. All ivory, silk, and heat. He

kissed the mound of her breasts with open lips, letting his tongue taste her tender skin. He heard her whimper, the kind a woman makes when lost in the pleasured heat of a man moving inside of her. He drew her closer; no doubt she could feel every inch of his erection against her thigh as his mouth moved closer to dangerous territory at the edge of her bodice.

He heard the creak of boards under carpet and the turn of a knob. He quickly flipped Lilith up. The door opened; he saw the swish of his mother's black gown. Dear God, he was as hard as an iron girder. But Lilith, that mysterious, infuriating, and amazing woman, realized his problem and mercifully stepped in front of him, blocking his trousers from his mother's hot gaze.

"You—you arrogant, unartistic lump-head!" Lilith shouted at him. "I see nothing wrong with my gown. It's lovely. You are all cruel to stifle my fashion, my soul's expression, my being."

"Miss Dahlgren, don't you dare talk such nonsense to the marquess. Put on a proper gown without delay. You will find that I'm not as diplomatic as my son in dealing with domestic matters."

Lilith rolled her eyes and stalked away, but when she reached the turn in the corridor, she glanced over her shoulder. "You promised," she mouthed and then disappeared around the corner.

"She is untamable and sadly misguided," his mother said. "It's that low Dahlgren in her. She has never been anything but resentful and ungracious to our kind overtures."

George didn't trust himself to answer. He spun on his heel and stormed to his study.

Not ten minutes before, George had been pondering courting a lady guest. Then he kissed Lilith's breasts. By all measures of correct behavior he should propose. But she could no more be the Marchioness of Marylewick than he could be a Whig.

Some things were simply too horrible to contemplate.

If she made a mockery of his party, he would… What would he do? He was running out of options for her. He threw money and marital threats at her and none of them stuck. How did one hold back a human gale?

He was going to read Colette until the first guest arrived. It was the only way he knew how to prevent homicide at this point.

In his study, he tried to focus on Colette's story, but his mind kept wandering to the box Lilith had found. Penelope had told him when he was thirteen that she had hidden his work in the attic, but he didn't care to see it then because it was filled with the relics of the boy he didn't want to be anymore. Why now at thirty-one did it matter what was up there?

He tried to focus on the page, but soon the words faded behind the memory of Lilith's beautiful eyes, imbued with awe and admiration, when she said, "I've seen your art. I've seen it. You're brilliant."

Just what was under that chamber pot?

Twelve

GEORGE WAS INFORMED THAT THE GUESTS HAD BEGUN to arrive an hour later. He straightened his waistcoat, smoothed his coat sleeves, and headed down to the great hall, feeling very much like a condemned inmate going to the scaffold.

He found his mother waiting in the hall like some version of a queen receiving her court. Penelope appeared distraught as she lurked in their mother's shadow. Across the hall, Beatrice traced her fingers along the leaves of a planted palm.

"Where is Miss Dahlgren?" George asked, turning about.

"She's probably off somewhere distracted by the colorful circus in her mind," his mother said. "Now let us be content. We are so content." She sang the last word. "Penelope, dearest, remove that sour frown or you'll get unsightly wrinkles. Beatrice, my darling girl, what are you doing over there by that plant? Why, no one can see you behind the foliage."

"This tropical plant appears to be blighted by a fungus or, perhaps, tiny insects." Beatrice turned a leaf. "Perhaps this is a new ailment from its nonnative environment? I wonder how I might get a proper specimen to study?"

"My darling, darling, darling," Lady Marylewick chimed. "Remember, delicate female conversation. The guests are arriving and I don't want to hear any more unbecoming, unladylike talk."

The bright, lovely fascination on Beatrice's features drained away. "I'm so sorry! I will be better. I will."

Before George could intercede, the front door opened. Mr. Pomfret strolled in a few feet ahead of his wife and daughter. George pretended not to notice Mrs. Pomfret discreetly fussing over her daughter's gown.

"Ah, Lord Marylewick, a fine day to begin your house party," Mr. Pomfret said congenially. He wore a plaid coat and trousers. His hair and whiskers were ruffled from the journey, yet this didn't bother the plain-spoken, unaffected gentleman.

His wife lacked all her husband's easiness. Her clothes were a little more adorned than was tasteful, and her ornate hair and hint of cosmetics gave the impression of someone who tried too hard. "Tyburn Hall is more magnificent than ever I imagined, Your Grace," she said, confusing his title. She performed an affected curtsy. "Is there a more superior home in England, my dear Cecelia?" She gave her daughter a tiny tug, pulling her forward.

"Y-yes, er, I mean no." Miss Pomfret performed a stiff curtsy, her hands trembling with nervousness. She broke out in a ferocious blush when he bowed in return and mentioned how delighted he was that she could attend.

Lady Marylewick further undid the poor young lady by gracing her with a compliment. "Such charming conversation," she said to the girl who had only stammered a few words.

Mrs. Pomfret seized upon the praise for her daughter. "Thank you, thank you, Your Grace. Miss Cecelia is exceedingly charming in conversation. Everyone says that they can't wait to converse with her." Her eyes flickered to George. "No doubt she will not be charming us with her conversation much longer. A gentleman will pluck her away now that she is out of the schoolroom."

"A lucky gentleman, indeed," George managed. All he could think was she wasn't near the woman Lilith was. *Why was he comparing her to Lilith?*

"Come, my dears," said Mr. Pomfret, realizing his wife teetered dangerously close to impropriety.

After they passed out of earshot, George's mother leaned in. "What a delightful mother. Not a hint of vulgarity or ambition."

"Mama," he growled under this breath.

Where was Lilith? Should he be relieved that she had chosen not to appear? Was he looking a gift horse in the mouth?

More guests began streaming in. Some were bachelors, whose eyes roamed around the hall, no doubt searching for the elusive Lilith Dahlgren they had heard so much about. Others were families of MPs or important political figures toting a decked-out, nervous daughter, granddaughter, or young female relative of marriageable age. Upon greeting each young lady, his mother would utter vicious little compliments such as "what a darling complexion" about the poor pimple-faced girl or "a delicate figure" about the young lady filling out her dress.

George was ready to walk out the door, shout *To hell with extending the Stamp Duty Extension Bill*, unhitch a horse, and ride away.

And where the bloody hell was Lilith?

The elderly Lord Harrowsby shuffled in, hunched over his cane. A serious young man attended him. Deaf in one ear, Lord Harrowsby spoke to everyone as if they were standing yards away. "Well, my boy, I almost lost my poor life on your roads. They get worse every year. Now I feel my gout coming on again." He jerked his head toward the man behind him. "I bring my physician along since that bout of painful indigestion after the Lord Chancellor's dinner party. Have a weak liver, you see. Vinegary wine brings it on every time. You never know what people are going to serve you."

"How's that weak liver, my lord?" an amused male voice said. "Still has you in the dumps?" In swaggered Lord Charles, with his father behind him.

Charles's eyes scanned the grand hall before lighting back on George and his mother. "Lady Marylewick, you are still the most beautiful lady in London after all these years. Pardon me, I forget we are in the country now. And how could I after bouncing and bumping about those potted roads? I positively feel my gout coming on."

"That's what I was telling him," cried Lord Harrowsby, not perceiving the joke was on him.

"Were you, now?" Lord Charles replied in all

seriousness, except for his eyes, which were aglitter as when he was at Eton, enjoying the casual torment of another boy.

George made a point to keep his fists from clenching. "I shall send my man to see about the roads," he replied civilly.

"Do that, my good man." Charles edged closer to George as his father greeted Lady Marylewick and Penelope. "Where is she? Where have you hidden her? Are we playing hide and seek?"

"I assure you that Miss Dahlgren will come down shortly."

"How she taunts me," he mock-cried to the heavens. "All day I dream of—" He faltered. The cynical, bemused expression evaporated from his face. A low hush blew through the room, all eyes turning up to gaze at an elegant young lady dressed in pale gold standing on the stairs. A hot, dizzying wave rushed through George's head. In his mind, he saw her as a picture, all dazzling gold, red, and light.

❧

Lilith cursed herself for being late. Even after she dressed, she had paced the room. Her mission had been simple: get George to see his art and then go on about her life. *See how wonderful you were before you turned into a flaming arse?* she would say to him. *See how your life could have been? Very well, then. There is nothing more for me to do. Ta-ta.* Using her feminine wiles, she had gotten him to promise. That had been child's play.

The problem was hers. When she had looked at him this morning, she didn't see the George she expected. She saw George and lovely blue robin eggs. And when he kissed her breasts and his body reacted to hers, he was George and lovely light dancing on the water. Now as he glanced up at her on the stairs, she had to grab the banister else she might go tumbling down, head over heels. She had always known George was handsome in an empirical, cold, assessing way. *George is handsome, and isn't that a lovely rug. What a fine view from this window, and, by the by, George is handsome.* His beauty assaulted all her senses.

She kept her head high and feigned the strength and confidence she didn't feel, as she had learned to do during those first excruciating days at a new school. She forced herself not to look at George but at Lord Charles, who gazed at her with a predatory gleam. She stifled a groan behind a gracious smile and swept forward to greet the duke.

"How wonderful to see you again, Your Grace." She curtsied. "And Lord Charles." Lilith tried to keep from peeking at George, else he would flood her senses once more. Nonetheless, her skin tingled at his proximity as if he was touching her all over.

Lady Marylewick gave her little laugh. "I didn't realize you were already acquainted with His Grace." The edges of her smile hardened.

"I attended school with his lordship's daughter," Lilith explained, in the gracious tones befitting a hostess. "Did you not bring her?" she asked the duke. "How I would have loved to have shared a little tête-à-tête."

"She was loath to leave my grandson," replied the duke. "He is almost half a year now, but she refuses to part from him."

"Of course she would be," she said. "A devoted mother. And Lord Charles, you look to be in fine spirits. I hope the journey from London wasn't too taxing."

"Like traveling on a cloud." Charles gave George a sideways glance, as though sharing a private joke.

A few more pleasantries managed to slip past before Lady Marylewick retook control of the conversation, at which time the duke noticed an acquaintance entering the parlor and excused himself.

Charles remained, taking Lilith by the arm. "I must talk to you," he said in an urgent whisper. "Of the most serious nature."

She wanted to resist, but she had to be careful. George needed the man's vote. She allowed him to escort her to a corner of the hall, partially concealed by a black and gold Greek vase hoisted on a pedestal.

"Lord Charles, whatever is troubling you?"

"That you are magnificent. A fine performance. Brava, my dear."

"Performance?" She had been lured away so that Charles could flirt! Now all she could do was patiently endure it until she could manufacture what looked to be a natural break in the conversation. She missed her old rag-mannered world where she could say *Go to Hades, Lord Charles*. Now she felt she was balancing on a spider's thread.

"Yes, England's most gracious hostess, and most beautiful, if I may boldly add."

"Lady Marylewick is the hostess. I'm merely a family member."

"Are you really a Maryle?" He leaned closer. "I prefer the Dahlgren. Exciting and enticing."

She edged back, but smiled so she wouldn't give offense. "Be careful, Lord Charles. You might be straying into territory others would call impertinent."

"I can't afford not to be. I must act boldly and swiftly. Look around, Miss Dahlgren, all eyes are on you, except for Lord Marylewick, the old boy, who prefers those proper, simpering, witless types. Ah, see now how this one curtsies before him, a shy, blushing, vacant young thing."

Lilith glanced over her shoulder. Another family had entered the hall, this one escorting a lovely daughter in a trim blue gown, her brunette hair falling in glossy spiral curls. She blushed when George greeted her. Lilith felt a nasty pang of jealousy as she watched the girl, but she kept her features cool. She knew Lord Charles, who only played the charming fool, watched for any twitch in her visage, anything he could use to dig into her.

"That particular female specimen is Lady Cornelia," he said. "This season's forerunner in the marital race for Lord Marylewick."

It seemed so obvious now, yet why did the knowledge suddenly strike her with such brutal force: of course every young lady of quality would be angling for George. The blinding light of the title marquess outshone the numerous deficiencies of his unyielding personality.

Why did this bother her? Who George courted shouldn't be a concern of hers, but that didn't stop her from wanting to stomp across the room and shout *Just so we are clear on the facts of the matter, he kissed me on my breast.*

"Now I have made you quite society's darling to get you invited to this little party and keep me entertained," explained Charles. "By Jove, I could not fathom a week of George's dull political romancing."

"This was all your little game? Why?"

"Do you not know?" He flashed an intimate smile as he set his elbow against the wall and rested his temple in his hand. "Can you not venture a guess?"

She remembered how George said that Charles had tormented him at school. She could see maliciousness lurking about the edges of his blond, wholesome face. The word "dangerous" drifted through her mind. "Someone to share your deep profound love of poetry?"

He tossed back his head. "Precisely." His face sharpened. "Ah, and here is Lord Fenmore now. I think a charming little family drama is in the brewing. Better than anything Drury Lane can offer. Shall we watch?"

She spun around. Penelope's husband ambled into the hall, carefree, roguish, as if the world were a big jolly toy for his amusement. Once he had been the type of young man to set girls' hearts aflutter. No doubt in his mind he still saw himself as that wild, carefree buck, but his exterior didn't match anymore. His fast living was beginning to show; his once chiseled, handsome features were bloated and lined.

Lady Marylewick greeted him by saying, "Lord Fenmore, has Penelope been so naughty as to desert you?"

"Lady Fenmore has been a naughty lady indeed." He chuckled, amused at his pathetic joke.

Penelope glanced at Lilith. She could see the distress beneath her cousin's composure.

Lilith didn't bother to make her excuses to Charles but swooped in. As she approached, Fenmore's gaze raked over her body in a way that made her feel squeamish. *Poor Penelope.*

"Greetings, Cousin Lilith," he said. "I can't venture too far in London these last few days without hearing your name."

Lilith made a point of not returning his smile. "How charming to see you again. I do not believe we've spoken since the occasion of your wedding." She rested her hand on Penelope's arm. "Dearest Lady Fenmore, I suddenly feel absolutely ill. Pray, let us sit in the parlor."

Lilith pulled Penelope away.

"I hate him," Penelope whispered. "And Mama is cruel. Why must she be so? I can't bear this house party, I can't. Don't tell George I said that."

"Don't think about Fenmore or your mother. If you get upset, find me. We'll get through this house party in Hades together."

Penelope's lips trembled, her eyes turned wet. Lilith panicked. She leapt at the first outrageous thing she could think of to shock Penelope from her anxious thoughts before they overtook her.

"Let us imagine that every person at this party is naked," Lilith suggested. "Now, take these young men congregating about the mantel. Who do you think is the most handsome without his clothes? I daresay the one with the blue plaid waistcoat, but of course he's not wearing it in my overactive imagination." Lilith was lying. The only naked man filling her mind's eye was George, all rippled with muscles and his sex exposed like Michelangelo's David. The effect her vivid musing had on her body was rather disconcerting.

Penelope giggled. "Lilith, you're terrible."

"But in the most delightful way. Oh, look, Beatrice is approaching. Now we must behave ourselves."

"Beatrice, dear, did you ever learn what fungus or insect blighted the palm?" Penelope inquired. Lilith had no idea what she meant.

"Lady Marylewick thinks it unladylike," replied Beatrice, her eyes darting nervously between Lilith and Penelope.

"Pooh!" cried Penelope. "It's very ladylike. Don't you dare let Mama tell you how to think or live!"

Lilith's jaw dropped, shocked to hear such open rebellion from Penelope. Then she broke into chuckles. Maybe there was hope yet. More people gathered about, wanting to share in their infectious laughter. Soon Lilith basked in the energy of the crowd, learning about the guests and hearing their stories. Every so often, she would glance about to find George studying her with his deep gray eyes. She would feel a little light-headed and quickly turn away for fear he possessed an amazing power to know her privates were wet and throbbing for him, only to find Charles or Fenmore also staring at her. That stopped that bothersome bodily throbbing quite nicely.

❧

After tea, the guests began returning to their rooms to rest and then dress for the evening.

Lilith's mind was whirling and she needed some

time to write and straighten out her tangle of emotions concerning George. She was turning a corner in the maze of corridors connecting the various wings of Tyburn when a powerful hand reached out of the shadows, grabbed her elbow, and snatched her into a room. Her first thought was Lord Charles or Fenmore. Those horses' backsides! She kicked her assailant hard in the shin. But as her foot connected with bone, the clove and pine scent of George filled her nose. *Oh no!*

"Good God, Lilith!" He groaned. "Why did you do that?"

"I'm sorry!" she cried. "I thought…I thought you were someone else."

"I feel sorry for that someone else if this how you treat them. Have you practiced that?"

"Yes, and other more painful kicks to strategic male regions." She found that George had abducted her to a small, paneled study. Glass cases adorned the walls but the shelves were empty except for a few knickknacks. A reading chair was pushed near the fireplace.

"I merely wanted to talk to you." He rubbed his shin. "I hope that doesn't warrant a kick in my strategic male regions."

"Not for you, George. Perhaps other men. Come." She supported George to the chair. Shadows had formed under his eyes and he appeared pale in the dim light. She wanted to reach up and ruffle his hair until it fell over his forehead. Then he would fit into any Paris salon, just another angst-ridden romantic artist. She knelt and began to massage his wounded calf through his trousers. The feel of his muscles did interesting things to her feminine regions.

"You look tired," she said.

"That dam—hanged bill. And Mama. And Penelope. And please stop soothing my leg. It isn't… it isn't… proper."

They had gone well past the line of proper on several occasions, so why stop now? She continued to rub. "Does it make you feel better?"

"That's immaterial. Many improper things make me feel better." When she didn't stop, he seized her hand and locked her wayward fingers between his. "I wanted to tell you that you were brilliant today. Thank you for helping Penelope. She… She won't confide in me. You have become such close friends these last few days."

Lilith studied their interlocked hands. "She's miserable. Her husband strays."

He released a long stream of breath. "I suspected as much."

"Why did you let her marry him? Was it the title, the old family, or the appalling lack of morals and human kindness?"

"She was in love with him. Father had just died and Mother was pushing the match." He released her hand. "I— I made a mistake." His words were labored, as if he had trouble admitting fallibility.

She wished she could tell him in that breezy, congenial manner not to worry, that we all make mistakes; the broken window could be replaced, an apology could undo the unintended insult. But this was no simple mistake.

"Anyway, I wanted to thank you," he continued. "You were wonderful today. Why can't you be like this always?"

She looked at him askew. "Like what?"

"Kind, welcoming, joyful, thoughtful, and—"

"My goodness, are you complimenting me?"

"Yes, and I would have continued had you not interrupted me."

She opened her palms. "George, I *am* like this always. Well, I admit I tolerated some behavior today that I wouldn't on another occasion. It's just around you…I'm all defensiveness, anger, and hurt."

He shifted forward in his chair. "Then what can I do, what can I say? How do I… How do I take the hurt or anger away to make this part of you stay?"

She didn't know why, but tears welled. Why was she crying? She had to turn her head and blink them away before he noticed.

"I-I must go." She tried to cover her lapse with a weak joke. "It would be unseemly if we were caught together. That roguish Lilith Dahlgren has tarnished many a man's sterling reputation." She hurried to the door before more embarrassing tears formed.

"Lilith," he called quietly. His voice sounded like a summer shower on a window.

She turned.

"I won't make a mistake with your husband," he said. "I will find you loyalty and kindness. And a home. Where…where you won't feel hurt or anger."

Oh, hang the tears forming in her eyes again. "Don't forget your promise to meet me in the attics," she whispered and fled.

Thirteen

COLETTE, IN A BORROWED CAFTAN, TIPTOED
through the sleeping palace. At every turn, she ex-
pected a powerful eunuch to catch her. Yet the palace
was strangely unguarded and she crept about unim-
peded. At last, she came to a lovely garden at the
very heart of the palace. A large white moon lit up
the fruit trees and lush flowers. Their sweet scents
drifted on the warm air.

Enormous carved doors painted in gold stood at
all the corners of the garden. She pivoted, unsure
what waited behind each one. A secret box, an an-
gry soldier, or the sultan enjoying his concubines?

A tree ruffled, a bird flew away, and out of the
shadows appeared the sultan. The moon's light glinted
on his sword. Colette cried out. In a graceful motion,
like a leaping panther, his hand was on her mouth and
his powerful chest against her back.

"Don't awaken the palace," he growled.
"Come to find the secret box, have you? Do you
truly think it will set you free?"

He released her and spun her around to look at

him. The pale moonlight softened his brutish features. His eyes glowed through the darkness.

"How did you know I was coming for the box?"

"My spies told me. I called off my guards and had the tigers caged for the evening. Then I waited."

He strode to a door framed by lemon trees. From within his sash he produced a key and opened the door to reveal a tiny room holding a red and gold painted table on which rested an unadorned wooden box.

He gestured with his sword. "Open it. You, the lover of secrets. Let me not stop you."

She hesitated. What game was this?

He laughed, low and rich, as he approached her. "Ah, but you fear the power of secrets now. What waits in this box you will never forget. What good is your free body if your heart and mind are forever enslaved by this secret?"

Colette's gaze lit on the sultan and then the garden's entrance.

"What will you find if you run from me?" He caressed her cheek. "Will you go home only to learn that it has been destroyed by another evil man who desires the secret to your Greek Fire? Where will you find safety? Where will you find freedom? Perhaps it is in the box. Open it and see what you find."

His lips brushed hers. Tender and warm. She cried out in anguish. How could the man she hated most in the world entrance her heart? Colette turned and ran away, tears streaming from her eyes. She refused to see his box even as he called to her. "Open it. Please."

❧

Unable to shake her giddiness, Lilith arrived in the hall outside the dining room, all blushing and nervous. Luckily, she fit right in with all the other nervous and blushing young ladies. George and Penelope were concealed behind a cluster of people. The matrons circled Lady Marylewick, her bell-like laugh ringing above the chatter as she basked in the toad-eating.

Beatrice hung about the corner. The bodice of her pale pink gown gaped on her thin frame. She clutched her little notebook, appearing quite distraught. Lilith debated going to her, afraid she would get a cold shoulder. But then Fenmore managed to catch Lilith's eye for a small moment, which he took as an invitation, and started swaggering toward her. She quickly zipped across the room to Beatrice.

"My dear, you seem upset," Lilith said, taking her arm.

Her sister was so distraught that she forgot she held a grudge against Lilith. "The ice cream isn't thickening. I told Cook to add more salt to the ice to lower the freezing point. She only huffed and told me to see to the dining room."

Lilith jumped at the chance to worm her way into her sister's affections. "But look at all you've done. It's wonderful. You should feel proud." She gestured to the dining room table set with china and gleaming silver. The servants were placing the last of the platters in a precise pattern around the candles and flower arrangements. "Don't allow yourself to be upset by one small detail."

"Good God, are we all waiting to go in by

precedence?" Lord Charles appeared at Lilith's side with several other gentlemen in tow. "I hope Marylewick, old boy, has consulted his handbook. I can never remember if I'm to enter before or after the Bishop of London."

"You have precedence over the Bishop of London," said Beatrice, taking him seriously. "But he is not here, of course."

Lilith stepped in to shield Beatrice from one of Charles's satirical remarks. "My sister has a brilliant mind. I'm quite envious. While I would wrack my poor brain trying to determine the precedence of a cousin of the queen's lady-in-waiting, who happens to be the widow of a Scottish lord, Beatrice remembers all. Her mind is like a camera."

Several of the gentlemen in the group turned their attention to Lilith's young sister. "How fascinating," they uttered, or "What a jolly fine talent." Beatrice's blush warmed Lilith's heart.

Across the room, the sea of men surrounding George parted. Lilith's breath left her body in a low rush. The rest of the room washed away, like rain on a chalk drawing. Everything was him standing there in his elegant evening clothes. The low chandelier cast shadows on the slight hollows beneath his chiseled cheekbones and along the lines running on either side of his generous mouth. And those lips, so soft against the hard contours of his face. So soft against her skin. Without thinking, she touched the spot he had kissed. He lifted his brow, his gaze finding hers. She thought her knees might stop working, along with her lungs. Meanwhile her heart thundered away.

I'm truly falling in love.
And with the sultan.
This can't be happening. Make it stop. He's the villain.
There must be a way to shut it off. A valve somewhere.

George offered his arm to a fashionable, elderly lady and led her into the dining room, followed by his mother and Lord Charles's father.

"And we are off," Lord Charles declared as if they were at the races. "Do you think a lowly third son of a duke and a Dahlgren will be seated near each other? Will that cluster too much dazzling conversation in one spot?"

"I believe Dahlgrens are seated in the scullery," she replied, her mind hardly in the conversation.

He laughed. "If I fall in love with you, it's your own fault."

The word "love" jarred her. "I think we've touched on the issue of *impertinent* behavior, Lord Charles."

"Good heavens, I seem to have forgotten," he replied. "Will you remind me at dinner while I ignore everyone else and gaze at you like a spoony moonling?"

❦

Lilith ended up seated near George's end of the table. Lady Marylewick presided over the other end where Penelope sat beside her husband.

Penelope glanced down at Lilith, a desperate look in her eye akin to a person drowning. Lilith made a discreet nod to her dinner partner, the gentleman formerly in the blue plaid waistcoat, whom Lilith had decided was the most handsome naked one. Penelope stifled a giggle.

Charles, sitting across from Lilith, did not miss the exchange. Amusement gleamed in his eyes.

"Mr. Fitzgerald, may I introduce Miss Dahlgren," he said. "Mr. Fitzgerald is a Tory MP and fond of cricket. Do you remember our games at Oxford, old boy?"

It soon became apparent that the winner of the naked contest was so fond of cricket that the subject formed the whole of his conversation. Lilith smiled and played along while Lord Charles, delighting in her misery, further goaded the man. "Tell me, Mr. Fitzgerald, do you believe yourself a stronger bowler or batsman?"

At the head of the table, the conversation wasn't faring much better. George asked how the weather was for everyone's journey.

Lady Cornelia, who, Lilith noted, was ravishing in blue silk, answered, "It was sunny in Harlow when we left, but when we reached London it started to rain a little." She blushed as if she had revealed some deep personal secret.

Lord Harrowsby bellowed, "It was damp and miserable in Melworte as always. I say, does this soup have a cream base? I'll be up all night with indigestion."

"Ah, it was all drizzle, drizzle, endless drizzle in London," waxed Lord Charles, displaying his feelings on the trite conversation. "The spirit-dulling type of precipitation that neither lets you bask in the glory of the sun nor wallow in the delight of a miserable drenching."

Lady Cornelia tilted her head, "I didn't mind the drizzle. In fact, I hardly noticed it. I bought the new *McAllister's Magazine* in the station."

Lilith's fingers tightened around her fork that was deep in a pile of peas.

"Ah, I missed it by a day." George shook his head. "And it is too late to send a footman down to the village."

George read *McAllister's Magazine*! Lilith's heart thudded like a carriage wheel hitting a pothole.

Dear Lord! Just look down at the peas. Think about peas. So green and—what if he read the story!

"I can lend you my copy," Lady Cornelia continued. "I have read what I wanted from it."

"And what was that?" George leaned closer to her.

Lilith wanted to leap up and cry *Let's stop this conversation right now. Back to the weather. It was rather cloudy here today. Isn't that fascinating?*

Lady Cornelia blushed even more prettily. "*Colette and the Sultan.*"

A slow smile curled George's handsome mouth. "My favorite as well."

God of all that's good on this earth! A huge, invisible foot swung down and slammed Lilith in the chest. *Keep smiling. Appear as if nothing is amiss.*

Lady Cornelia gushed as though she had found her soulmate. She said something, all breathy and flustered, but Lilith couldn't hear it for the roar in her ears. It was something about "Colette sees into my heart and says the words I would say, thinks what I would think."

"I agree," replied George. "Most female characters lapse into boring, moralistic prose. They are far too good to exist. But Colette," he paused to think, "you *feel* her. Her emotions are palpable as she struggles for…I suppose humanity, compassion in a merciless, meaningless world?"

Lilith took a large, impolite gulp of her wine. The

villain of her existence, the sultan himself, had cut open her heart with a few brief words.

"What is your opinion, Miss Dahlgren?" asked Charles. "Surely you have read the outstanding work. Is Colette seeking humanity in a merciless, meaningless world?"

How not to look guilty?

"I've read a few pages," she said in a breezy manner, setting down her glass. "I found it sensational claptrap. Hardly literature." She gave a false laugh that sounded very much like George's mother's. "So, Mr. Fitzgerald, when did you first start playing crick—"

"Sensational claptrap?" cried Charles. "Hardly literature? Sorry if I must rudely reference my university degree in the classics to differ with Miss Dahlgren."

"How odd that you feel that way, Miss Dahlgren," commented George. "I thought you would have enjoyed it. Especially the villain."

"The villain!" Lilith almost choked on her wine. "Why?"

"He is such a fascinating character. Obsessed and driven like Macbeth. She is all that he fears, all that he isn't, but he can only destroy her. As long as she exists, she gives voice to his own demons. A fine study of evil."

Lilith had no words to say to the man looking right at her, unguarded and happy, no idea that *he* was the fine study of evil. All she knew was how much she despised herself.

"Good God, Lord Marylewick," exclaimed Charles. "I never knew you possessed such profundity in that pragmatic, plodding mind of yours."

George's brow hiked a fraction, registering the subtle insult. Lilith could see the muscles of his jaw work, but he remained silent as Lord Charles gloated, so amused with himself. In that flash, Lilith saw the torment George had suffered as a boy at Lord Charles's hand. She had seen it at every school, the child who delighted in the misery of others, singling out the most vulnerable and sensitive.

How in her blindness and anger had she made a villain out of a boy bullied by his father and peers?

Dear God, get me through dessert without falling apart.

"I just find the sultan very scary," said Lady Cornelia. "Whenever he is on the page, ooh"—she shivered—"my skin crawls. But I can't stop reading."

"You are all so young," Lord Harrowsby bellowed. "Colette desired the sultan from the very beginning. He's not evil but represents her repressed yearning. She doesn't fear him but her own amoral longings. Women are chock full of amoral longings. If he kills her, which she also secretly desires, she will finally find relief from her darker nature. Good heavens, my lamb is stuffed with garlic. I must pick it all out."

Of course Lord Harrowsby's voice had boomed across the long table. Guests turned their heads, no doubt wondering about a conversation that included the words "desires," "repressed yearning," and "amoral longings."

Lord Charles explained, "We are discussing the literary masterpiece *Colette and the Sultan*."

The words blew up like fire on a haystack. Soon the entire table was ablaze with conversation about Lilith's work. The next two hours were akin to having her skin carved off, inch by inch, as she smiled.

And the most heart-wrenching part was how happy George looked, how enthusiastically he jumped into the conversation. A few weeks ago, this would have been a divine joke to share with Frances and Edgar. *Ha ha, my darlings, Georgie adores* Colette and the Sultan *and the starchy fool doesn't even realize he is the villain.*

Now the malicious joke was on her.

He wasn't the villain. She was. A deceiving, cold-hearted villainess.

"You are quiet, Miss Dahlgren," Lord Charles said. "Are you well?"

"Perfectly," she lied through her smile.

❧

After the ladies left for the drawing room, George motioned to the footmen to pour the port. During the dinner, his spirits had been lightened by the conversation, but now, with the ladies gone, dull despondency sank in. His gaze kept drifting to the seat Lilith had vacated.

He needed to stop thinking about her.

The ravishing Lady Cornelia adored *Colette and the Sultan*. She would make an excellent marchioness. He needed to transfer his thoughts and, if possible, his desires from Lilith to her. But even now when he should subtly guide the masculine conversation to politics, all he could think of was meeting Lilith in the attic. What magic did some childish, rubbish paintings possess to transform unruly Lilith into a docile, gracious, lovely, and—well—perfect lady?

Lord Harrowsby had begun a boorish diatribe on the dangers of port to the body, and George gently tried to steer the conversation away from liver ailments. "Now that we can't impose on the ladies with our dull conversation, I should like to hear your impressions of Lord Freddie's speech in Parliament."

"George, my dear boy," said Lord Charles, easing back in his chair. "For a moment at dinner I thought you could be saved, that underneath that stoic, implacable facade beat a lustful heart. But alas, no more talk of Colette, villains, and love but dull tariffs, taxes, and budgetary items."

"We are in debt from war after war," George replied. "This country cannot run its empire on fiction and your wit."

"Ah, but we cannot know, for I've never tried to run Britain on my wit. Shall I give it a go for the sake of experimentation?"

"We have only just arrived, let us relax," the Duke of Cliven said. "I haven't read this Colette and Sultan story. It sounds like a fine tale and Colette a jolly girl."

"Father, I must disagree. She is hardly a jolly girl but rather my ideal of womanhood. I shall endeavor to marry her."

"You may have an issue with her fictionality," quipped George.

"Ah, I do, I do," cried Charles. "But I shall come as close to the ideal as possible. Come, gentlemen, is not Colette the ideal woman? Are we not all sultans trying to capture a version of her for ourselves?"

The men rumbled in consent.

"Then let us play a little game called Who is

Colette, or the Ideal of Womanhood." Charles rose and began to amble around the table. "Here are the rules: When we join the ladies, let's beg the fair and kind Lady Cornelia to lend us her copy of *McAllister's Magazine*. Each young lady shall read aloud from the story, and based upon her poise, elocution, and grace, each of us bachelors shall secretly decide which young lady embodies our Colette."

"A fine game, indeed," slurred Fenmore, already inebriated.

"I believe we are playing whist this evening," George said, keeping his rage tamped down. The young ladies in his house were not there to be judged and compared like Drury Lane tarts.

"Whist?" Lord Charles echoed. "Oh dear, I didn't bring my spare pennies." He leaned against the chimney-piece. "Lord Marylewick, you adore Colette. Would you not be curious to hear her read from the mouths of your fair guests? Would you not want to choose the closest to your ideal?"

"If Colette is your idea of an ideal woman," George said, "it is because she was written by a man. Ellis Belfort is catering to a man's desires because he knows them so well."

"My foot Ellis Belfort is a man," said Lord Harrowsby. "A man couldn't write Colette. A man can only write about emotions for three sentences before distracting himself with a Grendel or one-eyed Cyclops."

"Let the ladies read," said the duke in that resolute tone that brooked no dissent. "Let them display their talents and beauty while they are still young. We can speak of politics another night. Tell us more of this game, my son."

ye

After the dinner torture mercifully ended, Lilith followed the ladies to the drawing room. At this point,
she just had to live long enough to show George his
paintings in the attic, then she could crawl into a
dark corner like a wounded animal and die of a lethal
combination of guilt, mortification, and regret.

Several of the young ladies tried to continue the
Colette and the Sultan discussion, but bless the selfish
Lady Marylewick. She would have no subject that
wasn't about her. Holding court on a sofa, she lectured as to how ladies in her day were more gracious
and better bred than today's ladies. The toad-eating
matrons all murmured their disapproval of preco-
cious modern ladies and their shameful divorcing and
demanding-the-right-to-vote ways. The young ladies
all assured her ladyship that they were of the simpering, submissive, old-fashioned variety of lady.

Across the room, on a matching sofa, Lilith sat
in between Penelope and Beatrice. Lilith could feel
Penelope stiffen, as if her mother's words were little
knives thrown at her. *Old-fashioned and simpering be
damned,* Lilith thought, and flagged a footman to ask
for a glass of sherry. Someone had to be an example of
the evil modern woman. Penelope added a quiet "one
for me also, please" to Lilith's request.

Lady Marylewick was deep in her lecture when
her son opened the door and strode in with the other
gentlemen guests behind him. Lilith didn't notice the
others because George took over her entire mind.
How had he managed to become even more handsome in the last forty-five minutes or so?

Stop thinking about George after you've made him the villain! After you've seen the beautiful art he made before it was beaten and bullied out of him. The throbbing stopped in her privates only to re-emerge in her heart.

George cleared his throat, and even that made Lilith's skin tingle with pleasure. Every tiny aspect of him now excited her. "Given our discussion of *Colette and the Sultan*, we have made a change to this evening's entertainment."

Lilith's belly tightened with dread.

"Lady Cornelia, may we trouble you for your copy of *McAllister's Magazine*?" Lord Charles asked.

"Of course." Lady Cornelia blushed prettily. Did she blush every time she spoke? "I left it on the writing desk."

"Thank you." George did no more than nod his head at a footman and the man shot off to retrieve the journal. "It has been suggested that each of the young ladies should read a page of the story."

Dear God!

If Lilith died at that moment and her soul descended into the fiery flames of hell, at least she could take comfort that she was no longer at Tyburn.

"What a wonderful suggestion," cried Lady Marylewick. "I was just saying how elocution and poise were so important when I was a young lady."

"Then let us make a little stage beside the fireplace." Lord Charles waved to another footman. "Push together the columns holding potted plants to arrange a backdrop of greenery."

"I believe the ladies may be more comfortable sitting," said George.

"But this is more theatrical," said Lord Charles, overriding the marquess in his own home. He shifted candlesticks on the mantel. "It is like a sultan's palace, you see."

"And now we can best view the elocution and poise," slurred Fenmore.

Lilith felt Penelope tense. She wished she could come up with something to say that would offer solace, but Lilith's head was a rush of dizzy panic. The most she could discreetly do was hold Penelope's hand beneath the folds of their gowns, as if they were two women comforting each other on a sinking ship.

A servant came running with the journal.

"Lady Cornelia, if you will be so kind as to read a page." Lord Charles gestured to the stage.

With a shy, blushing smile, Lady Cornelia crossed to the ferns and accepted the magazine. Lilith peeked at George, who rubbed his chin, enraptured, as he watched Lady Cornelia read. Lilith wanted to yank the pages away from Lady Cornelia's pretty hands. *Stop. Those aren't your words. You have no idea what you are reading.*

Why didn't Lilith just cut out her guilty heart for the evening's entertainment and have each young lady grind it under the heel of her dainty slipper?

One by one the ladies read. Lady Marylewick gave each a vivacious undercut in the guise of a gracious compliment.

"Now I believe it is Miss Dahlgren's turn," declared Lord Charles.

The room swam in Lilith's vision as if she were drunk. Did she look guilty? Could everyone tell she had written the story? Could she make toppling a candle and setting the curtains on fire appear accidental? She struggled to sound casual. "I said at dinner that I think the story is mere sensational claptrap. It would be disingenuous of me to read."

"Ah, but every young lady is reading," Lord Charles replied.

Lilith feared she would be pressing her luck if she declined again. If it was guessed that she was the author, George would be humiliated at his own house party.

It took all her strength to walk to the makeshift stage instead of running away. Lord Charles gave her the magazine and she glanced at the page. Colette had stabbed the sultan and now hid in a small cave formed by a fallen tree. This was the chapter she had written the night she and George had kissed. Lilith's throat burned. She glanced at the audience. Their faces seemed to fade into the furniture and walls; all she could see was George, his face, his eyes alight with anticipation. She had never felt more ashamed in her life.

"Miss Dahlgren," Lord Charles prompted.

Lilith wasn't sure if a sound would come out when she opened her mouth. But despite the breaking apart inside, the words flowed like silk from her lips. She readily knew their shape and tempo.

"Colette submitted to his kiss as her fingers patted about the ground until she found what she desired: the ivory handle of his sword. 'You heartless, vicious hobgoblin of a man. You are all that is evil and cruel. I will never give my secret to such a m–malicious t-tormenter.'" Lilith couldn't continue. Not with George's gaze heating her skin, unaware that each hateful word was about him.

"I'm afraid this is still sensational claptrap in my mind." She affected a breezy laugh. "What serious author writes 'you heartless, vicious hobgoblin of a man. You are all that is evil and cruel'?" *What detestable, ignorant, horrible author writes that?*

"But you must read an entire page," insisted Lord Charles.

Lilith could feel the tears coming. Her game was over. She had to prepare herself for the ramifications. She would plead on her knees to George for forgiveness. She would—

"No, she mustn't," said George in a low, grinding voice that dared anyone to refute him. "If she doesn't want to read, it is her decision. Thank you, Miss Dahlgren."

Her villain had saved her. Could she feel any lower?

Lilith returned the magazine to Lord Charles. By some miracle she made the short distance back to her seat without her quaking legs giving out.

"Lady Cornelia, would you be so kind as to finish?" Lord Charles said. "We have run out of young ladies and I am on tenterhooks to know what happens."

"You have not asked my ward, Miss Maryle," pointed out George.

Beatrice jerked her head from where she was studying the crystals hanging from a wall sconce, refracting the light. "Pardon?"

"I humbly beseech your forgiveness, my fair lady." Lord Charles performed a dramatic, hair-flinging bow before Beatrice. "Please do us the great honor of hearing you read from *Colette and the Sultan*."

Lilith's sister hurried onto the stage, her thin neck

bright red. Clutching the pages, she began to read in a fast monotone while swaying on her feet. Then she abruptly stopped. "Wait. Is Colette running away with the formula to Greek Fire?"

"Yes," Lord Charles replied. "Her father rediscovered its vile components and Colette, because she assisted her father, knows the dark secret. She doesn't want the secret of Greek Fire to be released into the world."

"Everyone knows it's resin and sulfur." Beatrice shook her head. "Is the sultan an idiot?"

"It's a work of fiction," Charles explained. "You must allow yourself the luxury of pretending."

Beatrice's brows furrowed. "But why is Colette running if she knows how to make Greek Fire and the sultan doesn't? What a puddinghead!" She thrust the journal at Lord Charles, her sensibilities clearly offended. "Here, you read it, since you adore it so much."

Lord Harrowsby said in a loud whisper, "If I were a young whippersnapper, Miss Maryle would be my ideal."

Fourteen

WHEN THE HELL WAS THIS PLACE LAST CLEANED? GEORGE surveyed the fortress wing attics with his lamp. Was his home a rubbish heap for everyone to dump their refuse? Was that a water stain?

And where was Lilith?

He released an exasperated breath and checked his pocket watch. Ten minutes past two. After he had spent the evening torn between excitement and dread, Lilith was late.

In the drawing room, he had tried valiantly to focus on the beautiful Lady Cornelia, but his eyes always drifted to Lilith. He had played Lord Charles's hateful game in secret and Lilith had won. Though she claimed the story was claptrap, the words came alive from her lips. She captured the nuance of Colette. She voiced Colette as he heard her in his own mind when he read.

He would give her a few more minutes while he shoved trunks and broken furniture away from the wall to determine the extent of the water damage. It would be easier to tear down this ancient wing than continue to sink money into it. Old castles littered England and the guidebooks wouldn't miss one less.

A gentle hand touched his shoulder, sending a warm current down his arm.

Lilith!

He wheeled around, ready to lecture her about timeliness, but the sight of her evaporated his frustrations. She wore that damned robe again. Her hair was loose, falling in waves over her breasts. The light from her lamp reflected in her glassy, red-rimmed eyes.

He seized her hand. "Lilith, are you well?"

She smiled and disentangled herself from his hold. "I'm just wonderful," she cried in false merry tones.

"You've been crying. What has happened?"

"Nothing. I'm— I'm merely cracking under the heavy strain of behaving myself." She edged past him. "Let me show you the paintings."

He wasn't going to let her change the subject. He grasped her elbow, again enjoying a flood of warmth.

"Has something upset you? Did someone say something troubling?"

"Yes, all manner of troubling things like cricket, the weather, proper behavior for young ladies, but nothing about radical art or lurid poetry. All the things that I adore."

"'Tis a pity you find *Colette and the Sultan* not to your taste."

She glanced at where he touched her and whispered, "Do you truly enjoy that story?"

"Why do I think that if I answer emphatically *yes*, you will think less of me…if that is even possible, considering I'm a fusty frog in your eyes."

She winced.

"Lilith, I was in jest. Tell me if someone upset you. Has a man made an improper gesture?"

"One."

His pulsed quickened. "Lord Charles?"

"No."

"Fenmore, that bloody cove. If I get through this house party without landing him a facer—"

"No, the man in question kissed me on my breast this morning. Very improper and compromising. I might insist that he marry me, but you wouldn't approve of him. He meets ladies in the dead of night alone in attics and he has quite a foul temper when provoked. And worst of all, he is an artist. You know how you feel about artists."

"I'm implacable in my poor opinion."

"A pity." She flashed him an impish glance from under her lashes and then led him through the rubbish.

"It's in here." She entered the back attic room.

When he crossed over the threshold, his mouth turned dry and his hands clenched. What the hell was wrong with him? He was just going to view some old drawings made by a little boy.

Lilith set down her lamp and tugged a huge trunk, trying to slide it atop another.

"Here, allow me." He stepped closer to her than necessary to milk the comfort of her body. Together they shifted the trunk. Beneath it rested an old chamber pot. Lilith reached for it, but he stopped her.

"A man must be chivalrous and hold a chamber pot for a lady," he joked to hide his nervousness. *Good God, man, what has come over you?*

Below the chamber pot waited a doll trunk with the childishly scrawled words "Kep Out." The work of his little sister.

Lilith knelt, opened the tiny latch. One of Penelope's old samplers rested inside.

"Ah, you've found my art," he joked, and tried to close the trunk. Why this dread? What was he afraid of?

She didn't laugh but gently slid his hands away and lifted the sampler. He recognized the roll of papers. *God, no!* He felt a sickening turn in his gut. He wanted to yank the art from Lilith's hand and keep it unseen.

The painting she revealed of Penelope beneath a tree punched out his breath. The visceral memory blossomed in his mind: the light reflecting on the water, the breeze blowing up his collar, the smell of grass, Penelope smiling, and the joy of being lost in the moment.

Lilith leaned against his shoulder and asked quietly, "Did you draw this?"

His burning throat closed up. She had exhumed a grave. Inside waited what was left of a hurt boy, a disappointment of a son, and a sensitive dreamer, whom George had destroyed in order to become a man.

He should muster a casual joke, insult his work, or call out Lilith for foolish behavior—anything to push this aching moment away.

She carefully removed the painting to reveal the one beneath. A maid sewing by the fireside. The model was the kind village girl who helped in the nursery and snuck him sweets after a spanking.

"Did anyone tell you how talented you are?"

Lilith asked. "Did they tell you how poignant your work was?"

The sorrow in her voice broke something inside him. How dare she feel sorry for him?

"I'm a marquess," he barked. He didn't mean to be gruff. She had done nothing except kick up the dirt of old memories. Yet he threw his anger at her. "See here, I've played your silly little game. These ridiculous paintings are the work of a feeble-minded—"

Her mouth stopped his words. Her lips were soft against his tense ones. Her fingers caressed his hard jaw. All the fury fled, leaving the raw hurt emotions beneath.

She withdrew and cradled the painting to her chest. "I couldn't let you say that your work wasn't beautiful."

She gently laid the picture on a trunk, and uncurled the painting he had done of the farmhands before his father had chanced to ride by and cracked his whip down on George's paints. "What the hell are you doing?" his father had bellowed. "Those lump-heads picking turnips are more responsible than you."

"Look at the beautiful composition." She traced the elements, careful not to touch the canvas. "The rows contrast with gossamer swirls of clouds and hunched-over workmen." She fixed her dark eyes on his. No trickery waited in them. "This should not be hidden in an attic under a chamber pot but cherished."

He couldn't bear to see the beautiful compassion on her face. He kissed her again, locking his hand behind her head so she couldn't escape and show him more paintings or say words that ripped into his heart. He pressed her mouth open and delved into her softness, his tongue filling her. She stiffened at his violent kiss.

He stroked her neck as an apology for his brusqueness, but he wouldn't let her go. Her body, her scent, her touch were a balm to his wretched feelings. Slowly, tentatively, she began to explore him.

Keeping her captive in their kiss, he gently lowered her until she rested on his thighs. He opened his eyes long enough to slide the paintings away with one hand. He caught a glimpse of a painted nest filled with robin's eggs. He remembered the day the gardener smashed them and how little George had wept. He closed his eyes again, letting Lilith's lips, mouth, and tongue draw out his pain and caress it away.

She finally drew away but only to rest on his arm. "Do you ever think about painting now? Tell me the truth. Don't get angry out of defensiveness."

He couldn't lie to those unguarded, vulnerable eyes.

"Every day," he confessed. "Right now, I wish to capture you. In this low light, your skin is almost white against the inky darkness of your eyes. You're all light emerging from darkness."

Tears shone in her eyes. "George. They shouldn't have hurt you. They should have encouraged you, loved you...they didn't know how lucky they were." He kissed a tear that spilled from her lashes.

"Tomorrow we will have to pretend this moment didn't happen." Her voice was brittle. "We will never share another moment like this. But promise me..." She swallowed, more tears fell. He wiped them away with his thumb. "That you'll draw and paint again. Please."

He smoothed an auburn strand from her forehead. "Why? Why is this so important to you?"

"Because I think who you are inside, the man you hide, is beautiful," she said. "He needs to be released. To know joy. Happiness."

Joy? Happiness? These were selfish words. He would be damned if he would go gamboling about like Lilith's set, seeking his joy while his tenants needed a roof over their heads and food to eat.

She rested her finger on his lips, hushing him even though he hadn't uttered a word. "But you are too busy to think about yourself. Yes, you must take care of everyone, especially that bothersome Lilith. But one day I'll be gone far, far away, married to some Timbuktu diplomat you've scratched up for me, if I don't run off, foolishly casting my would-be wealth to the wind. How will you console yourself without me to fight with, to refuse to put up with your mule-headedness—"

"I'm not mule-headed."

"—and force you out of the iron cage of your rational mind. Promise you'll make your art."

He couldn't make such a childish promise. But he would be damned if he would tell her that, not as she rested tame in his arms. "I must think upon the matter. Maybe if you kiss me again, I might be persuaded."

She smiled lazily, wrapped her arms around his neck, and raised her lips. The gentle touch soon turned fevered. Their tongues swirled against each other's, their bodies demanded more.

He groaned and released her mouth, letting his lips drift down her chin, neck, and chest. There he lingered, yearning so much to feel her breasts again, caress them, and learn their contours. He restrained himself. He must stop. But Lilith shifted under him, pressing her breasts up to be known.

He closed his eyes and found a hardened nipple. She gasped and her fingers dug into his arm as his tongue lapped the silken fabric over the tip.

"Dear God," she murmured, arching her back. She whispered his name, softening the hard consonants in a rush of breath.

He raised his head, letting his fingers play upon her. He studied her face. Her lips were parted in rapture, her lashes cast shadows on her cheeks. She was stunning in her wanton state.

His cock burned and he saw the moment she felt his arousal. Her eyes flew open. Conflict colored their surface.

"I'm sorry, Lilith," he said. "But you are too beautiful."

She sat up, keeping her eyes fixed on his face. She rested her palm, fingers spread, on his chest. Slowly, slowly, that hand drifted down until she reached his cock straining in his trousers. There her touch turned unsure.

"Lilith, please, you can't…I can't…" His words were choked. "What we've done already is improper. This is my fault. We must stop."

"Does my touch please you?" She kissed his neck.

"Please, woman," he begged.

"Let me," she whispered.

He slowly interlaced his fingers in hers and showed her how to stroke him over his trousers. He guided her until she needed no more instruction. Her touch was generous, she wanted nothing more than his pleasure. She quickly learned what heightened his arousal and gave him more. But she didn't know how to pace lovemaking to make it last and he carried too much pent-up frustration. The sensation built too fast, too powerfully.

"I'm going to climax," he cried through his tight jaws.

"I don—"

His mouth covered hers. He gently pushed her onto the floor and wedged his thighs between hers, wild for her magic.

"No!" she cried. "Stop! Stop! Please."

He sprang back, horrified at his loss of control. "I'm sorry! Forgive me. I would never take you against your wishes. Never! You know I would never hurt you."

She sat up and yanked the roll of paintings, now flattened from the weight of their bodies, from the floor and unrolled it.

"Thank heavens," she cried in relief. "The paint didn't crack. You must put them under some heavy books immediately."

He stared at her cradling his wounded paintings. "What?" he finally managed. "You were more concerned about that childish scribble than…than… It's nothing! The painting is nothing!"

"It's not scribble! It's beautiful."

He shook his head and rested his hands on his thighs. "Lilith, I don't understand you. Does the rubbish on those pages mean more than the disaster that almost occurred here? We almost had intercourse."

He couldn't decipher the emotions burning in her eyes.

"Yes," she said quietly. "Art means everything to me. My family didn't want me. I drifted from one school to the next, even my beloved Frances and Edgar betrayed me. Art remains true to me." She carefully swept her fingers over the pictures. "And it's not rubbish. A wonderful little boy lives on in the work. As long as this work remains, a piece of him is still here. 'A thing of beauty is a joy for ever: / Its loveliness increases, it will never / Pass into nothingness; but still will keep…' That's from Keats's *Endymion*." She pressed the painting to his chest. "Don't ever destroy these, George. One day they might save you." She rose and dusted off her robe. "There, I have shown you the paintings. That's all I intended. It's the only reason I behaved for the entire day. So good night."

"What?" he thundered. Thank God no one stayed in this wing. "No, it's not good night. What…what are we going to do tomorrow?" He came to his feet.

"Very simple. I'm going to keep my distance from you." She tried to sound matter-of-fact, but he wasn't fooled. He could hear the pain beneath the bravado. "I'm never going to utter a word about what happened if you honor your promise."

"My promise?"

She flung up her hands. "To paint, to draw, to make art."

He began to say something, many things in fact, but quickly shut his mouth. Technically, he had never promised. "Very well," he said, feeling very much like a careful solicitor.

"It was a near wreck. That is all. You almost sullied yourself with Lilith Dahlgren."

"Good God, Lilith, how can you say that?" How could she use the word "sullied" to describe the most loving and compassionate moment he had ever experienced?

"It isn't? Then George, you have compromised me. You must marry me now. Ah, the panic upon your face!" A sad smile graced her lips. "It is well. I would rather throw myself off St. Paul's Cathedral than be a Maryle." She picked up her lamp. "There, your kingdom is saved. Go marry Lady Cornelia. She will make a wonderful Marchioness of Marylewick." She started to walk away.

"Lilith, don't go."

She turned and gazed at him in that tender way that destroyed his heart. "Don't ever forget tonight or your promise."

"Let us talk."

"Whatever we have to say will only hurt," she whispered. "Good night."

She turned out of the room. He started to chase her and then stopped.

Bloody hell, let her go.

Just let her go.

He picked up his paintings and drawings, slowly studied them one by one, her words echoing in his mind. "A wonderful little boy lives on in the work. As long as this work remains, a piece of him is still here." He wanted to call her an irresponsible, grown-up child, anything to push away these feelings. But he couldn't. All Lilith had done was show compassion to his sister…and to him. His eyes burned. *Goddammit, you weakling!* He mentally shouted the words his father had once used.

He didn't need compassion. Nothing was wrong with him. He had obligations he had to honor.

He rolled up the paintings, restored them to their sarcophagus, and then encased it in its chamber pot tomb.

ᥫᩢ

In her bedchamber, warm tears streamed down Lilith's cheeks, dripped off her chin, and wetted the pages of her Keats that she hugged to her chest. She had done what she intended by showing him the paintings. She must let him go to Lady Cornelia or some other worthy wife.

But it was so bloody hard!

Her heart had shattered as she watched him gazing at his old pictures. She could see the fragile boy still inside him after all these years.

Why must she fall in love with the patriarch of the family she despised? She had been saving herself for a Keats-worthy man. Someone she could love with that trembling, ethereal delight she felt when reading a lovely poem or viewing a masterpiece.

She never thought she would feel such love for a man she could never have or want to have. George was her own Pre-Raphaelite painting. A lush, mysterious male beauty trapped in a canvas, forever unattainable.

It was all so bitterly useless.

At least she had made him vow to draw more. Some merit would arise from this horrid mess.

But on the crest of sleep, a tiny thought niggled in her mind. She bolted up.

He hadn't precisely promised to create art.

Did that sly marquess think he could get away with that not promising after she had all but given her body to him?

Fifteen

GEORGE DRESSED SLOWLY, LETTING HIS VALET FUSS over the minor details. He used that time to strengthen his resolve and drink another cup of black coffee. Until the first fingers of dawn, he had tossed and turned in his bed. Several women in his past had stripped him of his clothes and made love to his naked body, but Lilith stripped him bare in a way no other woman had. She ripped his skin off, exposing his beating heart, and released a host of demons. Long-forgotten memories came howling back to George in the darkness. His fingers itched with restlessness to do something, anything to get out the emotion that was burning inside him. When merciful sleep finally came Lilith returned to him in his dreams, whispering and giving him soft kisses on his mouth and other parts of his body. Suffice to say, a man over thirty shouldn't wake up alone in a bed with sticky sheets.

As he strolled down to breakfast, he was like Admiral Nelson sailing into the Battle of Trafalgar, refusing to go below deck even as the bullets were flying around him.

The dining room was humming with guests. He located the women in his life: his mother beaming majestically over her steaming tea, Penelope appearing pale and traumatized over her uneaten toast, and Beatrice discreetly removing an insect from the flower bouquet. But Lilith was missing.

He had a twinge of dread mixed with sadness at her absence. After he made the obligatory greetings to guests—"Jolly good morning," "I hope you slept well," "I assure you that we do not have mites in our sheets, Lord Harrowsby"—he turned to Beatrice and made a show of asking her a question. "My lovely Miss Maryle, what lively entertainment do we have for our lady guests this morning?"

Beatrice didn't hear, but was entranced by the green metallic bug circling her palm.

His mother cleared her throat. "Beatrice, my darling."

She jumped. "Yes! What can I do?"

George politely repeated himself.

"Oh!" Beatrice cried. She yanked out her tiny notebook and began to hurriedly read what sounded like a dictation from his mother: "In the morning, the young ladies can tromp down to the ruins, and once they tire of those dull, soggy things, they can see if there is anything tolerable in the village shops. Meanwhile, the matrons can lounge about eyeballing each other's fashion choices and gossiping in the morning parlor, while the gentlemen smoke, play billiards, and try to get those appalling Whigs to see the light of reason."

George locked his face in its polite expression.

Lady Marylewick forced a laugh. "How funny, you are so perfectly, darlingly droll, my little Beatrice."

Beatrice flushed bright red, suddenly realizing what she had read.

"By Jove, why, I can't think of a morning better spent than trying to see the light of reason," quipped Lord Charles. "I certainly hope Lord Marylewick can succeed where all those dons with their talk of Aristotle and Descartes failed."

"Miss Maryle inflates my ambitions," said George through his clenched jaws. "I thought a simple game of billiards would be enjoyable."

Before Lord Charles could make another clever rejoinder, Lilith burst into the room, clad in vivid blue and white stripes and hoisting a great roll of papers. Her vibrant beauty obliterated his train of thought.

"Isn't the morning glorious?" she cried. "I feel inspired. Look at the light. It's as if God is calling out, 'What a lovely day it is to sketch the ruins.'" She whirled on her toes, holding her roll like a dancing partner. Why did she whirl every morning? "I have brought enough paper and pencils for everyone."

He was ready to throttle her after he recovered from the quaver caused by the mischievous glance she flashed him. Her ruse was as thin as gossamer. Now she was on a campaign to *make* him draw.

"I'm afraid only the ladies will be joining you," he said in dampening tones.

"What?" Lilith was visibly crestfallen. "Mr. Fitzgerald, Lord Charles, you are not going? But what will happen if we are attacked by rabid sheep or…or a band of marauding art thieves?"

"My footmen have been specially trained for dealing with rabid sheep and art thieves," replied George.

"Deuce take it, Lord Marylewick," said Charles. "I couldn't let one of your footmen be the hero of the day. You know this county is teeming with art thieves and vicious sheep. Ladies, I shall be your protector. What do you say, Mr. Fitzgerald, care to be chivalrous this morning?"

"I do indeed," he replied.

Several of the other young gentlemen echoed this sentiment, as did Lord Fenmore.

The duke decided the matter. "Let the feeble old men play billiards. A fine day should be enjoyed by the young. Run along, Lord Marylewick."

George chafed at being told he should *run along*. Nonetheless, an hour later, he was *running along* the path to the ruins with his cane spiking the ground. Lady Cornelia and Miss Pomfret hovered around him, while Beatrice dawdled behind, lost in her own world. A retinue of servants carrying paper, easels, pencils, and jars of lemonade marched after the group of guests.

Lilith ambled gaily beside Lord Charles.

"Isn't it a lovely day?" she said, looking quite stunning amid the lush grass and pale sky. "I feel as though I've walked into a Claude Monet or Pierre-Auguste Renoir."

"Who is she talking about?" whispered Lady Cornelia.

"Inmates at Bedlam," he quipped, and then quickly amended, because Cornelia was an innocent civilian in his fight with Lilith, "I believe some people consider them to be artists."

"To capture such radiance!" Lilith carried on.

"My soul is enraptured," bellowed Lord Charles, matching Lilith's jubilance.

"As is mine," she cried.

"Mine's feeling right jolly," added Fenmore.

Lilith tossed her head, her curls flapping under the brim of her floppy straw bonnet. "What about you, Lord Marylewick? Is your soul not enraptured, enchanted, or in Lord Fenmore's poetic description, 'right jolly'?"

"Do you even have a soul, old boy?" queried Charles.

"But everyone has a soul," Lady Cornelia pointed out with puppylike eyes. Clearly she had never experienced a dark night in hers. No battles raged in its shallow depths.

"My soul is rather stoic," replied George. "It never does anything as vulgar as become enraptured."

It disturbed George how much Lilith's honest giggle lifted his spirits. *Turn back again, fair lady, let me see that wide grin below the brim of your bonnet. Can you make that errant curl lift in the wind again and blow under your eye?*

"Well, my soul is quite vulgar," Lilith said. "It positively dances in delight. Like a whirling dervish." Of course she had to whirl to illustrate. Every gentleman turned to witness the spectacle, each receiving a good eyeful of her trim ankles and shapely calves.

Lady Cornelia's shriek halted the dance. "Get it off me!" she screamed. "Get it off!" She hopped about, brushing at her shoulder.

"No!" cried Beatrice. "It's a marsh grasshopper. It won't hurt you."

Something large and green and red leapt into the air, only to be swatted by Cornelia's flailing arm. The great insect fell to the ground.

Beatrice gasped and hurried to the massive grass-hopper bumping about the ground. "No, its leg is injured." Beatrice's chin trembled. She resembled the small child George had held after her father died. "Why did you hurt it?" she demanded of Cornelia. "It had done nothing to you. Now it might die."

"It's ugly!" Cornelia cried.

Lilith knelt beside Beatrice. She removed her bonnet and gently picked up the struggling grasshop-per. She nestled it inside the bonnet, closed the brim around it, and tied it shut. "Perhaps you can help it," Lilith said, handing Beatrice the bonnet. "You are so smart about everything."

George watched Beatrice looking at Lilith, but he couldn't tell what Beatrice was thinking. He doubted anyone was capable of knowing her brilliant thoughts, but he believed he discerned a bit of awe.

"Thank you," Beatrice told her sister quietly, gath-ering up the bonnet. "Thank you."

‍❧

The guests sat in clusters on a small hill rising before the cathedral ruins. Lilith struggled to keep up her cheery facade as she found herself having to share a blanket and canvas with Lord Charles and Lord Fenmore, who sat so close her legs and shoulders touched theirs. Her eyes continually strayed to George.

He stood beside Lady Cornelia, studying her adequate composition, and paying trite, polite compli-ments, which caused the young lady to blush.

Lilith viscerally hated the kind Cornelia. Oh, jeal-ousy was a vile beast.

Would Cornelia be a complacent wife in bed? Would she tempt George? Would she drive him to wild passion? Would she hold him as tenderly as Lilith had? Would she even care to discover the true man beneath the title?

Pick up the pencil, George, Lilith thought, as if by sheer force of her mental powers she could influence his actions. *Draw. Free the winged Fancy.*

"I adore your addition of the rainbow," said Charles of their mutual sketch, breaking Lilith's concentration. "It really draws the eye."

She turned to her sad rendering. She was a good deal better at drawing than singing, but by no means a great talent. She was proficient enough to appreciate the brilliance of other natural artists like George.

"That's not a rainbow," she said. "That's the arch of the nave. Or rather it's my impression of the arch as it gleams in the sunlight. To the untrained eye it is a mere rainbow."

"You are a radical. Let me add some symbolism to our masterpiece." In a wild stroke, Charles made what appeared to be a bird atop her rainbow arch. "This dove is me, singing of the lovely, angelic Lilith."

George glanced over with an arched, disapproving brow. Lilith's heart lifted just from receiving his attention, even if it was in censure.

"This fuzzy blob down here will be me," Lilith said, milking that attention. "It's a chicken pecking about the ground." She had hoped to make George chuckle or even smirk. When he didn't, she asked, "What about you, Lord Marylewick, perhaps you could add your symbolism to our sketch or Lady Cornelia's."

"Please do," gushed Cornelia. "I will always treasure it then."

"A miniature copy of your bill in the sketch, perhaps?" Charles suggested. "I might be keener on it if it were presented artistically. You know, touched my aesthetic sensibilities."

"Because heaven forbid you should use your reason or intellect!" George snapped.

Even over the breeze, Lilith could hear the swish of collars and hats as heads turned toward George. The edges of his eyes tensed, a wince of sorts. She could tell he regretted his hasty words—a tiny chink in the self-control he prided himself on.

George muttered something about seeing to the servants and strode away.

"Did I do something wrong?" Lady Cornelia cried to Lilith and Charles. "Did I upset him?"

"No, I ruffled the old boy again," said Lord Charles. "Nothing to worry about. 'Twas a daily occurrence at Eton. He never could take a joke, but he'll be back in spirit soon enough."

Lilith wanted to run after George and embrace him behind some concealing bush. But she couldn't. She couldn't allow herself to get any more attached.

"Go to him, Lady Cornelia," Lilith advised. Her heart hurt as she watched the other woman hurry off to comfort the man Lilith wanted to hold so desperately.

"I say, Lord Fenmore," Lord Charles said. "Why do those ladies near Beatrice keep eying you? They've been doing it since we've been sitting here. Do you think they want something?"

Fenmore glanced over at the attractive women. "By Jove, I should ask."

"Yes, do be their humble servant and what," said Charles. He waited until the man had sauntered away and then turned to Lilith. "Fenmore and Marylewick gone. I say, fine work on my part. Now we may enjoy ourselves properly."

She leaned closer to Charles as if to speak in confidence. "You know Lord Marylewick drives me to distraction. Tell me how you teased him at school. In detail. Please." Lilith wanted to hear the damage done to George from Lord Charles's own mouth.

A slow smiled snaked over his lips and then he gazed off, as if remembering some dear nostalgic memory. "It was a game of how far we could push him. But we had to be careful, because he was a marquess's son."

Charles told of the cruel pranks he and his friends played upon George, who desperately had wanted friends and to fit in with his classmates. She listened with a rigid smile pinned on her face as her stomach turned. She had experienced the viciousness of other children in her boarding school years, but none to the degree that it had been perpetrated upon George. Charles had made the sensitive boy's daily existence a hell. Charles chuckled as he spoke, as if the horror he had inflicted was innocent play, no more than a skinned knee.

"For all our efforts, starchy George hasn't change a bit," Charles continued. "No one is a better Tory than Lord Marylewick. A true believer in the cause. He'll do anything Disraeli asks no matter how he is treated. It's the subject of every other *Punch* caricature, yet flustering, blustering George still can't see the joke."

Though the smile remained on her face, at that moment Lilith loathed Lord Charles. For all his fair looks and pretty words, he was a monster, like George's father and his mother. So many tormentors of her beautiful George.

"Now, darling, you owe me for this little titillating game of truths," he said. "There is much I want to say to you. Escape your many admirers and meet me in the gardens after tea."

All she wanted to do was run as far away from him as she could. And the fastest way to escape was to consent. "Yes," she said. "Of course. Now I must find my sister."

Her legs shook as she stumbled toward Beatrice. Where was George? As much as she was jealous of Cornelia, Lilith hoped the lovely young lady was holding him, saying kind things.

Beatrice sat just outside the cluster of ladies whom Fenmore was pestering with his boorish flirtations. She was engaged in creating a detailed rendering of the marsh grasshopper.

"Ew! She's sketching that horrid injured insect!" cried Miss Pomfret. "With its broken leg and ooze."

"Beatrice, that's unnatural," Fenmore said. "Why don't you want to sketch something pretty like the other ladies?"

Lilith couldn't control her temper any longer. "She can sketch whatever she blooming pleases!" she cried and stomped away.

⁂

An hour later, Lilith waited beside Beatrice on the bench outside the village church as the guests ventured into the shops. Lilith had declined to join them. She was content to watch the crows hop along the old tombstones and not engage in another emotionally trying conversation.

"Am I really unnatural?" Beatrice suddenly piped up.

So much for a brief respite from emotionally trying conversations.

"Of course not. Don't let an arrogant ignoramus like Lord Fenmore make you feel less about yourself. There are many wiser grasshoppers in the world than he."

Lilith's words didn't seem to help Beatrice. Little lines formed between her sister's brows. "I don't find pretty what other ladies think is pretty. I try very hard to like what I'm supposed to. Lady Marylewick probably thinks I'm hopeless."

"Well, you fascinate me. I think you are brilliant."

"I'm not. Don't say things like that."

"Are you insinuating that I'm a liar? Or that I'm not intelligent enough to recognize when someone is brilliant? I certainly hope not."

"No! I…I…don't know how to answer you now."

Lilith patted her sister's arm. "It's best to agree with me. I'm always right in these matters. It's one of my better traits."

Beatrice peered at the grasshopper through the pressed sides of Lilith's bonnet. "It's so amazing. A perfect life composed of thousands of tiny living miracles. I don't understand how a dress or bonnet could be as beautiful." She shook her head. "Sometimes I wish I had been born a man. It would be much easier for me."

"You're absolutely perfect as you are." Lilith

hugged Beatrice. "Don't let anyone tell you differently or try to change you. Keep studying this magnificent world and its inhabitants. Don't ever—bloody hell!" She saw Lord Charles emerging from the tobacconist's shop. She only had a brief window of time to escape before he tried to make eye contact and then demand her company. "I must go. I'm going to get some… some…toffee. Yes, toffee! It makes everything better."

She fled in the direction of the confectioner's around a corner. When she was safely out of Charles's view, she stopped, pressed her hand to her heart, and took several calming breaths before proceeding to the confectioner's.

Inside the squat shop were tiny mounds of toffee, meringues, and nougats behind glass. The scents of sugar, butter, and vanilla had the magic effect of easing her tense muscles and momentarily chasing away her anxious thoughts.

She opened her reticule and drew out some of the monies McAllister had given her. Penelope could use some toffee and Beatrice might enjoy the vanilla meringue. Lilith kept adding to her order, trying to linger a little longer in this sugary haven. She knew George wanted to marry her off to a respectable, genteel man, and she wondered how he would take the news when she ran away with a confectioner and lived happily ever after in his shop.

She took her candies, paper-wrapped, and stepped out. She still wasn't ready to face Charles, Fenmore, George, Lady Cornelia, and all the problems they represented. Nor could she leave Beatrice alone with wolves. She decided to take the long way back to the village church, giving herself ample time to eat enough toffee to fortify her defenses.

She was passing by an alley when a motion caught her eye. She turned, thinking a cat had sprinted by, but instead saw two men conversing deep in the shadows. George and Fenmore.

She concealed herself behind the brick front and peered inside the alley.

George hadn't visited a boxing parlor since leaving London. The tension in his mind and muscles roiled like a stoked-up engine. Last night Lilith had pleasured his cock, and this morning she sat shoulder-to-shoulder with Charles, smiling as the man taunted George. And those damned pictures she had shown him still circled in his brain, refusing to leave. Then, atop it all, to have Fenmore dallying about...

"It's one week," George growled at Fenmore and spiked his cane in the ground. "Can you show some semblance of proper manners toward my family for one bloody week?"

"Good God, man." Fenmore raised his palms. "I just accompanied the ladies to the ruins. Penelope didn't want to go. What? Did you think I would ravish a lady behind a bush? I wouldn't put it past that saucy ward of yours. She's always eyeing me like she wants something."

George dropped the cane and slammed the man against the wall, pressing his knuckles against his throat.

Fenmore gurgled for breath.

"When you are in my county," George said in a slow growl, "staying as a guest in my house, you will show bloody respect for my sister and my family. That includes Miss Dahlgren."

"Maybe your sister should show some respect to me," Fenmore choked. "Maybe she needs to learn how to be a proper wife."

He lifted Fenmore by his collar until the man's toes grazed the pavers and then slammed him against the bricks again. Air roared through George's nostrils. It would be so easy to punch the straying rogue. Again and again, with his bare knuckles, breaking apart that vacant, arrogant expression the man always wore.

Fenmore, realizing his peril, kept his stupid mouth shut, but he emitted humming, frightened whimpers.

George kept Fenmore suspended as he reined in his rage. His love for his sister was the only thing sparing Fenmore injury at the moment. He didn't want to further humiliate her with the talk that would arise if George beat her husband to a pulp.

"One week." George shoved Fenmore again, releasing his grip.

The man, dazed, slumped against the wall.

George turned on his heel, retrieved his cane, and walked away, fury still trapped in his veins and no relief in sight.

Sixteen

"I MUST KILL THE SULTAN," LILITH SAID, ALONE IN THE safety of her chamber. She broke off a bit of toffee and chewed nervously on it. "A merciful death."

After witnessing the scuffle between George and Fenmore, she had rushed down the lane and hid in the cheese shop as George passed. Amid the stinking cheeses, she had fought back her tears. The more she learned of George's sensitive heart and quiet honor, the more ashamed she felt. She was as guilty as his father and Charles of mocking him, except she had ridiculed him before the entire world under a cowardly nom de plume.

She was the cruelest one of all.

She couldn't continue writing, knowing that each word betrayed George. The best thing she could do in this tangled, heart-wrenching situation was quickly end the story. Everyone wanted the sultan to die, a classic good-over-evil tale. Why not give them what they wanted and be done with it?

The valide sultan allowed Colette neither food

nor water the next day. Colette's mind turned hazy,
but still she would not confess the formula of Greek
Fire. In her confused state, her memory drifted back
to the sultan's thrilling kiss in the garden and the
secret in the mysterious box. What was this secret
the sultan desired her to see?

In the early hours of the morning, weak with
hunger and driven by some dark compulsion that
she couldn't comprehend, Colette stumbled to the
garden. She found the sultan waiting, as if knowing
she would come.

He sat on a bench. His turban was gone and his
dark locks flowed freely. The plain box now rested
on his lap. In his powerful hands, he held a bunch
of grapes.

"My dove, you are ravenous," he said. "Come eat
the fruit from my mouth." He bit into a grape, letting
the juices drip down his lips and chin. Hunger drove
away her natural reservations. She readily sucked the
sweet juice from his lips and took in the fruit.

"You have come again because of the secret," he
whispered. "It drives you into the night. It pounds
in your mind like the beating of your own loving
heart. Do not torture yourself, my dove. Sate your
curiosity. Open the box."

She could resist no longer. She knelt before him,
lifted the lid slowly, and peered inside. In the dim
light she could see nothing.

"It's empty," she cried. "You have tricked me."

"It is merely too dark to see the thinnest of paper. So
old that the text fades, but I know the words by heart."

"What are they?"

"The secret to Greek Fire."

"W-what?" cried Colette.

"What!" cried the author too. "Muse, do you mean the sultan had the secret the entire time? You're supposed to be painlessly killing him via some dreadful accident, not turning the entire story around and…" Lilith paused, the implications sinking in.

"Oh," she said.

"Oh," again.

And then, "Ooooh!"

Her pen flew across the pages, barely able to keep up with her ideas.

❧

George sat in his study, surrounded by dour paintings of his forefathers. He pressed his fingers to his temples, trying to ease the dull throb in his skull. Between Fenmore, Lilith, his mother, his sister, Charles, the house party, and Disraeli, he felt as though he had been holding back the tide. But the waters were growing stronger.

He did the only thing he knew to do: work. He flipped through letters from his properties and various relatives, when he came to Disraeli's correspondence again. He released a frustrated "ahh." He couldn't resist and reopened it. There was Lilith, nude and waiting. He ran his pen over her curves, remembering the feel of her nipples as they strained beneath her silk robe. His mouth grew wet to lap and suck her once more. A blob of ink spread outward from her left breast, covering where Disraeli had written "a most critical objective." *Dammit.*

He glanced at the clock. In a few minutes the luncheon would begin, and he had to be the marquess again: restrained, congenial, diplomatic, and certainly not aroused. He didn't have the strength at the moment and that made him feel even weaker, especially as his father and grandfathers looked on.

He gazed at naked Lilith now marred by a huge blob of ink and Disraeli's scrawl. That was the last thing he really remembered until he heard a tap at the door and a timid voice on the other side announce "luncheon." He checked the clock. Thirty minutes had elapsed! But his headache had vanished, and on the letter, covering the prime minister's handwriting, rested Lilith's bare body, now contoured and shaded.

He slid the missive under a pile of letters. He rose, feeling the painted eyes of all his forefathers on him. He slicked back his hair, straightened his tie and collar, and ambled down to the dining room to find everyone assembled and waiting.

"There you are, my dear Lord Marylewick." His mother advanced with Beatrice in her wake.

"I hope I haven't kept you waiting."

"Of course not," she said in a tone implying exactly the opposite. "Now we can begin."

"Lilith isn't here," Beatrice pointed out.

"What a shame, dear," his mother said. "Do have a servant see if she is well and tell her not to trouble herself a bit on our account. She should rest in her bed for the entire day or week if need be."

George turned at the echoing footfalls of someone running through the corridors. Lilith halted at the corner and composed herself, smoothing her gown. It was a shock to see her clothed, as he had spent the last half hour envisioning her naked. Her hair was pinned up except for a long braid that curled down her neck. Color heightened her cheeks, but there was something different about her eyes. That usual tenacious glitter was gone, replaced with a dreamy, hazy glow.

"Hello," she said in a faraway voice. "So sorry that I'm late."

"Everyone's been waiting on you," his mother said sweetly.

Lilith remained distracted through luncheon even as Charles asked her opinion about various radical artists, boring the guests who didn't know them and offending the ones who did.

Lilith, usually enthusiastic for all subjects that outraged, mumbled a few comments and then gazed off.

Who was this incarnation? George had spent the last half hour capturing another Lilith only to have her turn up as someone else. Once he looked up from his roasted pigeon to find her staring at him, her mouth open, the tiny edge of her teeth showing beneath her lips. A wave of heat rushed through his body. Then she blinked, her face flushed, and she turned abruptly away.

A few minutes later, she stared with the same intensity at the salt cellar. Her lips moved slowly as if she were having a silent conversation with it. He began to wonder if dreamy, ethereal Lilith had been smoking opium in her room.

Before he could ascertain anything of her peculiar behavior, she fled again, leaving the other ladies to an afternoon of archery and giddy talk of the coming ball, and the men to billiards and not-so-giddy talk of politics.

❧

Lilith locked her door, fished her portfolio from her wardrobe, unlocked it, and drew out all her pages. She shouldn't leave Penelope alone with her mother and Fenmore, but *the muse's words* raged like a wild river swollen from days of rain. She scanned what she had already written—lines of impassioned prose splattered the page like mental vomit. Marylewick, Marylewick, Marylewick. His name jumped out as did the words "bare, engorged male instrument," "hard, burning tips," and "swollen petals of love."

Ye Gods!

Never mind that. She would change his name to Sultan Murada and mark through pulsating body parts later.

Without bothering to change into her robe or kick off her shoes, she sat, dipped her pen, and fell into the manuscript where she had left off.

Several minutes later she heard a tap on the door. Ugh! Could she work without being disturbed every fifteen minutes? She glanced at the clock to find that she had, in fact, been writing undisturbed for over four hours. Pages littered the desk; her pile of toffee had been reduced to a few pieces. Had she really eaten all that?

There was another tap.

She rushed to the door, cracked it open, and hid her ink-stained fingers behind her back.

A female servant curtsied. "Tea is being served, miss. Shall I help you dress?"

Tea already! She had left Penelope stranded all afternoon! And she had consented to meet Lord Charles in the garden after tea. She groaned and then thanked the servant, replying that she would remain in her current crumpled gown. She shut the door and locked it.

She would write a few more words…

It wasn't until she couldn't see what she was writing anymore for the dying daylight that she realized she had missed tea entirely, as well as her meeting with Lord Charles.

This time she truly panicked. *Muse, you need a watch!*

She popped her last toffee into her mouth and hurriedly hid her pages. Her fingers were so stained she turned her wash water blue trying to clean them.

She had finished putting away her portfolio when the servant tapped on the door again. "Dinner, miss. Shall I help you dress?"

                             ॐ

"Where have you been?" Penelope assailed Lilith as she entered the parlor outside the dining room. "Fenmore has been hounding me all day. I think I'm going to come undone, and I already ate all the toffees you gave me."

"I'm sorry…I…" Lilith so wanted to tell Penelope the truth. But what would she say? *I was working on the latest installment of* Colette and the Sultan. *My muse wants to redeem the villain whom I've based on George.* She doubted Penelope would be sympathetic. "I had a headache." What a weak excuse.

"I have one too," said Penelope. "I think Fenmore is drunk already."

Lilith squeezed Penelope's hand. "One day, you, me, Beatrice, and even George, if we can convince him to come along, are going on a lovely holiday. One where we get to live the lives we want and do as we please."

"I'm not sure I know how," Penelope said as the servant entered and announced dinner.

Lilith gazed across the room to find George studying her. Good God, the man was handsome in his formal evening clothes. She had to glance away before she melted on the spot, and came eye-to-eye with Lord Charles. She flashed him an I'm-so-sorry-please-forgive-me look. His upper lip twitched and he turned on his heel, giving her a cut.

Just capital! His feelings were hurt. He was like a little boy who had to be cajoled when things didn't go his way. Very well, she would play his game for George's sake. She straightened her spine and smiled, transforming herself into the charming, gracious lady. She could not let George down.

After dinner, Lilith followed the ladies to the music room, leaving the men to their port. The harp and piano had been moved to the center of the room with chairs and sofas clustered about. The ladies who were singing began warming up their voices, while others learned the feel of the instruments.

When the gentlemen joined them a half hour later, Penelope grabbed Lilith's hand. "Sit on the small blue sofa with me. Make sure our gowns take up the space. Don't let Fenmore near me."

Lilith obeyed, spreading her bustle across the cushions, which kept her distracted from ogling George. But she could feel him around her, causing her heart to quicken.

The ladies performed one by one as they had the previous evening. Afterwards Lady Marylewick bestowed each with a cutting compliment that the young ladies lapped up. Lilith remembered how George described the evenings as musical murders, and she allowed herself to sneak a single glance to see how he was holding up. He sat straight in his chair, hands on the armrest, appearing politely attentive. Dear George, who only wanted to do what was proper. His gaze flicked to her. She thought she would melt right there on the sofa. A puddle of Lilith.

Then Lady Cornelia rose to sing. Hers was a bright, lovely soprano that danced agilely upon the notes. George shifted forward in his seat, gazing at her with those smoldering eyes, enraptured. Lilith's heart squeezed into a tiny aching ball.

When Cornelia finished, she blushed and smiled shyly, clearly uncomfortable with the audience's enthusiastic applause. The performance was flawless and the guests awaited Lady Marylewick's praise.

A sinking sensation of dread filled Lilith for her rival, who so desired Lady Marylewick's blessing, like a puppy wanting to be petted. But Lady Marylewick preyed on weakness and couldn't stomach seeing perfection in others.

"Quite tolerable," was all her ladyship could muster.

An embarrassed pall hung over the room. Lilith saw George implore Penelope with his eyes. Lilith realized he couldn't say anything for fear of appearing partial. Yet his sister stared at her lap, her mind miles away.

"What a wonderful performance," Lilith said in gracious tones. "Thank you for delighting us with your truly angelic voice, Lady Cornelia."

"Yes, thank you," George safely agreed. "Quite nice."

Lady Marylewick shot Lilith a malicious look as Cornelia returned to her seat, a shy smile on her blushing face.

"My dear Lady Fenmore," Lady Marylewick said, seizing control of the evening again.

Penelope snapped to attention at her mother's voice.

"Why don't you play 'A Devoted Wife Adoreth Her Husband.'" Lady Marylewick clapped her hands together. "How I adored Lord Marylewick."

Penelope's mouth dropped with a soft cry.

"But I was going to sing that," Lilith interceded.

"You?" cried Lady Marylewick as if Lilith were a filthy street urchin who dared to speak up to the queen.

"Why, yes. It's my favorite song. I would be delighted to perform it now. Lady Fenmore, will you be so kind as to accompany me?"

Penelope stared, stricken, then broke into giggles. She could only nod her consent.

"I do not see anything funny," declared Lady Marylewick.

"Neither do I, your ladyship," Lilith replied as she stationed herself by the piano. Penelope gave Lilith her opening note, assuming Lilith could hit it, and then proceeded to play the first stanzas. Lilith sucked in a dramatic breath and then opened her mouth, releasing her voice onto the pandering piece.

She struggled to maintain an earnest face as she watched the uncomfortable twitching of the guests. Only George perceived the joke. He raised his hand to his face, his shoulders shaking with laughter. His joy, even at her expense, fueled her musical ambition. She reached mightily for those pesky high Cs and Ds and missed them by a good half note or more. Soon Charles had figured out the little jest. He watched on with a delighted grin.

"Brava!" he cried, when Penelope mercifully ended the torture. "A quite tolerable performance, indeed."

Lady Marylewick's smile had hardened to a rictus. "Aren't you a clever jester? I am so amused." Her laugh was devoid of all humor. In fact, it sounded rather murderous. Tension permeated the air.

"I enjoyed it immensely," said Lord Marylewick, overriding his mother and setting the guests at ease again. "My sister and ward are up to all the rigs. Thank you, ladies."

As Lilith returned to the sofa, she could feel Lady Marylewick's anger like a hot breeze rushing over her. But Lilith refused to be cowed.

&

The guests began to disperse after Lilith and Penelope's infamous song. Lilith lingered about the parlor, long enough to engage in a few conversations, and then made her escape. Her muse found her in the corridor, bursting with changes and improvements to what she had written.

"But I'm exhausted!" Lilith complained aloud.

"Are you now," a male voice said. Lilith jumped.

Oh God! She had been caught talking to herself. She spun around to find Charles.

"Whom were you talking to?" he asked, clearly amused as he swaggered forward.

"To the fairies, of course," she replied with dead earnestness. "Delightful conversationalists, all of them."

He tossed back his head and laughed. "Fair lady, you destroy me." In an easy, graceful motion, he clasped her arm and drew her into the library.

Really, it should be mentioned in the guidebooks that ladies visiting Tyburn are often yanked into various rooms without their consent.

"You broke my heart this afternoon," he said. "I tried to be angry with you, but then you sang and undid me again." He closed the door behind them. "I beg you, my dearest, to tell me who I am."

She made a point of reopening the door. "You are Lord Charles. You possess reddish-blond hair, blue eyes, and—"

"I am the third son of a duke." He captured her hands and held them between his. "My lair may not be a grand Tyburn Hall, but what I possess is rather impressive. I receive a generous annual income. In other words, I am a most desirable bachelor. Most ladies would cut off their toes to fit into the glass slipper I'm offering. But you...you..." He swallowed, losing his wry facade. "You treat me cruelly."

Not nearly as cruelly as you treat George.

"I'm sorry that I was unable to meet you after tea. I had a terrible headache—it must have been the wind this morning. I had a bit of laudanum and lay down for a nap. I remember being awoken for tea but falling back to sleep."

"You slept all afternoon and still you tell the *fairies* that you are exhausted."

Oh! A clumsy slip on her part. "I find this party very trying," she stammered.

His smirk blossomed to a half smile. "My poor, poor darling, you have my sympathy. George tries everyone's patience."

She bit back her retort that the only man greatly trying her patience was him.

"Ride with me tomorrow and all will be forgiven," Charles assured her. "There is a group riding out in the morning. We can wander off on our own and…" He raised her hand to his mouth and brushed it with his lips.

She tried to retract her kissed appendage. "I hardly know how to ride. I've spent my life in boarding schools and London and never had an occasion to learn."

"I would delight in teaching you." His fingers trailed down her arms, coming a little too close to her breasts. "Shall we enjoy our very first lesson?" He lifted her uncomfortably to her tiptoes. "To begin, you must properly mount the beast." His opened lips waited mere inches from hers. "Are you afraid of the beast?" His mouth descended.

"Pardon me, I thought I would enjoy a little night reading," a male voice said.

George! Lilith turned her head. Her knight in shining armor, or, in George's case, starchy black and white evening clothes, loomed in the doorway.

Charles took his time releasing her, as if to make

a show. George's expression didn't alter, but Lilith could see the tiny pulse at the back of his jaw.

"Alas, Ellis Belfort cannot write *Colette and the Sultan* quickly enough for me." George strode into the room. "Sorry to interrupt."

"Lord Charles has invited me to ride tomorrow," Lilith informed George like the proper ward. "But I don't know how to ride so he was giving me my first riding lesson: how to mount the beast."

Lord Charles coughed a laugh behind his balled hand, thinking the joke was on George.

George gazed to where Charles clasped her elbow. When he spoke, his words flowed out dark and slow. "What a negligent guardian regarding riding lessons and other matters. I must make remedies immediately. Along the lines of proper guardianship, allow me to escort you from this room, Miss Dahlgren."

Charles only chuckled as George led Lilith away. George had gotten her as far as the door before Charles piped up, "Shall we continue our lesson in the morning in the stables, then, Miss Dahlgren? All properly chaperoned, of course."

She wanted to say *bloody hell, no*, but knew the fate of George's bill rested in the man's hands. What an intricate little political knot.

"Yes," she said more breathlessly than she intended. Her body quaked from the sensation of George's powerful hand protectively holding her.

❧

"No man should ever treat you so disrespectfully," George growled outside her bedchamber door.

Lilith squeezed his hand. "It's well, George. Calm yourself. It's not as though I haven't had to extract myself from a dozen or so such situations before."

Although she never thought of herself as needing protecting, George's old-fashioned chivalry excited her. The shockingly wanton images that filled her vivid imagination caused an aching throb between her legs. She needed to get away from him before she did something very, very unwise.

But dash it if he didn't take her arm and slip into her chamber with her.

"Are you well?" His eyes were like warm feathery fingers that caressed her skin as he examined her. "Did he hurt you?"

"Of course I am well," she managed. "I'm not made of brittle china. I won't shatter if you touch me." *Touch me! See for yourself.*

Instead, he crossed his arms and leaned against the closed door. "I'm rather disturbed he didn't receive the same treatment that I did. My shin is still bruised."

She chuckled nervously and strolled to safety across the room at her vanity. "We need his vote. We can't afford to injure him."

"We? *I* need his vote. Not *you*. Lilith, don't compromise yourself for me."

"Compromise myself?" She jerked her head. "You're delightfully old-fashioned. I won't *compromise* myself, as you say. I'm not sure it's even possible for a woman like me—the wild bohemian sort."

"You are not a bohemian but a proper lady."

"I know disagreeing with you will make no difference." She began removing the pins from her hair.

"You see things the way you want to. Reality had better conform."

"What does that mean?"

She didn't answer, but undid her braid with shaking fingers. "Did you draw anything today?"

"What?"

"I realize that you never promised." She gave him an arch look through the reflection in the mirror. "Don't think I will let you get away with that."

"Please stop." He approached her, plucking out a missed hairpin. "I have enough to contend with without you hounding me, trying to turn me into…one of your addled-minded artist acquaintances. I know—"

"There is nothing wrong with being an artist! They are not addle-minded but visionaries."

"—that you keep talking about this little boy inside of me. But Lilith, he's gone. He's dead. You might as well have a funeral for him."

She studied his face. "I'm bereaved that little boy has passed. He had such a sad life. His father bullied him. At school the other boys hid his clothes and made him walk back to his dormitory naked. Destroyed his work so he would be paddled. Made him the butt of jokes and cruel ditties."

"How…how did you learn this?"

"I made Lord Charles confess." She cupped his handsome face. "George, I wish I could take all that away." He winced and tore past her, leaving her hand hanging in the air.

"For God's sake, who cares what happened so many years ago," he barked.

"I do. I—"

"Of course *you* do." He spun around; his eyes were black, shining agates. "You cling to the past. You refuse to let the past die. You want to nurse it, take every little hurt and explode it. Over and over, I have to hear about how you don't want to be a vile Maryle. How you hate Tyburn. How horribly we treated you! How I'm the reason for every terrible thing that ever happened to you!"

She flinched as if he had punched her. She knew he lashed out because she had brought up a painful memory, but her reason could not be a balm to her pain. She had spent the entire afternoon redeeming him on paper. She put up with Charles because of him. She had swallowed dozens of cutting rejoinders to his mother's nasty little remarks because of him. Bloody hell, she humiliated herself by singing because of him and his sister. "Get out," she hissed.

He pressed his fingers to the bridge of his nose. "I'm sorry. My nerves are rather frayed."

"I don't care. You shouldn't have said that. Get out."

He strode to her, his palms open in reconciliation. "Don't be this way." He gently lifted her chin. The touch that moments ago would have driven her wild with desire now angered.

She yanked away. "Go."

"I didn't mean what I said. What can I do to make you happy again? Tell me."

"You know what would make me happy." She flung up her arms. "You can draw, paint, and express all the beauty inside you. You can be the true George."

"This is the true me!" he burst out and then quickly

drew his emotions under control again. "My insides are not the beautiful palaces you envision but full of parliamentary bills and estate ledgers. I'm sorry if I can't be the man you want."

"But I'm supposed to be what *you* want! I'm not supposed to be the true Lilith, because she's too wild, too dangerous. I'm supposed—"

"Please keep your voice down."

"—to wear what you tell me. Read the etiquette books that you give me. Marry whom you order me to."

"I'm trying to help you."

"You're trying to control me. Help looks very different. It's often described as compassionate and kind."

His nostrils were flared. She could see the angry thoughts flying behind his eyes, yet in the end all he said was a curt "Good night," and walked to the door.

"Yes, good night. You really shouldn't be in my chamber. It's not proper. I should fetch my *trustworthy, gentlemanlike* guardian." She slashed where she knew it hurt him. "Oh, but you *are* him."

He glanced back at her and shook his head, his lips a hard line—so like the sultan's. Then he stealthily slipped out of the room to avoid detection.

"Yes, heaven forbid you are caught with me," she cried to the closed door. A tear trailed down her face. "Muse, I hate you. You see, this is why he is the villain in the first place. The sultan must die. He can wander in the desert, blinded by the bright sun, and die of thirst. He can awake to find his bed filled with extremely angry vipers."

❧

George strode through the maze of corridors, politely nodding to guests who were retiring to their rooms and wishing them a good night. Inside, his heart thundered. Why had he said those words to Lilith? Of course she would be angry. Hell, her own mother had rejected her. She'd never had a home, living like a jellyfish floating on the currents.

Damn him for being weak. He should have laughed off her little stories of his school experiences. Instead, he went for her throat like a feral animal backed into a corner. Why did her knowing the truth about those miserable years make him feel vulnerable?

He stalked into his study and began rereading the letters from this morning. He needed to get his mind away from her and focused on important matters of Parliament and maintaining his estates. He picked up a letter from the Lord Chancellor and there she waited beneath, in all her nude glory, gazing at him with those loving eyes. He pulled out the missive and released a long stream of breath. She had been different at this house party—compassionate to Penelope and putting up with Charles's advances to selflessly further George's bill. And he had hurt her because she ventured too close to old wounds and secrets. Damn him.

He rose and crossed to the bellpull. Minutes later a servant appeared. "Please try to conjure up a riding habit for Miss Dahlgren and deliver it to her room in the morning. Ask her to don it and meet me at the stables at six."

The least he could do was save her from a riding lesson with Charles.

Seventeen

MY WITS HAVE TRULY GONE A-BEGGIN' NOW, LILITH thought as she entered the stables in what Frances would have called "the middle of the night." She had been up into the early hours anyway, crying and thinking about all the things she wished she'd had the presence of mind to say to George in the heat of their fight. She whipped her skirts with her crop. She had reached across a vast ocean filled with decades of hurt to reach out to him, and he had mocked and belittled her pain. And all she had wanted was a simple sketch.

The only reason she was down at the stables at dawn was to articulate to him, in rehearsed words, just how much he hurt her last night. She tugged at her habit again, which pulled across the bust and bunched up around her waist. She didn't know where it came from except that it probably looked quite exceedingly fashionable about twenty years ago on a very trim and tall woman.

She stomped around the corner and there George stood, quietly holding the reins of a squat, spotted, and homely horse in one hand and peering at his watch with the other.

"How many minutes am I late, George?"

His head jerked up. His handsome face was pale, his eyes weary, the lines around his mouth etched a little deeper. Her heart weakened. Had he been up all night too?

"Good morning." He bowed properly. "You look lovely this morning."

"What a plumper. I look hideous this morning. Don't you dare say a thing about this ridiculous riding habit or I'll whip you with my crop." She brandished it in the air. "Dashingly useful accessory, a crop."

"It's the morning light," he said and gestured to his own face. "It sets off your skin and beautiful eyes."

Was this his way of making peace? It was working better than she wanted to admit. "Why don't you paint a picture of me and this horse with all its lovely spots? Bask, indulge in the morning light."

"Lilith, please," he said quietly. "Could we just have a lesson, or would you prefer Lord Charles to teach you?"

"Let me consider. Which is the lesser of two evils? Hmm. Alas, I'm already dressed and you are conveniently here, so you may as well teach me."

He placed his hand on his heart. "I'm honored. Now, I've already selected a horse for you. Her name is Maude."

Maude gazed up at Lilith with lovely eyes, those ancient, compassionate kind that made Lilith want to believe the Hindoos' theories of reincarnation. Her heart melted. "She is darling." She ran her hand down the mare's neck. "Maude, we shall be friends, I can see that already. Here, I have a gift for you to seal the friendship." She unfolded her hand to reveal lumps of sugar she had taken from her breakfast. Maude gently lapped up the offering.

"Please don't give her sugar," George said. "My horses adhere to strict diets."

"Don't listen to him, Maude," she whispered aloud in the mare's ear. "He doesn't understand females."

"I know Maude isn't much to look at. She is—"

"Don't hurt her feelings! She is stunning."

"—steady and intelligent. She often is stabled near my high-spirited stallion to calm him. As you see, I've had her saddled and bridled, but an accomplished horsewoman must learn to do these things herself."

"I have no aspirations to be an accomplished horsewoman."

"Your future husband shall desire a wife who rides."

"What if my future husband desires that I tattoo his boyhood pet name Jon-Jon Tushykins on my bum, should I do it?"

"Of course," he said in dead earnest. "You should obey your husband in all matters, horse, tattoos, and otherwise."

Lilith had to stifle a giggle. After all, she was quite irate with him.

"Give me your crop," he ordered. "You won't be needing it."

"I understand that manners are all the rage in those etiquette books you made me read. I remembered it prominently mentioned in *The Lonely Suitor's Guide*."

Her lips trembled, but she refused to give in to his infectious gentle laughter.

"Dearest lady, I humbly beseech you to bestow the honor of your riding crop upon me."

"If I must," she said airily, allowing him to with-draw it and set it on the stable ledge.

"There now." He knelt and placed his opened palm on his knee.

"I prefer you in this groveling position," she said.

"I know you do. Now I want you to place your foot in my hand. Yes, that's good. Now put your hand on my shoulder like so. Hold on to me and I will lift you into the saddle. Here we go." In an easy motion, he lifted her. She released his shoulder as she slid across the saddle, almost falling over the other side of the horse.

"George!" she cried, flailing.

He quickly caught her wrist and then secured an arm around her waist. "Hold on to me," he said. "I won't let you fall."

The heat of his body and the security of his firm grip caused her eyes to water. She tried to blink the embarrassing tears away, but one escaped and slipped down her cheek.

"Lilith." His voice shook. His hold on her tightened.

"Please say you didn't mean those words last eve-ning. They really hurt me." The long, angry speech that she had composed during the night was now reduced to a few plaintive words.

"Forgive me," he whispered. "I can't imagine how it felt to be exiled from your family. I trivialized your pain and I'm sorry. I only want your happiness." Poor Maude was so squat that George could draw Lilith close, letting his hand trail up and down her back. How could she hate and desire one man so fiercely? Why did she find the safekeeping she had sought in the man she had spent years running from? They silently held each other until the sound of stable hands conversing in another part of the stable drew them apart.

"Now carefully put your right limb around the pommel." George's voice was hoarse, laboring with emotion. He patted the hornlike things sticking up from the saddle.

She lifted her skirt, revealing the bottom of her pantalets, and lifted her leg, hooking it around the pommel. "Like this?"

"Lilith!" He glanced about, in case she might destroy some stableboy's innocence. "Have you heard of modesty?" He chuckled and yanked down her skirts.

"Modesty?" She shook her head. "No, I'm afraid I don't know that word."

Still chuckling, he placed her feet in the stirrups. His hand wandered up her ankles. She enjoyed the pressure of his fingertips even through the leather of her boots.

"Now I'm going to give you the reins," he said.

"The reins. I can go anywhere! You can't stop me."

"Maude will. She knows her master."

At the sound of her name, Maude whinnied.

"She's only pretending to agree with you," explained Lilith. "That's how we females work."

"You mean there's a method to female madness?" he quizzed her.

She gave him a playful swat. "I should never have relinquished my crop."

"No, you should not have. Now hold the reins with the first three fingers." He carefully tucked the reins accordingly. "And there you go."

He patted Maude on her hindquarters and the horse began to walk.

"Look at us, Maude!" Lilith cried as they headed for the corral. "Aren't we a clever pair?"

George was a patient teacher, if not a little too overprotective. Whenever Lilith began to speed up, he slowed her down, saying he didn't want to fetch Lord Harrowsby's physician that morning to see to her broken bones. She had to admit, as much as George carried on like a nervous mother hen, it was lovely to have someone care about her well-being and fuss over her.

After he was confident she could safely ride around the corral without his guiding hand, he had his own horse fetched. Studying him atop his stallion, Lilith felt no better than a fifteen-year-old in the heat of her first spoony crush. His powerful thighs straddled the steed. He sat high, his shoulders broad and strong.

Even Maude stepped a little lighter, no doubt feeling for that powerful stallion what Lilith felt for its rider.

"We are hopeless cases, Maude," she said.

⁂

Lilith laughing in the sunshine. Lilith clowning with her horse. George realized she would never be an excellent horsewoman. She was more concerned with being Maude's friend than mistress. George wished he could stretch out this moment for the rest of the day, him and Lilith with her eyes sparkling in the light.

"What have you done? What is this?" Charles entered the corral with Mr. Fitzgerald, Lady Cornelia, and Miss Pomfret in his wake. "What kind of mount

have you given the fair Miss Dahlgren?" he asked
George. "A dull stock horse?"

George watched anger tighten Lilith's features.
Then she quickly concealed the emotion behind a
breezy laugh. "Lord Charles, don't you dare insult my
dear Maude. I adore her and if *I* adore her, of course
you should, too."

Lord Charles's lips trembled with an unexpressed
smile. How deftly Lilith turned him. For years,
George had only received the direct heat of her vivid
personality. At its most intense, she burned away
any thought, any emotion that wasn't her. But now,
watching from outside as she focused her vivid energy
at others, he saw how nimbly she moved. Her dance
that he once thought chaotic actually responded with
perfect precision to the undercurrents of a situation.
How tired she must be, always to be dancing on her
toes. He wondered who Lilith was in stillness. How
could he capture her and keep her still? How did one
stop the beating of the hummingbird's wings?

"Lord Marylewick, do not think that I'm not
vexed that you stole my opportunity to teach Miss
Dahlgren." Charles tossed back his head in a casual
laugh, but George detected the lurking malice. "Now
I shall have to undo all your work and teach her to
gallop freely instead of in this safe circle. She cannot
be contained. Come, my ladies, Mr. Fitzgerald, let
us hope that we all have such fine horses as Miss
Dahlgren's." Lord Charles winked at Lilith. "Maude
is without equal."

After the guests entered the stables, Lilith leaned
down in her saddle. "Don't listen to him," Lilith told

Maude, but her glance flickered to George. "Charles may be handsome and charming, but he's an arse. We are not fooled."

⌘

George, concerned for Lilith, guided the party at a plodding pace along the flat fields. Cornelia discussed her favorite flowers and Mr. Fitzgerald entertained Miss Pomfret by analyzing the strengths and weaknesses of his favorite cricket players. Meanwhile, Charles pestered Lilith with his usual inane conversation, brimming with lascivious undertones. George gripped his reins, his muscles rigid. Each ridiculous word Charles uttered chafed at George's already raw nerves. Lilith bore Charles's flirtation with a charming smile that George, now knowing her better, recognized as feigned. He wanted to snatch her away, put her atop his horse and ride away, both of them escaping this life of pain hidden behind smiles.

"Lord Marylewick, my horse is dying of boredom," Lord Charles complained. "Let us burst forth in a wild gallop. Let Miss Dahlgren experience the exhilaration of a powerful beast beneath her."

"Enough!" George thundered. He turned his horse. "That is entirely inappropriate. Apologize to Miss Dahlgren at once!"

"I can tell she is bored to flinders with this humdrum pace—"

"You don't mean the pace," George shot back.

Charles smirked like a filthy-minded adolescent. "What *did* I mean, Lord Marylewick? I would like to know so that I might apologize for it."

It was Lilith who saved the moment. "This is my first real ride and I pride myself for not having fallen off, ridden into a branch, or knocked someone else from their horse." The dangerous tone in her voice filled George with dread. "There is nothing Maude and I love more than experiencing powerful beasts. Why don't all the gentlemen race across the field, and we shall see who is—I mean *has*—the the most powerful beast?"

"Miss Dahlgren, you are very naughty," said Miss Pomfret. She and Cornelia broke into schoolgirl-like giggles.

"Lilith—Miss Dahlgren—I don't think that is a good idea," warned George.

It was too late. She had already planted the vile seed in Charles's fertile mind.

"No, it is a smashing idea," he countered. "Fitzgerald, are you as good on a horse as you are on the cricket field?"

Fitzgerald's eyes had that glassy look of primal masculine competition. "Bloody hell, yes," he said, forgetting his company.

The ladies, other than Lilith, blushed.

"I apologize, ladies, for Mr. Fitzgerald's impolite language," said George.

"Uh, yes, I apologize too," muttered Fitzgerald. "I daresay, this horse ain't near as fine as my own, but it's the rider that matters."

"Precisely," said Lord Charles. "Are you coming, Lord Marylewick, or are you staying behind with the ladies?" Derision bled through his words.

"He's going," said Lilith.

"And you can't disappoint a lady, Lord Marylewick," said Charles. "It's ungentlemanly."

"Miss Pomfret shall make the call to start," Lilith said.

"The things we do to impress the ladies," Charles said as the men rode to the edge of the field.

They lined up their horses. The rivals' faces were stony and tight.

George wanted to shake Lilith. Why did she encourage this little race? What did she want to prove? He leaned forward in his saddle, his nerves on a razor's edge waiting for the call.

"Go!" shouted Miss Pomfret.

Then the only thing George could hear was the pounding of hooves on the grass. He stood in his stirrups, feeling the air stream over him. In his peripheral vision he could see Charles approaching. Rage, as black as the blood in his veins, boiled up from deep inside George. *That goddamned cove would not beat him.* He lowered his head until he was almost on the horse's neck. His anger flowed through his muscles into his horse's, combusting into speed and thunder as they sliced the air. Charles disappeared. All George saw before him now was grass and sky. For those seconds, he was free and powerful. He wanted to seize this sensation and put it into Lilith. Press his hardness deep into her softness until she cried out in ecstasy. *Lilith.* A mere glance back at her shattered the moment. Charles and Fitzgerald were at least six feet behind him. What would Disraeli say? George was destroying the Stamp Duty Extension Bill to show how big his cock was. He eased up.

❦

"What!" Lilith exclaimed as she watched the others pull ahead of George. But he was going to win. He was ahead for the entire race. How did this happen? Lord Charles sailed across the path first, then Mr. Fitzgerald, followed by George. "No." Her heart crumpled. George needed this win. He needed to show that he was the best man on all counts.

"Victory!" Lord Charles raised his fist and shouted to the sky. He bounded over to Lilith like a happy puppy expecting a reward. "Marylewick gave me quite a run. I didn't expect it from him. But alas, I prevailed. It would be quite a blow if I lost to Lord Marylewick. I would be tormented in the clubs for weeks."

She glanced at George. He wore the sheepish grin of a good loser.

He had lost on purpose!

"Congratulations," she told Charles. "Your reputation is preserved. How simply horrible it would be to lose to Lord Marylewick." She struggled to keep the bitterness out of her voice. She wanted to slap the congenial expression off George's face. *Why did you let the arse win? Don't tell me it was because of your stupid bill?*

"A horror, indeed," agreed Lord Charles, so puffed up with victory he couldn't conceive that it was handed to him. "What is the prize? I know, a kiss from a fair maiden as in the olden days of chivalry and armor."

"I don't think that's appropriate," said George.

"Of course you wouldn't," Lord Charles replied. "What do you say, Miss Dahlgren?"

The other girls giggled. Lilith wanted to suggest that perhaps they should kiss him if it was so amusing.

Charles didn't wait for her reply but positioned his cheek for the coveted prize.

Yet another frog kiss, Lilith thought with a sigh. But as she leaned closer an odd reaction welled up inside her. He wasn't George. How could she kiss a man who wasn't George? Her body rebelled, unable to perform even a casual peck on the cheek. An awkward moment passed; she wasn't sure what to do. Her savior came from an unlikely source. Maude decided to give Charles's horse a good bite for getting too close. His horse reared up and then galloped several feet away.

"I'm sorry. It seems my chaperone didn't approve." Lilith gave Maude a rub of appreciation.

"Don't worry, Miss Dahlgren," said Charles, resuming control of his horse. "I will get my prize."

❧

All the way back to Tyburn, Lilith had to listen to Charles boast about his victory and Mr. Fitzgerald breaking apart the race second by second. Lilith had to clamp down on her rebellious, vitriolic tongue. By the time she reached the stables, she was a bundle of pent-up rage. She thanked Maude and whispered that she would sneak her some more sugar. One thing she had learned from a shifting life was never to take a friend for granted, even if she were a horse.

In her chamber, she yanked herself out of her hideous riding habit, washed her face and hands, and was struggling with the buttons at the back of her fresh gown before a servant arrived to help her. Then she marched to George's study and waited for him, pacing about the room.

She assailed George when he entered, wearing a fresh gray coat and trousers and a blue waistcoat.

"You lost on purpose," she cried.

He jerked his head, surprised to find her there, and quickly shut the door.

"Perhaps you should not have forced me to race."

"I saw how you flew on that horse. You were magnificent. Why did you let that…that…arrogant, assuming arse of a man win? Why do you always let him win?"

"Because I need that arrogant and assuming arse's vote."

"To Hades with that blooming tax. Let some other Tory support it and kiss Lord Charles's backside. You've done enough."

He rubbed his forehead and strode past her to his desk. "I know you have a difficult time understanding the concepts of duty—"

"Stop being patronizing." She followed him, talking to his back. "It's time for grown-up boys like Lord Charles to do their share. He thinks everyone is here for his amusement. Meanwhile, you've done your duty over and over. You've done it so much, sacrificed so much, that you don't even know who you are outside of your responsibilities."

"I disagree." He shifted a pile of letters, picking up the top one. "I know very much who I am. I'm the Marquess of Marylewick."

"No, you are George, the gentle, profound, and soulful artist."

"Please don't start with that nonsense again. Enough."

She yanked the missive from his hand. "Do you

know what Lord Charles told me? That it's a joke how the prime minister leads you about like a dog on a leash. It makes great fodder for *Punch* magazine."

That caught his attention. The muscles worked at the back of his jaw. "I would seriously question any account you get from Lord Charles. Please hand me the letter. It's from my solicitor."

She offered it, but caught his hand when he reached for it. She caressed his knuckles with her thumb. "Did you draw today?" she asked softly. "Let your fancy wander?"

"Lilith, please stop." Yet he made no move to extract his hand.

She edged closer and pressed his hand to her chest, savoring the sensation of his touch. "Did you think about drawing? Did some image enrapture your imagination?"

"You're not talking sense," he muttered. "Now, I have some correspondence to return before luncheon and then we have croquet on the lawn."

"It's all so carefully planned. No little cracks in your day. No time to question ourselves. It's all work, responsibility, and croquet."

"Yes, every day," he quipped. "Work, responsibility, and croquet."

She transferred a stack of letters to the opposite corner of the desk. "Oh, look what I've done! It's out of place now. What shall we do? Our lives may shatter."

"Please put that back. It's all sorted."

She picked up a letter and placed it atop another pile. "I've ruined everything. It's all chaos. How will we ever find anything? It's all so hopeless…"

"This is not a game." He replaced the letter in its proper place. "Stop."

She seized the stack. When he tried to grab it from her hands, the letters scattered onto the floor. "No!" she cried in earnest. "I didn't mean for that to happen. Truly. I..." She stopped, tilted her head, and stared at a particular letter on the floor—the one with the nude sketch on it.

"Dammit!" He reached for it, but she was faster. She snatched the missive and rushed to the other side of the room by the window. She drew back a curtain, letting a shaft of sunlight penetrate the room.

"Please," he whispered, his arm extended, reaching for her. "Please, don't look at that."

"You have been drawing, after all," she said slowly, studying the face and eyes of a woman wanting to be seduced, to have her body ravished with pleasure. Lilith knew those eyes. They stared back from her mirror every day. Her head turned dizzy. "Is this... is this me?"

He sank into a chair and slicked his hand down his face.

"Oh God!" She released the letter and fled.

❧

George rubbed his aching temples. He should go to her, but what would he say? *I'm sorry but I dream all day about how to capture you in stillness and in motion. I want to know every aspect of you. But I can't have you. You must marry another.*

Never in any relationship in his life had the words "I'm sorry" been uttered so many times. He would give her a little time to calm down and then he would approach her. He carefully picked up the offending

letter and shoved it in his desk. Then he retrieved
the scattered correspondence, placed it back into its
proper piles, and returned to his work, because he
didn't know what else to do. However, as he read
the missives from his steward and man of business,
her horrified face bled through the lines. What had he
done? As he opened the drawer again and studied the
drawing, shame washed over him. But damnation, she
had fondled him and allowed him to caress her breasts.
She had to have some inkling of his desire.

That didn't matter. He hadn't behaved as an
honorable gentleman, and he had abused his position
as her trustee. Unless he intended to marry Lilith, he
shouldn't have allowed such intimacies between them,
much less sketched her nude likeness. He would apologize and refrain from touching her in an improper
manner again. He picked up her sketch, crossed to the
grate, and tossed it on the burning coals. As the paper
caught fire, he desired to yank it back, but forced
himself to keep it over the flame. *It must burn away.*

Lilith sent word that she suffered a headache and
preferred to stay in her chamber for luncheon. George
couldn't very well barge into her room and force his
apology upon her. So he remained in agony, unable
to talk to her, to understand her feelings, to beg her
forgiveness. While he concealed his disappointment
at her absence, Charles made public his displeasure,
uttering such inane statements as "My soul aches
without Miss Dahlgren" and "All is emptiness."

Luckily for Charles's aching soul, Lilith appeared for

croquet in the afternoon and stayed close to Penelope. Charles circled her like a wolf, keeping George and the other men away. Then she disappeared again.

That evening Charles cornered George outside the dining room as everyone waited to enter. "May I request a few moments of your time tomorrow, my good man?" he said.

Dread churned in George's gut. "Concerning?"

"Concerning a certain…" Charles faltered and then muttered, "Dear God."

All the conversation in the room dropped to a hush. George didn't need to look up to know *she* was near. Her presence charged the air. When he finally raised his eyes to see, his cock jolted. She wore a garnet-colored dress, cut low to display her creamy shoulders and generous bosom. Her hair was piled high, leaving her neck bare but for one teasing tendril that wound down her neck and rested on her left breast. She gazed about the room from under her lashes, her eyes glittered like a stalking feline.

He wasn't the only one feeling her powerful magnetism. Every man in the room was caught in its draw. Lilith was in heat.

Her gaze locked onto George and her mouth opened just enough for him to see the tip of her red, wet tongue.

"She's mine," murmured Charles. He pushed through the crowd to claim her, but not before George received another powerful flash of her dark eyes, sending a scorching rush of heat to his sex.

At dinner, his mother tried to launch into her tired "ladies in my day" conversation when Lilith cut her off and directly asked the Duke of Cliven, the most powerful man at the table, to tell her about the grand tour of his youth. She laughed at his tales, gently encouraging others to share their travel stories. Now that he knew more of her agile mind, George watched her work in awe. She deftly controlled the conversational current by encouraging everyone to talk. She added little except to smile and praise the words of others, helping them to relax and enjoy themselves. It was masterful diplomatic maneuvering that no book of etiquette could teach.

She turned her head and caught him watching. She hiked the edge of her lip and subtly glanced down. He followed her line of vision to see her spoon atop her knife. *Meet me later.*

However, after the men had hurriedly finished their port, they returned to the drawing room for an evening of cards only to find Lilith missing.

"Such a shame," Lady Marylewick said. "She had another one of those headaches that have been plaguing her. Poor thing. We shall miss her."

Eighteen

WITH LILITH GONE, THE OTHER GUESTS WANDERED off after a few hands. George, stuck in the role of host, had to listen to Lord Harrowsby's diatribe on patent medicine and healers for hours over whist. At one in the morning, the last guest mercifully went to bed. George headed to his study for quiet and a glass of brandy.

A low fire burned in the grate, folded blankets rested on chairs, fluffed pillows lay on the sofa. A refreshed decanter and clean glass waited by a lamp that was recently filled and lit. These attentive touches did little to combat George's hollow listlessness.

Even after the horrible episode before luncheon, he couldn't deny the red-hot anticipation he felt when he thought she was signaling with her spoon and knife to meet her. Then she disappeared, sinking him into a dingy brown despondency.

He reached for a letter from an elderly female relation, forcing himself to get Lilith out of his mind. He heard the quiet grind of a turning knob and lifted his eyes, expecting a servant, but instead Lilith stood in the doorway.

She wore a black coat decorated with glass beads, black lace boots, and a blue hat dominated by a brilliant ostrich feather. She concealed her hands behind her back.

Whatever misadventure she was proposing, he should adamantly refuse. But he couldn't deny her anything, especially after this afternoon's embarrassing episode. He rose, launching into his apology. "Miss Dahlgren, I want to apologize for my ungentlemanly behavior with regards to the, um, inappropriate sketch."

She said nothing, only watched him, an odd glitter in her eye. She uncharacteristically chewed the edge of her lip.

"As your trustee, I have broken a bond of trust between us," he continued. "But...but dammit, Lilith—" He flung up his arms. "After all we've done, you have to know that...that..." He couldn't finish.

She remained annoyingly quiet, swaying slightly on her feet.

He smoothed his waistcoat and straightened his tie in an effort to compose himself again. "You're a beautiful woman and I'm a man of natural lusty needs. Yes, I admit, I desire you." He raised a finger in check. "But I will not act upon these desires in any capacity. You can trust me."

Finally she spoke. "So I'm safe around you?"

"Yes. Please forgive any dishonorable behavior toward you. I am humbly sorry."

"Oh." She gazed down, continuing to chew on her lips. "I'm afraid I cannot easily forgive." He could scarcely hear her quiet words. "I'm quite upset and it will take a great deal more than mere words to make amends."

"I'm sorry. What can I do? Tell me."

"You can draw." She brought forward the paper and sharpened pencils she had hidden behind her back.

He closed his eyes and squeezed the bridge of his nose. "Please," he said. "Ask me something else. Just not that. Not now."

"You don't understand." She set the paper and pencil on the table beside the chair. "You…"

She didn't finish, but stared at him with beseeching eyes. What did she want? What was she trying to say?

Her hand slowly rose, past her bosom to her top coat button. She undid it. No gown or that familiar blue robe waited beneath, only luscious skin.

"Don't!" he cried, realizing her game too late. But the second button had been undone and the garment fell away, exposing her bare body.

Her loveliness hit him like a punch to his chest. He couldn't breathe but only stare as the firelight danced on her lush curves. "Good God, Lilith," he finally managed.

He had envisioned her all incorrectly. Her breasts were far rounder than he had drawn them and tipped with pale rose nipples. Her stomach tapered, further accenting her breasts and the generous swell of her thighs. The fire drew out the coppery tones in the auburn curls about her sex.

Her chest rose and fell with nervous breaths as she watched him studying her. Her arms edged up instinctively to cover herself, but she forced them down again. "Draw me." Her voice quaked.

"Please don't do this." He reached for her coat, offering it to her. "Please."

"But you said I could trust you."

He gave a rueful chuckle. "I might have lied to myself and you on that account," he admitted. "I didn't realize you were going to be the most ravishing lady I have ever beheld. Foolish of me, I know."

She drew the coat from his hands, only to let it fall to the floor once more. Stepping closer, her nipples grazed his chest. Her vanilla scent exploded in his mind, burning away any rational thoughts.

"Please have mercy, woman," he cried through his clenched teeth. He tried not to glance at her body, but good God, she was magnificent.

"I've never been truly naked before a man," she said quietly. "You are the first one. I've come this far. Don't turn me away. Draw me. Please."

He was unable to muster even a weak "no" to the raw vulnerability and longing in her eyes. Words like "duty," "trust," "responsibility," "inappropriate" shouted in his mind. He knew what he was doing was wrong. But he was going to do it anyway.

He reached up and removed her hat, letting her luscious tresses tumble down, down, down around her breasts as she watched his face. "Every day I secretly watch you, trying to capture your picture in my head," he whispered. "The essence of you. But you are never still long enough. You keep changing, like light striking an exquisite diamond, sparking the different facets."

"I shall be still for you, then."

His fingers trembled as he combed the glossy fibers of her hair. "How shall I pose a goddess? How shall she catch the light?"

The first choice of the sofa was too obvious. The flat, blackened leather would overwhelm her delicate coloring and curves. Then the image arose in his mind. He began violently yanking away pillows from the sofas and chairs, pilling them on the carpet before the fire. He then spilled a crimson blanket over them.

"Come." He patted a cushion. His hand shook as he lowered her, as if she were the most delicate thing he'd ever held. "Lie along the cushions so the gold light bathes your body." She tried to follow his dictates, but couldn't replicate the vision in his head. He wanted the light to illuminate her belly and peaks of her breasts and shine in her chocolate eyes but keep the rest of her body in the shadows. "Please, may I touch you?"

"Of course." She smiled.

He tried to ignore the hot electricity that ran from where his hand touched her smooth skin, burning a blaze down his arm, through his chest, down to his cock. He drew deep breaths, trying to keep his arousal in check.

He rested her shoulder flat against the cushion, drawing her hand between her breasts, gently curling the fingers as in repose and careful not to accidentally brush her nipples. The other hand he rested beneath her mouth, touching her lips.

"I'm going to remove your boots. I really think their blackness will put too much weight on the right side."

She laughed. "Of course, I meant to do that."

His trembling fingers struggled with the simple laces as he forced himself not to glance up to the deep red of her sex. But when he bent her leg to pose it, he caught a flickering glimpse of the peak of her clitoris peeking through her curls. Good God! It was more than he could handle. He had to step away for a moment.

"Are you well?"

"Yes, very. Just having my, uh, usual masculine ailment when I'm around you. I'm as hard as a blacksmith's hammer."

Her bubbly laughter was that of a mischievous imp on a wild adventure. It disarmed him, releasing his tension, and he found himself joining in.

He bunched the blanket around her, careful not to touch her intimate places. "Are you warm enough? Shall I stoke the fire?"

"I am fine." Her tender smile undid him. He could only stare, overcome by the exquisite image she made. The shimmer of wetness on her lips, the light from the fire casting her breasts, belly button, thighs in luscious gold tones as her hypnotic eyes pierced through the darkness.

"Don't move. Stay like that. Where is that paper?"

She started to point. "It's over by the—"

"No! Don't move!" He caught himself. "I mean, *please* don't move."

He snatched up the page and paced about his bookshelves, yanking out a large atlas. He drew up a chair and then studied her. How could he begin? How did he capture that ethereal, lovely energy that enwrapped her? He wasn't good enough.

"Come, George, don't be afraid," she whispered. "Draw."

He released a stream of breath and drew a single

line—the rise to the peak of her breast. Then another line sloping down her rib cage to the gentle concave of her belly. Then another line and another. He felt confined, his clothes constraining him. He feverishly tore off his coat and waistcoat and then yanked away his collar and tie. He grabbed his pencil again and began the extension of her legs. "You are lovely," he said, not thinking, the words streaming out. "My God, you are more than lovely. I don't have words to say it. Spirit-lifting gold, mysterious deep red, and the purity of white."

"You are quite beautiful too."

"Hush, you are the work of art and I the mere artist who can only capture a shadow of your brilliance."

"Spoken like a true, anguished artist."

He didn't object—how could he—as he struggled to capture the gentle line of her jaw and contours of her hair. He needed to get the preliminary lighter strokes done to make sure he had her dimensions correct before he began shading.

"You look so happy," she said.

"Shocking how a nude woman can cheer a man," he quipped dryly. He couldn't admit how fearful yet elated he felt in his heart, like a child finally freed to run wild outside after watching from the windows for weeks. Or was it years? Perhaps a near lifetime?

"I mean when you're drawing," she clarified. "Don't deny that it makes you feel alive. That this is your passion. Be truthful. I've taken off my clothes for you, after all."

He slowly raised his head. He couldn't deny her the truth. She deserved it no matter the painful memories of lashings and self-loathing he had to rise above to tell her.

"Yes," he said quietly, holding her gaze. "Thank you, Lilith. Thank you."

∽∾

The truth in his voice undid her more than the way his eyes studied her body. She could hide nothing from him, but let his eyes have their way with her, teasing her breasts, caressing her thighs, and examining her face. Could he tell she was throbbing inside, that her folds had swollen with aching yearning? Her heart swelled with a sweet, pure love for him.

As she watched him sketch with feverish joy, she realized that this drawing wasn't enough. He may capture her on paper, but she had not captured him. The artist remained elusive to her. She wanted to know the passion and vision that drove him, not with her mind and eyes, but with her body. She wanted that beauty inside of her.

She wanted *him* inside of her.

The realization frightened and exhilarated her. Did she come here tonight to let him draw her or make love to her? Somehow these didn't feel like two disparate questions, but the same. She came here to know his truth. To love all aspects of him.

She had never loved a man so profoundly. Even though he could never love her with equivalent depth and dimension, even though her love had no future but pain, could she leave Tyburn without fully experiencing it?

She eyed her coat lying on the floor. Should

she slink away before she completely destroyed her heart? Or was this her only chance to know such an ethereal love?

"Are you cold?" he asked. She realized he knew every twitch of her body and motion of her eye. He rose only to kneel before her. "I've finished your chest and hips, as best I can. You are too magnificent for my meager talent."

"Hush." She pressed her fingers to his lips. He kissed them.

"Lilith," he whispered. He closed his eyes and rubbed his cheek against her fingers. "We must be careful." The pleasure on his face and the bristle and silk of his skin drove her desire higher.

She didn't want to be careful but reckless. To love him so fully and purely in this one night that it would justify all the pain of parting.

And they *would* part.

He edged away as if afraid to touch her again, and carefully nestled the blanket to cover most of her body, except her calves and feet. "There, are you warm enough now, dearest?"

Her throat tightened as if she might cry. There was nothing sad about the moment except something in his caring voice that hurt her deeply. Suddenly she didn't want him to draw now but to hold her and whisper things such as not to be afraid of the dark and to tell her that he would stay beside her until she fell asleep.

He returned to his page. She didn't like being covered. She liked being bared before him. "I'm a little too warm now," she said and flung off the blanket.

He continued to sketch, his handsome face drawn in concentration, until he finally threw down his pencil. "Enough!" He raked his fingers through his hair. "You're stunning and I can only create rubbish. You defeat me."

"No!" She came to her feet, not bothering to cover herself. What had she to hide from him now?

He bowed his head, refusing to look at his creation. She peered at herself staring back from the paper. He had posed her so that her breasts formed peaks illuminated by the firelight; her leg, slightly raised and resting on the other, drew the viewer's eye into the valley of her sex. His desire bled through in lights and shadows contouring her body. Yet her eyes carried none of the sensuality evident in the rest of the image. Large and black with points of light, they dominated the drawing. Tenderness imbued them. And love. Did he see it too? Was she that transparent?

Tears rolled down her face. "You are brilliant. See the primal and sensual juxtaposing with the gentle compassion? She's a nurturing lover. But…is she me?"

"She is how I see you tonight." He wiped away her tears with the pads of his thumbs.

"I wish I could look inside your beautiful mind. I wish I could view the world the way you do."

"You overestimate the contents of my poor m—"

She placed her mouth on his. He couldn't destroy the lovely moment with deprecating words that weren't true. She released the sketch, letting it float safely away as her tongue slid along his and she felt his body harden with yearning. Her hand drifted down, exploring the rise of his chest to the firm plane of his belly and then to where his sex pushed against his trousers. "Let me recompense you," she said. "For your art." He groaned through their kiss. She let her fingers gingerly trace the bulge before sliding them into his waistband to find the buttons.

He tore away from their kiss, clamping his strong hand atop hers. His chest heaved with labored breath. "Please, woman," he said, low and hoarse. "I'm too weak to deny you as I should. You owe me nothing."

But she'd made her choice. Other women wanted a ring, husband, wedding night; she wanted pure beauty and truth—these rare things trembling between them. They might never come again.

"'O! let me have thee whole,—all—all—be mine!'" she quoted Keats. "'Withhold no atom's atom or I die.'"

"You don't know what you're asking of me. You're not...ahhh." His trousers fell away and his cock thrust up, rigid and wide. For a moment, she just took him in, letting her fingers gingerly explore, learning his contours. Slowly she caressed him, all the while watching his face. His eyes were closed, mouth opened in pleasure. "What we're doing is wrong," he said in a low rush of breath.

"Hush, my handsome lover."

He leaned forward, his mouth roughly taking her breast, letting his tongue flick across the top. The surge of pleasure caused her to halt in her work, his magic paralyzing her body. She felt another hand slide between her wet, swollen folds and a finger slide inside of her. She released a high whimper.

"Dear God, Lilith," he whispered over her breast.

What had been a dull, aching throb turned acute.

She pushed against him, thrusting her nipple deeper into his mouth, pleading for more of his magic. Her entire body seemed to balance on his finger as it delved into her. She arched her back and made a strangled cry. "I want to feel you inside me."

She toppled him to the floor beside his sketch. Now he lay before her. He was too powerful, too big. She didn't know what to do.

Her only knowledge came from silly illicit books circulating at school and from what Frances had told her. But nothing could prepare her for this.

She tentatively, cautiously straddled her legs over his sex. "I want you to show me how to love you."

"I can't resist you. Don't do this. I beg you."

She leaned down, letting her lips hover over his, her hair falling around his face. "Let me love you."

He closed his eyes. She could see the conflict on his stricken face. Proper, old-fashioned George trying to protect her virtue. She kissed around the edges of his mouth. "Let me."

"You're a virgin," he hissed, his jaw tight. "This isn't the best way." He drew her onto his body, running his fingers lightly up and down her sides. Then, in an easy motion, he rolled until he was on top. He rose to his knees, letting them push her legs apart. She had managed to cede her power. Now he could walk away.

Yet he continued to stare at her, her face, her belly, and her open, exposed sex.

"Please," she whispered.

He released a hard, anguished cry and threw off his shirt. The dim light and shadows contoured his taut, powerful muscles. He gently lowered himself onto her, sheltering her.

His tongue stroked and soothed hers as his cock progressed along her swollen folds, finding her core. He pressed gently, seeking entrance. For several long moments nothing happened, even as his pressure increased.

What was wrong?

He withdrew from their kiss to whisper "Try to relax" in her ear. She obeyed, letting go into his embrace, feeling the protection of his powerful body over hers.

A twinge of pain shook her. He caught her gasp in his mouth, his fingers tightening around hers. She stayed in his kiss, letting his caresses chase away the sting.

Gently he slid into her, letting her adjust his weight and heat until inch by inch he was snugly inside.

"My beautiful lady." He studied her, not with the hard concentration of the drawing but with dark want. Then he smiled tenderly, letting her know she was safe in this new sensuous landscape.

He began to move with gentle strokes, leaving tiny explosions of pleasure in his wake.

"Oh my, ohh…" Her words drowned in a high, soft cry.

"Does this please you?" he asked.

She wasn't capable of words and pulled him back into a kiss, letting her tongue answer.

His pace quickened, his strokes deepened. Her body moved in unison with his, rising in welcome with each thrust, and then writhing, grinding against him, trying to sate the hunger he elicited. Pleasure yearned for more pleasure, like air to fire. She began to rebel against his controlled and gentle motions, pushing harder, greedy for the sensation. Her body needed no guidance, instinctively knowing to shift her thighs and arch her back, allowing him to penetrate more fully.

He clenched his teeth and closed his eyes as if pain.

"What's wrong?" she cried, trying to rise up to hold him.

"I'm— I'm trying to control myself," he choked. "Dear God! I can't." His motion turned wild and savage. He thrust and thrust and thrust. She met every one, squeezing his cock, trying to relieve the mounting pressure within her walls else she would burn to death from the inside out.

She was so close to something she didn't understand. She dug her nails into his skin, her thighs quaking.

He drove deep inside her with a teeth-gnashing grunt, raising her thighs off the floor. Wet heat filled her womb as he shuddered. Then his frantic energy subsided like a storm passing. Yet she continued to move, rocking against his now quiet body, pleading for the same relief. All his tension was gone, but it remained in her, burning and painful. She whimpered in frustration, turning her head and biting down on her fingernail.

"My poor beauty," he said. "I was too excited. I was…" He didn't finish, but slid off her.

"No," she cried. He couldn't leave her in this torment.

But he hadn't left her; instead he stationed himself between her legs. He drew up her knee and opened her folds with his fingers.

"What are—" She gasped as his tongue brushed across her peak. He lapped, licked, played, toyed, letting her body grow rigid and her legs quake again, until she could almost reach a pinnacle of something. What was it?

Release? Ecstasy? Incineration? He tortured her with pleasure, seeming never to tire of the game. She was open and at the mercy of his tongue. He let it swirl on her apex until she reached that state again where she could scarcely breathe and her body trembled. A roar filled her ears, she opened her mouth to scream but only the shrillest thin sound escaped. In this place she was suspended. Then his tongue moved a fraction higher and her muscles contracted, waves and waves of tension gushing out of her. His tongue kept moving, milking her until the climax petered away.

He rose up to his knees and studied her spent body. "I think I should draw this—*Muse After Rapture*." He lay upon her, letting his cock, now aroused again, rest against the wet curls between her thighs, his arms resting on either side of her, keeping her close. Perspiration gleamed on his muscles.

"That was the most exquisite thing I've ever experienced," she confessed, once she could talk.

He chuckled and kissed each of her hardened nipples.

"No, no, I am wrong," she corrected. "It's the second most exquisite."

"Impossible. What could possibly be better?"

She twined her finger through a strand of his wet hair, drawing it roguishly over his forehead. "When I saw your art in the attic."

He didn't say anything. Light from the grate reflected

in his deep gray eyes. The scorching heat of desire now cooled, yet there remained inside her the feeling of safety in the embrace of a man she had despised for years. Whom she had penned terrible things about under the guise of fiction. Who created the most stirring, precious art. Tears gathered in her eyes.

"I didn't mean to hurt you," he said, distraught. "I tried so hard to be gentle."

"No." She traced along the lines cutting down his cheeks. "It's that I love you," she said softly. He deserved to know. "I love you with all my heart."

❧

She loved him.

The words should have incited fear. He should have been panicking over what had happened.

He felt none of this. Only a deep satisfaction arising from some place deep below his thoughts. Lilith was his.

Finally.

He would like to think he was under some spell of her beauty, as her addle-minded art friends would say, but he knew in a primitive way what he was doing as he entered her body. He knew the entire time. He had recklessly claimed her, driven by desire, with no care for the consequences. He had forced his own hand and there was no going back.

Lilith, the unruly family outcast, was to be the next Marchioness of Marylewick. There was nothing to be done.

He rose to his knees and studied the shadows from the fire dancing on her thighs and breasts.

"What is wrong?" she whispered. "Don't be upset. Come, let me hold you."

"I'm not upset." He chose his words carefully. "Having a wife who loves me is the ideal situation."

"Wife?" She propped herself on her elbows. "What do you mean, 'wife'? Are you suggesting that we marry?" She laughed, albeit a bit nervously.

"We must, after what I've done."

"My lover." She sat up and kissed his forehead. Her warm touch seeped past his flesh into the marrow of his bones. "We did this together. I came here tonight because I wanted to. I love you, but I don't want to marry."

He shook his head. "I ruined you. There is no choice in the matter."

"Ruined me? Did we somehow tumble into the medieval age? Don't talk such nonsense. You're turning this beautiful moment ugly." She kissed his lips.

Her words chafed. How could she say she loved him and then brush him off in the next breath? She had a responsibility to him now.

"This will turn ugly, Lilith, whether you want it to or not." He rose to his feet and paced to his desk. "I promised your grandfather I would take care of you. You are my duty and I took your maidenhood. There is no other course."

Anger lit her eyes. "I'm not another duty! I'm someone in your life who only wants to love you and not to make demands on you. I want…I want this pure moment in all its beauty, not polluted by an unpleasant past or a future of demands."

"You are naïve. You just told me that you loved me. What if I've fathered a child?"

"Frances told me about precautions I could take."

"Those kinds of precautions don't always work. I know it doesn't mean much to your wild set, but what respectable man will want to marry a woman already known by another? Some medieval notions carry over. The future will find us regardless."

She opened her palms. "Why can't you just let me love you? Why can't that be enough? Come back. Let me kiss you."

Her response only enraged him. No, a kiss wouldn't do. He could not set her free now that he had captured her. Now that he had mentally committed himself to their union.

"Please," she said.

How could he work on her?

He knelt before her. She came to her knees, pressing her belly against his cock, her breasts against his chest. She gently kissed his chin, his neck, his shoulder, all the while saying, "I love you." Whatever magic she possessed filled him again. Everything was Lilith, the soft brush of her hair against his skin, her scent of citrus and vanilla mingled with earthy lovemaking, the lilt of her voice, the pressure of her nipples. Her hand found his cock, caressing it until it was hard with want again. He trapped her in a kiss while lowering her to the floor.

He entwined his fingers with hers and locked them to the floor, to hold her there, and then he slid his thighs between hers, letting his cock wait outside her folds. She writhed, straining to feel him, but he clung to every last shred of his self-control.

"P-please, don't torture me like this," she whined.

"If you could behave as you have at this house party," his words rushed out, "you could make an extremely competent marchioness. I've watched how you navigate people and situations. You are brilliant."

"No, I want you. Now. Not your name, this estate, all the horrible memories. I certainly don't want to behave. Please love me again. You see how I want you."

"Do you think I want this estate, this life, these mem—" He faltered. "You can't give your maidenhood to me and then pretend nothing has changed. That I wouldn't act honorably afterwards."

"I'm not another duty in your life. I just want you to draw. I wanted to see you smile, a true smile. I wanted to hold the real George and know his touch. I wanted to be his art."

He gently entered her again. Her body rose with her sigh, welcoming him. He groaned, feeling her snug around him. He released her hands and came to his elbows. "If I drew for you," he whispered, kissing her ear as he rocked gently inside her.

"What?"

"When we're alone, if I drew and painted for you. If I promised you kindness and loyalty." His voice turned to a labored whisper. "If you behaved like a proper marchioness, as dazzling as you have been these last few days, but when you were alone with me, you could be as wild and high-spirited as you want to be. Would you marry me then?" He pressed deep into her, using pleasure to weaken her resistance.

"This isn't fair how you are asking me," she cried.

He altered his tactics, trying to cut closer to her heart. "You said that all you wanted from a husband was kindness and loyalty and a home. I will give you all. I promise that you will never be lost and wandering again."

Tears wet her eyes. "But you don't love me as I love you. You need to love whom you marry. You need to love and be loved. You need it so much."

The words "I love you too" caught in his throat, burning there. They frightened him. He knew if he uttered them, he would relinquish his control over her.

And himself.

"Say yes," he urged, moving inside her.

"I can't—I—"

"Be my wife and I will draw for you." He kissed her jaw, her cheekbone, her wet eyelids. "Say yes. And I will be a loyal husband."

She whimpered and squeezed her eyes shut, a tear rolling from the edge. She could not turn him down now that he had finally captured her, like an exotic butterfly, wings spread, pinned beneath him.

"Please, let me give you a home. A family. Come in from the cold, Lilith."

"Yes," she said, the word flowing on her breath. "Yes."

"Lilith." His mouth covered hers. He moved in rhythm with her, plunging and withdrawing as her body commanded. The words he couldn't say, the fear and ecstasy that pulled him apart, he put it all into his sex, letting her take it away as her thighs quaked in climax and he released deep inside her.

Afterwards, she laid her head on his chest, her arm across him. His heart filled with a sweet sensation of happiness he hadn't known for years. And this same joy scared him to his core.

❦

Lilith felt the warm glow cocooning them begin to crack and she clutched him tighter.

Had she agreed to marrying into the family that had rejected her? Had she promised her life to the very man she had spit such vitriol about in the pages of her story? A man who couldn't say he loved her but looked at her with raw, vulnerable yearning? Who created art that broke her heart?

How could she say *no*? His words had shot right into her emotional Achilles' heel. *You will never be lost and wandering again…Let me give you a home. A family.* She grabbed for what he offered like a hurt child reaching blindly for comfort. And his body, so power-ful and strong, covered hers, blanketing her in safety.

He would draw for her. Let her live in the gardens of his mind.

But now her secret betrayal wormed in her heart.

She couldn't begin a life with such a wonderful man keeping the dark secret of her authorship. But she couldn't dare tell him now when everything was so fragile. She would redeem the sultan. She would show the reader how Colette was confused all along. She would make the reader love the sultan as she now did. Only then would Lilith tell George the truth: that forever he could have his own Colette.

"Now, we have to be in agreement about some-thing very serious before we continue this marriage endeavor," he said.

She lifted her eyes to meet his. The tenderness in them warmed her with the same sensation of being immersed in sun-heated water.

"We must have no disagreement on this point," he continued.

"It's too late for more terms," she teased. "You should have made me agree while we were making love."

"It is this," he whispered in her ear. "We will tell our children that I proposed to you in the study with our clothes on." He kissed her earlobe.

She couldn't imagine their children or their future. This was what the other young ladies at the party did—daydream of having his title and home. She just wanted to love him and that was all she knew.

Nineteen

"MUSE, THESE NEED TO BE THE BEST PAGES I'VE written in my life." Lilith opened her portfolio, her body still bearing George's scent and the feel of his love-making. "We need to approach the brilliance of Milton and Shakespeare. We may even consider iambic pentameter."

She leafed through what she had written, her horror increasing. Her art wasn't nearly as good as George's. Her words floundered like dying fish on the land. Not the light and lushness of George's work, but page after page of stinking, dying fish.

She had a vision of handing him the pages and exclaiming, *Guess what? The sultan is redeemed. He was good all along.* Only to have George say, *Dear Lord, you mean you wrote that hideous chapter? I couldn't possibly marry the author of such claptrap.*

Still, Lilith dipped her pen and forged on, desperate for the life George offered. "Brilliance or death, Muse."

∼

Lilith came down to catch the last of breakfast. She

slowed her steps as she wove through the labyrinth of corridors. Her nerves were giddy at the prospect of seeing George again. This frightened her. Her life couldn't possibly be this good. Something bad was clearly going to happen.

Lady Marylewick's tinkling laughter flowed from the open breakfast room. Lilith's stomach clenched. Was she really ready to have Lady Marylewick as a mother-in-law? But George could tell her to trek across the burning sands of the Sahara and she would do it for him.

The room was alive with a crackling, wild current or perhaps it was only Lilith's nerves. Warm morning sun bathed the walls and tables. From all corners, she could hear the rustling letters and newspapers, the scents of tea, sugar, and cream, and the murmur of excited conversation. The servants were beginning to carry away the empty serving platters from the sideboard. She glanced about, finding her heart's obsession conversing with the Duke of Cliven, their heads down, eyes serious as if engaged in deep, parliamentary contemplation. George glanced her way for the tiniest of moments, long enough to let her know he saw her and remembered all the delicious details of last night. Lilith's heart wanted to do things that would make a chemist marvel—rising, melting, and bursting into flames all at the same time.

"Miss Dahlgren, you shame the very sun." Lilith jumped. Lost in sweet memories of George holding her safe and snug, she didn't see Lord Charles materialize at her side. He closed his eyes and took a deep breath through his nose. "Ah! Can you feel it?"

he asked. "Is not the air alive with romance, or I do mean to say *ambition*. All the ladies are abuzz like honeybees in spring about the ball tonight. Crazy for the sweet taste of the title marchioness. Will the mighty Lord Marylewick finally fall this year? The suspense! It just bores me." He leaned closer. "We must steal away from the maddening frenzy this evening, Miss Dahlgren. We true romantics."

Oh no. She knew what he meant. In her real life—her life away from Tyburn and among her artist friends—she could say, *I would never consider marrying a man who maliciously enjoys taunting others and thinks himself more clever than everyone else.* But now she had to come up with the words that gently let him down, without upsetting George's political aims. In that moment, a future of political intrigue, as twisted and tangled as the old French court, opened before her. Was this what her life was going to be like? Careful, lithe words and smiles that concealed? Would she get her head lopped off at the end like Marie Antoinette?

Some god in the heavens took pity on her.

"Son, would you care to join Lord Marylewick and me for a small discussion in the smoking parlor?" The duke strolled over with George in his wake. He bowed. "Good morning, Miss Dahlgren, you are quite lovely this morning."

"Miss Dahlgren is lovely every morning, every hour," Charles corrected before Lilith could thank the duke. He then shifted his attention to George. "Will my robe and wig be required for this little discussion? I really must make a note for my valet to pack them for your house party. He keeps assuming I'm on holiday."

The duke chuckled. She lifted her eyes to George, saying in their depths: *I'm sorry you must put up with two utter arses. I shall make up for it later, my poor darling.*

She watched the men saunter out of the room, or more to the point, she admired George's powerful back. Small fingers wrapped around her elbow. "Let us come away," Penelope said. "One more word from Mother and I'll burst into a violent rage."

"Of course, but mind you, I would adore to see your rage."

The ladies left the room, heading in the direction of the entrance hall.

Penelope released a long breath. "Are you sure we can't go on that lovely holiday right after this house party?" She shook her head. "I shouldn't tell you this, but I can't keep words to myself anymore. Fenmore came to my room last night. He's...ugh...how could I have imagined that I loved him once."

"Please consider a divorce."

Penelope looked at Lilith as if she had uttered something in another language. "I couldn't do that to George. Ladies, real ladies, don't get divorces."

"I don't know. Many ladies get divorces these days. And they seem very real from what I can tell—arms, legs, mouths, brains, everything—and they are very happy too."

Penelope pressed her hands to her lips and giggled. "How do you make me laugh when I'm despairing the most?"

Lilith lowered her voice. "I have some news. Something that might cheer you up. But I can't tell you here. Let us—"

"Penelope, there you are," Lady Marylewick cried. Her voice was like icy fingers trailing down Lilith's spine. "My darling, darling daughter. I was particularly disappointed in you at breakfast. How you sat there Friday-faced. I had to do all the work as the hostess. And where is your husband? What have you done with him?"

"He was too sick from brandy to leave the bed this morning," Penelope said flatly.

Lady Marylewick gasped, pressing her hand to her chest. "Don't be vulgar. I don't want to see any more of this unbecoming behavior. Where are you learning it from?" Her eyes flicked to Lilith. "A lady must always strive for beauty and gracious manners. She must never give cause for reproach."

"I..." Penelope faltered, tears sprang in her eyes. "How can you..."

Lady Marylewick's vicious smile did not alter at her daughter's misery.

"I believe Penelope is the perfect lady," said Lilith slowly. If Lady Marylewick was to be her future mother-in-law, they needed to have an understanding. "She would never give cause for reproach or speculation for people of true intelligence and understanding. All mothers should be so lucky to have such a kind daughter. You should be more appreciative."

Lilith received a blast of that Arctic smile. "How everyone flutters around Lilith. Flutter. Flutter. Flutter." Lady Marylewick moved her fingers like little wings. "Everyone must adore you. I see you are trying to steal them away from me. You're jealous of me. You always have been."

"W-what?" Lilith's shoulders shook with laughter and disbelief.

"Mama!"

"And if anyone should be appreciative, it's you, Lilith," Lady Marylewick continued. "For the charity this family has extended to you. Who knows where you would be without Lord Marylewick. I always tell him not to pull you from your scrapes. 'Let that mindless dear learn the consequences of her behavior,' I say. But he is so like his father." She sighed, feigning a misty-eyed nostalgia. "Always taking care of everyone, no matter how ungrateful they are for his efforts."

"I do not believe Lord Marylewick is anything like his father," Lilith responded.

"How dare you!"

"Lord Marylewick is a greater man than his father ever was."

Lilith could see the confusion in her ladyship's face. She was trapped. Whatever she said would insult either the son or the father.

"Lady Marylewick!" Beatrice came running down the corridor, clutching her notebook. "Cook says that there are no proper brussels sprouts to be had!"

Lady Marylewick's nostrils dilated. "Must I do everything! This whole party would fall apart if it weren't for me." She stalked off in the opposite direction of the kitchen. "You don't care how I suffer."

Beatrice flinched as if stung. "Did I do something wrong?"

Lilith put a calming hand on Beatrice's arm. "No, you are well. Let's talk to the cook."

❦

Cook was a wiry woman with an obstinate face and stony eyes. She yielded a large, cracked wooden spoon the way a soldier held his gun.

Beatrice had her notebook open, nervously pointing to the menu. "Lady Marylewick specifically requested brussels sprouts with the venison."

"What her ladyship requests and what God deems the ground should grow are two different things," retorted the cook.

Beatrice shook her head. "But—"

"Let us not quarrel over mere brussels sprouts," Lilith suggested and then directed her attention to the cook. "What would best complement venison that is readily available?"

The cook blinked, no doubt accustomed to fighting for every inch. "Well, perhaps carrot pudding," she stammered. "Or smashed turnips and capers."

"I think either would be lovely," Lilith said. "Thank you for your wise help. I have enjoyed all the meals. You and your staff are quite capable."

The cook stared, her thin-lipped mouth flapped open.

"Come ladies, let us visit this lovely kitchen garden. You can smell the rosemary from here." Lilith linked her arms through Beatrice's and Penelope's elbows and led them though the sculleries and into the yard.

Beatrice gazed at Lilith, awe on her features. "How...how did you do that?"

"Years of boarding school experience. Always value people, that is, unless they are real pains in the backside. Now let's do something very naughty."

"Naughty?" Beatrice said. "I-I can't."

"Of course you can," Lilith said. "Let's make

everyone believe we are locked in our chambers, busy curling, powdering, and bejeweling ourselves for the ball. Meanwhile, we'll sneak off."

෴

An hour later, Lilith sat beside Penelope and Beatrice on a blanket inside the old ruins. Around them cooed pigeons nesting in the crevices while overhead cottony white clouds blew across the cerulean sky. At their knees rested an open box of toffee and a bottle of red wine.

"I think this is my favorite part of the house party," Penelope said. "Well, except when you sang the other night."

"I was thinking of joining the Royal Opera." Lilith took a swig of wine. "Do you think they will take me?"

"You would be atrocious, and everyone would enjoy the opera for once," Penelope said.

"I believe all true pleasure is bad at its core," mused Lilith. "I'm philosophical that way."

"Did you know that Kepler advanced infinitesimal calculus by determining the volume of wine in a barrel?" asked Beatrice as she studied the bottle of wine.

"No, and that is absolutely fascinating," Lilith said. "Have you studied calculus?"

"Secretly—don't tell Lady Marylewick." Beatrice twisted a strand of grass around her finger. "Can—can I confess something else? You can't tell."

"Confess away to Monsignor Lilith."

"I've also secretly studied astronomy, biology,

chemistry, physics, Latin, and Greek. And I know more than my brothers. I could be first in the classes if I could go to college."

"Did you know that Oxford is accepting women this year?" Lilith said.

"They are!" Beatrice sat straight up and then lowered her head. "But proper ladies shouldn't attend."

The plaintive tone in her sister's voice inspired Lilith. She rose and plucked a humble white wildflower growing between the old stones. She distributed the tiny petals between them.

"What is this?" Penelope asked.

"An ancient ritual that I've just made up." Lilith raised her arms and cried, "Great sun god Helios, I present thee with candidates for the sacrosanct Maryle sisterhood."

Penelope and Beatrice broke into giggles.

"This is very serious!" Lilith admonished. "Don't anger the sun god." She gazed upward. "O great Helios, for you to know that I am your true servant, I shall perform the most sacred dance of the sisterhood." Lilith began to move with the graceful motion of a ballet dancer, before breaking into a rowdy jig and then bowing to the ladies and casting her up skirts, giving Helios her pantalets-clad backside. Penelope and Beatrice clapped.

"Once you are inducted into the Maryle sisterhood," Lilith said, "all the transgressions of the past are forgiven and you must promise to love your sisters with all your heart and keep their secrets for the remainder of your life. If you are prepared to enter this hallowed order, take ye toffee in your left hand and repeat the age-honored words which I'm making up: 'By all the delicious bits in this toffee, I swear my lifelong allegiance to the sisterhood.'" Lilith paused while they repeated the words. "By ingesting this confection, we affirm our desires to join the sisterhood and share in the joys and sorrows of our sisters' hearts. May our lives be sweet like sugar, filling as cream, and joyous as nuts."

"You are wildly silly," Penelope said, after chewing and swallowing her sacred toffee. "And I adore you."

"Here is my secret and I hope my sisters will share in my joy." How to say it? The words didn't seem real. Had she dreamed last night? Yet the dull soreness between her thighs was definitely real. "Lord Marylewick—George—and I, we…" The words stuck in her mouth. "We are…going to be married."

Penelope and Beatrice only stared. Lilith began again. "I'm going to be the new Marchioness of Marylewick."

Penelope broke into laughter. "You are darlingly funny. I love your little pranks. You are so kind to me after Mama and Fenmore. Sometimes I feel like I haven't laughed for years."

Lilith cringed. "I'm not jesting. George asked me to marry him last night."

Penelope's laugh petered out. "You're serious. He asked you?" She blinked, shaking her head, unable to comprehend what she had heard. "Why?"

Lilith's feelings were rather hurt. "Because he felt it was proper."

"Proper?" Penelope's eyes narrowed with carnal understanding. "Did you seduce my brother?"

Lilith didn't appreciate the outrage in her cousin's voice. "Things just happened."

"You mean, you...you...performed the mating dance with Cousin George?" Beatrice said, wide-eyed.

Lilith grabbed the bottle of wine, took several big gulps, and then wiped her mouth. "I love George. I love him. And I'm going to be a good wife."

"But Lady Marylewick truly abhors you," Beatrice protested. "Yesterday she blamed you when she tipped over a fire screen and broke a lamp. And you weren't even in the room."

"Never mind that," Penelope said. "Does George love you?"

Lilith swayed on her feet. "The way he touched me and his eyes..."

"Did he say he loved you?" Penelope emphasized each word as if Lilith were hard of hearing.

"No," Lilith confessed.

Penelope gazed off. The wind blew her hair under her bonnet. "I cannot approve. I cannot. You knew George would do the proper thing. Why did you do that to him? I know most marriages in society are not based on love, but I wanted something different for him. He deserves more for all he's suffered."

"I am going to make a loving home for George," Lilith cried. "Where it is safe for him to be the sensitive man that he is inside. I thought we could all be together, including my brothers. Penelope, you could get away from Fenmore, and Beatrice, you could... could study at Oxford. We could finally be a true family with love and acceptance." She knelt again. "We shall be happy. All of us. I will make it so."

"You can't be a marchioness," Penelope said. "It's not your station. You know nothing of finer society."

"I love your brother with all my being," Lilith fired back. "*That* is my station. I decide what society I move in. I govern my own life."

The two ladies stared at each other.

"Um, I...I don't think Lady Marylewick would approve," Beatrice ventured.

Penelope's shoulders shook. For a moment, Lilith thought she was crying. "Of course she wouldn't approve!" Penelope broke into laughter. "Love him well, Lilith. Promise me. Never betray him or speak spitefully of him. Give him all the love he deserves."

"I promise," Lilith whispered, not without feeling a tinge of guilt over the horrid sultan business. But she would remedy that. She would make all of Britain know what a wonderful man the sultan was. She raised the bottle. "To the Maryle sisterhood."

"The sisterhood," the ladies repeated.

Lilith could hear the hesitancy in their voices.

Twenty

LILITH, PENELOPE, AND BEATRICE, ALL A LITTLE TIPSY on red wine, sauntered back to Tyburn an hour or so later. They were giggling like schoolgirls when the long window by George's study opened and he peered out. Lilith's heart quickened at the sight of him. She was no better than a spoony lovesick thirteen-year-old.

"I feel there is mischief in the air," he said. "Is that an empty bottle of wine?" He shook his head in mock disapproval. "Naughty ladies. Miss Dahlgren, may I speak with you for a moment on a serious matter? Ladies, can you pardon us?"

Lilith's smile faded. Was he teasing? She couldn't tell anymore. Or she was so terrified that everything would fall apart that she searched for a sign of doom in every little word.

"Of course," she stammered.

"One moment, please." He disappeared into the chamber.

Penelope kissed Lilith's cheek and then she and Beatrice continued around the wing. Lilith waited, her belly tight with nerves.

What if he had changed his mind? No, he wouldn't do that. He would sooner be tied to a medieval torture rack than rescind his word. Why was she so skittish? Where was her confidence?

He stepped through the window and closed it. His features were stony. "I'm very upset with you."

"You are?"

"Come with me, please," he said curtly and offered his arm.

She hesitantly latched on. "I can't stand the suspense. What have I done to upset you? Tell me now."

"You will see soon enough."

Surely he was jesting. But what if he wasn't? Her vivid imagination lit up with every possible horrible scenario.

He led her through the garden. Finches flitted about the boxwood labyrinth and the sun sparkled on the water flowing from the center fountain. He stopped by a stone bench against the back brick wall that was shaded by a conifer tree.

"Tell me," she whispered, ready to respond to the three dozen or so disasters she had already envisioned.

"I've had numerous directives handed to me by the prime minister that I need to attend to. The very financing of the British Empire and her interests hinges on this party. I should be very busy, but instead I spent the morning doing this." He fished out a sheet of paper from his coat and handed it to her: a sketch of a curious wren, its head cocked and tiny feet clinging to a branch. "This little fellow visited the tree by the study window."

A smile blossomed on her lips as relief washed over her. "It's lovely. May I keep it? I'll treasure it."

"Then perhaps you will be delighted by this dull

decanter? I sketched it instead of seeing to my tenants' welfare."

"You've been seeing to your tenants' welfare for years. They won't miss a few minutes of capturing the beautiful light on the glass. The composition is perfect in its simplicity. How dare you call it dull?"

"Aye, but this one I can't explain. My fingers just itched. I had to draw. I call this *The Common Inkwell*."

"You are a master." She laughed. "Amazing detail in the ordinary. I shall cherish it as I do you in all your amazing detail." She didn't know if it was a trick of the sunlight or the unguarded smile on his face and in his eyes that made him appear years younger.

"When Disraeli asks, I'm going to blame the entire debacle on you," he said.

"Whatever can I do to make up for it?" She feigned horror. "Please don't get me in trouble with the prime minister." She rose to her tiptoes and brushed his lips with hers. "Will that make it better?"

"Hardly." In a quick motion, he pulled the drawings from her hands, tossed them onto the bench.

"George, no—ah!" He lifted her from the ground and slid her on his lap as he sat.

"People could see!" she cried, but didn't stop him when he raised her skirts to anchor her thighs around him. Her crinoline formed a ridiculous humplike circle behind her.

"I expect a little more spirit from the daring Lilith Dahlgren, especially when we are alone." He kissed the fabric covering her nipple. Damn the gown and corset. She could barely feel him. He couldn't tease and lap as she loved.

"Who is this George?" She tried to pull her skirts over her folded crinoline. "What have I created?"

"Do you really want to know?" He drew her closer still until her sex, exposed through the slit in her pantalets, met his erection straining against his trousers.

"Hmm, what shall I do?" she teased.

"I think you know."

Their hands met as they undid his trouser buttons. He kissed her chin and neck. She giggled, rose up, and then sank onto him. How dangerous and reckless, yet how perfect and natural she felt in union with him in a garden. He and she were no better than the birds and rabbits making uninhibited, unabashed love. She held his face between her hands and kissed his lips as she rocked against him.

She wished she could stop time from moving forward. No chapters to be written, no past to haunt, or fear to fester in her heart. Only this moment lasting forever.

"Lilith," he murmured and released into her. She continued to hold him, feeling his heart beat against her breast. Yet she still couldn't brush away the scary thoughts. *Your life can't be this wonderful. Something terrible has to happen and take it all away again.*

"Should we make an announcement tonight?" He kissed her earlobe.

Instinctively she cried, "No." She could feel his muscles relax and knew she had given the right answer.

"I think it would be too much for your mother," she explained. "We must break the news to her slowly, giving her room to scream and not be heard. And let us resolve the Stamp Duty Extension Bill issue."

"We mustn't wait too long, because I won't keep

away from you. And I don't want you to give birth to one of those shockingly premature babies which comes out of its mama's womb all chubby and bouncing."

The idea of having his children, all lovely artists like their papa, moistened her eyes. She wiped the tears away before they could fall.

"What's wrong?" he asked gently.

"I'm so happy. And that scares me."

"Hush, now." He started to kiss her just as they heard voices coming from the other side of the wall. They sprang apart and quickly smoothed each other's clothes.

Lilith had to hurry into the house through the servants' entrance. Despite her and George's efforts, her poor skirt was wrinkled in the most damning fashion that shouted *I've been tupping in the garden!*

In her chamber, the muse graced Lilith with lovely, flowing words. Poetry in prose. Her pen flew across the lines of *The Redemption of the Sultan*.

"Muse, I should make love in the garden more often," she concluded.

❧

George took the grand stairs to the ballroom. Not twenty-four hours ago, he would have been filled with that same old weary dread. He hadn't realized how alive yet dead he had been until Lilith awoke him. At the end of this night, she would fold him into her arms again and whisper that she loved him and how wonderful he was.

He only had to draw for her.

He merely had to be himself.

Yet "himself" felt like a whole new man whom he

hardly knew. Now everything was brilliant colors. The vibrancy of the dust sparkling in the light streaming from the window, the loneliness of the cup against the saucer, the optimism of the pink-budded rosebush. It was all silly and the old George would have dismissed it, but this kind of foolishness made Lilith smile that tender smile which bathed him like clean rain.

He marveled that although he had made love to her all through the night and again not a few hours ago in the garden, he hungered afresh for her. The more he loved her, the more he desired her. He would unravel one mystery of her, only to find another waiting inside. He had never been so profoundly enthralled by a woman.

He was relieved that she didn't want to announce their engagement tonight. He didn't want his new-found joy tarnished by exposure. He wanted to keep it a beautiful secret for as long as he could.

He stepped into the grand hall where the servants were busy shifting about large flower arrangements and the orchestra tuned their instruments. Lord Charles leaned against the wall, smoking and watching the activity without any emotion. George refrained from saying that he didn't appreciate smoking outside of the smoking parlor.

"The extension of the stamp duty." Charles gazed at George through a swirl of smoke. "I'm going to frame the discussion to the House of Commons leaders as thus: We are seeking this extension to relieve the income tax of those who shoulder the greatest burden of financing this country. The great peers and businessmen, to whom we owe the prosperity of this great nation, deserve a reprieve for their sacrifices."

"I believe you are making the correct decision for this country and her—"

"Yes, yes." Charles made a shooing gesture. "I have given you what you wanted and now you must give me what I want in return."

George's belly tightened. He knew what Charles desired. This wasn't the conversation he wanted to have at this delicate juncture.

Charles turned and strolled into the parlor opposite the ballroom, letting George follow.

Charles picked up a decanter from the side table. He poured two glasses and handed George one. Then he crossed to the sofa, sat, and stretched one arm along the back. "I want her," he said. "To honor and cherish till death do us part. And don't bother me with such trivial things as a dowry."

"Are you speaking of Miss Dahlgren?"

Charles didn't answer but only looked at him, head cocked, and eyes that said "don't toy with me."

George drank his brandy, buying himself some time to think. "I'm afraid Miss Dahlgren's affections are elsewhere engaged," he said after an interval.

"I don't believe you. She has done nothing but wildly flirt with me all week."

George stifled his smirk with another sip. The poor man was so sure of his romantic prowess that he had misinterpreted Lilith's attempts to hold him at bay. "I'm sorry," he said quietly.

"Let me talk to her."

"I would not advise that."

Charles bolted to his feet, his muscles corded with anger. "I see. You've always held a grudge against me for some mere boyish pranks and now I must pay." He opened his arms and bowed. "Very well, I'm sorry for my past transgressions. I was wrong. Please forgive me. Now I've conceded my vote and some of my pride. Concede your ward."

"I'm afraid you've misread the situation."

"Have I? Who would provide for her better? Tell me, old chappie. Despite her dazzling charm, she has the faintest claim to your family's great honor and name. She is, in fact, far beneath me by society's measure."

George crushed his molars together, feeling the primitive urge to smash Charles's handsome face for insulting his future wife.

Charles stuck to his dangerous course. "You're hurting Lilith by your own obstinacy and resentment."

"I'm sorry," George said again, this time with gritty menace.

"No, I'm sorry." Charles tossed his cigarette into the fire. "I wanted to be honorable about this for your sake, ask your permission and what not, but Lilith will do as she desires. She answers to the true call of her heart. I know her."

"I beg to differ. You've only known her a few weeks at most. Lilith is not who you think she is."

"I have known Lilith six months at least. And I have heard about her for almost a decade now. I know her mind, her imagination, and the landscape of her heart."

Lord Charles refused to lose gracefully. George flung up his arm. "So, you've carried on a clandestine relationship with that even she doesn't know about?"

"Your sad attempt at satire belittles you. You are not that clever. Don't assume you know this situation." Charles approached, putting a thumb's length between them. "Think of it as some clan bride barter. Lilith makes the peace between us. I'm the best man for her, despite how you dislike me."

George struggled to tamp down his rage. He flexed his fingers to keep them from curling into a fist. The political issues at stake were far bigger than two raging men. But a massive wave, rolling and foaming with years of anger, was building inside George, ready to crash.

"Give her to me," Charles said. "Or I'll steal her away."

"Lilith is already engaged," George admitted.

"To whom?" Lord Charles kept his pale eyes fixed on George's face. "Tell me his name."

George remained quiet.

Charles chuckled and stepped back. "You're a terrible liar, Lord Marylewick. You always were."

"She's engaged to me," George barked.

George's anger didn't stem Charles's mirth. His taunting laughter only grew stronger. "You, my dear fellow, *are* strongly opposed to her marriage to me." A smirk smeared his mouth. "Lilith wouldn't possibly consider marrying you. You know nothing of her true nature. Or her secrets. You couldn't keep her even if this 'engagement' you invented were true."

"I am a marquess," he said through his clenched jaw. "You are nothing but a younger son. You have an estate. How pleasant for you. I have several. I've known Lilith most of her life. I know her heart, her mind, her…" He silenced the word "body," refusing to demean Lilith before Charles.

"If this is true, well, it's utterly delicious." Lord Charles finished his glass and stared at the empty bottom, shaking his head. "So, old boy, Colette is going to marry the sultan. I admit, I'm shocked you had the stomach to forgive her after how she portrayed you before everyone in England."

"What are you talking about?"

Charles flung up his arm and shook his fist. "Good God, this is brilliant. A masterful farce. Why are we not on stage with this genius?" He sat again, casually crossing his legs and draping an arm. "I have a darling story to tell you. You will find it quite enlightening. In fact, I think you may want to reconsider your little 'engagement.'"

George could scarcely hear the man. His words seemed to be coming from miles away. Lilith wrote *Colette and the Sultan*? Impossible. If it were true, she would have shouted it from the rooftops of London. Or at least admitted it as he held her, her eyes tender and earnest, incapable of such a malicious secret.

"Last summer," Charles began his tale, "in an attempt to recover from the horrible ailment known as Parliament, I sojourned to Paris. There I came across the most interesting people, as one always does in Paris. A delightfully roguish fellow by the name of Mr. Edgar Dahlgren and his charming wife, Frances. We met in a gallery and he struck up a conversation about art. I was intrigued as ever I am when a British gent speaks of art. It's very rare, you know. Soon the conversation moved us to a wonderfully bohemian establishment, where it was made clear to me that Mr. Dahlgren sought a patron. So desperate was the poor chap that he told me an extraordinary secret. Care to hear?"

"I have no interest."

Nonetheless, Charles forged on. "It was about this darling lady Lilith Dahlgren and her wicked guardian Lord Marylewick. This piqued my interest, as my sister attended school with Lilith, and by Jove, I've certainly had the displeasure of our friendship for years. So I poured a drink—a rather pricey cognac that my new acquaintance had selected—settled snugly into my chair, and asked the man to go on." He uncrossed his legs and leaned forward. "It seemed the poor girl had transformed you into a villainous sultan and was venting your mistreatment of her for all England to enjoy." He paused for effect and then feigned a yawn. "Unfortunately, I was not able to help the Dahlgren cove, but I say, the story almost made up for the expensive bill they left me and my gold cigarette case they stole. But I admit, after a day or so, I lost interest in the story written by a seemingly bitter spinster, except to keep it in the back of my mind in the event that one day it might prove useful. You know, dear fellow, it's just politics, after all. Then one dreary evening, after suffering through an equally dreary play, I picked up an issue of *McAllister's Magazine* trying to escape my ennui. Oh, but Colette was glorious. I was determined to meet this Lilith Dahlgren."

Charles rose and began pacing, his energy turning frenetic. "Unfortunately, the bill and the cigarette case incident kept me away from their gallery, but I found that Lilith Dahlgren was moving around me, that our lives were parallel. I would go to galleries to learn she was just there. Oh, the allure of knowing she was near but just out of touch. What a cruel and utterly delightful game. It wasn't until that day when we met in the park that I assimilated the entire Lilith. She was," he paused and gazed out the window, "far superior than I had imagined her. The most striking and charming woman I have ever met."

Charles turned. The light glowing from the window turned his eyes a translucent blue. "You tell me I do not know Miss Dahlgren. But I beg to differ. You do not know her at all, it seems. She has been making a mockery of you this entire time. And to be honest, my man, I adore her for it." He crossed to the decanter. "Speak to me of this engagement," he said, pouring another drink. "I want all the details. Where is the wedding to be held? Has she picked out the bridesmaids? I wonder about her gown."

"You are wrong in your assumptions. Lilith would never—Miss Dahlgren has more integrity than the lies of which you accuse her."

"Go ask her. By all means, prove her innocence. I, however, never understood the allure of innocence."

Lord Charles's words rang in George's ears as he strolled from the room. "I say, this has been a most enjoyable house party, Lord Marylewick. The crush of the season. To think I dreaded coming a few weeks ago."

George's body trembled as he navigated the corridors to Lilith's chamber. What was he doing? Why did he have these doubts? She couldn't have done this to him. She was many things, but not viciously cruel.

He didn't bother to knock or request Lilith's presence in his study, but slipped into her chamber. She wore only a white corset and petticoat. She and a maid sat atop the bed, sewing on a gown turned inside out.

The maid gasped as George entered and seized Lilith's robe, draping it over her.

"Pardon us," he said, more harshly than he had intended. The servant scurried out, her face crimson, eyes averted.

"George." A tentative smile wavered on Lilith's lips as she slipped off the bed. "Is something wrong?" Anxiety quivered in her voice. She didn't approach him but began edging away, her hands clasped together as if she were praying.

Black heat rushed into his brain. His temples throbbed. No, she wouldn't have done that to him. She wouldn't have betrayed him. "Lord Charles asked for your hand." He was barely able to manage the words.

"Your bill! Was he very angry?" She reached out to him, but didn't touch his arm.

A rueful bark of laughter escaped his lips. "Never mind the bill. He told me an interesting story. One I'm sure can't be true." He paused, trying to put his words in order. He never could spin beautiful webs with words. All he had was color and emotion—the stark white of her chemise and the fear in her dark brown eyes. "It seems that in Paris last summer your cousin Edgar confided in Lord Charles a most extraordinary secret: that you penned *Colette and the Sultan*. Not only that, I was the model for the sultan. I was your villain." He flicked his hand. "Naturally, I told him that he was wrong. You could never be so cruel." He lifted a brow, waiting for her answer.

She closed her eyes, her shoulders sinking with her exhale.

Dear God! No!

"How?" he cried softly. "Why?"

She had betrayed him.

He didn't want to acknowledge how like a hurt little boy he felt. The pain was raw and fresh, all the cynicism he had built up in this thirty-something years of living afforded no protection. His mind flooded with precious images: the beautiful light in her eyes as she held his childhood art, the ivory of her skin bared for him as he sketched her, the burnished tones of firelight in her hair as he held her and made her agree to marry him. All these colors now ran together to a muddled brownish-black.

"I'm sorry." Lilith's eyes shone with tears. "I didn't know you—the real you—when I wrote those words. Forgive me. Please. I beg you."

Now he was supposed to forgive her? Was this merely another scrape she'd landed in? Was she that oblivious to his pain? To all he had done for her? No, he was a villain. He had no forgiveness for her, only rage.

"That's right," he growled. "You only knew the *unreal* me when you lampooned me in those pages. The one who took care of you and pulled you from the suds again and again. The evil man who paid your rent and stayed with you when your cousins left you. The *unreal* me oversees this estate and the well-being of its tenants, attends Parliament to see to the welfare of this country, and serves as a guardian to my greater family, including your siblings whom you abandoned."

"It's only a story." Her words were a choked squeak.

"Was it funny? Did you and your Dahlgren cousins, the ones that were *so* loyal to you, laugh behind my back the way Charles did to my face?"

Again she was quiet. She pressed her hands to her mouth.

He paced and raked his hand through his hair, unable to tamp down his fury.

"I am not a villain!" he thundered. "I have sacrificed everything. Every moment of my life is spent worried about this country, this estate, this family. I…I…" He swallowed, remembering the harsh lessons his father taught. The boyhood taunts he suffered from Lord Charles and his ilk. And now every day he had to be strong and responsible for others, when he wanted to walk away. When he only wanted to paint.

"I admit I laughed behind your back." Tears dripped down her cheeks. "There. I wrote those stories using your name and then I would change it to the sultan before I gave it to the publisher. I didn't know you. I didn't know I would fall in love with you. You wanted to find me a husband. But I…I wanted to…this is hard to explain… I wanted to know something true. I wanted to love a man for his lovely spirit. And it was you. And I couldn't see it all those years. I was ashamed. So I redeemed the sultan in the next chapter."

"Now I need redeeming," he quipped ruefully as she rummaged through her wardrobe. She returned to him, holding pages. There was his Colette in Lilith's handwriting. The evidence was damning. Colette, the fictional lady who had taken him from his troubles all these months, who articulated his emotions, mocked him. He was a big, dumb joke.

"You are just brilliant," he whispered, broken. His father would be ashamed at his weakness. "Go to Lord Charles. You belong together." He tossed the pages on the bed.

"But we're engaged—"

"As you aptly pointed out, the false me is responsible. The real me…" Of course he would marry her. He had given her his word and now he was trapped in this painful joke. All his life, his strivings, reduced to a silly character on a page for the amusement of others. It wasn't the false George who turned and headed for the door.

"That's right, leave." Her cold tones stopped his progress. "I should've known better than to love you. How foolish I am. I should have thought, *So he drew a few pictures as a boy? So what? He's a Maryle. He will leave. He speaks of loyalty, yet he has none when it comes to me, a lowly, scorned Dahlgren who doesn't merit loyalty.*"

He turned, his temples throbbing. Lilith's eyes were dark and shiny as wet obsidian.

"For every so-called scrape you pulled me from," she spat, "for every penny of my own money that I had to beg for, I was told how irresponsible and addle-minded I was. How I burdened you. I was never good enough for you or this family. I do not say this out of feeling pity for myself. I merely can't explain why I spent my entire young life being hidden away."

"You misunderstand."

"No, I do not," she fired back. "You did not want me at this party. This *annual* house party. It is by the trickery of Lord Charles that I am here. Even in our betrothal…" Her voice thinned to a high, brittle pitch. "You made contingencies on our marriage that I behave, meaning if I wasn't me." She clutched the thin fabric over her heart. "And do you want to know the truth?"

"There's more?"

"The truth is, you came to my parties because you had to. Because deep down, you wanted to belong to my world. I know that now. You didn't come to scold me. You came because you needed to be there. Don't deny it."

How naked he felt under her penetrating gaze. "Enough of your artist mumbo jumbo! I certainly don't need your silly artist friends and your ramshackle mode of living."

"Just go, then! How stupid I was to think things could change. How stupid I was to give myself to you because you drew a few pictures." She screamed the last words.

"For God's sake." He flung up his arms. "Of course I'm going to marry you. I have to. I gave you my word. You couldn't honestly believe that I would leave you. "

She laughed through her tears. "What a lovely marriage this will be. I'm another responsibility and duty. Maybe you can give me a separate house, so you won't have to see me. I can beg for money every month during my allotted fifteen minutes. It will be

the way it was before. Wasn't that wonderful? I…I…"
The mocking tone drained from her words. Her body
convulsed with sobs. "I wanted a true home. Where I
was wanted. I thought you would g-give—"

"Lilith." He grabbed her gown from the bed and
draped it over her shoulders. "Get dressed and come
down to the ball. We will pretend that nothing happened and then we will talk. Calmly."

He tried to cup her chin in his hand and draw her
gaze to his face. But she resisted. "I'm sorry. I'm not
so good at pretending."

"Really?" He gave a snortlike chuckle. "Because
you pretended for pages and pages."

She lowered her head. Her gown fell, puddling
on the floor by her feet. He felt like an arse for being
cruel. There was enough pain already.

"I'm sorry," he whispered. "Please come down."
He had to stop the shedding of further emotional
blood. "We will find a way through."

Tears rolled down her face, dripping off her chin.
Her sadness muted his anger. He wished this moment
had never happened and he had remained in igno-
rance. He gently brushed away a teardrop with the pad
of his thumb. He said her name, savoring the rush of
air over his tongue.

In a quick motion, she clasped her arms around him
and pressed her cheek against his coat. He shuddered
and drew her snug, trying to keep her from floating
away in the fast, invisible current of their pasts that
rushed through the room, toppling the present. He
didn't want to go to the damn ball, try to influence
that bloody bill anymore, or dance politely with each

of the ladies. He had grown so weary of his life. It streamed out before him—a sun-faded sand color, cracking from the dryness. He clutched her tighter and bitterly reflected on the cruel paradox that the woman who could cut him the deepest was the only one who could soothe away the pain. "We'll find a way through," he said again.

For a long minute they said nothing, but held each other. Finally, he had to pull away. He couldn't shrink from what needed to be done.

His rational mind began clicking along. "Let me go down first. I'm not sure what Lord Charles has told everyone. I'll try to smooth any damage before you arrive."

She nodded and said something too quiet to be heard.

He wanted to kiss those lips again. Get lost in them. Allow their bodies to balm the hurt. Instead, he forced himself to turn and slip out of her chamber.

He cut through the traffic in the corridors to his study and paced, giving himself some time to strategize.

❧

Lilith stared at the closed door for a long time. Her life had been beautiful for a few hours. She should have known better and not attached herself so strongly. He had once asked her if she wanted love in a marriage and she had said no. That was when she thought love, the beautiful ethereal kind of love she desired, was too much to ask for. She didn't expect that she would ever find something so precious. But she had and it had ruined her. She could not enter into a marriage with George who did not return her love with the same fierce desire and need. Nor could she keep George from loving another with the profound depth that she loved him.

She must take to the road again. Another painful good-bye.

She gathered the pages, the lovely chapter in which she had redeemed the sultan, and stacked them on the commode. She carefully hung up her ball gown, smoothing the delicate pale gold fabric. Then she sat at the writing desk, her Keats by her arm, and penned a letter.

Twenty-one

THE SECOND GEORGE STEPPED INTO THE BALLROOM, HE realized that Lord Charles had blabbed to everyone. He could feel it as sure as a coming rainstorm.

His mother assailed him. "My dear Lord Marylewick," she said with hollow politeness and gave one of her tinkling laughs. "I'm sure Lilith isn't feeling well and must stay in her room." She seized his arm, lowering her voice. "Else I might put my fingers around her darling neck and choke her." As she uttered this vitriol she gave a little finger wave to one of the guests. A sign that nothing was wrong. The Marylewick world was as wretchedly perfect and pleasant as ever.

George glanced around. Everyone peeked curiously at him while trying to feign polite disinterest. Then the room appeared to shift in his eyes. The detail turned to rushes of color and splotches, illuminated in the light falling from the chandelier. He stared, transfixed by the stunning image.

"George, tell me it isn't true. Lilith would never play such a cruel joke." Penelope appeared at his side with Fenmore trailing behind her.

"She's a saucy minx to make a hay game of you," her husband said, lurid admiration in his drunken voice.

"Of course that little monster did," his mother replied. "All—"

"It was a joke between Lilith and me all along," George cut in, unable to bear his mother's nasty jibes a second longer. "I want you to tell everyone that." He recoiled at how similar to his parents he sounded, glossing over an ugly truth. He wanted to live with integrity and dignity, not with the veneer of them. "Let me get through this first dance," he muttered and turned to face the ballroom.

The room continued to swim in his vision, a whirling, teeming sea of color, energy, and light. He wanted to capture this moment on a canvas and show it to Lilith. Lilith. The thought of her made him angrier, but not at her. At this damn ball, Lord Charles, the bloody bill, and at these images he couldn't get out of his head. Paintings waiting to be painted. Why did she have to write those stories when he only desired to lose himself in her body again? He forced himself to keep moving forward, one step and then the next, smiling politely. He had to think about England's future.

He bowed before Lady Cornelia's father. "May I ask your daughter's hand for the first dance?"

Panic seized Cornelia's features.

"She would be honored," replied her father. He clasped Cornelia's arm and tugged her forward.

She appeared like the frightened virgin of some indigenous people, about to be sacrificed at the yearly ritual to appease the harvest gods.

"A-are you really the sultan?" she stammered as he escorted her to the floor. Something about her high, girlish voice and vacuous eyes made him want to answer, *Of course—apart from the times you've see me, I live in the sixteenth century, wear a caftan and turban, and maintain a large harem of highly intelligent, cultured women who live to pleasure my body and mind. I merely pretend to be a marquess and go to Parliament as a diversion. The life of an evil, murderous sultan can be so tedious.* Instead he replied in cool tones, "'Tis an old joke between Miss Dahlgren and me."

She tried to smile. However, his explanation didn't entirely wipe away the fear in her eyes that George might somehow contrive to murder her on the dance floor.

Other couples came forward to dance. Fenmore, staggering from inebriation, led Penelope. She glanced at George as if to say *help me!*

Lord Charles, escorting Miss Pomfret, brushed George's shoulder. "How are those wedding plans, old boy?" he muttered low enough for only George to hear.

George's hands balled. Black rage burned in his heart and contracted his muscles. His dance partner made a frightened squeak. *For God's sake, woman!* He glanced toward the door, hoping to see Lilith in all her creamy loveliness. Yet the threshold was empty. Where was she? He needed her.

The music began and the dancers swayed to the first steps of a waltz.

George's eyes blurred with the colors of the dancers' clothes—black, white, gold, rose, and blue, all bathed in the chandelier's light. He forced himself to concentrate on the dance rhythm. One-two-three, one-two-three, one-two-three.

Charles swept near again. "Where, oh where is your intended?" he quietly taunted as George spun Cornelia. "Clearly, it's true love."

George almost missed securing Cornelia's waist. The ballroom transformed to splotches of angry color, like black and red paint tossed onto a canvas. Like the painting he'd created after the robin eggs were smashed. He needed Lilith. She understood what was happening. She *knew* him. He glanced toward the threshold only to see a servant entering, hoisting a platter of wine glasses.

Charles waltzed close again, his eyes shining with malicious, mocking blue light as when he was George's childhood torturer. "I may vote on your little bill after all. I may—"

Charles couldn't finish because a fist—George's—had smashed his vicious mouth, silencing him. George wasn't sensible of what happened until after the fact. He remembered his muscles flexing, fist flying forward, and knuckles hitting teeth, all the while shouting "To hell with that bloody bill."

Charles was flung away from his partner, stumbling backward into the center of the floor. A drop of vivid red blood oozed from the side of his mouth, contrasting with his fair looks. Gasps resounded. George knew he should feel shock or remorse, but not the sheer exhilaration pulsing through his veins.

Charles charged. George didn't flinch but leaned in with anticipation. Every morning he'd spent in the boxing parlor made it all rote. George easily deflected the oncoming punch and then rammed his fist into Charles's ribs. George braced for a jab to his chin; a more seasoned fighter would have made such a move, but Charles was not as nimble or potent as his vicious words. He left himself unguarded for George to deliver another blow to the gut. Charles dangled on George's fist and then crumpled to the floor.

The orchestra stopped with an ugly flat note of the French horn. An electrified silence crackled in the air, broken only by Lady Cornelia, who cried "He *is* the sultan" and fled to her father's protective embrace.

George stared at Charles, who lay huddled, clutching his belly. George wanted to growl, *Get up and fight through the pain.* But Charles couldn't follow through his flimsy cruelty with real strength. His facade ripped away, Charles was as substanceless and cowardly as George's father had been.

The Duke of Cliven rushed onto the floor. "Son! My son, are you well?" he cried, as if Charles were nine and had tumbled from a tree. "Speak to me."

Charles rolled over, cradling his bleeding face. "You bloody cove!" he hissed at George.

Lady Marylewick materialized in the center of the scene. The tightness around her forced smile and fluttering eyes formed a grotesque picture. "Ha, ha, ha," she said lightly. "How very funny. Men roughhousing like little boys. Come, let's all dance again. Play the music. Play it! What a darling little jest it all was. Just darling. But it's over."

"Darling?" Charles quipped. "He attacked me." Charles came to his feet with his father's aid. "Find another supporter for your ridiculous bill," he told George. "I've grown weary of you, as has all of Parliament."

"Lord Marylewick, you will answer for yourself!" warned the duke. "You shame this nation, the prime minister, the Tory party." He paused for dramatic effect, dropping his voice to a low, gravelly tone. "And your late father."

Wasn't George supposed to be ashamed for dishonoring his father? But the duke's words rested as heavy on his conscious as baby-bird feathers.

"Now, now," cried Lady Marylewick. "It was merely a tiny misunderstanding. Everything is…is… perfect." She glanced desperately about. Finding no one who shared her view, she turned to her daughter. "Penelope, look happy."

Penelope bit her lip and began to shake her head. "I'm not happy."

"Yes, you are," retorted his mother. "You are perfectly content. Stop talking nonsense. Everyone is content. Perfectly, perfectly content."

Penelope looked at George. Pain in her eyes. "I want…I want a divorce." The words seemed to burst from her mouth, as if she couldn't silence them any longer.

Another gasp rippled through the crowd.

"You can't divorce me," barked Fenmore. "A proper wife can't divorce her husband. Tell her, Lord Marylewick. She's embarrassing me."

George began to pivot, taking in all the silent faces contorted in horror. Laughter began to flow through him like a spring breaking through the earth. England's big, dumb joke, the plodding, starchy

George was the sinister villain. Who would have thought? He had done something truly terrible and his bill was destroyed, his house party was in ruins, the secrets of his family exposed for everyone to see. All the things he fought so hard to maintain were crashing down, becoming gossip fodder for people he never really liked nor admired anyway. He should care, but he didn't. He should be on his knees apologizing; instead he just laughed, the weight of years flowing off his shoulders.

"Yes, she can," George choked through his mirth. "She can certainly divorce you, Fenmore. Good God, I would divorce such a faithless rogue. She's been the best wife she could and now she can live the life she wants. That's right, Penelope, my dear, don't look happy, *be* happy. There is a huge difference, you see."

Penelope burst into tears that transformed to wild laughter. She rushed to her brother and he wrapped her into his arms. He could hear the whispers around him. He realized that his guests didn't understand the liberation he felt. They would only censure him, but he didn't care what they thought anymore. All his fears, the things he thought so important and weighed on his mind, scattered like dandelion seeds in the wind. All that was left was what was true.

"Lilith Dahlgren!" his mother screamed, losing any semblance of propriety. "This is her work. She has ruined this family. This is all she ever wanted."

"No," George said. "She never wanted to destroy this family. She wanted to be a part of it. She only desired to be…" Loved. And he, too, had withheld it from her out of his own fears. "Oh, God. I *am* the sultan."

He had to get back to her. His Colette.

He clasped Penelope's hand and they rushed from the room.

Behind him, he heard someone clapping and then Lord Harrowsby said, "By Jove, a wonderful house party this year. The best I've ever attended."

❧

George slipped through his betrothed's door, ready to take her in his arms and tell her the words *I love you*.

But her chamber was empty. On the commode, a letter with his name on the envelope waited atop a stack of papers. He could hear the roar of his own blood in his ears.

"Don't you dare have done something rash," he hissed. He opened the letter and his stomach clenched.

Dearest George,

I was selfish to keep you for myself. I'm childish in my belief that my love for you was strong enough to overcome our history. That you would come to love me as I love you. You always said I was naïve in my beliefs and you were correct. And now, despite the deep pain I feel in leaving, I do not regret for a single moment sharing my love with you. You are an extraordinary man.

Do you think time really heals all wounds? I don't know. I think it all remains, all the love and hurt. You will always reside in my heart, so, in truth, I will always have a part of you. My true home—loyal and kind—is somewhere else and I

*will find it. I couldn't keep you in a marriage of
duty. I can't deny you the same love that I feel for
you that you will know for someone else. I wish us
all that kind of love—you, Penelope, and Beatrice.*

*I know you will want to look for me. You will
be inflamed with that old-fashioned chivalry that I so
adore. You think that I can't care for myself. But I
can. I will send you letters so that you know I am well.
Never forget to draw or be a joyous little boy sometimes.*

*Please tell Penelope and Beatrice that I have not
forgotten the vows of our sisterhood. When I am
stronger, I'll return.*

Love Always, Lilith

"No! No! No!"

Don't look for her be damned.

He tore out of the room and down the servant stairs.
"Has anyone seen Miss Dahlgren?" he demanded of
passing servants. A footman answered that he had seen
her around the morning room, which opened onto
the back gardens.

He rushed to that chamber to find it empty. He
flung open the door to the outside. The velvet night
was cold and windy. The whistle of a train broke the
silence. Along the horizon traveled the black silhou-
ette of a train and its long smoke trail.

"No! Lilith!"

He sprinted through the gardens and around the
side entry for delivery wagons. He didn't stop running
until he reached the train station. The tired travelers descending the steps stared at the frantic man in

evening clothes cutting through them. At the ticket counter, a young ticket agent with a fresh face and hair that spiked around his cap was idly stacking coins while reading from a journal that lay open below his lamp.

"Pardon me," George said.

The agent didn't look up from his periodical but continued reading, his lips forming the words.

"I said, pardon me." George slammed his palm down on the page, obscuring the text. "I'm Lord Marylewick."

The man jumped back, fear entering his eyes. He crossed his arms over his face and cried, "I'm sorry, I'm sorry." He began backing up, bowing at the same time. "Don't harm me."

"What in God's name are you talking about?"

The agent lowered his arms and peered at George. "You're… You're the…the sultan, my lord."

"Oh bloody, bloody hell!" George boomed.

The young man yelped and crouched under the desk while the remaining people in the station took a few steps back.

In a matter of minutes the news had hit the village. It would only take a few more hours before the entirety of England knew.

George groaned and leaned over the counter. "That's right. I'm the dangerous, evil sultan. Now, you had better tell me if you've seen a beautiful woman with auburn hair and luminescent eyes. A mole rests just above her lip."

"Yes, my lord. We held the train a full two minutes for her."

"You did?" All the breath left his lungs. Lilith! He had lost Lilith.

He could scarcely move his lips to muster the words, "W-when does the next train for London leave?"

"Eight twenty-five in the morning, my lord," the agent said from under the desk.

George slicked his hands down his face, his eyes moistening as if he had received a nasty punch. How was he going to find her? She may think she could take care of herself but…

But who would take care of him?

The agent peered cautiously over the counter.

"You may come out," George's voice broke with a faint, bitter chuckle. "I won't murder you. Today."

George staggered down the station steps and then walked home in the darkness. The towers of Tyburn obscured the waning crescent moon. She had been like the moon, moving around him. Since he became her trustee, he always knew where she was, he knew the dimensions and path of her orbit. And now she was gone. His universe in disarray.

He entered Tyburn through the garden doors. No music filled the house. All was silent, as though a death had occurred. He continued to Lilith's chamber. There, he picked up her letter, folded it, and slid it into his pocket. He took the pages stacked on the commode over to the grate. He stirred the coals until they burned bright enough to read by.

Colette had been captured and taken to the sultan's palace. George could see very little of how Lilith had redeemed his character until the story twisted.

"Do not torture yourself, my dove. Sate your curiosity. Open the box."

She could resist no longer. She knelt before him, lifted the lid slowly, and peered inside. In the dim light she could see nothing.

"It's empty," she cried. "You have tricked me."

"It is merely too dark to see the thinnest of paper. So old that the text fades, but I know the words by heart."

"What are they?"

"The secret to Greek Fire."

"W-what?" cried Colette. "You knew all along. Why did you drag me from my home? My father died. I've lost everything because of you."

Shadows concealed his face, but still she could see his eyes, glowing with tender light. "The secret couldn't fall into the hands of my enemies. They are savage beasts, willing to stop at nothing to destroy the prosperity of my kingdom. For the safety of my people, I fostered a reputation as a merciless tyrant to frighten my enemies."

He plucked a yellow budding flower from a bush and tucked it into her flowing tresses. "I came for you and your father, not knowing what I would find. I was ready to kill you both for the protection of thousands. But I found that you were neither cruel nor ambitious, only a loving woman desperate to save her ailing father and to keep a devastating secret from falling into the wrong hands. Alas, it was too late for my physicians to help your father and too late to garner your trust."

"Why didn't you tell me?"

He caressed her cheek. "You wouldn't listen.

You believed the lies that I had propagated in your lands. So I made you think me the barbarian of your imagination in order to get you to safety. I knew that villains far worse than I would have no compunction about torturing you to death. These monstrous men are still out there, waiting. They want to hurt my Colette." He gently kissed her lips. *"Can you trust me? Can you find peace in my garden? Can you call my palace your home, my fair and loving Colette?"*

She was a mere slave girl now. A nobody in a foreign land. He probably kissed all his concubines with the same tenderness. *"At my home, my father loved me. My home had love. Here, there are so many men demanding your time, so many ladies who desire you. My love would be nothing."*

"There are many who desire me because I am the sultan, but none love me with the spirit I feel in you. I'm rapacious for your heart's contents." He cupped her chin in his hand. *"I shall keep unto you only, sing in the garden to you, and feed you grapes from my lips. This can be your home, full of beauty, for the rest of your days."*

Colette had found a home in the sultan's lovely gardens. But her creator was still wandering, lost and hurt.

Twenty-two

THE NEXT DAY, GEORGE AND PENELOPE STEPPED ONTO the platform at Euston Station in London.

"Are you sure Beatrice can manage Mama?" Penelope asked for the fifth time.

"No, but Mama won't murder her as she will us."

"I'm going to insist she come to us in Grosvenor Square. Mama will squash her sweet spirit. I can't let what happened to me happen to her."

"I'm going to unite us all once I find Lilith. We're never going back to the way our lives were before."

She squeezed his hand. "Tell me we'll find her. That all will be well."

He wished he could. His voice stuck in his throat. "Yes," he managed, but didn't truly believe it.

He clutched his walking stick and portfolio that held Lilith's chapter. He kept his head bowed as they waded through the travelers. All around him he could hear the sensational buzz. As with all gossip, the mundane truth was twisted to something grotesque. "Ellis Belfort is really a female ward of Lord Marylewick. The stories are about his cruel treatment of her. He locked her in the cellars of Tyburn for days, giving her only broth to eat." "Lord Marylewick punched Lord Charles and threatened to murder him." And "Lord Marylewick and his entire family have gone mad. Lord Fenmore must divorce his insane wife." The inanity was spreading like an aggressive cancer. He held Penelope's arm and whispered, "Don't listen."

They took a hansom cab to his London townhome. He told the driver to wait outside and stepped in long enough to settle Penelope in and interrogate the staff about whether Lilith had called during the night or morning. No one had seen or heard from her.

He had the cab drive him to Lilith's old home. His fingers shook as he unlocked the door. The house had the silent feeling of having been empty for some time. Nothing was amiss in Lilith's bedroom, nothing to give any indication that she had come here in the night. He let his fingers drift over her books, reading the titles—all the things that she loved and thought about. He drew up the bed covers. They smelled of citrus and vanilla. Lilith. His throat burned. Through the second-floor window, he could see the rooftops— sloping, peaking, rising far into the horizon. Would he ever find her?

He couldn't think about it. He had to keep moving or he would be paralyzed.

He had the cab driver deposit him at Fleet Street in front of a brick building with "McAllister's" printed across the top. George clutched the portfolio holding Lilith's chapter under his arm. As he crossed the walk, he accidentally rubbed shoulders with a lady in a vibrant orange dress and possessing a yellow parasol.

"Pardon me," he murmured.

The woman gasped. "You! It's you!"

George raised a brow. "Are we acquainted?"

"You're Sultan Murada."

"No, I'm Lord Marylewick," George explained nervously, realizing this woman was off her nut. "The sultan is fictional."

"Murderer! Murderer!" The woman shook her parasol at him. "How dare you hurt dear little Colette?"

People were stopping on both sides of the street and not to observe the mad, ranting woman but the vile sultan. They pointed to him and whispered to each other.

"What?" George flung up his hand. "I didn't murder Colette. At most, I tried to…" Wait! Was he trying to defend some fictional version of himself? He spun on his heel.

He opened the door to find a narrow set of stairs and a sign that read "Office" with an arrow pointing upward. The floors shook with the pounding of presses. He lifted his cane and took the steps two at a time, coming to an open stairwell where a young clerk with an air of put-upon sullenness hunched at a desk. The man peevishly thumped the stack of papers he was reading with his pencil. "Relative clause! For God's sake, use a comma!" he cried in agony and then added one with a great flourish.

"I am seeking the editor of this paper," George said. "Presumably, a Mr. McAllister."

The clerk's indolent gaze drifted from George's

face to the portfolio he held. A bored glaze came over his large, slightly bulging eyes. "Mr. McAllister is busy. If you would like to leave your manuscript for consideration, I shall add it to my pile." He flicked his pencil toward a mini Leaning Tower of Pisa made of paper and stacked suspiciously close to the rubbish bin.

The clerk continued in a bored drone, returning his attention to the pages he was reading. "You may expect an answer in four to six weeks. Any inquiries before that time will be politely ig—"

"I'm Lord Marylewick."

The man's mouth dropped. He shot out of his chair, scurried to a closed door, and tapped it. "Mr. McAllister. You have a v—"

"Not now!" a voice boomed from inside.

The clerk gave George a nervous smile and knocked on the door again. "Mr. McAllister, Lord Marylewick is here. Standing right here. Eyeing me. He's very angry."

Not five seconds later the door flew open and a man with unkempt, greasy curls and a beard that needed trimming scrambled out of his office. His shirt, waistcoat, and brown plaid trousers had the ruffled appearance of having been slept in. He performed a series of curt bows as he approached George.

"Lord Marylewick, you honor us with your presence. A great honor, indeed. We are humbled." He glanced around and behind George and added, "I see you are alone?" There was an arch in his voice that left his question dangling. George looked at the man's anxious eyes and guessed the reason for worry.

"My solicitor is attending a funeral—his mother's," replied George in a deep intimidating voice. "I elected to visit you myself."

"Sorry to hear about your solicitor's mother. Very sorry indeed. Please come in." He made a shooing motion to the clerk. "Stuart, bring us some tea."

The man's small office appeared to have been hit by a tidal wave of paper. Great towering stacks on the verge of tipping over covered every surface. Pages were even tacked to the walls. McAllister removed a stack of illustrations from a chair. "A new artist we are considering for future volumes. Please, please sit down."

George sat, keeping the portfolio in the crook of his arm.

The editor leaned against his desk and rubbed his hands together. "I want to say that Miss Dahlgren never gave me any indication that the sultan character was inspired by anyone she knew. I see no reason to get the courts involved."

"That remains to be seen," replied George coolly, even though he would cut off several of his less-needed appendages before dragging his name through the courts. "Do you know where I might find Miss Dahlgren?"

"Of course, of course, let me get her address." He began to flip through the mountain of documents on his desk. "Now, where is it?" Seeing the futility of this scavenger hunt, he opened the door and shouted. "Stuart! Fetch Miss Dahlgren's address."

"When did you last see Miss Dahlgren?" George continued.

"Over two weeks ago. She turned in the installment of *Colette and the Sultan* that we last published.

Naturally, we'll cease to print the story." He forced a chuckle and then his features turned hawkish. "Unless, of course, you would care to write a letter releasing us of any defamation and libel. Not that those terms apply in this case." Another forced chuckle. "No, no. Merely a precaution. Better safe than sued—I mean sorry!" He wiped his damp brow with this sleeve.

"Whether I sue depends on my meeting with Miss Dahlgren."

McAllister edged toward the door. "Stuart, hang the tea. Get the address."

Stuart walked into the office holding a teapot that he set down on a stack, and pulled a random page from the sea of disorganization. "Ah yes, here it is," said Mr. McAllister. He read off the address of Lilith's old residence. The one George had visited. His spirits flagged.

George rose, restless to continue his search. "Please let me know if you hear from her in any regard, else my solicitor might bandy about those terms of defamation and libel. Do not print any work of hers until you talk to me."

"Perhaps we could work out an agreement. A most lucrative agreement. The story is very popular. People will be quite angry if we couldn't finish it."

"Perhaps not." George strolled from the office, letting his cane strike the floor.

❧

He stepped outside and gazed at the soot-filled sky cluttered with hundreds of roofs and chimney stacks. The image began to shift. The building, sky, street all turned to a watery, despondent gray with thick black lines outlining the streetlamps and roofs.

"Murderer! Sultan!" The crazy woman had waited for him. Her vivid yellow parasol broke through the gray. A crowd had swelled around her.

Bloody hell.

He quickly waved down a hackney to head back to the safety and sanity of Grosvenor Square. Outside the carriage window, London passed. Building after building. London housed three million people. The metropolis could easily swallow Lilith. If she were even in London. She said she would come back when she was stronger. But could he wait that long? What if something happened to her?

What if…

What if she found someone else?

He couldn't stomach the idea of another man touching her. She was his. She was his art. He would find her if he had to seek out every tormented artist and writer in England.

Two streets later, he tapped the window, halting the carriage. He stepped down and asked the driver to wait. He walked into the art store. A hunched woman with metallic silvery hair and pale, almost translucent blue eyes was busy organizing paintbrushes into canisters according to size.

George removed his hat. "Pardon me, I would like to know where I might find some prominent artists' studios…and…and…"

"Yes?" The woman smiled, forming kindly crinkles at the corners of her eyelids.

"I would like to purchase some paint."

❧

Day after day, the headlines became more ridiculous. Penelope continued to read them, fretting, upset, questioning her decisions. George recommended that she stop paying the stupid rags any heed, as he had. He had spent a lifetime catering to people and this was how they treated him? To hell with them. He accepted no visitors nor replied to any summons. He pushed to the back of his mind that Parliament returned in a week's time. A letter from the prime minister lambasting his behavior and demanding an audience remained unanswered. He couldn't muster his old self, the conscientious George who kept everything in its place.

But as George faltered, his secretary eagerly assumed more responsibility. He competently handled all the business correspondence and interactions with the housekeeper and butler. Rather than wander idly about without direction, George's staff worked harder when their master loosened his rein on them. Why had he not trusted them sooner? Why had he tried to control everyone?

During the day, he urged Penelope to stay at home and wait for any letter or communication from Lilith while he wandered off, in disheveled clothes and a hat worn low, to the haunts of artists in the underbelly of London. If he found no refuge in proper society, he was offered plenty by the artist community. Humbled by his desperation to find Lilith, he had to temper his usual contempt and request help. He learned Lilith possessed a great number of interesting friends, albeit poor. Everyone had a story to share about her wild spirits but also her kindness and charity. It only broke his heart even more.

None of the artists knew her whereabouts, sending him on to someone else, but only after offering him tea and a look at their work, explaining their artistic vision. What he once scoffed at now intrigued him, and even inspired him. He understood in a deep, wordless way why capturing the pure moment when the white light slanted across the empty glass was far more important than shoring up the crumbling walls of the fortress wing. In fact, Tyburn Hall could fall to the ground as he stayed up late in his study, trying to capture the way that same white light had bled through the breakfast-room window and danced on Lilith's face. The first few nights he struggled with his fears as he put his paintbrush to the canvas. It had been so long since he painted last, secreted away in a closet at Eton. But soon, he was lost in his work again.

Penelope, also unable to sleep, would join him late at night and ask what all those blobs were that he had painted and if he needed glasses, because everything was blurry on his canvas. He would launch into a lengthy discussion about the reality and subjectivity of experience. By God, he was losing his mind, but it felt so much better than droning on about stamp duty and other such nonsense. Even in his sorrow, he'd never felt more alive. At least he felt pain—deep, acute, throbbing pain—and not the dull nothingness that had characterized the last decades of his life.

After a week with no news about Lilith, George went around to *McAllister's Magazine* and bandied about the word "lawsuit," but it didn't help. They hadn't heard from Lilith either, and she had missed her chapter due date. He wanted to tell them that she hadn't been negligent. A new chapter waited beside his bed, atop his drawing of Lilith the night he made love to her. The pages were worn from reading and rereading.

He returned to his study and hung his head in his hands. "Please, Lilith, please," he pleaded. "Have mercy, woman." He picked up his brush, mixed a little red paint into brown and added a stroke to his canvass. As if this were a prayer to her.

"She's here! She's here!" he heard his sister cry outside his door. He dropped his brush, his heart pounding. He turned, expecting to find her tender, forgiving smile.

"I love—" he stopped.

Beatrice and his sister rushed through the door.

Beatrice stopped in her progress and gazed about the study, taking in the paintings of Lilith and then his ruffled appearance.

Concern wrinkled her brow. "Are you well, Cousin George?"

"He has taken up painting again," Penelope explained. "Aren't the canvasses beautiful?" She tried to sound unconcerned, but he knew that she was as anxious about him as he was of her.

"And your face," said Beatrice.

"He's growing a fashionable beard," Penelope interceded again. She beckoned Beatrice to the sofa. "Come, come, how did you manage to escape? I was terribly worried about you. Did you receive my letters?"

Beatrice described how the guests had politely scattered from the house party the morning after the ball. Lady Marylewick had raged to Beatrice that she hoped everyone in England saw what underserving children she had and how poorly they treated their mother and dishonored their family's name.

"She said that if I left, I was as horrible as you," Beatrice concluded. "I didn't mean to say that you are horrible, I'm merely repeating her." She twisted her hands in her lap. "But…but…Lilith was correct when she said Oxford was allowing women to attend. I can't stop thinking about it. I know I should care about finding a husband and dresses and other stupid things, but I—I so want to learn about astronomy and physics and what really matters. I can't help—"

"Good God, Beatrice, if you desire to go to Oxford, just tell me to whom to write," George said. "However, my reputation as an insane, cruel sultan might affect their decision."

"Really?" Beatrice rushed to his arms, embracing him. "I love you, Cousin George. They can't turn away the Marquess of Marylewick's recommendation, even if you are insane."

He chuckled to himself. Yes, perhaps he was insane. Did an insane man know he was mad?

There was a gentle tap at the door and the butler slipped inside. "A telegram has arrived, my lord."

George and Penelope exchanged glances.

The butler handed him the slip of paper and bowed. "I shall be happy to send a return should you require it." Then he left.

George read the sparse words. They weren't what

he wanted to see. He closed his eyes, swallowing down the pain.

"What does it say?" Penelope demanded. He couldn't bring himself to form the words. Penelope gently took the page and read aloud: "I am well. Don't worry. Love to you, P, and B. Don't forget to draw with joy." She turned the page over. "There is no return address or originating office. No way to find her."

A glum pall permeated the room.

"She has always been like this," Beatrice said quietly. "She never wanted anything to do with us. Yet she told me about Oxford, and we made that silly sisterhood vow. I wanted to believe that she really desired to be my sister. True sister. How could she leave after she wrote those silly stories and performed the mating dance with Cousin George? How could she be so cruel to everyone?"

"What?" George cried. "She told you about the, um, mating dance?"

"It's hard to love Lilith." Penelope embraced Beatrice. "When she's near, she shows you this sparkling, wonderful world in which you so want to belong. She says yes when everyone tells you no. She fills your heart with hope, but now that I'm holed up in this house, reading the dreadful articles in the papers and watching poor George suffer, I realize she offered a false hope. I feel very misled." She released her cousin and slumped onto the sofa. "Maybe I shouldn't divorce Fenmore. I'm only causing more pain. Mother is angry. I've embarrassed George. The things those hideous papers say…"

"No!" George said quietly. "Lilith didn't deceive

you." He paced to his painting, letting his gaze follow along its lines. "She felt horrible about *Colette and the Sultan* and begged my forgiveness. We fought that night. She left because she thought I didn't love her. She didn't want to burden me with a loveless marriage of responsibility and duty. She wanted me to love someone as much as she…" He faltered. "As much as she loved me. She so much wanted us"—he gestured to Beatrice and Penelope—"to be the loving family that she had never known. Everything she wrote, she wrote out of pain, not vengeance. She showed me that sparkling, wonderful world of which you speak and I slammed the door in her face."

"But you *do* love Lilith, don't you?" said Beatrice. "After all, you did the mating dance with her and painted these pictures of her."

He raked his hands through his disheveled hair. "I didn't tell her. I kept it from her. Because I was afraid of…of…"

"What?" asked Penelope.

"Myself," he confessed. "My *real* self. The one she loved."

Penelope stared at him, tears glistening in her eyes. "Oh, George," she cried, and then her sweet voice hardened with anger. "You lost Lilith, you idiot! You lost our sister. Her heart must be broken. That poor lady. Come, Beatrice." Penelope linked her arm through Beatrice's and began leading her to the door. "You and I must do something to find her. We made a sacred vow, after all."

"Wait," George said. "I can find her."

"You haven't succeeded so far," was the nasty and unhelpful response he received from Penelope.

"There is one course left," he admitted. One desperate and humiliating course.

Twenty-three

LILITH LAY ON THE WORN SOFA IN THE MORNING parlor, the only quiet room in the Brighton Artist Colony, and stared at the cracked ceiling. This particular ceiling had a W-shaped fissure. The one in her cramped bedchamber, which she shared with another writer who enjoyed writing through the night, while smoking and asking Lilith's opinion about every paragraph she scribed, had an S shape. Lilith had been staring listlessly at ceilings for days and days, hoping in the plaster heavens to find the words to end the cruel Colette story, but all she thought about was George. He would have fixed the ceiling. He took care of the smallest things others might view as trivial. He saw the wonderful details, shapes, and colors that others missed.

Now the newspapers were ablaze with the stories that her sensitive George had inspired the villainous sultan. Of course, the simple truth was too dull and must be embellished for the audience's insatiable taste for scandal. Sensational tales circulated that George had punched Lord Charles at the Tyburn ball and then threatened to murder him with an ax. Some papers claimed George had gone mad and his family had hidden him away in an asylum. The lurid accounts didn't stop at George but extended to Penelope, who, according to the lowest of scandal-mongering rags, had run away with her French lover and demanded a divorce from her husband, and that Lady Marylewick burned down Tyburn Hall in a fit of rage.

Lilith had set off this storm of inanity. All those years she had huddled in her boarding school bed, plotting her revenge of the Maryle family. Never in her most cruel fantasy had she desired this horror.

She had always been able to rally herself after a disappointment, raise her sails and catch a fresh wind. For the first time in her life, she felt truly broken. She had hurt the man she loved most in the world. She wasn't going to recover for years, if not a lifetime. Memories of George throbbed, physically aching the way Lilith imagined the leftover stump of an amputated arm or leg would.

All she could do was mercifully end Colette and the story. Colette deserved to die for being a blind, self-righteous fool. Lilith had tried to explain this to her muse, but her muse remained silent. Lilith suspected that her muse never made the switch to the Brighton train at the Euston station.

So that morning, Lilith decided to forge on without the help of her muse or toffee. She began from where she had left off the day Frances and Edgar abandoned her, forgetting about the tantalizing love scenes in the tent, the magnificent palace, and the gentle kisses in the garden.

Colette fled deeper into the forest, a knife clutched in her hand. The briars and brambles cut her legs. The footfalls of soldiers thundered behind her.

She ran and ran, until her lungs burned. At last, she came into a clearing amid the trees. From all turns, the sultan's men, holding swords, materialized from the dark wood.

"Surrender, Colette," she heard the sultan say. He strode forward, his blood staining the silk robe where she had stabbed his shoulder. "You have nowhere to go. The lands are filled with other men who want your secret. You cannot win. Come with me and I shall show mercy upon your misguided soul."

Her will to fight was gone. Her spirit destroyed. Her fingers trembled as she aimed the knife to her own heart and—

"There you are!" A young actress barged into the room. "I'm going to read the lines again. I've spent the entire morning walking along the beach, trying to feel the anguish of Lady Macbeth. Now listen: 'Out, damned spot! Out, I say!—One: two: why, then, 'tis time to—'"

"It is as wonderful as the last dozen times you've performed it for me." Lilith concealed her ire at finally making literary headway, only to be interrupted.

"But this time was different. A different inflection, a different angst in my heart. Could you not hear it?"

"Yes, of course. A little."

"A little!" The actress's face fell. "You don't understand," she wailed and fled the room as Benjamin, a soul-ailing poet, stumbled in. He threw himself down on the other sofa and tossed an arm over his eyes. "I've been rejected again! I'm in hell. I ought to quit and go back to the farm." He flung the letter at her.

She swallowed a sigh and picked the missive from the floor. When did her tolerance for drama so sharply decrease? She could easily see why George limited everyone to fifteen-minute appointments.

"Ahh, the publisher says you show promise," she said, skimming the correspondence. "And asks you to submit more poems in the future. This is all very good."

"Promise, merely promise? I spent two years working on that. I'm horrible, and no one has the gumption to tell me."

"We've already talked about what a great poet you are." Ad nauseam. "There, there, I'll just go get us some toffee. That will make it all better." In truth, she was down to her last shillings and would have to kill off Colette in the next week or so to have enough money to pay for her keep. But for now, she had to get out of this raucous house with its uncared-for ceilings and insane, needy inhabitants.

After going down the stairs, Lilith came upon the resident composer playing the piano for some lovesick village ladies.

"Hello, Lilith, luv." He winked at her. "Come sing for me and be my inspiration."

He hadn't heard her sing or he wouldn't utter anything so foolish. "You are beautiful, you speak the poetry of angels, and you are the all-knowing goddess of etiquette, but, dear God, you can't sing," George had said that lovely evening in London when they had enjoyed their musical murder.

"You have enough inspiration." Lilith nodded to his audience of spoony ladies and continued through the great hall painted with murals, and out the door. Upon the lawn, a semi-nude man stood, draped in a cloth and with laurel leaves in his hair. Artists with canvasses on easels formed a loose circle around him. None were as talented as George. And his beautiful body put to shame the model's.

George. Everything reminded her of George. When would come a time when he wasn't in her every other thought? When suddenly she might realize she hadn't thought of him or felt the dull throb of her unrequited love for ten full minutes?

That time seemed far, far away as she walked down the road, remembering making love to George in the garden. The contours of his muscles under her finger-tips, the power of his thighs thrusting against hers, the hard set of his jaw as he shuddered in climax. And his eyes afterwards, lit by the brilliant sunlight, glowing with tenderness.

She had held truth and beauty for a fragile moment. Nothing would be as amazing again.

Outside the confectionary shop she told herself to buy just two toffees. No more. One for Benjamin and one for her. Of course, once inside, the tiny pieces of heaven behind the glass only made her pine again for the lovely day with Penelope and Beatrice and the vows of sisterhood they had made over toffee. She wondered what her sisters were doing now. If they were angry with her. Could she ever make them understand why she had to leave?

She took her two meager pieces of toffee and

ventured further into the town, desiring not to return quite yet to the asylum for the obnoxious and insane. Against a public house rested a little boy in rags with matted hair and red, raw, bare feet. She tried to walk past the human misery, but her conscience badgered her until she turned back, giving him a toffee and her last half-sovereign.

Now she had to finish Colette or she might be huddled barefoot on the street too.

She continued toward the booksellers, where she could easily hide for several hours, perhaps even find a book that would relieve George from her mind for just a while. Yet she couldn't reach for the door for the women crowding around a magazine vendor outside.

"The sultan!" cried a girl who looked about fifteen. "The sultan!" She released a long squeal of ecstasy that shook her bonnet and her red spiral curls. Her acquaintance performed an amazing feat, reading *McAllister's Magazine* while jumping up and down and crying, "I love him! I love him! I love him!"

What was this? McAllister's didn't publish today and she hadn't turned in any pages.

Another woman used her edition as a fan to cool her perspiring face. "I always loved the sultan. Always. I didn't care what anyone said. I *knew* him." She waved her magazine faster. "Oh, oh, I must get home. Oooh."

Lilith edged through the women until she reached the crusty-faced magazine seller.

"What are you selling?" Lilith shouted over the crowd.

"A special edition of *McAllister's Magazine* and *Colette and the Sultan*. Aye, but it's gone now."

"What!" Lilith grabbed the man's filthy brown coat

sleeve. "I must have a copy. You can't be out. You simply can't."

"I ain't a magician, miss."

"But…but…that story is about me! That's my story."

"It's my story too!" cried the squealing redhead.

"No, it's *my* story!" shouted her jumping friend. "I loved the story from the first installment. I told you about it. Remember? So it's *my* story."

"No, it really *is* my story," said Lilith. "May I see your copy? Please. I beg you."

The girls shot her a nasty possessive look and hugged their treasured magazines to their chests.

"I'll give you my last toffee for a peek," Lilith beseeched. "A tiny peek. Please. What must I do? This means the world to me."

The redhead reluctantly relented and snatched up the offered toffee. Lilith opened to the first page. *The Redemption of the Sultan by Lilith Dahlgren. Illustrated by the Marquess of Marylewick.*

What!

Her heart thundered. Her head was so light she could scarcely hold on to her flying thoughts. She flipped the pages, reading the words she had written, yet drawn through George's amazing mind.

The illustrations were intricate and detailed. He saw Colette's world with more depth than she could ever have imagined it. Tears blurred her vision. She wiped them away and continued to a stunning full page illustration of Colette and the sultan in the garden. The sultan and Colette kissed against a background of lovely intertwining flowering vines. The image could have been mistaken for a romantic sketch by Rossetti or Millais. The caption beneath it read, "This can be your home, full of beauty, for the rest of your days. I love you. Consent to be my wife. Marry me."

Lilith gasped. She was certain she didn't write those last sentences. They weren't in the story. Why had he added them? Was he telling her that he loved her? "I must…I must go to him."

She blindly thrust the magazine at its owner and ran to the train station. Clothes, toiletries, her Keats book—she didn't need such trivial things. She scrambled into the great hall where the news of the sultan echoed in the high ceilings. "Lord Marylewick, the sultan, illustrated the story!" "I always knew he wasn't the villain!"

She used all her restraint not to push ahead in the long queues waiting for tickets. For God's sake, turtles could crawl to London faster than this line moved.

"I need to get on the next train to London," she cried, when she finally reached the ticket window. "I have no luggage. I have nothing. I need to get to London as soon as possible. I'm desperate."

The ticket agent was a young, unamused man with a critical gaze. "It leaves in thirty minutes," he said. "Nine shillings."

She opened her valise and dug deep into the folds and crevices searching for every last coin. Oh, had she not bought that toffee! "All I have is eight shillings and three pence. Is that enough? Please say yes."

The ticket agent shook his head. "Sorry, miss." He beckoned forward the somberly dressed elderly man and his wife in line behind her.

Lilith spread her arms and grabbed the counter,

refusing to leave. "Oh, please, please, you must let me on that train. My life, Colette's life, all depend on it. I'm Ellis Belfort...Lilith Dahlgren. I wrote *Colette and the Sultan*. I wrote it! I have to get back to Lord Marylewick. I really hurt him, you see."

The ticket agent was getting that weary look in his eye, as if he were dealing with a made-up sob story from someone trying to board a train without paying full price.

"I'm not lying!" she cried. "I didn't tell Lord Marylewick about *Colette and the Sultan* until it was too late. After I had fallen in love with him. He's not a villain, he never was. I was the villain in a way, because I couldn't see the truth." The entire story tumbled out in an incoherent tangle of words, starting from Lilith's father's death and ending with the horrible night of the ball, leaving out, of course, the more intimate details. The others in the queue inched up to listen, as did the people in the next two lines. "So I ran away so he could have the life he wanted," Lilith concluded. "But now he's illustrated the entire story for everyone to see. He told the world that he loved me through his art. My God, man, is that not the truest, noblest love? I must tell him that I love him with all my being. He is my truth and beauty. Please give me a ticket. I beg you." She was ready to climb over the counter and snatch away his tickets and stamper.

"I'm sorry, miss, the ticket remains nine shillings," replied the heartless man. "I don't set the rates. Perhaps you shouldn't have run away from the marquess and caused all this trouble."

"What!" Tears burst in Lilith's eyes. "You cruel, unfeeling—"

The elderly man behind her set a shiny florin on the marble counter. "Young man, people in love don't always act rationally." He patted his wife's arm. "One day you will learn that lesson. Now allow this young lady on that train."

The people in line burst into applause.

⚜

George painted in his study as he waited for a word, any word, from Lilith. Beatrice sat quietly by a lamp reading a book, while Penelope took turns about the room. He scratched his chin where his beard was growing in, sipped black coffee, and then mixed in a little white paint to lighten the flesh tones along Lilith's forehead. "It's getting dark," he said aloud to his sister as she paced by the window. "Are they still there?"

Penelope drew the curtain slightly and peered out. Even through the thick lead, he could hear a female cry, "I saw the curtain move. It's him! It's him! The sultan!" A chorus of female squeals rang out. The crowd of women had been gathering throughout the day, waiting for him to leave or open a window. Wild for any glimspse of him. No doubt the neighbors were not amused with the special edition McAllister had printed.

"I think there may be three dozen now," Penelope marveled. "You've gone from a feared, dastardly villain to a desired hero in a matter of hours."

Capital. Now if he could only attract the one woman he desired. If he could be her hero.

Penelope read his anxious thoughts. "It was published not twelve hours ago. Give her some time."

"I can think of multiple scenarios to detain her," said Beatrice in that cool, rational manner of hers. "She could be on the continent and a magazine won't arrive there for another few days and then, perhaps, she won't go to a store with English papers for a week or—"

"Thank you, Beatrice," said Penelope. "I'm not really fond of that scenario. Let us try another."

"She is in London and has seen the paper and decided not to come." Beatrice closed her book and clutched the edges. "That is not a very good scenario either."

"Why don't we all go to bed early," suggested Penelope. "It is no use to stay up fretting. Maybe tomorrow we shall awake to find Lilith here, sharing breakfast with us in a ludicrous ensemble just to raise George's ire." Her small chuckle turned hollow and bittersweet, like remembering a funny story of someone dearly departed.

"Yes, yes, sleep," said George. "A grand idea." He set his brush down and wiped his hands with a damp cloth. In truth, he wanted to be alone with his worries, fears, and aching heart. He began herding the ladies to the door. "'Sleep that knits up the raveled trouser leg of care' or whatever Shakespeare said. Lilith would know."

"Sleeve, not trouser leg!" corrected Beatrice. "'Sleep that knits up the raveled sleeve of care.' It's from *Macbeth*."

"Very good," he said. "You must know these

important scholarly things when you go to Oxford, young lady." He kissed her cheek. "Now off to bed. Let me do a little more work and then I shall follow suit."

Penelope hugged him. "Don't worry, brother. She will come. She loves you."

She hurried and caught up with Beatrice, linking arms as they strolled down the corridor to the stairs.

He returned to his study, hung his head, and released a low stream of breath. What had he done by publishing that story? He had opened himself up to all of England for ridicule, yet she hadn't come. No one would take him seriously anymore. He didn't know if he could even take himself seriously. He glanced at the correspondence that his secretary said required his attention waiting on the desk. He couldn't wallow in this pathetic hole of self-pity anymore. He had to put some semblance of order back into his life. He just couldn't muster the strength at the moment.

She hadn't come.

After he had told the world he loved her. After he had humiliated himself by letting out his artistic secret. He still couldn't shake off the shame of his work. His father's words and the slash of a leather whip echoed too strongly in his memory, and Lilith wasn't there to silence them.

She hadn't come.

Unthinking, he picked up his brush and added another dab of paint to Lilith's forehead. If this painting had a name, it would be *A Fading Memory of an Afternoon in the Park*. He was already beginning to lose her precious details. He remembered the glorious sunlight dappled through the vivid leaves and the sensation of her sadness as she said that all she wanted from a husband was loyalty, kindness, and a home. But he didn't recall how the sadness rested on her features, only that he'd felt it as she clutched her book to the bodice of her lavender dress, which dulled her earthy coloring. He had the oddest desire not to draw her face at all but leave it as a blur of emptiness and hurt contoured with harsh black lines. He cleaned his brush, dipped it in the black paint, and poised it a half inch from the canvas.

"I knew you would be a wonderful painter," a familiar voice reverberated in the room. He hadn't heard the door open, or footsteps. He didn't move, afraid to turn and find she wasn't there, that he'd imagined her voice.

"It's beautiful and expressive," she said.

"Lilith," he whispered, still afraid to look.

"I remember that day." The swish of a skirt and she was beside him. Her citrus and vanilla scent filled him, bringing back memories of holding her. He trembled, afraid she would disappear like a ghost. "I remember that I felt betrayed because Edgar and Frances had left me. But you saved me and forced me to walk in the park to lift my spirits. I was angry, but that was because I didn't understand you then. I didn't realize you were trying to take care of me as best you could. Or maybe I was taking care of you. Either way, that day in the park we, the sultan and Colette, struggled with so much we couldn't fathom. See her faceless face." She gestured to the picture. "And the vivid world around her, but she can't see it, for she has no eyes to see outside herself. How you captured me then."

He laced his fingers between hers. They were trembling.

"Poor Colette running from the very man who could save her." Lilith lifted his hand and caressed it to her cheek. Her eyes sparkled with tears. "She didn't realize…" Her voice broke.

"No, my love." He kissed her falling tears, stopping them in their tracks.

"She didn't realize that the man she despised, the most narrow-minded and starchy of men, saw the world deeper and vaster than she could imagine in her meager words. Inside him were beautiful palaces and lush gardens."

"And a terrible secret he kept hidden in a box high in an attic under a chamber pot." He kissed her chin. "And here was that heinous, unfathomable secret: that Lilith, the woman who infuriated him and drove him to distraction, and he were kindred spirits. For that crime, he couldn't let her near. He couldn't tell her that he loved her, because he was afraid she would tear his world apart. Ahh, but the flimsy thing fell on its own and then he punched Lord Charles."

"Wait, you really punched him?" she asked, breaking the precious moment of heartfelt confession. "That rumor was true and not some sensational story for a rag?"

"I punched him three times and in the middle of the annual Marylewick house party ball."

"That's perfect!" She pressed her hand to her mouth and giggled, then turned serious again. "I guess that ended hope for your bill."

He shrugged. "I suppose so."

"What about going insane, is that true? Or that Lady Marylewick, in a rage, burned down Tyburn

Hall? Or that Penelope vowed to divorce Fenmore and run away with a French lover?"

He gently finger-combed her hair from her face. There were many dark times in the last days when he'd entertained the terrible thought that he might never be able to hold her again or have that little mischievous smile light up his senses. Now she was back, filling up his eyes and heart. He would never let her slip from the safety of his love.

"Well, I have gone insane, that is true," he quipped, letting his fingers trail down her jaw and along her neck. Oh, to touch her! "Insane and lovesick. My mother is in a rage, but my secretary received a letter yesterday concerning a roof leak in the fortress wing, so I assume Tyburn is still standing. Penelope is getting a divorce but not running away. I don't think she has a lover, French or otherwise. And Beatrice is going to Oxford, provided she is let in."

"Truly?" Lilith caught her breath. "Truly?"

He nodded, marveling at how he felt her joy as if it were his own.

"Such wonderful news!"

"I have more to tell you." He cupped her face in his hands and gazed at her. "I'm relinquishing your grand-father's money to you. It's yours. You were right. I didn't know it at the time. I controlled you with the trust to keep you near me. You are free now. All I have to offer is my love, if that is enough for you?"

She closed her eyes, her shoulders shook, and she broke into sobs.

"No, Lilith."

"I've been so miserable," she cried. "I've been

trying to have Colette commit suicide. I could only imagine the most horrible of endings for that love we made. And then your story arrived. Please, please tell me this is forever and that it won't disappear." She clutched his arm. "I never want to feel the excruciating pain of parting from you again."

His lips brushed hers. "I am going to hold you close to me for the remainder of our lives, my muse. My love." He groaned and relaxed into her kiss, drifting in the soul-settling peace of her body pressed against his.

She drew back, smiled, and gingerly touched his chin.

"My beard, or the beginning of one. Does it bother you?"

"I adore it. It's perfect for the artist that you are. Don't you dare think of shaving it or not painting."

"Very well, then, but you, my beloved, better get busy writing. What am I going to read now that you've finished *Colette and the Sultan*? You know I adore Colette. In fact, I'm thinking of taking her as a mistress." He winked.

"Oh, there will be all new stories to tell. Many exciting, exotic mistresses for you from all over the world. A whole harem of mistresses. You won't be able to keep up. In fact, I hear my muse calling."

"Your muse must wait." He drew her back into his arms. "You're in my thrall now. No imaginary mistresses for the moment, only one loving, intelligent, spirited, beautiful Lilith. She outshines them all." Enough with soul-settling peaceful kisses, time for scorching lovemaking. They had so much time to make up for, after all.

The door flew open and the impassioned lovers jumped apart as Beatrice and Penelope scurried in, their robes flapping about their ankles. "It's true!" Penelope cried. "She *is* here."

"Sisters!" Lilith rushed to meet their embrace, their laughter ringing about the room.

Their hug turned into a simple dance. They circled, arm-in-arm. Lilith, flushed with happiness, held out her hand, beckoning George to join. A profound sense of well-being rested in his heart. All the lines and colors of his life were coming together to form a beautiful new picture to be painted: *The Maryle Family Dancing.*

1847
Stuke Buzzard, England

ISABELLA LIFTED A DELICATE, PERFECTLY COILED tendril of hair in the "luxurious shade of raven's wing" from the Madam O'Amor's House of Beauty package that she had secreted into her bedchamber.

Her black cat, Milton, who had been bathing his male feline parts on her pillow, stopped and stared at the creation, his green eyes glittery.

"This is not a rat," Isabella told him. "You may not eat it."

Unconvinced, the cat rolled onto his paws, hunched, and flicked his tail, ready to pounce.

The advertisement in last month's *Miroir de Dames* had read *"Losing your petals? Withering on the vine?*

*Return to your full, fresh, feminine bloom with Madam
O'Amor's famous youth-restoring lotion compounded of
the finest secret ingredients, and flowing tendrils, puffs, and
braids made from the softest hair."*

Isabella typically didn't believe such flapdoodle.
But at twenty-nine, she was dangling off the marital
cliff and gazing down into the deep abyss of childless
spinsterhood. Now she finally had a live, respectable
fish by the name of Mr. Powers, her bank partner,
swimming around the hook. After he walked her
home from church on Sunday, she had decided
not to take any chances and had broken down and
ordered Madam's concoctions. Even then, a little
voice inside her warned, "Don't lie to yourself. Who
would want to marry an abnormal, cracked, freakish
girl?" All those things Randall had called her years
ago. Strange that words uttered so long ago still had
the power to sting.

After making excuses to loiter about the village post
office for almost a week, Isabella had been relieved
when her order had finally arrived on the train
that morning, just in time to restore her full, fresh,
feminine bloom before Mr. Powers called on bank
business. Little did the poor gentleman know that for
once she couldn't care less about stocks and consuls.
She was hoping for a more personal investment with a
high rate of marital return: a husband.

Standing before her vanity mirror, she opened the
drawer, drew out a hairpin, and headed into battle.
Her overgrown, irrepressible mane refused to curl
tamely, held a fierce vendetta against pins, and rebelled
against any empire, Neapolitan, or shepherdess coiffure

enforced on it. She secured the first tendril and studied the result. It didn't fall in the same easy, elegant spiral as in the advertisement, but shot out from behind her ear like a coiled, bouncy spring.

"Oh no, this looks terrible." She tugged at it, trying to loosen the curl. "I'll just secure the other. You can't tell from just one; it's not balanced."

Meanwhile, her cat eyed her, scheming to get at those strange yet oddly luxurious rats on her head.

The second tendril was no better than the first. "I look even more abnormal, cracked, and freakish, if that were possible. I knew this was a stupid idea. Why did I even try when I knew it was stupid?" She sank into her chair and buried her face in her hands. She just wanted a husband and children. Why was it so difficult for her? Why couldn't she be like her mother—graceful and gentle?

Tap, tap.

"Darling, I hate to nag," Judith called through the door. "But the Wollstonecraft Society meeting is in less than two weeks. You really must practice your speech."

Oh fudge! Isabella didn't have time to remove the offending curls. She grabbed Madam O'Amor's box and shoved it under the bed. Milton, who was teetering on the edge of the mattress, saw his moment and took a nasty swipe at her head.

Judith, founding member of the Mary Wollstonecraft Society Against the Injurious Treatment of Women Whose Rights Have Been Unjustly Usurped by the Tyrannical and Ignorant Regime of the Male Kind, strolled in. Her auburn hair was pulled into a sloppy bun and secured by crossed pencils, her reading glasses sitting low on her Roman nose. Before her face, she held Isabella's draft of her acceptance speech for this year's Wollstonecraft award.

"My dear, this is interesting information, but it's rather, well…boring," she said. "Unlike you, most people don't remember numbers and—my goodness, what torture have you inflicted on your poor hair?"

Isabella extricated Milton's claw from her head and drew herself tall. "I've styled my hair into tendrils," she said firmly. Her companion was bossy and a relentless nagger. Isabella had to put up a strong front.

"Tentacles?"

"I said *tendrils*."

A tiny pleat formed between Judith's eyebrows. "I hope you aren't doing all this for a *man*?" Her face screwed up tight, as if the word *man* emitted a foul stench.

"No, no, of course not." Isabella had been careful to hide her little infatuation with Mr. Powers. If she didn't, Judith would launch into her standard marital lecture, that Isabella shouldn't give over her freedom and money to a simple-minded, barbaric man who would just gamble away her wealth. "W-what would I do with a man?" Isabella laughed nervously, trying to sound innocent. Her gaze wandered to the bed, and her mind lit up with all manner of things she would do with him.

Thankfully, Judith didn't pursue the subject, but reverted back to her usual obsession: the Wollstonecraft Society. "Now, darling, you need to make an emotional connection with the society members in your speech. You must speak to their desires and pains. Remember how we discussed showing our emotions when writing your book."

Isabella groaned. "We agreed never to talk about the book again."

A fellow member of the Wollstonecraft Society had recently bought a printing press in London. Judith had thought it a wonderful idea for Isabella to write a volume educating women about investing and the stock exchange. She'd pestered Isabella for months. Finally, when the weather turned brutal in the winter, Isabella produced a work she titled *A Guide to the Funds and Sound Business Practices for Gentle Spinsters and Widows* by "A Lady." She gave the pages to Judith to edit and happily forgot about it. Three months later, her companion returned a bound book retitled *From Poor to Prosperous, How Intelligent, Resourceful Spinsters, Widows, and Female Victims of Ill-fated Marital Circumstances Can Procure Wealth, Independence, and Dignity* by Isabella St. Vincent, majority partner in the Bank of Lord Hazelwood.

The entire village must have heard Isabella's mortified scream. To make it all the worse, Judith had taken her modest examples, such as "Hannah was a plain spinster with only the limited means left to her by her late father," and added such Gothic claptrap as Hannah having been used and abandoned by some arrogant lord of a manor.

She had hoped the book would languish unread on some library bookshelf until it disintegrated into dust, but it was now in its fourth printing. And Isabella, who was only a member of the society because Judith sent in her membership letter each year, was to be awarded the society's highest honor: the Wollstonecraft—a large gold-painted plaster bust of the famous advocate of rights for women.

Judith pointed to a paragraph on page two of Isabella's scribbled speech. "Now, where you say consuls return three percent, you should perhaps say, 'an infirm widow whose husband, a typical subjugating, evil man, had gambled away their savings before drinking himself to—'"

"I can't say those things." Isabella flung up her arms. "You know I'm a horrid lecturer. I just stand there mute or start babbling nonsense. Please go to the London meeting and accept the award. You had as much to do with the book as I. And you know Milton gets mad when I go away, and wets my bed out of spite."

"Isabella!" Judith gasped. "It's the Wollstonecraft! Do you know how many ladies dream of being in your shoes?"

Isabella couldn't think of more than six. "But... but..." *I've almost got one of those subjugating, evil men hooked and squirming on my marital line. I can't leave now. To Hades with the gold bust of Mary Wollstonecraft! If I don't know a man soon, I'm going to spontaneously combust.*

"No *buts*," her companion said, handing Isabella back her pages. Surrounding her neat, efficient words and tables were arrows pointing to her cousin's scrawled notes that read "Young widow must support ailing child," or "Honorable, aging spinster turned away from her home."

"This is wrong. Investing is about numbers, not

whether you are abandoned or caring for your dead sister's husband's cousin's eleven blind and crippled orphaned children or such nonsense."

"Now you sound like a *man*." Judith scrunched her nose again at the terrible m-word. "The women of Britain need your help. They have no rights, no vote, no control over their lives. Money is their only freedom." She placed her palm on Isabella's cheek. "I know what a brave, kind soul you are. Inside of you remains the grave child who didn't cry by her mother's casket and the young woman who waited stoically every day by her dying father's bedside. Don't be afraid of your vulnerability and pain. Use it to talk to your sisters in need."

Isabella's throat turned dry. Judith didn't know what she was talking about. Emotions were wild and confusing variables. Their unpredictability scared Isabella, making her feel like that helpless child unable to stop her mama from dying. Logic was, well, logical. It had numbers, lines, formulas, and probabilities. If she could teach those ladies anything, it would be that the key to good investments was to discard those useless, confounding emotions that only muddied the issues and look at the cold, hard patterns in the numbers.

"I knew from the earliest moments of our acquaintance that you would grow into a brilliant leader of women," Judith continued. "Now you must go to London and accept your calling." She turned and sat in the chair by the grate. "Let's rehearse. So chin up, shoulders straight, and begin."

Isabella stared down at the pages and began to drone, "Thank you, ladies of the—"

Mary, one of the servants, slipped through the door. *Mr. Powers is here!* "Pardon me," Mary said with a bob of a curtsy. "Lord Randall has called."

"Lord Randall," Isabella said, disappointed. "What is he doing here? Isn't his parents' annual house party starting today? Oh bother. Put him in the library." At least she could use the loathsome viscount as an excuse to escape this oratorical torture. "I'm sure this is about extremely urgent bank business that needs attending to immediately," she told Judith.

❦

After the last session of Parliament, what Lord Randall, the House of Commons' famed Tory orator, needed to fortify himself was twelve uninterrupted hours in bed with a lovely lady before heading home to his parents' annual house party and shackling himself to a powerful Tory daughter, living unhappily, but politically connected, ever after.

If things had gone as planned, at this very moment he might have been leisurely arriving on the train after one last good morning tumble.

Of course, things hadn't gone as planned, as they hadn't for the last six months. Instead of feeling the soft curves of a stunning little ballet dancer or actress, he had felt the bump and rumble of a train as he traveled alone through the night, staring at the blackness beyond the window, his mind swirling with scenarios of political ruin. Now he stood in the library of a woman he was desperate to see. But hell and damnation, he would rather gnaw off his own leg than share twelve uninterrupted hours of frolicking with Isabella.

He raked his hands through his hair, feeling little strands come loose. *Great.* On top of everything, he was losing his hair. *Could something else go wrong?*

And where is she?

He paced up and down the Aubusson rug adorning her somber, paneled library. Some books lined the shelves, but mostly financial journals in leather boxes labeled by date and volume. A large oak desk was situated between two massive arched windows, its surface clean except for a lamp and inkwell. He tugged at his cravat as if he were choking. How could Isabella live in such oppressive, silent order? It stifled his soul.

He strode to one of the windows and watched the line of carriages and flies from the railroad station heading up the hill to his father's estate. Inside them rode Tories of the "right kind" as his mother had phrased it, along with their daughters, all vying for Randall's hand in marriage. He leaned his head against the glass. "You've got to save me, Isabella," he whispered.

"I'm surprised to see you," he heard that familiar soprano voice say behind him.

An odd, warm comfort washed over him at the sound. He turned and found himself gazing at the fashion tragedy that was Isabella. She wore a dull blue dress or robe or something that made a slight indentation around the waist area and concealed everything else from her chin to the floor. Her glasses magnified her gray eyes, and she had styled her wild hair in some new, odd, dangly arrangement. Still, a peace bloomed in his chest at the sight of her frumpy dishevelment, like that nostalgic, grounding feeling of coming home. Well, not his real home, where, despite all British rules to the contrary, his strident mother ruled. As the rest of his world was coming undone, Isabella remained the same old ungainly girl of his memory—his faithful adversary.

"Just 'I'm surprised to see you'?" he repeated in feigned offense. "Perhaps 'Good morning, Lord Randall. I've missed you terribly. You haunt my dreams. I'm enamored of your dazzling intellectual and manly powers. There is a void in my tiny, black heart that only you can fill.'" His anxiety started to ease as he settled into the thrust, glissade, and parry of their typical conversation.

For a beat, she just stared at him. The old girl took everything at face value. Then the realization dawned in her eyes that he was ribbing her. "Oh, I was about to say that, if you had waited…for several thousand years," she retorted. "What I meant was that I thought you would be busy at your house party, choosing a wife. At least, that is what the papers claim."

"As you often say when avoiding something messy and emotionally taxing, 'I don't want to talk about it,'" he quoted her back to herself. "Except to say it's a shame that Napoleon could not have enlisted Mama; I believe the war might have turned out differently. The Duke of Halsington sent a late reply, upsetting Mama's meticulous arrangements. He will be joined by his wife, who requires a room conveniently adjoining the Earl of Worthsam's, while his grace much prefers comfortable quarters beside Mrs. Kettlemore's. That little farce resulted in ousting me from my chambers to the Fauna chamber, named for housing my late uncle's stuffed avian collection. I spent the early hours of the morning being stared at by dead birds. But enough about nightmares of being eaten by African lappet-faced vultures." He gestured to a chair. "Would you care to sit down? Oh, wait. It's your home. You were supposed to politely suggest that."

"Would you care to sit down, Lord Randall?" she said, with mock sweetness.

"I don't mind if I do; how thoughtful of you to ask." He pulled up a chair before her desk. "Ah, I have something to tempt you with." He withdrew some folded pages from his pocket and wagged them before her. "I did retrieve the list of new clients for the London bank as you ordered—pardon, I meant *requested* in your last letter."

She snatched up the papers, her face glowing with the same delight he had seen in his mistress's—ex-mistress's—when he had given her a ruby necklace. Isabella was an odd bird. Any man who dared to romance the shrew would have to forgo the floral tributes—and not because of her adverse reactions to certain flowers, grasses, and hay—and arrive with bouquets of financial reports instead.

She took a seat in her late father's massive leather chair on the other side of the desk and scanned the lines of patrons. "This is much better than expected," she said, a small smile playing on her lips—soft and cushy lips, he noted. Rather kissable, not that he would ever consider kissing her. It was merely an empirical observation: the sky was blue; the sun was yellow; Isabella had the kind of lips that should be ravished.

"And by the way," he continued, drawing her attention back to him, "I wouldn't write to someone, calling him a flaming ignoramus of the grandest magnitude for his vote on the Scottish banking bill, and then ask him to spend the afternoon at the new bank building kissing babies and welcoming new customers." Despite the panicky economy, when nervous customers were putting runs on another bank every day and sinking their savings, the Bank of Lord Hazelwood was rapidly expanding, "discovering new markets," as Isabella would say, taking offices in London and Manchester. He and his father's profiles and the family's coat of arms appeared in journals all over England above a caption that read "For four hundred years the name Hazelwood has inspired trust. Place your monies where you place your trust."

"It must have been such a hardship being adored and fawned over," she mocked. "I'm sure every unmarried lady in London was beating down the bank door." She waved the documents. "Incredible. There must be five hundred and fifteen names on this list and about three-fifths of them are women."

"I seduced the Hades out of those stodgy old ladies and spinsters for their pennies. I still have bruises in the sensitive areas where they pinched me."

She paused, then a spark lit in her eyes as she realized that he was jesting again. She laughed, a beautiful, silvery sound. Again, he felt that flood of peace. He had an urge to hide in her library, behind that unfashionable skirt of hers and away from his political woes and his parents' damned house party. But alas, the world marched on. Or marched *over* him, as it seemed these last weeks.

He drummed the great oak desk with his fingers,

suddenly feeling vulnerable. He had never let his guard down around her before, always keeping a protective wall of lithe, barbed words between them.

"Speaking of being pinched, perhaps you read about my little set-to with George Harding in the parliamentary railroad committee meeting." He tried to sound casual, even as his heart sped up.

"Little!" She raised a single brow, comically screwing her features. "It's an epic scandal! The financial columns criticize you for standing in the way of England's progress, the political columns believe you have committed electoral suicide with the election coming, and the society columns wonder whose powerful Tory daughter you'll marry to patch up the mess." He couldn't miss that little hint of glee under her words.

He found that he was too restless to sit after all, and rose to his feet. "The railroad committee voted Harding's line down. I merely asked if he was spread too thin. The very words you used at the bank board meeting last winter when we decided against investing in his other lines."

She blinked. "You actually listened to something I said?"

"I didn't mean to. I was just about to drift off when your words hit my ears. *Splat!* Then they wouldn't come out, just rolling around in there. Anyway, I thought you might be right and—"

"Stop right there!" She held up her palm. "Say those words again."

Despite his worry, his lips cracked into a smirk. "I said I *thought* you might be right."

"Oh God." She flipped open a ledger and reached for her pen. "I must make a note: On this day of our Lord, May 17, 1847, Lord Randall has finally admitted that I was right."

"No, you weren't," he barked. "And I'm glad my troubles amuse you." His words came out harsher than he intended.

Her head jerked back. "I'm…I'm sorry."

He pinched the bridge of his nose, cursed under his breath, and crossed to one of the windows.

She joined him there. Her eyes were tense, conflicted between fear and concern. She reached out, letting her hand hover an inch from his before pulling back. He knew she struggled to connect with others and messy emotions scared her. He remembered the days surrounding her father's funeral, when she'd tried so hard to hide her sorrow, but he still felt her deep grief ripping her apart.

"You'll sail through this tiny setback with no trouble," she whispered, her voice shaky and unsure. "You'll win your seat. You lead a charmed life." He discerned a hint of bitterness under her last words.

"Well, it's been quite difficult lately, for all its charm," he quipped. In the distance, a fly rambled down the long drive to the Hazelwood estate. "I think Harding is plotting against me," he confessed.

"Why?"

He ran his hand over the cleft in his chin, pondering what he could politely repeat about the previous night's bad turn. He probably shouldn't mention to Isabella the desire for twelve uninterrupted hours in bed with a beautiful woman, which had made him stick a red rosebud in his lapel and stroll into a gaming hell off St. James's early last evening. How he had drained a couple of brandies, trying to wash away the anxiety of the last weeks, until he felt the shine of his old, cocky charm return. That he had been about to amble over to the perfect quarry—curly, raven hair; large, luxurious dark eyes—when he heard a sweet, breathy voice say his name.

He had spun to find Cecelia, his ex-mistress, standing there, ravishing in pale blue. His throat had gone dry. The entire room stopped mid-roll, play, bet, or conversation and watched her, as though the famed actress were onstage in her own production. Before he could manage a "good evening" to her, George Harding had stepped forward, flanked by three personal flash men, and placed a possessive hand on her shoulder.

Randall didn't think that Harding stealing his mistress was relevant to Isabella and the business at hand. Nor did he want to admit to Isabella that Harding was damned handsome, in an exotic way. While Randall was tall, the railroad baron towered over him. The man had bronze skin, a muscular build, a flint-like jaw, and a shiny, bald head. His black brows were slashes above eerie, unblinking eyes. So, essentially his version of the story for Isabella's ears began with, "I went to a club and saw Harding. He asked me to sit down for a drink, something about clearing the bad blood between us."

"Why did you take my railroad, my lord?" Harding had asked, setting his glass of cognac on the table and opening his palms. "I try to be a good Tory. I back your candidates."

Harding's flash men rushed to agree. "That's right, Mr. Harding. You're a Tory's best supporter," and "You've always done right by the Tories."

"Do you pay for this personal audience of yahoos?" Randall had asked. "Or do these cullies follow you around because they don't have any bollocks of their own?"

Harding's flash men had glanced at each other, as though deciding how to react. The consensus was menacing until Harding broke into deep belly laughter. "Oh, you're a funny, funny man." The railroad baron leaned over, plucked the rosebud from Randall's lapel, and twirled it under his nose. "Smells nice. With your title, pretty words, and face, you could have gone far, maybe prime minister. But you supported child labor laws and the repeal of the Corn Laws, instead of building railroads and prosperity. What will become of our golden boy with his empty head and glorious ambitions if he isn't reelected?"

Randall had let a slow smile crawl cross his lips. "Careful there, old chap. One word from me and you might lose another railroad."

Harding replaced the viscount's rose. "With your title, you think I can't touch you. The world is about to change; you need to choose which side you're on before the election. Enjoy your house party. I hope you find a lovely, connected wife. I understand you've been a bit lonely of late."

Randall decided it wasn't important to tell Isabella how everyone in the gaming hell had watched the railroad baron leave with Randall's beautiful mistress—*ex*-mistress—or the stream of colorful curses he'd released under his breath.

Now he gazed out the window in Isabella's library. In the distance, at the entrance of his home, he could make out ladies in expansive skirts stepping from the carriages. His mother must be cursing him for not being there to greet them.

"I know you make fun of me," he said quietly. "I know you, like my critics, think I'm shallow and overly ambitious and you disagree with my views." He turned to Isabella, latching his gaze on her face. "But dammit, I'm a good politician. I've all but given my life to this country. I try—"

"You need something solid to hold against Harding."

"No." The motivation for his visit sounded so conniving, almost dishonorable when echoed back to him. He sank into his chair, rubbed his forehead, and conceded. "Yes."

About the Author

Susanna Ives started writing when she left her job as a multimedia training developer to stay home with her family. Now she keeps busy driving her children to various classes, writing books, and maintaining websites. She often follows her husband on business trips around Europe and blogs about the misadventures of touring with children. She lives in Atlanta.

A Gift for Guile

The Thief-takers

by Alissa Johnson

— ❧ —

Never Trust a Thief

Once a famous officer of Scotland Yard and now a renowned private detective, Sir Samuel Brass has better things to do than shadow a reckless hellion in her misguided quest for atonement. But when the daughter of a notorious criminal—and a former thief herself—returns to London to right an old wrong, Samuel is drawn back into the dangerously exciting world of Esther Walker-Bales.

Beautiful and conniving, maddening and brilliant, Esther is everything he shouldn't want. She's a liar. She's a con. She's a thief. And God help him, but he'd do anything to keep her safe.

Esther knows she's put herself in terrible danger, but nothing will stop her from making amends that are long past due—not her family's enemies, not old fears, and certainly not the domineering, interfering, and undeniably handsome Sir Samuel Brass. Yet whenever he's near, Samuel makes her long for a life that can never be hers…and wish she was worthy of being saved.

— ❧ —

"Sweet, sexy, and completely irresistible."
—Cecilia Grant, author of *A Lady Awakened*

"Witty, quirky, and altogether fun."
—*Publishers Weekly* Starred Review

For more Alissa Johnson, visit:

www.sourcebooks.com

A Scandalous Adventure

Victorian Adventures

by Lillian Marek

They're hiding a scandalous secret

When his monarch's flighty fiancée disappears, Count Maximillian von Staufer is dispatched to find her. His search leads Max to discover not the princess, but a look-alike who could be her double. Desperate to avoid an international crisis, he conceives a plan that will buy some time—and allow him to get to know a beautiful Englishwoman.

And time is running out

Lady Susannah Tremaine and her young friend Olivia are staying at the Grand Hotel in Baden, where so far the most exciting part of the visit has been the pastries. But when a devastatingly handsome royal Germanic officer asks Olivia to impersonate a missing princess, Susannah finds herself drawn into a dangerous world of international intrigue as she tries to protect her friend—and her heart.

Praise for *Lady Emily's Exotic Journey*:

"Captivating…fabulously intriguing locales…a roller-coaster ride of adventure." —*RT Book Reviews*, 4 Stars

"Richly detailed romance with unexpected characters readers will love." —*Fresh Fiction*

For more Lillian Marek, visit:

www.sourcebooks.com

Discovery of Desire

London Explorers

by Susanne Lord

⸺ ❧ ⸺

The one man who's not looking for a wife

Seth Mayhew is the ideal explorer: fearless, profitable, and unmarried. There is nothing and no one he can't find—until his sister disappears en route to India. His search for her takes him to Bombay, where Seth meets the most unlikely of allies—a vulnerable woman who's about to marry the wrong man.

Discovers a woman who changes his dreams forever

Teeming with the bounty of marriageable men employed by the East India Company, Bombay holds hope for security for Wilhelmina Adams. But when the man she's traveled halfway around the world to marry doesn't suit, Mina finds instead that she's falling in love with a man who offers passion, adventure, intimacy—anything but security…

⸺ ❧ ⸺

Praise for *In Search of Scandal*:

"Smart and sexy." —*Booklist*

"Beautifully written, deeply romantic, and utterly magnificent." —*New York Times* bestselling author Courtney Milan

"Delightful… Passionate characters and personal adventures come alive." —*Booklist*

For more Susanne Lord, visit:

www.sourcebooks.com

The Girl from Paris

Paget Family Saga

by Joan Aiken

───── ❦ ─────

Ellen Paget's life is irrevocably changed when she accepts a position as governess for the radical Comte and Comtesse de la Ferte, in whose Paris salon Ellen is introduced to the most illustrious artists, writers, and philosophers of the day. The charming Benedict Masham, second son of an earl and an old family friend, makes it his business to look out for Ellen's welfare. That would be nice, if it wasn't so annoying to Ellen, who wants to flout convention and spread her wings in Society.

Ellen soon sheds the stifling conventions of her proper English upbringing, and contends with the questionable affections of a beguiling writer, whose attentions to Ellen dismay the steadfast Benedict.

When tragedy and scandal force her to beat a hasty retreat back to England, it takes all of Ellen's ingenuity and fortitude to solve the mysteries of the past and present—but can she do so in time to save her father and brother from the machinations of those who mean them harm?

───── ❦ ─────

Praise for *Mansfield Park Revisited*:

"Delightful and charming." —*Becky's Book Reviews*

"A lovely read—and you don't have to have read *Mansfield Park* to enjoy it." —*Woman's Own*

For more Joan Aiken, visit:

www.sourcebooks.com

Wicked Little Secrets

by Susanna Ives

— ❧ —

It's not easy being good...

Vivacious Vivienne Taylor has finally won her family's approval by getting engaged to the wealthy and upright John Vandergrift. But when threatened by a vicious blackmail scheme, it is to her childhood friend that Vivienne turns: the deliciously wicked Viscount Dashiell.

When being wicked is so much more exciting...

Lord Dashiell promised himself long ago that his friendship with Vivienne would be the one relationship with a woman that he wouldn't ruin. He agrees to help her just to keep the little hothead safe, but soon finds that Vivienne has grown up to be very, very dangerous to all of Dash's best intentions.

— ❧ —

"With *Wicked Little Secrets'* intriguing plot, quirky characters, witty escapades, and heartfelt dialogue, Ives has created a read that's as thought-provoking as it is romantic." —*RT Book Reviews*, 4 1/2 Stars

"If you love historical romances, this book is a must!" —*Long and Short Reviews*

For more Susanna Ives, visit:

www.sourcebooks.com